WITHDRAWN

Olivier Bleys was born in Lyon in 1970. He holds master's degrees in modern literature, computer graphics and cultural project management. At the age of twenty-two he won the Lyon young novelist's prize for *L'Île*. Three years later his second book, *Le Prince de la Fourchette*, received the Prix Saumur. His third novel, *Pastel*, was translated into several foreign languages and was awarded the Prix F. Mauriac by the the Académie française. *Le fantôme dans la tour Eiffel* was awarded the Prix du Roman Historique in 2002. Besides writing novels, Olivier Bleys designs interactive cd-roms, lectures on multimedia, manages cultural projects and organises exhibitions. He has a wide range of interests spanning medieval history, music and science-fiction. He lives in Paris.

J. A. Underwood has translated many French and German authors including Gaston Bachelard, Sartre and Kafka. A former joint winner of the Schlegel-Tieck Prize for his translation of Kafka's *The Castle*, he has also worked as part of a team re-translating the works of Sigmund Freud.

Also by Olivier Bleys

Pastel (Gallimard 2000)
Le Prince de la Fourchette (Arlea 1995)
L'Île (Jaques Grancher 1993)
Madagascar (Fer de Chances 1997)

THE GHOST
IN THE EIFFEL TOWER

Olivier Bleys

a novel
translated from the French by
J.A. Underwood

MARION BOYARS
LONDON · NEW YORK

Published in Great Britain and the United States in 2004 by
MARION BOYARS PUBLISHERS LTD
24 Lacy Road, London SW15 1NL

www.marionboyars.co.uk

Distributed in Australia and New Zealand by Peribo Pty Ltd
58 Beaumont Road, Kuring-gai, NSW 2080

First published in France in 2002 by Éditions Gallimard

10 9 8 7 6 5 4 3 2 1

A CIP catalogue for this book is available from the British Library
A CIP catalog record for this book is available from the Library of Congress

ISBN 0-7145-3094-8

This book is supported by the French Ministry for Foreign Affairs, as part of the Burgess programme headed by the Institut Français du Royaume-Uni for the French Embassy in London.

The Publishers would like to thank the Arts Council of England for financial support in the publishing of this book.

Printed in the UK by Bookmarque, London

For Laetitia
'de la Tour précieux homonyme'

THE FOUNDATIONS

1

Armand left a franc in the coachman's palm and strode off without waiting for the change.

He had asked to be dropped off some way from the gate, precisely in the corner formed by the office buildings and a brick depot. What should he do now? Present himself immediately? He preferred to give himself some time. No one was expecting his visit, no one even knew about him; so Armand could choose his moment, quietly installed in a nearby café, thinking about the interview that his career might depend on.

'A coffee… Excellent idea! They say Paris is where you get the best coffee.'

The young man from the provinces looked around him but there was no bar or restaurant in sight, not a single inviting signboard. The deserted landscape did not offer so much as a porch in which to shelter.

'So this is where Eiffel has his den? What a strange fellow!'

Armand walked round the cab to get a better view. How different from the way he had imagined it! He had expected a bustling street but instead there was this grassy track where, pressed down by heavy loads, the paving-stones lay half-buried. Rather than a line of elegant façades, there was a broken fence revealing a scrubby patch of open land. The sun was rising behind a row of factory chimneys that looked like wild snakes dancing.

'Pah! Who cares what the stage looks like – what matters is the play!'

The youth was aware of his collar pinching. He was dressed as if summoned to appear before a government minister. What must he look like in his fancy frock coat, diamond cravat pin and fob watch? A fool, undoubtedly.

Such was his disappointment that he thought of turning back. His hand was already reaching out towards the coachman when, remembering the latter's grin – the fellow would of course be very happy to collect another fat fare – the traveller experienced a surge of pride. No, never let it be said that he had given in!

'What are you waiting for? Be off with you!' Armand said with as much authority as his twenty-five years could command.

The coachman, a kindly soul, gave a shrug. Then, flicking the whip at his horse, he sent the cab on its lumbering way back towards the city.

Armand was now committed. There was no turning back. He took a deep breath and set out amongst the puddles, treading carefully, not to say daintily, to spare the patent-leather shoes that had cost him 2 francs to hire. The squeak of a catch made him jump. In the low building flanking the road, a window had just opened. Nimbly, Armand removed his hat.

'Can I help you, sir?' a man asked, poking his head out.

Armand replied with his name and the reason for his being there.

'Come in! I am Gustave Eiffel.'

For all Armand's care, he stepped straight into a puddle of mud.

His career nearly ended as a result of this insipid encounter.

'Can't stand shilly-shallyers!' Eiffel told him by way of qualifying their handshake. Blood rushed to the young man's cheeks.

Nevertheless, Armand thought it remarkable – and said so – that a man as busy as his interlocutor, who had just begun work on the world's tallest monument, should be gazing out of his window and hailing passers-by.

'We're being spied on, you see,' the entrepreneur confided, one thumb wound into his watch chain. 'The gossip columnists! They send their runners out here to Levallois-Perret to beg for sketches.' And with a thin smile that quickly vanished, Eiffel unsealed the letter Armand had handed him.

'I knew your father well,' the engineer said, reading the signature. 'A most estimable man…'

However, a steady look through a pair of pince-nez spectacles warned the visitor against expecting any advantage from this. Eiffel began to read, his eye rapidly scanning the opened sheet.

The interlude gave the youth time to examine the engineer's physique, which he knew only from pictures in the newspapers – flattering pictures if the papers were well-disposed, ugly if they were hostile.

At first glance, one was struck by the man's shortness, which his stooping shoulders further exaggerated. While hardly a freak in this respect, Armand stood at least a head taller, which left Eiffel, even wearing a hat, somewhere around the level of his breast-bone. What made so short a man dream up such huge structures as the Gabarit Viaduct, the Duoro Bridge in Oporto and now the 300-metre Tower? 'He's compensating,' the young man assumed.

A certain girth partly made up for the man's vertical inadequacy; one noted the heavy neck, the spreading waistline and the thickset limbs filling out the suit. The silhouette was that of a peasant rather than an engineer, someone more gifted in the muscular department than in the realms of the intellect.

However, the face corrected this impression. Without forfeiting an underlying sprightliness that Eiffel owed to his Burgundian roots – whence the ruddy cheeks, the rebellious quiff – his features spoke also of reason, of scholarship and finally of the pragmatism that enabled this brilliant man to translate his ideas into actual structures. A groove followed the arches of his forehead, the mark of the truly pensive, not those who frown at difficult questions but those who raise their eyebrows in the effort of replying. The bear-cub countenance, anchored by a light-coloured beard and sprinkled with freckles, held the attention less than the eyes, which were of a mottled blue like the patina on an iron locomotive, burning or ice-cool depending on the mood of the boiler.

'So, you fancy a bit of metal construction?' Eiffel resumed, hauling the young man out of his daydream. 'Want to build bridges, do you? Or maybe work on the 300-metre Tower?'

Armand responded with a manly 'yes', hoping to correct the somewhat spineless impression he had given before.

'We don't need you,' the great man informed him in the same tone. 'We've already got our team.'

Handing the letter back, he went on, 'You're sure to find employment elsewhere. Everything's going to be metal at the World Exposition! What they're calling the "Hall of Engines", for example, that will involve nearly as much iron and almost as many calculations as the Tower.'

This last was spat out with a rapidity in which Armand sensed the irritation of a man who blamed himself for wasting time. It did not stop the young man from clutching at Eiffel's sleeve with the desperate impulsiveness born of timidity.

'I can't go back to St. Flour with that answer! What would my father say?'

A light flashed from beneath Eiffel's eyelids.

'St. Flour, you say? Isn't that the little town down near Garabit? I thought your father was in Limoges.'

'We lived in Limoges when he was working on the bridge over the River Vienne,' Armand replied with fresh hope. 'Later, hearing about your great viaduct project, he moved the whole family to the Cantal. St. Flour has been our home ever since…'

'Charming tale,' said the contractor with a grandfatherly smile. 'Sir, I'm delighted to have made your acquaintance.'

Eiffel gave him a second handshake, this one as final as a full stop. He quit Armand's company without another word, leaving the draught to show him where the door was.

'Well, really!' was the indignant reaction of the aspirant from the tiny provincial town of St. Flour.

He tried to summon the self-assurance to press his case, but the attempt failed. On the contrary, at the very moment when all his hopes crumbled to nothing, a sense of peaceful resignation came over him. What was the use of beating at a door that refused to open? All of a sudden the fatigue of the train journey, the boredom of those long hours spent in a third-class compartment made themselves felt on the visitor. He made up his mind; he would use his return ticket that same day.

His hand was already pushing the door open when a voice

hailed him. Armand turned his head and saw a man walking towards him.

At the same time he took in the whole setting. This he had quite failed to note during his conversation with Eiffel: the rows of desks, each with an oil lamp upon it, the blackboard with its chalk dangling at the end of a piece of string and, seated on swivel chairs amid rolls of paper, men in cravats with the look of engineers. Some of them, weary of calculating, sat with their elbows on their desks, chin in hand, contemplating the visitor. So he had been spied on, talking to the boss. They had all witnessed his humiliation.

An expression of proud rebellion came over Armand's features. He gave short shrift to the man in gold-rimmed spectacles who was holding out his hand.

'Would you care to take a seat?' offered the stranger.

'I would not,' replied Armand, ostentatiously propping himself against the door jamb.

'Allow me to introduce myself: Adolphe Salles. Monsieur Eiffel has asked me to oversee the mechanical aspects of the Tower.'

Armand nodded curtly. He was impatient to be outside and this chit-chat was merely an unfortunate hitch. Also, the fellow's appearance put him off: the finely chiselled face, the slender build, like that of a fashionable fencer, the horseshoe cravat pin, not to mention the waxed moustache with the curled-up ends that smelt of pomade. He grasped his hat.

'Monsieur Eiffel, you know, thought highly of your father,' Salles went on, one hand going to his buttonhole. 'He was a very fine carpenter. I never met him myself, but what I can say is that, in this office, his departure was much regretted.'

'Oh, yes…' thought the young man from St. Flour, 'the glib condolences…' He eyed the engineers, alert for the smile that would be his cue to leave. But no one was paying any further attention to him and Salles was already following up with:

'We should be flattered to associate the Boissier name with the 300-metre Tower.'

'My father has quit the business,' the young man retorted drily.

'I'm not talking about your father, I'm talking about you.'

Armand started. Had he heard correctly?

'You mean…you're offering me a job?'

'Absolutely! Building the Tower may require a team of intellects such as science has yet to furnish. Do you realise that we have here one hundred and fifty metallurgists, thirty draughtsmen, twenty-two engineers, five architects – all men at the top of their profession? And it still isn't enough. We need more manpower.'

'But Monsieur Eiffel…'

A wink caused the gold-rimmed spectacles to jiggle.

'Monsieur Eiffel is a very busy man. Do you think he can spare the time for the minor requirements of a research department such as recruiting staff to process basic calculations? That's one job we can take off his hands.'

'But you hardly know me!' protested Armand further, testing his good fortune.

'True, but we believe the good things your father says about you. You've been through college, you got an excellent degree. That's enough to take you on probation. If you measure up, you'll join Monsieur Backmann, who's been asked to look into the question of elevators.'

'There'll be elevators in the Tower?' Armand exclaimed, on hearing this magic word.

'If ever a building needed elevators, this is it! So, do we have a deal? Will you come and work for us?'

Armand's delight was such that words failed him. All he could do was take the hand that Adolphe Salles was proffering and work it like a pump-handle.

What a friend the man seemed to him now!

The Jules Boissier residence was a scaled-down version of the splendid buildings that lined Rue de Bruxelles.

With fewer storeys, a narrower front door and a less spacious garden, it contributed little to the uniform row of façades, rather as a leather patch sits ill on a holed rug. The building's stonework appeared less dazzling and its decoration less sumptuous. Above all, it made little identifiable concession to the historical style then in vogue, which everywhere else was to blame for a plethora of sculpted tympani and mullioned bay-windows.

But it was fit lodging for a simple man, whose wallet and reputation were both on the slender side. Indeed, Jules Boissier was neither a banker, nor a journalist, nor a successful author, but a retired engineer, having left ten years previously the humble career of railway and locomotive builder. When he moved into the small Rue de Bruxelles house this was, for his neighbours, a sign of social contamination, an unpleasant return to the past. People thought they were back in the days when rich and poor lived on top of one another, from cellar to attic in the same apartment block, whereas the new order spread them out in districts, finally remedying the twin problems of uncongenial neighbours and the throwing-up of barricades.

As things turned out, though, Jules Boissier had proved a tolerable neighbour. That is to say, he passed unnoticed. He seldom went out and when he did his reserve was such that he spoke to no one, for which his neighbours were grateful, since they would not have replied. It was as if the years spent calculating rails of constant gauge had taught him the habit of observing a similar distance from others.

Jules Boissier filled the days of his retirement as he would have filled his days as an engineer. He rose at dawn and, after a sparse toilet, sat down at his desk without delay. On it, plans of an electric locomotive or a self-cleaning gun shared space with a dirty supper plate and several piles of coffee cups.

There, bent over his papers, Jules Boissier worked for his customary fifteen or sixteen hours before going to bed exhausted to sleep until the next day – which he would spend in precisely the same way.

So his uncle was at his desk when, on the evening of March 9th 1887, Armand called at the house. The young man had entered unbidden, simply pushing wide the front door, which Jules left open, even in winter, since he liked the way the cold kept his thinking clear.

The old man was somewhat surprised to see his nephew, whom he had expected the next day.

'I left earlier,' the lad explained. 'I couldn't wait.'

Jules embraced him fondly then cleared a seat of its litter of books.

'Sit down, won't you? Good trip?'

The detached, somewhat dreamy voice made Armand smile. In the Boissier family, Jules was thought of as an eccentric. His passion for work was remarked on, the studious distraction he had shown for some time now, often to the point where he lost all contact with reality.

Armand skipped the formalities to impart his good news straight away.

'I've just been talking to Gustave Eiffel.'

'The structural engineer?'

'The very same! He's offered me a job in his research department. I start the day after tomorrow. I'll be involved in the 300-metre Tower!'

Jules stepped back, hands on hips. He appeared to consider his nephew in a new light, one brightened by respect and not untinged with envy.

'But that's wonderful! Congratulations! What a fine start to your career!'

Then, after a moment's silent thought, 'Do you know what part of the Tower Monsieur Eiffel wants you to work on?'

'We didn't go into details. I believe he's thinking of the elevators.'

'The elevators?' echoed Uncles Jules with some disappointment. 'Well, why not? It's something new, after all. The newspapers are saying they represent a huge challenge because of the height of the structure and its concave profile. Probably several machines will be necessary, linked together… I read that somewhere.'

As he spoke, Jules slid a newspaper cutting from a pile of papers. The margins were full of scribbled notes, calculations and geometrical sketches.

'Are you interested in the Tower, then, uncle?'

'Who is not interested in the Tower? It concerns us all in different ways. The engineer wonders how it will be built, the architect wants to make it look good, the soldier asks what role it can play in the defence of Paris, the doctor studies the benefits the altitude will provide. Everyone down to the priest has food for thought here, because this monument to science will reach more than twice the height of the highest thing raised by religion – and I'm talking about the spires of Cologne Cathedral, which soar to 156 metres!'

The young nephew mused dreamily, 'It's scarcely conceivable!'

'True, our minds are not in the habit of thinking on such a scale. Even our eyes will have to learn to take in an object that, for someone standing at its foot, will fill the whole horizon and half the sky as well. Nevertheless, we must accept the challenge. The difference between man and beast is not only that the former walks erect whereas the latter goes on all fours; it is also that man scans the sky while the beast keeps its eyes fixed on the earth.'

Armand gazed up at the ceiling, the white, slightly soiled bareness of which offered him a negative image of the depths of infinity.

'300 metres! What a height! Is it true, uncle, that someone had the idea of sending up a balloon to give a visual impression of the projected monument?'

'Yes, with four cables anchoring the gondola to the sites of the piers and flags marking the platforms, but the plan never materialized. They were afraid it would attract crowds of the idle curious.'

'Another thing I read was that the Tower will top the combined heights of Notre-Dame, the Statue of Liberty, three Vendôme Columns, the Arc de Triomphe and a six-storey building!'

Jules snorted in scorn.

'Another journalistic formula! To be sure, the gossip-columnists have been the most rabid fanatics about the Tower. It doesn't yet exist and already they're scribbling about it! No royal visit was more eagerly awaited!'

The old man was becoming quite heated. He had already made three tours of the room, taking large strides and several times changing direction. A sudden idea would send him off at a tangent, causing him to strike out from the desk across to the window or from the stove towards the hat-stand, as a horse might shy away from each crack of the whip. On his third tour he picked up some empty cups from a shelf before seizing a fat file and tossing it into Armand's lap.

'The full dossier on the Tower!' Uncle Jules affirmed with pride.

The young man undid the leather belt around the file, revealing a sheaf of newspaper cuttings with dates and issue numbers jotted in the corners. Each one bore an article about the Tower.

'I didn't know you were making this collection.'

'It helps pass the time on bad days,' Jules confessed. 'Don't think the artist owes his entire work to inspiration. The engineer too has moments when all is going well, when the most complicated calculations come out effortlessly, and others that are the reverse. Some evenings, all I'm good for is reading the papers. So I fritter away my time on this little undertaking…'

Armand leafed through the cuttings, which had been assembled hastily. Some were still sticky with glue; several of them had a margin or a whole column projecting beyond the rough alignment of the heap.

'Which are the most interesting?'

'That one on top came out last month. It's a gem!'

Armand took up the article and moved it into the yellow lamplight.

'Oh, no! A petition against the Tower. In *Le Temps*, one of our top newspapers.'

'Didn't Eiffel mention it? I'm not surprised. He must have cast a glance over it, though.'

The nephew read passages aloud:

'We, the undersigned writers, painters, sculptors and architects, passionate lovers of the hitherto untouched beauty of Paris, wish to lodge the strongest possible protest…against the erection, in the very heart of our capital, of this useless and monstrous Eiffel Tower… For make no bones about it, the Eiffel Tower, which not even business-minded America would wish for, will disgrace our city…a dizzying, ridiculous Tower…a huge black factory chimney…hateful column of bolted sheet iron…venal imaginings of a man who normally builds machines…'

'How about that?' his uncle interjected. 'Don't mince their words, do they? Look at the signatures: Alexandre Dumas, Guy de Maupassant, Leconte de Lisle, Charles Gounod, Sully Prudomme, François Coppée, Charles Garnier…and to what end? To preserve, as the minister so eloquently puts it, that "matchless square of sand we call the Champ-de-Mars"! He's even asked for the petition to be displayed in the Exposition showcases. There'll be some red faces then, I'll be bound!'

Armand exhaled through his teeth, stung by a piece of criticism that he now took personally. Henceforth, any attack on the Tower was an attack on him. Knowing none of them as yet, he nevertheless felt solidarity with the engineers called to serve this monumental work. After all, he would soon be their colleague.

'And what comes then? Eiffel's reply?'

'Exactly. And it's not a bad piece of prose. The fellow can write! When he promises that the Tower will have its own beauty because the conditions of force correspond to the laws of harmony, one believes him.'

'And what about this: "Why should what elicits admiration in Egypt become hateful and ridiculous in Paris?" Comparing the Tower with the pyramids, that's pretty audacious!'

'It's the accusation of uselessness that Eiffel answers best. The Tower, he states, will enable interesting observations to be made in astronomy, meteorology and physics. In time of war, it will keep Paris in constant signalling contact with the rest of France. I'm not aware of anyone capable of pooh-poohing that argument, twenty years after the Prussian siege!'

'Oh, uncle, you're teaching me so much!' the young man from St. Flour said delightedly. 'But tell me – which is the earliest cutting in your collection?'

'That would be an article published in *La France*, a civil-engineering journal, in December 1884. Three years ago! Notice that it was in the same year and almost in the same month as the decree deciding in favour of a World Exposition. Doesn't that say it all? Eiffel had the ear of the government from the outset. When the architectural competition was published last year, his project was already well-advanced and the jury already selected. The hundred or so other candidates (poor things!) flogged themselves in vain to turn out, in two weeks, a design for a "300-metre Tower, made of iron, standing on a square base," plans for which had been lying idle in Eiffel's drawer for two years.'

Whenever the engineer came in for criticism, Armand's attention waned – if he listened at all. As a diversionary tactic, he asked a question.

'Did the article in *La France* mention the Tower?'

'At the time it was only an abstract idea, a disembodied calculation. Eiffel showed no interest in the project submitted to him by two of his engineers, Kœchlin and Nouguier. Later, of course, he changed his mind!'

'You mean the idea for the Tower was not in fact Eiffel's?' Armand asked with a chuckle.

'Oh, no! The foreign press are always taking him to task over that, particularly in Switzerland where Kœchlin comes from. Still, it fell to Eiffel to build the thing. Who gets the crown: the person who comes up with the idea or the person who turns it into reality?'

Armand rose from his chair with a yawn.

'That's a discussion we can have over supper, uncle. I've been travelling all day and I've had nothing since breakfast. I could eat a horse!'

'Right you are! Of course!' Jules exclaimed, clapping a hand to his forehead. 'Whatever was I thinking of? Here, take off your coat. You're still wearing your travelling clothes. I'll go and heat up the soup.'

2

In the annals of the Boissier family, Armand's first day with Gustave Eiffel & Co. was to assume some importance.

The day before, Jules had dispatched his nephew to his own personal tailor to order a made-to-measure suit. 'You need something smart but sober,' Uncle Jules had pronounced. 'Stiff material and a straight cut. These people appreciate precision.' Liberal purchases at the shirtmaker's and the perfumer's, followed by a prolonged visit to the barber, completed the realisation, in Armand's person, of his uncle's idea of 'how an engineer should look'.

So sure was Jules Boissier's sartorial aim that, when the young man from St. Flour pushed open the door of the Eiffel offices, no one noticed him. His high collar and frock coat with narrow lapels blended with the décor and had the effect of making him indistinguishable from the dark-suited men passing to and fro in the corridors. The visitor might well have been left standing at the door had he not finally approached the nearest member of staff.

'My name is Armand Boissier,' the newcomer announced

politely. 'The day before yesterday, Monsieur Adolphe Salles...'

Without leaving him time to complete his sentence, the employee pointed to an empty desk.

Unfortunately, it was a long way from the stove and quite near the windows, so there would be no shortage of draughts. Armand could be in no doubt that it was meant for him because an envelope with his name on it lay waiting beneath the lamp. God, how crowded the office was! A pygmy could scarcely make do with so tiny a space, half of which was filled by the desk itself!

Armand was coming to terms with his disappointment when a small man accosted him.

'Good morning, Monsieur Boissier. My name is Pluot, I'm the manager of the Detail Design Office.'

The visitor was happy to be addressed. Monsieur Pluot appeared to be in a hurry, however, and was disinclined to make conversation. He was already unrolling a plan on the desk.

'Here's a drawing of a girder. Our draughtsmen have just inked up this final version. Don't forget the blotter to rest your arm on. A clumsy smudge means a rivet in the wrong place and the whole Tower collapsing!'

This was said with a wink – but one as humourless as a whiplash.

Armand had no time to smile, for the manager had already departed, leaving a little block of pale rubber on the desk – a common-or-garden eraser.

'What's that for?' the engineer wondered. Vaguely, he eyed the outspread plan, which was so large that it spilled over the edge of the desk and fell to the floor in folds. His gaze returned to the eraser, which lay where Pluot had left it, slap in the middle of the drawing.

Suddenly, he understood what they wanted him to do…

'Me, an engineer, rub out pencil marks on drawings?' the youth snorted.

Whom did they take him for? Had they so low an opinion of a college graduate that they were giving him the jobs usually reserved for trainees?

Frowning rebelliously, Armand sat back in his chair and took out a cigar. The cigar had been a gift from Uncle Jules, who had slipped it discreetly into his nephew's pocket without the latter's knowledge. The young provincial had never smoked a real cigar, discarded butts of which were collected professionally along the boulevards and even bought and sold in the capital. At engineering college, most men had smoked only cigarettes, finding them more fitting than an art student's pipe or a bank-manager's Havana. Also, the mechanical manufacture of the cigarette, the smooth cylinder chopped off neatly and containing a precise, unvarying measure of tobacco – these things appealed to their scientific rigour. How different from the nauseating fog of pipe tobacco!

At this point in his thoughts, Armand became aware of a coughing noise. He noticed a young man whose desk abutted his own and might have been its mirror image: the same lamp with the green-glass shade, the same polished-oak chair, the same case of John Mitchell pens, even the same eraser placed on the drawing. The only difference was that some white rubbings showed that the eraser had been used, whereupon Armand felt immediate scorn for his colleague.

Haughtily, he looked away.

'I shouldn't light that cabañas if I were you.'

Striking a match on the wall, Armand looked back at the stranger.

'And who's going to stop me?'

'No one, to be sure, but Monsieur Pluot would give you the sack. Smoking is forbidden for anyone handling plans. It's a rule.'

Tempted to make a lofty rejoinder, Armand nevertheless restrained himself. Why reject the friendship he was being offered? Opting for reason, he extinguished the match and returned the cigar to his pocket.

'Are you an engineer?' he asked, making a quarter-turn on his chair.

'Yes, I studied here in Paris, at the École Centrale.'

'Really? The top college! And you're rubbing out pencil marks on plans? But tell me – isn't that where Eiffel himself trained? So he's taking it out on you, is that it?'

Armand laughed out loud and the other man was good enough to join him.

'Look, Eiffel & Co. is an old firm,' Armand's neighbour said indulgently. 'We've just been taken on but there are some who've worked here for fifteen years! It's understandable, surely, that they should want to cut new recruits down to size a bit.'

'All right! I bow to your sweet reason. If rub out we must, then let's get started!'

And the two young men, rolling up their sleeves in tandem, bent over their drawings and rubbed.

The friendship between Armand Boissier and Odilon Cheyne blossomed from that moment.

It was marvellous to see two beings so well matched, two characters blending so harmoniously. Many things brought them together: age (they were both young), schooling (they were both engineers), talent (here they seemed more or less equals) and finally experience (virtually nil).

As they conversed from desk to desk, it was not like two men talking but only one, holding a discussion with himself.

Their working at adjoining desks threw the resemblance into relief. The very large plans, which required several tables if they were to be unrolled completely, always covered theirs. People got used to seeing them together around the workshops and speaking of them in the same breath. Even Eiffel, who rarely joked, dubbed them 'the eraser twins' – a reference to the thankless chore they performed side by side.

It was at Eiffel's instigation that they were given two-man jobs. Their gifts complemented each other perfectly. Odilon was very good at first drafts, quick sketches on a blank sheet of paper; Armand then made the final plans. The working drawings passed from one desk to the other, appearing in the process to be following a natural path, feeding a well-oiled machine.

In one respect, though, Armand and Odilon differed radically, and that was socially.

Armand was a product of St. Flour, a small provincial town in central France. Everything he had read and learnt, even his college and its uniform, had been unable to expunge completely the rustic tinge that coloured his whole behaviour. This ruddy-complexioned youngster still stared after trams and had trouble tying his laces. Shoes were altogether something of a novelty for him; as a child, he had always worn clogs.

The young man made no secret of the fact that he had never worn a frock coat before his interview with Monsieur Eiffel and that the capital, which he was likewise visiting for the first time, teemed with inventions he did not recognise. This 'hick from the sticks' had to be taught in the space of a month what civilisation had spent a century producing: electric light, which illuminated some of the rooms of

Établissements Eiffel; photography, several prints of which he had admired in Adolphe Salles's office; even his uncle's telephone. Armand did not admire these novelties in equal measure – far from it. Though the gramophone inspired him to the heights of fairground fervour, he found the telephone harder to accept, accusing it of enslaving those who used it. 'There it goes again, your telephone,' he said when the strange device announced itself. 'It rings and you answer it. That's what a valet does.'

Odilon, on the other hand, had all the hallmarks of the city-dweller. From his long hair, styled like an artist's, wafted subtle perfumes, which he had made up for him especially at Lubin's or at Houbignant's and of which, apparently, he had quite a collection. His handkerchiefs were imbued with the appropriate floral essence to match the fine specimen he wore in his buttonhole – red carnation, narcissus or nutmeg geranium, depending on the time of year.

Despite his youth, Odilon walked with a stick, proud to flaunt this handsome object, which had cost him a months wages. It was a Malacca cane with a handle fashioned from a warthog's tusk, and it was admired by all, including Eiffel, who had a taste for finery.

'Where did you get that stick from?' the boss had asked him one day.

'It's an heirloom,' Odilon lied, uncomfortably aware of the futility of such expense.

But Eiffel was not fooled. The following week he had a cane exactly like it – only his was adorned with a silver model of the 300-metre Tower.

It was difficult to imagine a more sophisticated creature than Odilon. His foulard shirt, mother-of-pearl waistcoat buttons, and beaver-fur hat (which he occasionally exchanged for an

English boater) all proclaimed him a man of taste and refinement, a champion of civilization. Indeed, he valued the company of painters and assiduously attended private views. He dabbled in portraiture himself in a semi-bohemian way, and a number of promising ink drawings bore his signature. He was known to have attended the Beaux-Arts before switching to engineering, hence his delayed entry into the profession.

Odilon's penchant for the arts was so pronounced that his taking up a career in engineering caused astonishment. People wondered whether his talents might not have been better invested in painting. Whenever Monsieur Pluot levelled this mild reproach (as he did occasionally, given the somewhat free line of Odilon's working drawings), Odilon replied that science required intuition as art required discipline. Nevertheless, the young man felt a certain kinship with the few artists involved in the Tower: Stephen Sauvestre, for instance, the monument's architect-in-chief, who like him wore a lavalliere when everyone else wore an ordinary black cravat.

The friendship of Armand and Odilon reflected these dissimilarities but on the basis of a deep complicity. Very early on they had assumed the roles of teacher and disciple, or rather, mystagogue and initiate. The four years seniority that Odilon had over Armand, but above all his intimate knowledge of a city in which the young provincial had only just set foot, dictated the tone of their relationship.

'We must see to your Parisian education,' Odilon had announced one day.

His friend had taken this amiss.

'My education? What do you mean by that? You may sport a cane and affect high and mighty airs but what have you got to teach me?'

'I'd like you to meet some of my friends...'

'What friends? The kind of people you go around with? Those dandified fops? No, thank you! My tastes have nothing in common with theirs. I'm not interested in pigeon-shooting or horse-racing or playing baccarat. I've never corresponded with a shirtmaker to review the shape of my cuffs or with a tailor to discuss the cut of my waistcoats. Life in the grip of fashion is not for me. Anyway, how could I afford it? When my father dies – or "pops off", as your friends say – my only inheritance will be debts!'

'All right, keep your hair on…' the Parisian smiled. 'My friends upset you? Fine! We'll go out without them. Would you like to see something of Paris?'

'Would I? Of course!'

Whereupon the two friends had drawn up a programme of outings in the capital. These would take in cafés and museums, the cabarets Odilon thought most suitable for what he called 'breathing in the air of the city'.

'The only air like it in the world!' he said, becoming animated. 'You'll see: all things creative, every idea, everything that excites admiration has its origin on the banks of the Seine. The loveliest women and the most famous men are to be found on our doorstep.'

'When do we start?'

'Soon, soon…don't be in such a rush! Come Sunday, we'll take a stroll round the Alma district. Care to see where the Tower's going up?'

'Why not? I'm drawing it, but in the abstract. Is the site interesting?'

'Not very. They're still digging; building has yet to start. Still, Eiffel's solutions to the problem of the foundations, two of which are on poor ground – they're worth a look.'

'Right, then! Sunday it is, at the Champ-de-Mars!'

Armand had been looking forward to his Parisian excursion like a schoolboy in feverish anticipation of the holidays.

As dawn was breaking and the delivery boys were sliding newspapers beneath doors, he climbed into the cab ordered the day before for the drive to the Champ-de-Mars. Except for the municipal sprinkler wagons, the streets were deserted; the gas-lamps had yet to be extinguished. In an instant, it seemed, they were at the café Dupuy.

Armand could see that the iron grating was still down.

'Good grief! It's closed!'

'The Dupuy doesn't open till eight o'clock, it's a bourgeois establishment,' remarked the coachman, who occasionally drove patrons home.

Armand buttoned up his frock coat. It was bitterly cold this winter morning. Not the raw, diffused cold of the countryside but a different kind of cold: keener, as if the steely glints off the river had become knives, slicing along the dark streets. Long blades of wind whetted themselves on the bridges as on a grindstone before testing their edges on the tall façades.

'Brrr! I need a Turin vermouth, piping hot!' the young engineer said imploringly, blowing into his hands.

No less foreign to him than the quality of the cold were the sounds he could hear. The quiet of a rural daybreak, barely disturbed by a distant cockcrow, became a roaring, almost thundering sound here in the city. Early as it was, the clatter of trams could already be heard, as could the panting of steam barges, the cries of street traders and the tramping of crowds that swelled by the instant, noisily beginning the daily round.

In this medley of sound, one note stood out clearly: the busy, juddering rattle of machinery. It came from the direction of the Champ-de-Mars. 'The Tower site!' the engineer realised with a surge of emotion. He consulted his watch. 'I'm in plenty of time! I'll take a look around.'

The Champ-de-Mars was then simply a stretch of flat ground, a huge empty space at the heart of the capital. Of its earlier uses, which included vineyard and market garden, nothing remained but shreds of undergrowth, scraps of clothing on a vast expanse of nudity. For over a century, soldiers had contested every centimetre of that square of sand, simulating charges and digging trenches. When war did not rage over the Champ-de-Mars, the space was used as a fairground or horse-races were held there or balloons released, one bearing Nadar with his photographic cabinet. Unfortunately, despite being graced by World Expositions every ten years, despite being ringed with a plank fence – the planks were promptly filched by the gypsies – the Champ-de-Mars invariably returned to wind and dust. Thus it had always been, and thus it was still: one vast, useless plain...

Armand strode towards a high fence. The only things visible above the wooden screen were a mast with ropes suspended from it and a number of gibbet-shaped structures. But from the vibration of the earth one sensed that great works were going on below. Impatient to see, he scaled the plank wall.

What a sight! The whole area had been churned up. As a building-site, it was certainly imposing – but quite incomprehensible: an open-cast mine where construction and demolition seemed to be proceeding simultaneously.

Here processions of horse-drawn wagons hauled earth from the depths of a crater. There a number of curious metal barges, each with a shed on top, seemed to float on the sandy surface. Having worked on the designs, Armand recognised the compressed-air caissons that made it possible to excavate underwater.

Only a professional could identify the positions of the four piers of the Tower, as yet ill-defined amid the jumble of blocks, ramps and heaps of ballast. In places, the work the labourers were engaged in conjured up ancient ruins: Rome, in those thick rubble-stone walls; Egypt, in those inclines of dressed stone suggesting the foot of a pyramid.

'Sir! No climbing the wall – it's forbidden!'

Surprised, the engineer tried to leap down but stumbled. Odilon, laughing, ran to help him up.

'What do you mean, playing tricks like that! I nearly died of fright.'

'What are you so scared of? You're not scrumping apples. Come on, plenty of people do what you've just done every day. That tree over there could tell some stories, I'll bet!'

'But what a sight!' Armand said, dusting off his hat. 'It's difficult to make sense of it all.'

The Parisian steered his colleague towards a gate in the fence.

'That's because the four piers require different treatments. For those on solid ground, it was only necessary to excavate tons and tons of clay and gravel, which were dumped on public tips. But for the piers nearest the Seine, we found water.'

'Water! But it's not exactly on the river bank.'

'It was for our ancestors. Where the north and east piers will stand was once an arm of the river with three small islands: Treilles, Vaches and Longchamp. The islands were made into one and that was where duellists made their appointments, hence the name, Malequerelle. On occasion, it was also used by farmers, who took their animals across to graze. At other times, butchers rinsed offal in the clear waters of the Seine. The Sun King raised birds there, behind high fences, and from then on the place was known as Swan Island. Eventually, it was joined up with the riverbank before the Revolution.'

'You certainly know your stuff,' said Armand, admiringly.

'The subject interests me… I don't believe the decision where to build a monument should be taken lightly. One thing's for sure, when this site was chosen for the Tower rather than the Bastille or Montmartre, there were other reasons besides ground solidity. Did you know human skeletons were unearthed during digging? They were the bones of Huguenots killed at the time of the Massacre of St. Bartholomew. The Tower, built on top of a graveyard! Makes you think, doesn't it?'

Odilon had spoken these words with an air of mystery that Armand found intriguing. He tried to catch his friend's eye but the Parisian had fallen into a stubborn silence, which he maintained throughout their visit.

While the twins were investigating the Tower site, two other strollers had entered the Champ-de-Mars. Their slow, meditative steps seemed those of a funeral procession.

The first was a tall man, wearing a chequered suit, supple boots and crossover braces in a style that betrayed his American origins. The other was all in black except for a tiny red spot in his buttonhole, like a drop of blood in a lost duel, the Revolutionary rosette.

'Oh dear, they've started digging,' sighed Gordon Hole, his French mangled by a transatlantic accent.

A sceptical frown creased the second man's brow.

'They're digging, but will they build? Digging is child's play. Erecting a tower 300 metres high is something else entirely.'

Hole made a pensive, sucking sound.

'Monsieur Bourdais, if I may address you as a professional colleague. You are the famous architect of the palace across the river, the Trocadéro. The skyscrapers for which I drew up the plans have also brought me a certain reputation across the ocean. We both know that this metal tower is an absurdity and that it will never be built…Or, if it is built, it will collapse. No one has built anything so high before!'

'Never was there a worse idea!' Jules Bourdais agreed vehemently, kicking at a stone. 'If only they'd chosen my project, "The Sun Column", which would be 360 metres high and built entirely of granite!'

'Five storeys with galleries all around.' Hole recited. 'A permanent museum of electricity. Balconies for TB sufferers up where they can breathe best and at the very top, a giant lantern.'

'Yes!' roared Bourdais, punching the air above him. 'An electric beacon, magnified by parabolic mirrors, so that all night long, all over Paris, there'd be eight times more light than a person needs to read a newspaper. Darkness sent packing, banished from the "City of Light". There's a serious ambition for you.'

'A marvellous project, worthy of the master that you are. But alas! The spirit of science that crowns your beacon will never gaze out over Paris. They go and choose the tinkerings of a bridge-builder in preference to the grand designs of the architect. Art has been sacrificed to engineering. The devil take Eiffel!'

On hearing his rival's name, Jules Bourdais seemed to collapse inwardly. His shoulders drooped, the whole man appeared to become shorter. He walked with head bowed, eyes fixed on the toes of his shoes, gloomily absent.

Hole chose this moment to take his colleague's hand in a warm embrace.

'Can you keep a secret, Monsieur Bourdais?'

The architect threw him a forlorn look. He was like a hurt child, waiting for a word of comfort.

'I know Gustave Eiffel better than anyone. Thirty-five years back we shared a bench at the same engineering college. Then he was only interested in the chemical side, hoping for a position in his uncle's vinegar distillery. His results hardly fitted him for any other career, he came eleventh in his first year, twenty-second in his second and thirty-third in his finals. Above all, he had a horror of drawing.'

'How curious! I'd never heard that story,' said Bourdais, his interest aroused.

'At the time, I was already a fan of metal construction. It seemed to me that wrought-iron could usefully be employed in the construction of major works without having recourse to the ancient techniques of arch, vault or dome. Wrought-iron is cheap, I thought, and incombustible, and does it not offer more resistance than cast-iron to all kinds of forces? So I spent my evenings working out a system. In class, I made a presentation to my fellow-students. Eiffel listened... Oh, if only I'd held my tongue! I was misled by his apparent lack of interest in the subject, but he was taking extensive notes, even copying formulae over my shoulder.'

Bourdais gave a powerful squeeze to the American's hand, which still held his own.

'Eiffel – a plagiarist!'

'There's no other word for it. Take the ugly-looking section of his tower: two legs, an arch, then a spire topped by a crude lantern, the whole thing criss-crossed with a loosely-woven lattice of metal struts! The spitting image, surely, of all those steel viaducts they've spent the last forty years throwing over every chasm in the world? Think of the Crumlin Bridge in Britain, the one across the Sarine near Fribourg in Switzerland and here in France the bridges at La Cère and Le Busseau d'Ahun.'

'You're right, by God!' Bourdais conceded, folding his arms.

'In any case, it was certainly my calculations that Eiffel used as the basis for his model. I, sir, designed the world's first skyscraper, the Home Insurance Building in Chicago, completed over two years ago. Well, if you strip that building down and look at the wrought-iron armature, you'll find it contains all the secrets of the Tower. The plain truth is: Eiffel robbed me!'

All the time Hole had been speaking, Jules Bourdais had listened very attentively. Eyes half-closed, he had appeared to savour and slowly assimilate the American architect's every word. Then suddenly, turning to Hole, he stopped him with a hand on his chest.

'Sir, what you are saying is serious. In the name of science, such things must be exposed. Are we to stand idly by and see a swindler triumph? Shall we simply allow this tower about which there is nothing new, let alone beautiful, to shoot up like a weed? No! We must fight. I know people in Paris: journalists, judges… This scandal is going to hit the roof.'

The American's smile was restrained.

'Right, you talk about alerting the press. So you should, I quite agree. In fact, I would urge you to. But don't imagine that any amount of printing-ink will ever topple the Tower. Work has begun, Monsieur Bourdais, we have the site before us, less than three months from now we shall see the ironwork starting to climb! No, there's only one way to stop it.'

Jules Bourdais stiffened like a soldier awaiting his orders.

'So be it! I'm listening, sir. How can it be stopped?'

Gordon Hole stared hard into the Frenchman's eyes. On and on he stared, probing the man's soul, searching for a response. Finally, with a brief exhalation of breath that made his nostrils quiver and carved two malevolent dimples at the corners of his mouth, he pronounced one word…

'Sabotage.'

A sudden pallor came over the Frenchman's face. He looked at Hole as if he had seen a snake rearing up behind his head.

'Are you out of your mind?'

Hole seized him in a convulsive grip. His voice sounded tense, as if drawn out by fear.

'An act of sabotage, Monsieur Bourdais. There is no other way. I wanted to make your acquaintance because I saw you as a man of resolution, even of daring, if circumstances required. I cannot act without back-up, this is not my country, but together we can accomplish anything. We'll bring the Tower down! Gustave Eiffel has invested everything in its construction. He'll never recover. So, are you with me?'

Violently, Bourdais wrenched his sleeve free.

'No, I am not, you old fool! Above all, I have no intention of joining you in prison!'

Whereupon Jules Bourdais turned on his heel and strode off without so much as a word of farewell.

Gordon Hole watched the Frenchman disappear rapidly in the direction of Avenue de Suffren. His formerly contorted features now assumed a relaxed expression, leaving only a single deep furrow descending all the way from his hairline to the bridge of his nose. One hand reached into an inside pocket of his jacket, which some heavy object had pulled badly out of shape. He took out a revolver, a 41-calibre nickel-plated Remington Deringer with his initials engraved on the double barrel.

'No silly tricks, now!' he reasoned with himself, putting the weapon away and walking towards a carriage parked nearby.

Gaspard Louchon took up the flask and drew the cork. His

gaze rested on the thick glass. The flask was half-full of a viscous liquid. He shook it, releasing a stimulating, spicy smell.

'Ah, this is the stuff!' he said contentedly.

Then he stuffed the neck of the flask up his left nostril and threw his head back. In seconds his mouth fell open like that of a fish out of water. A milky fluid dribbled down his chin.

Just at that moment Gordon Hole climbed into the carriage.

'Damned dreamer!' the architect exclaimed on finding Gaspard with a bottle up his nose.

He grabbed the flask and threw it out of the window.

'If I catch you swallowing that poison again, I promise you…'

But the other, slumped on the seat, his chest heaving spasmodically, appeared not to hear. His tongue was strangely swollen.

'Are you listening to me, Gaspard?' Hole asked, shaking the addict without ceremony.

He slapped the man's face, which threw his head back against the door, right beside an advertisement reading, 'Visit Faussillon and Co. for a huge selection of odd gloves, perfect for the one-armed gentleman.' A second slap, followed by a third, progressively restored Gaspard to consciousness. His pupils swam through a curtain of tears.

'Sir…,' the addict gurgled.

'That's one more time I've saved your life, you damn junkie, but it's the last time too! What do I want with a man who takes poison? Are you some sort of poet, that you smoke camphor cigarettes all day? Joined the Zutistes, have you, or the Hirsutes, or the Hydropaths or some such crazy sect? Go to hell!'

Hole banged a fist on the padded door and the carriage lurched into motion.

'Is something the matter, sir?' enquired Gaspard, who was slowly recovering his wits.

'Yes, I have a headache. It's your language that does it, French gives me unbearable migraines! I honestly hate the language, particularly when I wrestle with it to no purpose.'

'Monsieur Bourdais didn't…?' Gaspard ventured, then blew his nose.

'No!' the architect thundered. 'What do you think? Bourdais is a coward and a fool! In actual fact, when all's said and done I'm not too sorry he declined our offer. Who, in a job like this, wants anything to do with a man who still builds in stone? Stone, for Christ's sake, like back in the Ancient World! Stupid reactionary! Did the Washington Monument teach him nothing? That granite obelisk was meant to reach 183 metres but they were forced to cap it at 169, after thirty years work! So Bourdais isn't with us? Good riddance!'

'If you're happy, I am too,' Gaspard mumbled through his self-induced fog.

Hole threw him a black look and pulled down the blind.

'They're all dreamers, these Frenchmen. No enterprise, no Anglo-Saxon spirit! What have been the masterpieces of architecture in this century? The Crystal Palace complex – in London! Brooklyn Bridge – in New York! The French have built nothing decent.'

'All the same,' interjected Gaspard, the drug stimulating his patriotism, 'the competition for the 300-metre Tower produced some very novel projects.'

The architect snorted with derision.

'You don't say! You mean that building in the shape of a watering can, designed to keep Paris moist in case of drought? Or were you thinking of the giant guillotine, that shining reminder of the Revolution? Ah, there was Monsieur Hénard's design, an Indian-style temple supported by elephants! Really, you had to laugh!'

Seizing his American employer by the coat-collar, Gaspard broke into a storm of spluttering.

'The 300-metre Tower will be French, sir! French and Parisian! It is our country's revenge for the defeat of 1870, a limb of iron to replace the one the Prussians amputated: Alsace and Lorraine!'

The American needed only to shrug his shoulders to release himself from the addict's flabby grip.

'I pity you, Gaspard. A life thrown away sketching urinals and newspaper booths! What do you know about the 300-metre Tower? Anyway, that's not what it's called, the proper name for it is "the 1,000-foot Tower". Your fellow-countryman Sébillot brought the project back from America, scene of his birth half a century ago. Our engineers dreamed up that beacon long before yours. In a fair world, they'd have built it, too!'

The architect gently massaged his temples.

'We're going to have to change our plans. Looking for allies is a mistake, the truth fights alone!'

Gaspard was using a twisted corner of his handkerchief to fiddle inside his ears.

'What do you have in mind, sir?'

'I haven't decided yet. Would sabotage work? And if so, what's the best way to do it? Dynamite one of the piers? Cause the first platform to collapse? Make one of the elevators plummet? Topple a crane? Or what about waiting for the inauguration ceremony and replacing the fireworks with real shells?'

'It'll be expensive!'

Hole gave his associate a cold stare.

'Quite a sensible comment for a dreamer. Don't you know how powerful explosives are? What a man can do alone with a flask of nitro-glycerine?'

'Go to his death – I know that much.'

'Enough!' the American roared, losing his temper. 'Don't say another word! Your French is addling my brain!'

He turned his back on Gaspard, who calmly continued fiddling in his ears.

Before long, the carriage drew up outside a private house. Gaspard got out and knocked on the front door. A marble slab bore the inscription: 'Structural Engineers' Club'.

Having finished viewing the site, Armand and Odilon left the Champ-de-Mars on foot.

The fascinating panorama of the excavations had dispelled Odilon's troubled mood. His laugh had returned, he told jokes and winked at the pretty girls who went by. His zest for life, too, seemed restored, and he talked non-stop about Paris and its wonders, especially the ones in skirts, and promised his provincial companion those legendary 'kisses under every streetlamp'.

'Really, people kiss all over the place?' the young man asked, enraptured, taking everything at face value in his candour.

'Yes, they do, in a manner of speaking. Nothing could be more natural than falling in love in Paris! It's as though it were always springtime here. Look at that bridge and that square with its pretty green kiosk, don't they seem made to stage a love scene?'

'Oh, yes, indeed!' rejoiced Armand, clapping his hands together. 'How glad I am to be here!'

Odilon shot his friend a sly look.

'You're looking for a fiancée, aren't you? Your face gives you away. Well, take your pick! Across the river, for example, up near the Opera House, on Boulevard des Italiens you'll see more nubile girls than windows. Milliners, dressmakers, florists… The most sought-after are linen laundresses, every young man dreams of having one of those on his arm – so pretty, so clean, white as swans and smelling of fresh linen!'

'Oh, show me! Lead me to it!'

A captivated Armand was all for hurrying straight there. He tugged at Odilon's arm like a dog pulling on a lead.

However, doubts assailed him at the first crossroads they came to, where choosing one pavement meant missing the other and possibly missing a treasure within easy reach. The great theatre that was Paris gave shows round the clock and one could never be sure where the stage shone most brightly.

Odilon, of course, had a more rounded idea of what they should see.

'I know – the Louvre!' he said. 'Let's start with the best!'

But Armand disagreed.

'Oh, damn museums! Time enough for them when we've got hair growing out of our ears. Let's go to one of those cafés with singers. You said they were so wonderful…'

The discussion dragged on, Odilon holding out fiercely for the finer things in life, Armand as fiercely defending his pleasure. The sun was already high when they reached a decision, they would follow the nearby Seine. The two friends descended to the embankment and began walking along it.

It was the start of a comfortable stroll, following the winding course of the river and rounding the obstacles placed here and there in the shape of heaps of goods.

Armand and Odilon walked side by side, noses tucked into their scarves as protection against the cold. Down by the water it was even colder and icy beards hung from the mooring-posts of the lighters, many of which were frozen in. The strollers stopped opposite a sailing-barge surrounded by a sheet of ice. Its rust-red canvas and the copper piping round the boiler made it look like a Golconda ruby in its casket.

For Armand, everything was an object of curiosity. He gazed in wonder at the mattress-makers leaning back against the parapet, tearing out handfuls of grey stuffing from old beds. He looked closely at the floating wash-sheds with their rows of stout women working beetles; and he looked even more closely at the swimming establishments where the very occasional lady bather was braving the icy water. He was captivated by the sight of a steam dredger, the rising and plunging motion of its mechanical shovel mesmerising him like a child.

Porters hurried to and fro, making little piles of merchandise. In one place, pyramids of yellow or green fruit filled the air with a blaze of colour, like light from a stained-glass window. In another, there were stacks of coal or sawdust, hillocks of sand that, shovelful by shovelful, were migrating from barge to quayside. On Solferino Bridge, opposite the Tuileries Gardens, a lone fisherman watched his line, which was threatened by blocks of ice floating down on the current.

Towards noon, Armand and Odilon took a table in a cheap restaurant frequented by the stevedores. Over lunch, they discussed these intriguing impressions.

'You said you'd tell me why that man was toting a basket filled with cobwebs,' said Armand, picking at his food.

'He sells them, of course!'

'He sells cobwebs? Noble trade!'

'No, it's true. I've seen how he does it. He mixes the spider's silk with glue, slaps a coat on a glass bottle, then sprinkles the whole thing with sawdust.'

Odilon passed his knife over a piece of bread and butter to mimic the cobweb-merchant's work. Armand followed the operation, fascinated.

'But who on earth buys that kind of thing?'

'Bar-owners. A bottle covered in cobwebs gives a good effect. It looks old and commands a higher price.'

'Amazing!' Armand exclaimed in delight, his mouth very obviously full. 'You don't get that in St. Flour!'

Such innocence made Odilon smile.

'Oh, Paris holds many mysteries! For instance, you spotted that old man, working his way upriver on a raft?'

'Towing a string of dead dogs? How could I have missed it!'

'What do you think his trade is?'

The young man was silent for a long moment, sipping his wine reflectively.

'Don't know, but one thing's for sure: he won't have a private income!'

'That man manufactures maggots. From dawn to dusk he paddles up and down the Seine, collecting drowned animals – those hideous, bloated corpses that drift down on the current. He harpoons them and ties them up behind his raft. Other times he buys dead cats from the ragman for a few pence. All that carrion goes into a big box in his attic, where he leaves it to rot. A week later, the maggots are ready; all he has to do is scrape them off into tins.'

Armand's stomach heaved and he pushed his plate away.

'How disgusting! I shouldn't like to shake his hand. You certainly have some stories.'

'Oh, I do! There's no shortage of characters in the capital. What do you expect? Poverty propels the imagination...'

'Tell me more,' his provincial friend pleaded.

'In Paris, you can set up a leech-hire service, there's this woman who, for thirty sous, will provide the worms and also apply them. Her services are in great demand with the sick. If you have a good surname, why not become a putative father and pass it on to children no one has acknowledged! You like smoking? Be a pipe-seasoner, a lazy job that involves puffing away all day to blacken the bowls of pipes. Gypsies used to do it before pipe-seasoning factories were invented. I could give you a thousand other examples: hair-implanter, dogshit sorter, a person who wakes up nightworkers, cricket-seller – for people who like to have one chirping in the hearth – live-in shepherd, to look after your pet sheep or goat, and that's not all…'

'Stop! Stop!' Armand cried through his laughter. 'You'll make me regret that I practice so ordinary a profession as engineer!'

Their meal paid for, the friends climbed a steep flight of stairs and came out on the embankment. Odilon pointed out a nearby footbridge, 'The Pont des Arts, the first iron bridge built in France!'

It was a shock to be back in the Parisian traffic, a many-layered affair of pedestrians, horses, carriages and trams that roared only steps away from the peaceful riverbank. It was like another river, a more turbulent one, flowing along beside the first.

A disabled veteran of the last war was displaying books and medals in a box on top of the parapet and the engineers lingered to leaf through his wares. They found some engravings of the Tower, rather badly done. One sensed that the artists, trained on monuments of solid stone, had trouble capturing this delicate network of metal, full of glints and highlights.

'Look, it's getting late. Let's hire a cab, or a *sapin*, as we say in Paris… I've done enough walking.'

So it was in the comfort of a hackney carriage that they continued their trip. Armand felt annoyed with himself for having spent so much time strolling aimlessly. Queues were already forming outside theatres and the lines of cabs crawling along the boulevards increased his unease.

'Oh, how stupid! We've wasted the whole day!' he sighed regretfully, picking at the padding of the seat.

Soon they reached the Latin Quarter. 'Student country!' commented Odilon for his friend's benefit as Armand leaned out of the window. The latter nodded distractedly and signalled for them to move on.

In a moment, the cab came out on Boulevard St. Germain. Here everything looked very different. The bohemian façades of the Left Bank gave way to handsome town houses, their porches surmounted by stone escutcheons. The pipes smoked by the students were replaced by cigars, gripped between the teeth in holders of precious amber or meerschaum. Armand remembered his cabañas, which he now drew from his pocket and lit.

Through the window of the cab, the different quarters of Paris succeeded one another: the Chaussée d'Antin, the financial district; Nouvelle Athènes, where the artists lived and worked; the Faubourg St. Honoré, home of the foreign embassies. Without wishing to stop anywhere, the young man from St. Flour delighted in the richly-coloured tapestry of scenes that first entered, then faded from his field of vision.

After a two-hour journey, the carriage drew up at the Louvre.

'End of the line!' the driver barked, tugging on the reins.

'Already?' said an astonished Armand. 'We've been all round Paris?'

'We've seen the best bits, certainly!'

'It's not enough! I've seen nothing! Where are the girls you were bragging about? And the Opera House and the fancy-dress balls?'

'A week wouldn't be enough!' Odilon protested as he counted out the fare into the cabbie's hand. 'We'll do that next time!'

Armand pretended to throw a tantrum, banging his heels on the floor of the cab.

'Oh no, we won't! I'm not going back to my uncle's without something to remember! Those were the best bits of Paris, you said. Show me the worst!'

He refused to let the matter rest. Their tour of Paris had left him hungry. He'd been expecting something stronger, meatier, more like the novels that had woven his 'dream of the capital', as he called it.

'Dream? More like a nightmare!' Odilon laughed. 'All right, you want a thrill? You shall have one!'

And the engineer whispered to the coachman, naming a mysterious address, their new destination.

The 'eraser twins' were dropped at dusk at the 'Quay of Flowers', as it was called, the easternmost tip of Île de la Cité, behind Notre-Dame. It was well-named: the parapet and part of the roadway were given over to the flower-sellers, who had set out displays of the lovely creations that constituted their trade in bunches, in pots or on cardboard or wooden extensions. Wearing smocks as grubby as those of painters, they tastefully assembled perfumed bouquets.

'A little corner of heaven!' the young provincial breathed admiringly.

'The flower market, which every Sunday becomes the bird market. This way!'

Just after Pont St. Louis, the street curved around to hug the island's tip. The area was in darkness, night already blanketed the pavements and the lamp-posts cast regular pools of light. There were no gas-lamps here, these were carcel lamps burning oil. Their blood-red light bathed the flagstones.

At the end of the street was a little square with, on the far side, a building half-buried in the embankment. Odilon pressed the bell.

Just then, a wagon drew up at the arched entrance. The open side of the vehicle revealed the interior, where Armand made out a policeman with his distinctive coat and white truncheon, two other silhouettes well back in the shadows, and between them the outstretched body of a woman. The woman was headless.

'We're closed,' came a grating voice from the spyhole.

'Open up, Old Man Modesty★. It's Odilon Cheyne.'

The lock slid back with a thud. In the half-open doorway stood an elderly figure holding a candlestick. He resembled an eighteenth century print with his carpet slippers and the embroidered skullcap crowning his long white hair. A strong smell of embalming fluid accompanied him.

'This isn't right,' the old man growled. 'It's late. Anyway, there's no seance today.'

'A courtesy call…' Odilon explained, wholly at ease.

Old Man Modesty stood aside, shaking his head. 'It's not right…,' he went on muttering as he followed them down t he passage.

'Odilon, where are we?' Armand asked uncertainly.

'At the morgue!'

They were ushered into a dark room. Only the echo of their footsteps gave any indication of its size. Old Man Modesty's candle was surrounded by profound darkness, a murky obscurity that seemed almost viscous, one sensed it as

★Père la Pudeur was indeed the name of the morgue attendant at the time. The 'modesty' alluded to is of a sexual nature, and the title was bestowed in a spirit of ironic ridicule, given the shameless nudity of the man's 'charges'.

something tangible, one felt that if one opened one's mouth one would be able to taste it. Armand was surprised at how cold the room felt, colder than outside.

'May we have some light?' he asked, having just stumbled over a step.

Still muttering, the old man found a firebrand and lit a series of weak jets, one by one. Gradually, the shiny edges of glass cases emerged from the gloom, followed by the shapes of arms, legs and outlines of heads under shrouds…The darkness gave up its prey reluctantly, dripping from each slab like a melting iceblock. It was like a winter of death breaking up.

The last jet was alight. The whole room was now visible.

'Great heavens!' exclaimed Armand, clutching a rail behind him.

Six corpses of men and women lay on slabs of black marble arranged regularly about the room. These were no ordinary dead bodies waiting to be laid in coffins; these were murder victims whose wounds, whose pus, whose twisted and broken limbs were here placed shamelessly on public view. Nothing separated the dead from the living but a frail glass box. So the curious could study close up the evisceration of a woman, or trace in a man's chest the path of a bullet or sword-blade. Some of the bodies were still soiled with a mixture of dried blood, brain tissue and other spatterings.

Armand had never met such a sight before.

'We're in luck!' Odilon remarked, walking among the cases. 'During opening hours this place is packed. Lots of people come here in the middle of the day in summer for the coolness of the refrigerating machines. It's even worse the day after a murder, they want to see the body with the slashed throat they've all read about in the papers!'

'Odilon, why did you bring me here?' gasped Armand,

aware that his stomach was starting to turn.

'But this is the Paris the novelists write about, my friend! Several of us have got into the habit of visiting the morgue late at night, when the crowds have dispersed. What better place to contemplate the finite quality of human existence?'

'I…I feel ill,' Armand groaned.

Leaning back against a wall, he fumbled with his shirt collar.

'Well, well!' murmured the Parisian. 'Who's an impressionable fellow, then!'

At that moment, a dreadful racket was heard. A pair of double doors burst open at the back of the room, admitting a stretcher borne by two men. The young engineers recognised the headless body they had glimpsed in the wagon. A third figure, the policeman, followed carrying a tray: on it was the head, wrapped in a piece of cloth as if it had been a ham.

Armand swivelled about and vomited.

'Hey! My floor!' protested Old Man Modesty.

'Don't worry, grandpa, we'll clean it up,' Odilon retorted, moving to steady his friend.

With a shrug, the attendant turned back to the newcomers, who were laying out the body on an empty table.

'They're strange fellows, these…' the Parisian confided under his breath. 'Do you know, anatomy demonstrators and medics can buy bodies here very cheaply? I mean, they have to have something to practise their scalpel technique on! Some steal a march on the morgue collectors and purchase murder victims while they're still warm! They pay 30 francs for an adult male, twenty for a child. It happens out at Clamart or Faubourg St. Marceau…'

'For pity's sake, can we stop talking about corpses!' Armand begged, sniffing at a handkerchief sprinkled with alcohol.

The policeman had unwrapped the head and was trying to

fit it to the body, inclining his own head to judge the artistic effect. Eventually he compromised by standing it to one side.

It was at this point that a curious phenomenon occurred. Armand looked up to see the severed head, which the policeman was still holding by the hair. The dead woman's eyes were wide open. And although the dark pupils held no sign of life, they did have an expression – the agonised expression of a soul wrenched from existence without being able to yield up its secret or name its murderer. The young engineer felt something drawing him into the depths of that look, a kind of suction, as if he were a dinghy trapped in a whirlpool. He cried out.

At that very instant, several panes of glass in the morgue shattered.

'Good God!' the attendant swore. The other witnesses of the scene just stood there, stunned. Shards of glass covered the floor.

'What…what happened?' Armand wanted to know, sensing all eyes upon him.

Odilon was staring at him with particular intensity.

'Nothing at all!' he said at length, helping his friend to straighten up. 'A gas explosion, probably. Miners are familiar with the danger. Come on, it's time we were going! We're in these gentlemen's way.'

Odilon dragged Armand from the room, pulling him vigorously, almost authoritatively, by the arm as if their lives depended on their being outside as soon as possible.

The two friends emerged from the morgue. By good fortune the driver, dozing on his bench, had not yet left. The sound of the cab door closing made him stir.

'What address, sir?' he enquired with a yawn.

'My place, Rue de Berri!' Odilon told him. 'You can take my friend home afterwards.'

The cab set off, its shiny hood gleaming beneath the crimson street-lights.

Gaspard Luchon took the proffered quill and wrote his name in the leather-bound register. As he made to close the book he noticed, entered on the same page, a long list of diners. There was a whole group of them, bracketed together as 'Engineers'.

'Is there a reception this evening?' he asked the porter of the Structural Engineers' Club.

'There is indeed, sir. Jules Boissier is celebrating his nephew's being taken on by Gustave Eiffel.'

'Eiffel, eh? Must be a promising young man. Why didn't I get an invitation, I wonder?'

'An oversight, I'm sure,' the porter murmured discreetly.

Gaspard Louchon gave him a coin and retired to the toilet. Using a soft cloth and a silk brush, he smartened up his jacket. A bar of mimosa-scented soap removed all trace of grey from beneath his perfectly manicured fingernails. The finishing touch was supplied by a circular pill, which he dropped from a pill-box. Swallowed with a mouthful of water, this brought a pink blush to his cheekbones and a limpid breeze, as it were, to his spirit. He winked at his reflection.

A velvety half-light filled the billiard room. Gaspard nodded to the bored scorer, who had no players to attend to. The reading-room with its comfortable armchairs and the music room with its Érard piano in the centre were similarly unoccupied. Members were all heading for the dining-room, from which came the sound of groups of people engaged in conversation. Gaspard handed his card to the chief steward, who intoned sonorously: 'Monsieur Gaspard Louchon, formerly of the Department of Public Works'.

A jovial-looking gentleman promptly approached him, bearing two glasses of champagne. One of these he offered to Gaspard.

'Welcome, Monsieur Louchon! I am Jules Boissier, railway engineer, now retired. I have not, I believe, had the honour of meeting you before…'

'Indeed so, sir – forgive my intrusion. As a long-standing member of the club…'

'You were quite right to come. My colleagues will be delighted to make your acquaintance. A number were with the Department.'

His reception duties performed, Jules Boissier was on the point of withdrawing when Gaspard raised his glass and touched it to his host's.

'Well, then… To your nephew's health!'

'How kind, many thanks,' said the old man, somewhat surprised. 'But how did you know?'

'The porter may have been indiscreet. So, the lad has been recruited by Monsieur Eiffel?'

'A fortnight ago and he's doing well. He's only an office-boy at the moment, working on drawings of small parts and checking calculations. But my nephew is ambitious and a hard worker. I'm sure he'll make his way.'

'I've no doubt of it,' Gaspard said flatteringly, licking golden champagne foam from his lips. 'And what is the young man's name? I have a friend myself in a high-up position on Eiffel's staff.'

'Armand Boissier. His name is Armand Boissier.'

'Armand… Very good!' said Gaspard with approval, writing in a little tortoiseshell-bound notebook. 'I shall not fail to recommend him.'

'That's very good of you,' said Jules in conclusion, shaking him by the hand. 'And now, enjoy the evening!'

Gaspard Louchon bowed with a smile. The satisfaction of having drawn so much information from Uncle Jules, coupled with the expansive effect of the pill, gave him a feeling of happy self-contentment. He mingled with two or three groups of engineers, who were discussing construction prices. Then, emptying his glass into a large flower pot, he left the room.

The club had a brand-new telephone. No one had yet tried the apparatus, a gleaming mahogany Ader No. 4 enshrined in a corner of the smoking-room with an instruction manual beside it. Gaspard pressed the call button several times, waiting for the ring. When it came he unhooked the two receivers and asked the operator for the Hôtel Britannique. Several minutes later another ringing sound told him that the connection had been made.

The receptionist answered. Gaspard had to wait while a bellboy went to wake Gordon Hole politely. Eventually, the American's drowsy voice came through both receivers.

'Gordon Hole speaking…'

'It's me, sir! Gaspard Louchon!' said the engineer, his lips almost brushing the pine panel.

A hiss of irritation was heard at the other end of the line.

'I hope you've got a good excuse, ringing me at this time of night. But for this damned headache, I should have been asleep by now.'

'I have an excellent excuse, sir! I've found a young man who works for Gustave Eiffel. He's called Armand Boissier.'

With Hole refusing to speak the language of La Fayette any longer, the conversation switched to English. The American architect's voice was obscured by the crackling on the line and as Gaspard's vocabulary was limited he grasped only one word in three. This was in fact fortunate because the rest were not ones he would have wished to hear.

'You sound angry, sir. I fail to understand… Would it not be very much in our interests to make an accomplice of this young engineer? What better way could there be of getting our hands on plans of the Tower in order to prepare our move?'

'That would be a smart idea – if the engineer was a man of forty. But a novice who's just joined a firm, a young man on the threshold of his career, do you think he's going to betray his boss by sabotaging the man's life's work? Never!'

'But with money…'

'Money isn't everything, Gaspard. In fact, it's rather a feeble lure compared to fame. End of discussion. Drop the idea.'

Sensing that the other man was about to end the call, Gaspard went on hurriedly: 'Just a second, sir! Would you let me tail the young man?'

'You'd be wasting your time.'

Then, after a pause for thought:

'Still, why not? I've nothing planned for you… Up to you!'

This time the connection was terminated.

Gaspard hung up the two ear-pieces and rubbed his hands. He was exultant. 'A splendid evening's work! Really!' This fresh success certainly deserved a treat. Gaspard promptly took out his pill-box and helped himself to one, no, two more 'happy pills'. He washed them down with a mouthful of Dutch bitters to enhance their effect. His head lolled back against the armchair.

A moment later, the door of the smoking room opened. Jules Boissier entered, yawning, and crossed towards the telephone. He was startled when one of the armchairs swivelled round to reveal a beaming Gaspard Louchon, cheeks as bright as Father Christmas, a glass of genever in his hand.

'I'm so sorry! I didn't realise…' said the old man in some confusion, backing towards the door.

But the other leapt to his feet, bowing like an acrobat.

'Think nothing of it! Think nothing of it!' he almost sang. 'I was just speaking to my sister. It's all yours!' he added, indicating the telephone.

Much taken aback by his companion's manner, Jules nevertheless thanked him. He sat down at the desk, waving vaguely towards the door, for Gaspard showed no sign of leaving.

'This won't take a moment. The reception is in honour of my nephew, who is rather late arriving. My guests are becoming impatient. I'm going to call home.'

'A fine young fellow!' the engineer remarked, donning his hat. 'But I warn you! Communications with the Left Bank are not good.'

'I live on the Right Bank. Moreover, the line to Rue de Bruxelles is a good one. Several celebrities live there and they are all subscribers. Émile Zola, for instance.'

'Oh, well, you'll have no problems.'

Unable to postpone his departure any longer, Gaspard left with a huge laugh, a booming laugh that accompanied him down the corridor and across the vestibule and could even be heard when he was out in the street.

'Curious fellow!' mused Jules Boissier as he unhooked the receivers.

Having begun so strangely, the twins' night finished in an unremarkable fashion.

Odilon had himself dropped off at home and parted from his friend with a handshake. Neither had discussed the morgue episode. The Parisian in particular seemed to prefer silence, as if afraid that Armand might pester him with questions. He alighted from the cab with obvious relief.

Armand initially gave his uncle's address but then, remembering the invitation to the Structural Engineers' Club, had the driver change direction. By the time he arrived, the reception was almost over. It was only because a small number of guests had stayed on that he avoided his uncle's remonstrances.

Even so, 'Good heavens, where have you been?' Jules wanted to know as they negotiated a bend in the corridor.

Armand found it extremely difficult to formulate a lie. The evening's events had left him in a state of nervous exhaustion that even now projected people and things behind an impenetrable gauze screen.

He swallowed two or three glasses of champagne, unenthusiastically toasted his engineering career and, as soon as he conveniently could, took his leave of the company, pleading fatigue.

'Off already?' asked Jules in astonishment.

'A friend took me on a tour of Paris. I'm exhausted.'

'You must pace yourself. Others have been known to be shown the door for finishing their night's sleep on the drawing-table!'

Armand smiled obediently as he donned his overcoat. Back at the Rue de Bruxelles house, he climbed the stairs in a torpor and, without even lighting a lamp in his room, slept on the bed as he was.

3

Next day, Armand and Odilon were back at their desks in the Gustave Eiffel offices.

A certain awkwardness had come over them, not because of the adventure at the morgue but because of the silence that had followed it, a silence that neither had dared break. This betrayal of their friendship had left a bitter taste – as does the first kiss, between lovers, exchanged through force of habit.

Their colleagues were not slow to notice this. Nothing had changed in the arrangement of the two desks and their two jackets still hung from the same peg, but an unusual silence reigned in their corner of the office.

At lunchtime, the eraser twins found themselves at their usual table, left alone by the other diners. A heart-to-heart was unavoidable. As the elder, Odilon felt obliged to make the first move, which he did as soon as the soup course was over.

'Armand,' he began, 'It's silly of us to give each other the cold shoulder like this. Anyway, I don't mind admitting it: I was a fool, taking you to the morgue…'

There was no reply at first. The Parisian found this

disturbing and cursed himself for having gone straight to the point, thinking he ought perhaps to have been less blunt.

In fact, the pause had simply been due to Armand finishing his current mouthful.

'Something odd happened there,' he said, stabbing another morsel with his fork. 'When I saw that woman's head, it was as if… No, you'll think I'm mad!'

'Go on!' the other encouraged him.

'Well, the moment I met the dead woman's gaze, I sort of entered into her, drawn by the eyes as if by a lodestone. Unless it was the other way around. Could it have been her entering into me?'

Odilon appeared interested in what his friend was saying. However, as had happened at the building site the previous day, a certain opacity came over his features.

'Oh, no, you're making that face again…' Armand said with a sigh. 'In that case I'll shut up.'

'No, please continue, please do,' his friend said, putting as much warmth into his words as he could.

'The feeling of being somehow *occupied* stayed with me for the rest of the evening. My head was no longer all mine. It seemed to be shared by two minds, subject to two wills, another besides my own. What's more, the feeling didn't leave me until I fell asleep.'

'That's extraordinary!' Odilon said, chewing a piece of bread thoughtfully. 'Two minds, you say? That kind of language is nothing new to me, you see. In fact, it may hold the key to the riddle!'

The Parisian's look of intensity might have indicated close attention but it might equally have indicated mockery. Armand made the natural choice.

'You're teasing me!'

'I am not!' Odilon protested. 'Not in the slightest! This is too serious a matter for teasing.'

Pushing his plate away, the Parisian leaned over and spoke into his friend's ear.

'I wasn't going to say anything. After all, we hardly know each other. You'll have seen me as a bit of an eccentric, possibly to the detriment of our friendship. Besides, it's not a subject one can bring up with just anyone, it needs a careful approach in this sort of setting…'

'What are you talking about, for God's sake?' Armand burst out. 'Don't be so mysterious!'

Odilon drew back a little, still staring into his friend's eyes.

'You're not ready yet, not quite… In a few months time I'll introduce you to the group and everything will be clear.'

Odilon poured himself a glass of wine and fell silent. It was impossible for his colleague to find out more. Armand tried every trick he knew including flattery and threats but it was no good. Odilon would tell him nothing. The Parisian simply intoned, 'You'll find out eventually,' investing the words with an air of impenetrability.

'Oh, I give up!' Armand said finally, having run out of arguments. 'Let's talk about something else!'

And they did – about many things. But there was no further mention of their visit to the morgue.

At midday precisely, the Palais-Royal's time-keeping cannon thundered on its granite bollard.

Hundreds of passers-by in the nearby streets simultaneously took out their pocket watches to check that the minute hand was exactly on top of the hour hand, bringing them together by turning the knob if necessary. For one individual, on his way to a luncheon appointment with a mistress, the sound of the gun resulted in a definite quickening of his pace – noon already! For another, an older man, the sound produced a quickened heartbeat as myriad heroic memories were conjured up by the voice of the brass cannon. A third, deaf man began to sniff at the air, intrigued by the smell of gunpowder.

The explosion had left no one indifferent – except Gordon Hole. At the moment of detonation, a well-honed razor blade was sliding over the American's neck, yet it neither wavered in its course nor nicked the skin under the smooth covering of perfumed shaving-cream.

'*New York Herald*! Paris edition! Get your copy of the *New York Herald*!'

Hole tossed a coin from the window and a rolled copy was hurled back in. He tore off the band and spread the newspaper out on the bed.

On the front page there was an engraving of the 300-metre Tower, as already widely reproduced in all the French papers. It showed the building in its initial, rather graceless design, standing tall amid other famous monuments of human history.

At the foot of the Tower were the Cheops Pyramid, the dome of the Parisian Hôtel des Invalides and St. Peter's Basilica in Rome, all dwarfed by the spectacular height of the wrought-iron mast. The boldest of these constructions, Cologne Cathedral with its soaring spires, barely reached the second platform. Above, the sky belonged to the Tower alone; no other building came close to challenging it there.

But the main thing was this: the Tower was printed in bold, using a broad line that made the tiniest metal strut stand out, whereas the other buildings were only sketched in faintly, blending into the grey background. It was as if they, not it, were awaiting existence. It, a mere ghost, was more substantial than their reality.

Hole skimmed through the article. The journalist stated that work on the foundations was going ahead, that the schedule was apparently being adhered to, certain technical complications notwithstanding. 'Before long,' he announced, 'we shall see the first iron girders rising into the air. The vertical will throw down the gauntlet to the horizontal. This will be the challenge of homo erectus to the four-footed beasts.'

The article then adopted a more critical tone, listing the obstacles that still stood in the way of the project's realisation. A professor of mechanics had calculated that the Tower would never exceed 221 metres, above which height it would collapse. People living next to the Champ-de-Mars site were taking the City of Paris to court in an attempt to block construction of the Tower...

Even so, behind the usual criticism one sensed sincere admiration for the undertaking and a feeling of regret, almost of amazement, that it was not American.

Hole discarded the paper in irritation. Lighting a cigarette, he began to pace the room. The idea of sabotaging the Tower still struck him as very obvious and since his abortive encounter with Bourdais he was determined to act alone. One night had been sufficient to persuade him. All his thoughts now centred on this fresh project, much as iron filings are aligned by a magnet.

Nevertheless, something still held him back from committing to it completely. He was troubled, almost undecided, when he should have shown himself resolute and active. Why this unease?

A glance at the newspaper gave him the answer. He heard a voice whispering that, if he wished to bring the Tower down, he must wait until it was up. What could be more obvious? But the American could not bear to wait. If he had only known how to stop the Tower now, at the foundation stage, as the life of a snake can be snuffed out in the egg! However, prudence counselled the reverse. The higher the Tower grew, the greater the chance of dealing it a fatal blow. To be effective, sabotage was going to require patience.

The architect smoked his cigarette down to the very end. He kept the nails of his thumb and middle finger long in order to waste none of the burning tobacco. He had learned this trick from a beggar child, except that for the boy's grubby paws Hole substituted pink, freshly manicured nails.

When the last flakes of ash had dropped like snow from between his fingers, the American picked up his jacket and left the room.

Gaspard Louchon checked his equipment. In the pockets of his overcoat, several of which had been sewn especially, he was carrying the complete toolkit of the spy, including a pair of opera glasses capable of magnifying distant objects, a set of false hairpieces for altering his appearance, gloves to prevent fingerprints, several round files, a skeleton key, a small mirror...

A particularly deep pocket below the left armpit held a roast-pork sandwich. Buttoned into a gusset in the lining Gaspard kept a flask of phenobarbitone ('to combat fear', was this hired man's excuse).

His disguise had been pondered at length. There was no question, clearly, of displaying his normal appearance or his natural features. Even wearing a cravat, Gaspard would not be able to wander around the Eiffel offices for long without attracting attention. Also, what would happen if things went wrong and he had to flee with the police after him? He would have to wear a disguise for the rest of his life!

After much thought, Gaspard had chosen to dress as a ragman. Such a costume was cheap to assemble and cheap to maintain. Above all, it was a disguise that operated at the psychological level. The streets were so full of ragmen that no one noticed them any more. Or else they gave such creatures a wide berth, as if they were somehow unclean. It was the ideal cover.

So it was that, early one morning, Gaspard donned a moth-eaten jumper, set an old plush hat on his head, slipped his feet into a pair of unlaced boots and cautiously descended the stairs of his apartment building.

It so happened that, as he passed the caretaker's flat, the caretaker himself popped out with a mop and pail.

'Ah, Monsieur Louchon!' he said, showing no surprise at the tenant's get-up. 'Come to pay your rent, have you? It's getting on for five days since I asked you…'

'Of course, of course,' mumbled the spy.

How had he been recognised? 'I know,' he reasoned with himself. 'He opens the door to me every day. Anyway, people in his job never forget a face.'

Gaspard passed through the door and out into the street. A watch hung from his lapel. He consulted it and quickened his step.

On Boulevard de Clichy, the spy tried to wave down a cab. As it happened there was one just coming, but when the driver spotted the fare he went on by, completing Gaspard's disguise with a generous splash of mud. Not that the spy took any offence; he was happy that at last someone had mistaken him for a ragman!

This was good news, but there was a down side. In vain did Gaspard hail cab after cab, even when he was waving a banknote and running to jump on the step none would agree to take him. 'You'll dirty my seats!' some drivers cried. 'You stink like a sewer!' others opined. And they all had whips, which they wielded vigorously. Several times the spy felt a sting on his legs. Bus and tram drivers likewise wanted nothing to do with him. Before long, the cruel truth dawned. He was going to have to walk in those painful boots all the way to Levallois-Perret – a distance of 2 kilometres or more!

By the time Gaspard reached his destination he was staggering with fatigue. The boiled-leather boots were excruciatingly painful. On top of this, the sole on the left one was coming off in such a way that it formed a sort of shovel, scooping up the mud as he walked and forcing it inside the boot. Not caring whether he was recognised or not, he slumped against the wall of Établissements Eiffel and dozed.

The feeling of a coin being dropped into his palm brought him round. The spy opened his eyes just in time to see a group of employees going in at the gate. 'Poor fellow!' one of them was saying. Gaspard stared at the coin in his hand. He was being given alms like a beggar!

Incensed, the spy flung the money to the ground, though he then picked it up again almost immediately, thinking that it would help defray expenses. He took up a less visible position behind the fence opposite. A glance at his watch reassured him that these employees were very early and most of the staff would be arriving later. Gaspard settled down to wait.

The next hour did indeed see many workers arrive. Depending on their means, they alighted from cabs or private carriages or came humbly on foot from the nearby omnibus stop. Their status was also indicated by their dress. The engineers sported high collars and tightly-knotted cravats, sometimes adorned with a jewelled pin, whereas the manual workers had scarves tied around their necks and wore sheepskin caps.

Faced with this human tide, these waves of humanity rolling into the workshops, Gaspard was seized with doubt: how was he going to identify Armand Boissier among all these engineers, many of whom might be around the same age? He had only seen the fellow's uncle, after all.

The spy took comfort from a quick draught of his phenobarbitone. What did it matter, anyway? If he failed here, he need only keep an eye open back at Rue de Bruxelles. He would be very unlucky to miss someone whose name he knew and virtually his address.

Just then a tall young man appeared, dressed in the style of an engineer and with an aquiline profile that was directly reminiscent of Jules Boissier. He was walking arm-in-arm with another young man who swung an ivory-handled walking-stick.

'Good grief!' the spy swore under his breath, flattening himself against the fence. But the pair had already entered the building.

Gaspard clapped his hands together excitedly. He had his man! With a nose like that… No one could have that nose and not also share the same name. The thing was crystal clear, the one with the hooter was Armand Boissier! That had been quick work. But should he thank his lucky stars or should he congratulate himself on the investigative skills that had put him in the right place at the right time?

'Gordon would be proud of me!' the hired man breathed in triumph. And, like a lion-tamer rewarding an obedient beast, he treated himself to another tot of phenobarbitone.

Now all he had to do was wait until closing-time. The

minute Armand came through that door, he would latch onto him and dog his steps. Then he would do the same thing the next day and every day thereafter until he had a full and detailed picture of the young engineer's habits. At which point the prey could be shot down and retrieved for the hunter: young Boissier laid at the feet of Gordon Hole…

The spy was delighted with the easy turn events had taken. With time on his hands, he conceived the idea of putting his character (who had the clothes but not the behaviour and certainly not the equipment) to work for a while. Parisian ragmen constituted not one community but several, forming a hierarchy in accordance with the profit they made from rubbish: there were *piqueurs* or 'pickers', who went about on foot with baskets on their backs; *placiers* or 'travellers', who combed the wealthier neighbourhoods with horse and cart; and finally *chineurs* or 'dealers', whose stalls, out near the fortifications, sold low-level trash at knock-down prices.

Gaspard found a pointed stick in the gutter. It was all he needed to become a 'picker', even without the basket. With a spring in his step, whistling as he went, he set about examining the cobblestones in search of litter. Each time he found a piece of peel or scrap of paper, his stick picked it up and carried it to a pile he had started at the side of the road. He injected an element of imagination into his work. Having speared, say, a potato he might flourish his stick in imitation of a golfer's stylish swing.

The spy had been at work for two hours and the pile was by now knee-high when another ragman rounded the corner. This was a genuine 'traveller', straight from some posh suburb and doing very well for himself, to judge by the cartload of garbage being hauled by his ancient mule. Hence, possibly, the hostile grimace that was his response to Gaspard's fraternal smile.

'Here comes trouble!' the spy predicted, avoiding the man's eye.

Nevertheless, he continued to spear litter in keeping, so he believed, with his costume and the implement in his hand. The traveller left his mule-cart in the middle of the road and began to walk over to his colleague. Gaspard cast a sideways glance at this huge man bearing down on him in a coat of cats' fur that looked – and almost sounded – as if it was seething with fleas.

Fortunately, the ragman did not offer a hand but stopped some distance away. Too far, Gaspard hoped, for any fleas to jump the gap.

'Clear off!' the man roared.

'Steady on, friend!' Gaspard whined pathetically. 'The streets belong to us all.'

'This street is mine! You have no right to pick litter here!'

'Really? I didn't know that. Let me finish off today, then tomorrow I'll go somewhere else.'

'No, you'll leave now – this instant!' the traveller insisted, spitting at his feet.

Gaspard felt his pulse leaping. What foul luck, this oaf happening along when the case was going so swimmingly! And right outside the Eiffel offices, too, with the entire staff looking on!

The spy felt the weight of the stick in his hand. Would it make a good weapon? Did he have the energy to hit the ragman over the head, knock him out and drag the inert body behind the fence? He sized up his tormentor, who had not moved. No harm in trying, surely?

'Oh, look – a comet!' he said, pointing skyward.

He seized the moment when the ragman glanced up to deal him, using all his strength, a massive blow to the head.

Unfortunately, the 'weapon' missed its aim and came down on the man's shoulder, where there was an extra layer of fur. The wood was rotten and the stick broke in two.

'Help!' Gaspard yelled as the man seized him by the collar.

He fought like a fish on the end of a line, whirling his arms about and pedalling with both legs to escape this humiliating hug. He was not sure what horrified him more: the promised thrashing or the invasion of the insects, which Gaspard could already feel administering tiny bites all over his face.

'Help!' the spy shouted again, even more loudly. 'Murder!'

His cries had alerted the employees. Gaspard saw windows flung up, heads leaning out... The last thing he saw was the gate opening, before a fist made brutal contact with his chin.

When the spy came to, he was lying in the road. Close to his face was the light-brown toe of what looked like an expensive shoe. A group of men surrounded him, their hatless heads etched against the pale sky. Bobbing about at the end of a shifting funnel was the ragman's dark-coloured coat, flanked by the buttoned jackets of two policemen. A pale truncheon appeared to be stroking the fur.

Summoning all his strength, the spy propped himself up on one elbow. The effort sent a flash of agony down his arm. Under this stimulus, the pain extended to other parts of his body, some so distant he was not sure they belonged to him. With the pain came a certain lucidity, and Gaspard recognised faces around him. Young Armand Boissier was among them.

'Gaspard!' came an authoritative voice.

Who was calling him? The spy rolled eyes like lottery balls.

'Come on – get up!' the voice continued.

Hands hooked into his armpits. Gaspard felt himself raised from the ground.

'Well, well! You *have* been in the wars!' said Gordon Hole, dabbing the spy's temples with a handkerchief. 'Get in the carriage and we'll clean you up.'

But a policeman intervened.

'One moment, sir! We need to speak to this man.'

'This man is my brother,' the American announced. 'I can vouch for him absolutely.'

'Your brother?' the uniformed man said in surprise. 'A ragman?'

'A soldier who no longer has all his wits about him, a bullet having shot some of them away on the battlefield… A poor madman whose wounds return to plague him from time to time, involving him in all kinds of outrageous behaviour. That's the reason,' the architect added, reaching inside Gaspard's coat, 'why my brother is never without his phenobarbitone.'

Spotting the flask in Hole's hand, the officer drew himself up and made a military salute. His colleague did the same with his left hand, the other being wound tightly around the travelling ragman's arm.

Hole climbed into his carriage, followed by two men supporting Gaspard. The driver gave his horse a brisk touch of the whip.

'What odd visitors!' Odilon was heard to observe as the eraser twins, together with their colleagues, went back inside the building.

Inside the carriage, with his back to the driver, Gaspard sat between the two men.

The seat was not wide enough for three, so they shared it with an ill grace, digging and prodding with their elbows, often at the expense of the one in the middle. In return, the passengers by the windows had to suffer the proximity of this pretend ragman with the very real filth.

The two men appeared relieved when Gordon Hole dismissed them with a generous tip. The spy, too, was happy because he now had the whole seat to himself.

'Don't doze off on me, now!' the architect said with a smile, giving Gaspard's face a gentle tap with a finely gloved hand. 'I'm interested in what you have to say.'

Gaspard propped himself up as best he could against the side of the carriage, a cushion under his head.

'Your face is certainly a picture!'

'Sir, if it hadn't been for you…' the Frenchman began, taking the handkerchief Hole was offering him.

But he stopped, exhausted.

'Whatever were you thinking of, swinging sticks at your age? You may have grey hair, but you haven't a scrap of wisdom.'

The spy shucked off his boots and threw them out of the window.

'I was tailing the lad. It might work!'

'The idea is good but your method of execution was poor. Honestly, what did you hope to achieve with that charade? You read too many cheap novels!'

Gaspard half-smiled, basking in this partial approval. In a gesture of docility, his hands returned to the hot-water muff on his knees.

'How lucky that you found me!'

'It wasn't hard. A moment's thought… Where could your search begin except at the Eiffel offices? I had a feeling things might go wrong, so I hired those two layabouts and hurried over there. Good job I did!'

The American lit a cigarette and went on.

'I saw Armand Boissier, he gave a statement to the police.

He's a nice boy, but watch out! The innocent ones are sometimes the hardest to bamboozle, their openness protects them. Also, he now knows your face – and mine!'

'Oh, sir!' Gaspard groaned. 'I'm so sorry about that!'

He was trembling with emotion. Hole removed his own cloak and offered it to his companion.

'You're the older man, yet you're like a son to me,' the architect said in a softer voice. 'I'm fifty-four, I have neither wife nor child, and for my only company – an elderly lunatic I need to keep an eye on day and night. Poor me!'

This intimate tone was so far from his employer's usual style that Gaspard gaped in amazement. Not surprisingly, he misunderstood.

'It's the same for me, sir! I'm a bachelor, too! Actually, I'm quite glad of it, a wife only means trouble!'

The carriage had just turned into Avenue Victoria. Before alighting, the American gave his employee further instructions.

'Carry on watching Armand Boissier. Make a note of the hours he keeps, his habits and the people he sees. When the time comes, we'll put it all to use.'

'Sir, you can count on me!'

Hole took back his cloak and entered the Hôtel Britannique.

A steward approached the American in the lobby.

'Sir, there's a lady to see you in the red drawing-room.'

Gordon Hole adjusted the knot of his cravat and walked stiffly towards the drawing-room door.

Seated in an armchair tucked away behind a screen, the woman was drawing at a long-stemmed pipe, from which occasional wreaths of smoke rose into the air. A cloud billowed gently beneath the ceiling of the room, its greenish whorls contrasting with the deep red of the curtains.

Without a word of greeting, Hole brushed a hand against the call-girl's dress, whereupon she stood up and followed him. The elevator was available but he chose the stairs, stepping aside to let his guest precede him. The woman was no fool, and on the very first half-landing she arched her back, accentuated the roll of her hips and thrust out her bottom – almost in the American's face. Hole feasted his eyes on the teasing movement, which was accompanied by a crackle of shiny silk. And when, entirely by design, his visitor bent down to re-fasten a shoelace, he caught her up with one bound and planted a wet kiss on the corpulent lure.

'I beg your pardon!' the woman said with an amused start. 'I've got the right day, then?'

'My body is on fire!' Hole growled, this time loosening his cravat.

Reaching the second storey, they withdrew into the suite. Hole lost no time in bolting the door behind them.

Having located the bedroom and the bed by instinct, the woman began to undress with professional efficiency. Her attire, though studied, was uncomplicated. In particular, it had no more buttons, hooks and pins than were strictly necessary. Certain garments, such as the camisole, were designed to be removed almost instantly: it peeled off easily at the slightest touch, falling to the floor almost unassisted.

Hole watched the spectacle from the hallway of the flat. He had removed his coat and jacket, but as he was about to do the same with his waistcoat he hesitated. The fever he had felt inside him was beginning to cool off. 'Why has she got undressed already? Stupid slut!' thought the architect, attributing his unease to this.

The fact was, the stockings draped carelessly over a chair,

the ankle-boots flung on the floor and other preparations for the act of love did little to arouse the architect. On the contrary, he felt inhibited by them, as the diner entering a restaurant feels his hunger subside if he spots the chef sharpening his knives.

Nevertheless, Hole went to the woman and helped her to undo her corset. His fingers were shaking with irritation, which she took for desire.

'Such eagerness, my friend!' said the call-girl, lying down on the bed. 'My efforts have not been in vain, I see!'

She turned her head to one side and waited, legs spread, humming a music-hall chorus.

'Quiet!' commanded the American, slipping off his socks.

The girl's practised eye rested on the front of her client's trousers, which remained quite flat. Sighing, she hoisted herself up and crawled towards him.

'Stop right there!' ordered Hole, stepping back sharply. His hand flew to his crotch as if to shield it from some biting animal.

'Relax!' the call-girl said with some insistence. 'I'm beginning to lose patience. Are you paying me to chat or what? I don't know which are worse – clients who want too much or those that don't want anything!'

'You don't know what men want!' Gordon retorted accusingly.

'So why send for me? Three times this week!'

'Because you speak English!'

The call-girl fell back and crossed her arms. The ensuing silence enabled the American to finish undressing, which he did calmly and methodically, placing his shirt on a hanger and inserting his trousers into a press, like a meticulous schoolboy tidying away his uniform.

Now also naked, the architect approached the bed. But

instead of lying on top of the woman he merely sat down beside her. However, his penis showed definite signs of arousal and this cheered the girl up.

'About time!' she said, putting an arm round the American's neck. 'Let's get on with it before it gets cold!'

But Hole disengaged himself, barking:

'Turn over on your stomach!'

'As you wish, but it costs more,' the woman warned, complying.

The architect slipped a hand under the call-girl's left leg and bent it upward. Then, taking hold of her right arm, he angled it across her back before turning it at right-angles.

'Ouch! You're hurting me!' the woman protested.

Silencing her with a click of his tongue, Hole continued with his strange game, arranging the woman's limbs and head as a sculptor might manipulate his model or a puppeteer his marionette – briskly and quite roughly. Occasionally, he paused to assess a fresh pose before resuming his task. 'This is going to cost you!' the woman hissed, suddenly afraid. Hole took no notice.

The American kept looking down at his penis, gauging his desire the way a taster searches for the poison in a mouthful of wine – half-hoping, half-dreading. But desire did not come; desire consistently escaped him. Every so often Hole would straighten up, his eyes on the call-girl, his hand gently stroking himself; his penis would become engorged, then shrink again as soon as he released it. At other times his scalp tingled at the sight of a spread thigh – that damp fold of flesh, fringed with shadow. Next moment he saw only a play of muscles and tendons, an insipid composition of skin and flesh.

Meanwhile, to an ever-increasing extent, the woman's body appeared to him as an abstraction, the complex solution to certain problems of dynamics: standing up, walking on two legs, performing various movements without losing balance...

Everywhere, his trained eye saw the laws of architecture at work. The voluptuous buttock encased the hip joint, a trite assembly of one bone with another in the arrangement known in his trade as 'haunching'. The leg made him think of the shaft of a pillar, the shoulder-blade suggested a roof-truss. He decided on the woman's poses as a designer chooses his angles to study a monument.

A wave of nausea swept over Gordon Hole.

'Go!' he shouted. 'Be off with you!' And he slapped the woman's bottom.

Reaching for his jacket and extracting a bundle of notes from a pocket, he flung them on the bed and left the room. A small sofa stood against one wall of the hallway. He sat down to wait for the woman to leave.

'Get a move on!' the architect ordered sternly. 'I don't wish to see you here any more!'

The New York Herald with the Tower on the front lay on the seat beside him. Picking it up, he spread the newspaper on his knees.

Never had the Tower seemed to him so radically virile. Despite the effeminate curves of its base, despite the great arches intended to soften the angles of the lower storey, this was undoubtedly a male member rising up there: the apotheosis of a phallus, stiffly triumphant, standing ready to fecundate the universe with the seed of progress.

For centuries, buildings had been designed to please women; moated châteaux, intimate pleasure gardens, curvaceous fountains... In the past broad expanses of smooth cobbles had cradled cities in laps of rounded stone. Now a new era was dawning, a male era of iron and machinery.

Buildings would no longer spread sideways; they would shoot skyward, storey upon storey, up and up, taller and taller, reaching ever higher!

In truth, what could the Tower be likened to but a giant erection? And how could anyone doubt that the engineer who was going to build it was anything but an exceptional male?

The call-girl appeared in the doorway, dressed, her hair re-arranged, the pipe between her lips. Before her, she saw a naked man reading a newspaper, the picture of the Tower, by an unhappy fluke, rising precisely from his groin. A fruity laugh shook her whole body.

'You wish!' she hooted. 'Dream on! Yours will never bear any resemblance!'

The woman swept out of the door, still laughing. Gordon Hole suppressed a sob.

4

One week after the morgue incident, Armand and Odilon no longer referred to it. It was a bad memory, apparently effaced, as was the misunderstanding to which it had given rise between them.

In any case, there was no shortage of topics to enliven their lunchtime conversations. Parisian life was one they touched on frequently. The eraser twins had made some fresh excursions; indeed, planning these had become a custom and undertaking them something they much looked forward to. They met every Sunday just north of Place de la Concorde, at the corner of Rue Royale and Rue St. Honoré, and set out together for the day's destination.

Sometimes, to supplement these Sunday outings, they made use of their Thursday breaks. Monsieur Pluot, their immediate superior, gave a day off to those whose heavy workload had kept them late at their desks in the early part of the week. That was why the two friends lingered over their drawings some evenings: they were hoping for one of these free Thursdays.

It scarcely troubled their youth, which was capable of

sustaining this rhythm without flagging and made a reveller of the assiduous employee – or the other way around – at the drop of a hat. There were times when they even forgot to go to bed. Armand and Odilon would leave work to make merry, then leave their merry-making to go back to work without a moment's sleep.

In April, having gone out relentlessly for the past month, the twins felt they had done nothing yet. They drew up a list of things they had seen and were astonished to find it so lengthy when so many places remained to be discovered. Armand culled new ideas on every page of his guidebook, a much-thumbed copy of *Paris Guide* with a preface by Victor Hugo.

A debate began between the two of them, the motion at issue being whether their future excursions should aim for novelty or re-visit familiar places. Predictably, Armand was for change, Odilon for staying true.

'Aren't you happy to go dancing?' the Parisian asked, astonished. 'The masked ball at the Opera Garnier, the "Blind People's Ball", the "Montesquieu Ball", the "Negro Ball"…'

'But they're winter dances!' retorted the young man from St. Flour. 'Noisy, smoky, full of girls with colds who snuffle on your shoulder…and do they drink punch! A chap could be bankrupted!'

'Iced lemonade is no cheaper. Anyway, the summer dances haven't opened yet. I know of only one interesting place just now.'

'What's that?'

'The "Dance of the Loonies" at La Salpêtrière. The asylum holds it once a year, in the middle of Lent.'

Armand was taking all this down.

'The "Dance of the Loonies"? That's a fine advertisement!'

'The Lionnet brothers, who run the place, thought inmates might find it entertaining and maybe it would attract visitors, too – and bring in money! The lunatics wear costumes that they sew for themselves, sometimes reflecting how strange their illnesses are. Sirens and odalisques you get plenty of, but you might also find one dressed as a bar of soap, say, or a jug or a vase of flowers! You have to be prepared for all kinds of odd behaviour on their part: some hand out sheets of paper containing their thoughts, crudely rhymed; others frantically wave fans loaned by a department store. You wouldn't believe your eyes!'

'A sad form of entertainment, by the sound of it! No, you can keep your "Dance of the Loonies."'

Their chats tended to go on long after the official lunch break. Sometimes it was the café proprietor who threw them out on the grounds that he was about to close but usually it was Monsieur Pluot who came to fetch them, tapping his pocket-watch and muttering, 'The Tower awaits!' – which soon became a catchphrase.

Then the two friends would return to their desks. In the studious silence of the office, the conversation might continue for a while in lowered voices. Only when Eiffel himself entered the room did they finally stop talking.

The possibility was mooted that the eraser twins had something to do with Eiffel's habitual visit, every afternoon around three o'clock. That was what the staff thought. It certainly matched the style of a man whose neatly compartmentalised mind filed minor facts alongside major ones, with no apparent regard to their importance.

Every afternoon, then, Eiffel would come bursting in and cross the room at an angle towards the far door. He stopped occasionally to read a plan or leaf through a register; more often, pausing as he drew level with Armand's desk and peering over his spectacles through the blue smoke from his pipe, he would flash the young man a look of fond reproach.

Eiffel's appearance had an electrifying effect on the twins. Instantly, they bent to their work and with such enthusiasm that in an hour they had made up for three.

However, it would be wrong to assume that Armand and Odilon were in any way slackers.

They might linger over lunch, but they drew out their evenings in much the same way, staying out until midnight or later without there always being a day off to follow. Their lockers contained a blanket and pillow for sleeping at the office. They were known to work twenty, even twenty-five hours at a stretch, sometimes falling asleep ruler in hand; there were times when they got cramp from holding a pen too long.

But even when they were tired, their handwriting remained firm and their brains alert. Not once did Monsieur Pluot find a wobbly line or a sum calculated wrongly. Model employees, they could stop instantly, like machines. One moment Armand – or it might be Odilon – was wholly focused on his work; and the next, his head fell back and he was asleep. The other would then arrive in a rush to remove the eraser from his fingers, fold his arms and slip a pillow behind his head. It really was the strangest sight.

This shared zeal in the service of irreproachable work did not, of course, escape the notice of the head of department, and it was not many weeks before Monsieur Pluot realised that the eraser twins deserved better than tidying up other men's drawings.

So he entrusted the young men with sketches, studies and increasingly complicated calculations – though without ever giving them any real responsibility. Such tasks might, for example, involve checking the logarithms that determined the placing of a rivet, or straightening out a part that had too much curvature.

This added sufficient variety to dispel boredom, yet Armand could not conceal his impatience for greater things. His ambition, not unnatural in one so young, was nevertheless more a matter of temperament. Albeit at the bottom of his profession, he retained the presumption of the student. 'Trivia!' the young engineer complained bitterly. 'That's all they'll let us do!'

His friend's diplomatic advice fell on largely deaf ears. The work they were given to do still struck him as pathetically rudimentary and the problems thrown up by the design of parts for the Tower appeared negligible. The fact that most of those parts were oblique, dissimilar, each involving a different angle – that he did not find intimidating. It was all 'child's play' to him.

Repeatedly, the young engineer pleaded for a 'real challenge' to which to apply his talents. Had he not demonstrated what he could do? Had he not shown evidence, in mathematics as much as in drawing, of a quite remarkable facility?

If it came to it, Armand would have consented to his salary staying the same, since he had enough to live on. However, it seemed to him a cruel injustice that his career should be forced to mark time. 'I will not be messed around!' the young hothead protested. 'I shall defend my point of view!'

Countless times, Armand had thought of seeking Eiffel out. After all, the boss had already granted him one appointment and might well agree to see him again!

Armand had already prepared for this interview by covering sheets of paper with his demands and Eiffel's likely objections, for which he sought definitive rebuffs. The whole thing filled several dozen cardboard boxes, which he went through every evening before going to bed. To strengthen his defence, Armand learned by heart words that famous writers had penned about right and wrong. Zola supplied a number of quotations, but his principal resource was Victor Hugo, a writer whom he loved for his concise way of putting things. Hugo's sentences had the brevity and punch of an advertisement for soap.

With this armoury of arguments at his back, Armand prepared to go into battle. He chose the time – the following afternoon – and place – a small courtyard behind the offices – and he set his ambush.

'You're mad!' Odilon warned him.

'Let him hear me out or strike me dead!' Armand replied, as if writing his own romantic novel.

Initially, everything went according to plan. Eiffel set out, alone, across the courtyard at three o'clock, even pausing to fill his white china pipe. Lurking behind a stack of wooden crates, the young man waited for the operation to be completed before showing himself. The boss, he reasoned, would not appreciate being interrupted at such a time.

It was at that moment that a glance from Eiffel, piercing the latticed crates like an arrow, froze the young man to the spot. Their eyes had not met for more than an instant, nothing suggested that Eiffel had even seen him, yet Armand felt his resolution drain away. The same thing happens, apparently, when hunters find themselves looking into the eyes of their prey; it is not uncommon for them to lose all motivation. His pipe alight, Eiffel climbed into the carriage that had come in through the gate. The opportunity was lost and Armand had a confused sense that it would not recur.

Nevertheless, in the weeks that followed the young

engineer made several further attempts to accost Gustave Eiffel. Each time he was unsuccessful.

Something about the man's appearance kept the importunate at bay. Eiffel unwittingly fended off intruders as a current repels the swimmer. The challenge was physical as much as moral – and few withstood it.

Speaking to Gustave Eiffel meant first matching his pace, because the man was forever on the go. An accomplished sportsman, who taught his own grandchildren rowing and fencing, he exuded a burning energy with every movement of his body. It was exhausting, trying to keep up with him. How long would Eiffel need to climb the staircases in the Tower, once it was up? That was the absurd question posed by one member of his staff, who was taking bets on it.

Also, to meet with Gustave Eiffel one had to be sure of one's facts. Even accosting him was a daunting prospect. The moment never seemed quite right. Would such trifles as one's salary or promotion simply irritate him when he was preoccupied by the important question of elevators in the Tower? Was one going to tackle him about canteen menus at a time when he was studying the plans for the Panama Canal? Of course not!

The result was to turn the great man into an intimidating if not unapproachable personage, a living remedy against inefficiency. No need for him to discourage visitors; visitors put themselves off. Enthroned behind his huge oak desk with its panoply of secret drawers, Eiffel was an all-powerful, undisputed monarch. At times it seemed as if the Tower was a 300-metre pedestal for his personal glorification.

The eraser twins worked for three months without any promotion at all.

Then, one day, without warning, Monsieur Pluot

conducted the young engineers into the office used by Adolphe Salles. They found Salles in the process of unrolling a plan of the Tower. It was the first time they had seen a detailed drawing of the construction on a scale large enough to show the rivets as tiny pinpricks on the steel legs. Before, they had handled only one-fifth scale plans of major parts and half-scale plans of small parts; that day the scattered bones came together to form a complete skeleton. Their eyes feasted on the novelty.

'The 300-metre Tower!' proclaimed Adolphe Salles, holding the drawing up. It was almost as tall as he was.

The twins murmured respectfully.

'Gentlemen, I have asked you here to talk about your future. It is not my habit to summon employees in pairs for a career interview, but they say you are inseparable – also that you have as much to say to each other as those pet birds that chatter together incessantly!'

This pleasantry drew the man's shiny moustache into a curve of amusement. Odilon smiled politely and with a discreet nudge urged his friend to do the same.

'You joined us back in March,' Salles went on. 'Your skill at drawing is widely acknowledged and people also speak highly of your aptitude for mathematics. Monsieur Pluot has drawn my attention to the excellent work you have been doing for him. Such talent deserves recognition. It is my pleasure to inform you that you are both being promoted.'

Odilon patted his friend on the back and Monsieur Pluot stepped forward to shake them both by the hand. Only Armand showed a certain hesitation. His voice was suspicious as he asked:

'Where are we to be posted?'

'You will both be upgraded to Assistant Engineer. Monsieur

Boissier…,' he turned to Armand, '…will help Monsieur Backmann to plan the elevators. As for Monsieur Cheyne, he will be looking at the safety of the Tower and in particular how to insulate it against atmospheric phenomena involving electricity. These are two key areas where the Exposition's Consultative Committee has asked us for fresh guarantees.'

This second announcement punctured the delight occasioned by the first. The twins, it appeared, were to be separated!

'But that's impossible!' was Odilon's spontaneous reaction.

Then, in more measured tones, he continued:

'We have worked side by side since the day we were taken on. Not to mention the friendship that has grown up between us, our output is far greater when we are together.'

'So rumour has it. However, the same source informs us that you lack discipline,' Salles remarked pitilessly.

'We can do something about that!' Armand threw in. 'We promise to be more responsible!' Salles banged his fist on the desk.

'I don't want any haggling! You're not at school now! I'm not reproaching you, I'm offering you promotion. You can either accept it or reject it. Would you rather go on being the "eraser twins," I believe that's what they call you?'

This harangue plunged the young engineers into an emotional silence. They exchanged looks, each weighing the other's resolve to say 'no' against the hope of off-setting his own fears. However, the ambition of Armand skewed the balance. He was the first to sign the contract that Adolphe Salles was offering. Odilon followed, but with the face of one writing his name in a register of burial.

'About time!' huffed Salles, laying a piece of blotting-paper over the signatures.

That concluded the interview; no compliments, no

handshakes. Leaving the presence of Adolphe Salles, the two friends felt like youngsters who, on being offered one drink by a naval recruiting-officer, unthinkingly sign on for ten years.

'What a shame!' sighed Armand, wishing to sound kind.

'We've done a stupid thing! What's the good of more pay if we can't spend it together?'

'Still,' the other countered soothingly, 'Won't you be glad to put down that eraser? It'll be good, surely, to be in a larger office where there's room to flex your arms with no risk of knocking the lamp over?'

'You're right… The thing is, I'd got used to having you nearby. Who will there be to talk to from now on? Who's going to wink at me whenever I yawn? No, the good times are gone!'

Odilon was overcome with emotion. His condition was infectious. Armand, too, felt a vague queasiness in the pit of his stomach. Taking his Parisian friend's hand, he gave it a squeeze.

'I'll not abandon you, never you fear! We'll still go out together on Thursdays and Sundays. We'll still take the bus together, share the same seat upstairs, watch our smoke whisk away… We'll still have fun!'

More than the words themselves, Armand's evident desire to impart comfort did something to revive Odilon's mood. Rallying, the eraser twins returned to their desks and began to pack their things.

THE FIRST STOREY

5

As soon as the foundations of the Tower were laid, at the beginning of summer, earth was thrown over them.

These shovelfuls of earth falling funereally on the still fresh stonework called to mind a burial, and many people were happy to interpret the operation as meaning that the project was being consigned to an early grave. The silent efforts of the labourers would, it was said, soon restore the Champ-de-Mars to its previous appearance — a dreary piece of waste land, a second cemetery digesting the remains of human follies.

However, from the flattened ground there emerged sixteen huge blocks of masonry, as tall as a man and three times as wide as a man is tall. Onlookers were informed that these blocks would serve to support the piers of the structure. They found the announcement bewildering. With the masonry 'hoofs' at an angle, how was the Tower to stand upright? Was a wall ever raised on slanted footings?

As work on the foundations was completed, the task of assembly began. The last cartloads of excess soil passed the first convoys of iron components and handshakes were exchanged between the departing labourers and the incoming metal crews.

The two workforces differed as greatly as their functions and their equipment: on the one hand, men of the world of darkness – former miners, some of them, used to wielding picks in the dank shadows of underground tunnels; on the other hand, creatures of the open air, ex-topmen from the navy whose contempt for vertigo made them ideal for high-altitude work.

It was the latter that mainly captured the imaginations of journalists. Were these the harbingers of a new class of workers, the 'acrobatic' or 'flying' operatives who specialized in high-rise buildings? They quickly acquired a nickname, the French press dubbing these steeplejacks *ramoneurs* – 'chimneysweeps'. By contrast, men who worked on the ground became 'cow-level men'.

The 'chimneysweeps' worked to such good effect that the Tower quickly put on its first few metres. All the time the foundations were being prepared, the parts were being machined at Levallois-Perret, ready for on-site assembly. At the beginning of July 1887 they began to arrive on large horse-drawn wagons. A travelling crane took over from the horses, then smaller wagons transported the parts along four divergent tracks towards the piers. There, 22-metre jumbo derricks hoisted them into position for fixing.

Work proceeded swiftly. The Eiffel method was for each part to be offered up with holes already drilled and two-thirds of the rivets inserted, like a piece of some giant construction kit that only had to be put in place and secured (and could be dismantled in the same way). Because the girders were relatively light, none of them weighing more than 3 tons, the operation could be done by a few men in a matter of hours.

At no time was this enormous building site, which rivalled that of the pyramids in size, peopled by more than 250 workmen.

The progress of construction could be noted day by day: the Tower grew almost as one watched. Office staff, leaving for work in the morning, would gauge the height of the piers with a pencil, and they would do the same in the evening, on their way home; the difference was sometimes a fingernail's width. A Monsieur Durandelle was commissioned by Eiffel to take photographs of the Tower's advance, documenting the miracle, as it were.

The sixteen masonry hoofs already supported quite long iron stalks, with cross-struts running between them. From a distance, it was as if sheaves of vegetation were emerging from the soil like monstrous metal plants. 'They've made iron girders germinate!' passers-by exclaimed in wonder. And indeed, in a patch of earth that had been tilled as if to receive seed, in the determined upthrust of the iron, in the thin, knotty headers now reaching for the sky, many people believed that what they were witnessing was the inexorable, organic growth of a tree.

'But trees can topple!' the sceptics retorted. The fact was, towers of wooden scaffolding had risen alongside the ironwork. There were so many of them and they were so densely strutted that they obscured the actual piers. And the same people as had been alarmed by the slanting hoofs took fright at these crutches – which inevitably spelled danger, admitting as they did the possibility of collapse.

As the Tower rose, so too did the tide of fear that it inspired. Its very tangible presence lent substance to more diffuse anxieties. It was a nightmare from which there was no waking. Some watched the Tower going up as the condemned man watches the scaffold being erected for his own execution. It seemed to be saying two things simultaneously: while it hailed the world that was emerging, it also bid farewell to a world that was passing. A true monument to the approaching turn of the century!

Apolline Sérafin fluttered a vellum fan before her face. The black-lacquered guards contrasted with her nails, which were varnished a vehement red.

The young woman was the sole occupant of the omnibus seat. Her dress of dark gauze, its sleeves decorated with bead embroidery, spread over the seat unimpeded, falling to the floor on either side. A small smoke-coloured bag and a silk umbrella floated on this sea of fabric. Her right hand rested on the knob of the umbrella, a tiny hand that might have been that of a puppet or doll with the same pure quality as porcelain.

Apolline Sérafin was like a flower that has just opened – but a jungle flower, deep and venemous. Her fan spread a heavy scent of iris and benzoin. A veil obscured the upper part of her face.

Opposite Apolline sat three young men. They had shoulder-length hair. Long waves of brown curls stirred in the draught from the fan. Dark cravats, knotted loosely as if by hands lacking strength, hung down outside their waistcoats. Their suits did not draw the eye; they were invisible, so to speak, all that sombre velvet soaking up the light.

The remaining benches accommodated other men and women, also dressed in black. The vehicle, a double-decker, was already full, and the sounds that penetrated to the upper deck suggested that it was ingesting even more bodies. The whole omnibus appeared to have been hired by a funeral procession.

A voice was heard from the rear: 'Where are you taking us, Madame Apolline?'

'To the Champ-de-Mars.'

There was a murmur of surprise among the passengers. A man sitting by a window put up his hand like a schoolboy requesting permission to speak. He had a black patch over one eye.

'Why the Champ-de-Mars?'

The fluttering of the fan slowed, as if checked by an invisible breath.

'A spirit is summoning us there…'

'But the Champ-de-Mars is where they're building the 300-metre Tower!' gasped a fat man with mutton-chop whiskers.

'What's that got to do with it!' the man with the eye-patch retorted scornfully. 'How could the Tower be of any use to spiritualism? One wonders, one really does!'

The fat man inserted a monocle into the folds of flesh around one eye.

'Come on, it's obvious, isn't it? The Tower will be built of iron, and iron is a perfect vehicle for electricity, so what better agent could there be for the magnetic phenomena so beloved of our discipline?'

'That's not all!' interjected an old man's wheezy voice. 'According to the newspapers, the Tower will have room for ten thousand visitors at a time. Imagine all those pairs of legs, connected by the iron of the stairways and galleries and platforms! It's by placing our hands on a table, is it not, that we sometimes communicate with spirits? On the Tower, thousands of people will be connected to each other without realising it!'

A mighty voice boomed out across the upper deck.

'The Tower will join earth and heaven! It will bring us closer to the spirit world!'

'Nonsense!' the one-eyed man protested. 'Spirits don't live in the sky, any more than they flock to human gatherings. If they did, imagine the hosts of spirits that would assemble every time the Prefect throws a banquet!'

Apolline's fan closed with a snap.

'A little discipline, gentlemen! Let us not forget that the spirits are among us! What will they think of a spiritualist society whose members fritter away their time in squabbling rather than put it to good use increasing their store of knowledge?'

Clearly, the young woman had real acting talent. Something about her furrowed brow, her quivering nose and her furious, Medusa-like stare commanded respect. Unless, as a minority contended, she had been using some of what a certain Professor Ninon advertised as his 'eyebrow fluid', a product that – the professor claimed – would endow a woman's face with an almost magnetic attractiveness.

Apolline's words had restored silence. Members were nodding penitently. Some had screwed up their eyes in an effort to detect, through the smoky interior of the omnibus, signs of spirits on the prowl.

Sensing that the reproach had been aimed at himself, the one-eyed man came clean.

'We're afraid, Madame Apolline, we're afraid… Nothing is as it was. You proclaim major changes, predicting that the Tower will exert a pernicious influence upon spirits and in particular upon our society. How? What does fate have in store for us? We need to know!'

A silent Apolline merely shook her head.

At this, a man sitting opposite her smiled, revealing yellow, decaying teeth. The ailing incisors appeared shorter than they should be as their points were bevelled like the edges of a mirror.

'Apolline is saying nothing because her prophecy is so terrifying. What the spirits are murmuring to her, what the future holds for us really is…the end of the world!'

The spiritualist eyed her colleague with compassion.

'Poor Samson, you're not well at all. Your teeth are rotting. And your eyes, there's virtually no colour left in them, just a sort of pale opacity…'

'It's the syphilis, Madame,' Samson sighed, fluttering his eyelashes. 'They liken the illness to the manchineel tree, you know, fatal to all who fall asleep in its shade! I take care of myself, but the mercury and iodide injections are useless.'

'Still, you take your medicine, at least? Some people cultivate the pox out of a taste for the macabre or to give themselves the appearance of vampires. The fools!'

Then, raising her voice, she addressed the group.

'Listen to me, all of you! People who take pleasure in the weird and in black masses have no place in our group. Only an idiot can worship death! Our destinies are played out here on Earth!'

'I disagree,' Samson retorted, passing his tongue over his unwholesome teeth. 'We're surely closer to the dead than to the living? Don't spiritualists dwell in the other world?'

'You dwell here, Samson, on Earth! Your spirit is one with your body!'

'Not, I fear, for much longer, Madame…'

Samson drew a wicker case from beneath the seat and unfastened the clasps. His neighbours shrank back. So sombre was the expression on the syphilitic's face that they feared to see a dagger or a pistol emerge. But the case contained only two delicate crystal goblets, nestling in cavities lined with red velvet, and a flask stopped with wax. Samson broke the seal. A strong smell of ether spread through the omnibus.

'A toast, if you please, to this degenerate world!' cried the young man, filling one of the little goblets. 'Let's drink to universal corruption! Here's a health to the putrefaction of all things!'

A smoking stream of ether cascaded into the second glass. Apolline pushed the proffered goblet away with her fan.

'As you wish, Madame!' said Samson, offering the glass to someone else. As he did so, his heavily-veined hand caught the light, presenting a glittering array of rings: a St. Hubert ring against rabies, a magnetic ring against migraines, an electro-voltaic ring against rheumatism…The collection was a curious blend of science and superstition, suggesting that while its owner vested hope in the machine, he placed his faith in spectres.

Samson took a handful of cherries from his pocket. Selecting the finest specimen, he dropped it into the goblet of ether. An icy bubbling enclosed the fruit, which became almost blue in its bath of liquid.

'Cheers!' said Samson, greedily swallowing the stone.

The drinker's fixed grin, with its ruined teeth and with beads of blood on the lips, was ghastly to behold. Yet it excited more pity than fear.

'You shame us, Samson!' protested Apolline. 'Please! Put the bottle away!'

'My apologies for upsetting you, Madame. Yet the merest glance at the world will reveal that we are surrounded by the symptoms of an inescapable decadence. They burn dead people like the carcasses of animals. There are now brothels where men offer themselves to other men. Writers complain that no one any longer speaks anything but that barbarous, wholly artificial Volapük. Worse, a doctor once hinted to me that masturbation is becoming dangerously prevalent, and the evils of self-abuse are well known. Tell me honestly, are such things to be rejoiced at? Is there any decency left in the state of abjection to which we have declined? There is not! Prisoners in this ghastly age, each of us has a duty to welcome death, even to invite it…'

'Yes, yes, we all know that tune,' intoned the man with the eye-patch. 'The end-of-the-century lament, youngsters nowadays sing nothing else. Bah! This post-war generation has no mettle!'

The fat man with the mutton-chop whiskers was now in his element.

'He's right! Less than twenty years ago your fathers were fighting at the barricades, but you – what do you have worth defending? The lives of young people today are all idleness and debauchery. One might feel pity for them, but for the fact that they compound the felony by committing the most heinous, least pardonable sin of all: debasing religion. Your generation claims to be mystical. All that means is that it is infatuated with prayer and ceremony as well as with black masses and witchcraft! Young ladies purchase dresses called 'the phantom', 'the neophyte' or the 'martyr' in a desperate attempt to ape the stars of today's satanic theatre. Their young men hum the religious airs performed at the Black Cat nightclub or attend Rosicrucian art exhibitions. It's a swamp they're living in! Their whole world's a swamp!'

Samson's wall-eyed gaze held only defiance for his elders. From time to time, the milky opacity of his eyes lit up from within, as a dull metal surface may still give off flashes.

'Pity the young, indeed, but their elders are no better! What kind of example do you set with your passion for money and your adulation of power? There's nothing in your behaviour to edify us!'

'Of course there is!' the one-eyed man exploded.

'What, then?'

'Well, the healthy life we once knew, far from cities and their corruption. The countryside we grew up in, where we spoke the local dialect...'

Samson took up the theme, mimicking a provincial accent:

'...and where we had honest fun at our village fairs, stoning a goat tethered to a post or a chicken strung up by its feet, and where we applauded the ratcatcher as he killed his biggest catches by biting them to death!' Resuming his normal voice, he went on, 'I hate countryfolk with their cunning and their greed! It's their fault, when all's said and done, that milk today doesn't taste like milk any more. To make it smoother they add plaster, lime, lead and even dried brains! And isn't it the case, too, that cream goes off very much sooner than it used to? As if nature is now so enfeebled it has no more strength to invest in a food supposed to boost growth!'

'My curds! Who'll buy my curds? Who wants a healthy body?' recited the fat man, imitating the cry of the street vendor.

'It's nothing to joke about. This is the poison that, up and down the country, sucklings are imbibing with their mother's milk! And just as alarming is the olive oil mixed with honey and chicken fat, the coffee bulked out with clay beans, the snails that are really calves' lights stuffed into old shells, the wine containing bulls' blood, the radishes carved from beets... The whole monstrous menu of adulteration!'

Apolline's fan had resumed its pensive motion.

'Listening to you, Samson, one would think all hope was gone! One might as well hang oneself. Yet you never have. What cowardice holds you back?'

The sick man's response to the challenge was to sigh. His clouded gaze contemplated a second cherry that he had just dropped into the ether. Attacked by the liquid, it began to decompose into shreds. The pink inside was like that of an open wound.

'What cowardice, you ask? Why, that of the flesh, Madame! The body clings so fiercely to life. Who knows what instinct in the folds of the brain or in the crevices of the organs checks the fatal gesture? Consequently, one seeks what distraction one can from a constant sense of unease… Since life will not leave us, it is consciousness that escapes. People of modest means readily take comfort in cordite, the drug of war, preferring it to veronal or chloral. The wealthier among us choose to cultivate our neuroses with the old Pravaz syringe, dosed with a drop of morphine. And which of us has never submitted to the charms of opium? The drug is available at most pharmacies.'

This sober assessment was only half understood by the fat man.

'It's one thing to flee the vulgar materialism of our time, quite another to stupefy oneself with absinthe and bad wine. So you recommend opium-smoking, do you? But do you also justify those sinister dives where people may drink till they drop for a penny an hour? Do you approve of lacing children's soup with brandy from the age of three or four? Such abuses disgust me, sir… As a man of the law, I come across alcohol-related crimes every day. In fact, they're so common that the courts have recently downgraded them. The pity of it is, being drunk will often constitute an extenuating circumstance for a murderer, leading to a lighter sentence.'

The second cherry, now ready, was gobbled greedily by Samson.

'Any kind of gut-rot is better than white coffee, that

enervating drink, that rank woman-killer!'

'Not such a killer as Terminus absinthe, I'll bet! And everyone knows women drink more than men!'

'That goes to demonstrate their superiority over our sex!' the young invalid replied, winking at Apolline.

Then, recharging his goblets:

'Drink up, friends! Drink up! Let's toast the dying century! Let's get soused!'

And Samson put the bottle to his lips, downing fearsome great gulps of ether. The liquid ran down his chin, mingled with blood and perhaps also with tears.

'Champ-de-Mars!'

The cry diverted the spiritualists from the dreadful sight. All eyes turned to the omnibus boy, splendidly identified by his braid decorations and scarlet trousers. He gave two tugs on the cord. A bell tinkled beside the driver, who brought the vehicle to a halt.

'Champ-de-Mars!' the boy shouted again, unhooking the chain that blocked access to the running-board.

Two groups of passengers formed: one from inside, the other descending from the upper deck by the spiral staircase. They met at the doors of the omnibus and alighted in order, each person nodding to the boy in passing.

The sombrely clad gathering looked out of place, so far from any cemetery. A sudden shower prompted umbrellas to unfurl, forming a flowerbed of greyish blooms.

'This way!' ordered Apolline, picking up her skirts.

Led by the young woman, the spiritualist society moved off towards the Champ-de-Mars and the site of the Tower. In the distance, gleaming in the rain, bare girders rose in stooks.

'Are you daydreaming?' barked the coachman, leaning out from his seat.

Lugubriously, the bell tolled somewhere inside the omnibus.

The eraser twins continued to meet each Sunday for their weekly excursion. On one occasion, Odilon arrived at their meeting place more promptly than usual – and with a look on his face that Armand scarcely recognised.

'What a ghoulish expression!' he observed. 'Do you have an appointment with the tooth-puller?'

Odilon took his friend's arm and drew him along the boulevard. Several omnibus routes converged there, generating a continuous roar like a waterfall that caused the ground to shake and set the windows rattling. One after another these bulky horse-drawn carriages, painted green, yellow or brown, debouched from side-streets behind their teams. Most were drawn by a pair of horses, though a third was added if the route was hilly. The animals were pathetic specimens, drained by the effort of hauling their twenty-six passengers; not a few were destined to die in the prime of life.

To Armand's surprise, they shunned the omnibus that was their usual mode of transport towards the city-centre and hired a cab by the hour.

'Where to?' the cabman asked, and Armand, echoing the driver's question, asked simultaneously, 'Where are we going?'

'The Gingerbread Fair, near Place du Trône!'

Armand waited until they were seated before voicing his astonishment.

'The trip merits a cab? What about your lessons in saving money?'

'We're expected,' the Parisian replied by way of justification. 'The omnibus wouldn't get us there in time.'

The cab deposited the engineers at the ticket booths. They

paid the entrance fee, and each received a gingerbread figurine with his name inscribed on it in icing.

'Hey, this is fun!' said Armand, biting off one of the little character's ears.

He hung the figurine around his neck and pushed through the gate, followed by Odilon, who brandished his own like a pass.

A crowd entered with them and it became even more congested inside. There were so many people that it was impossible to choose one's direction. If one wished to go left, the movement carried one to the right. If one tried to slow down, the throng accelerated. One had the feeling one was not making ground oneself, one was involved in the locomotion of some animal. It was like being a segment of a millipede. Many visitors must have entered the fair and left again without experiencing it as more than an unfolding decor.

The twins had passed the waxworks, the big wheel, the Alpine panorama and the cabinet of anatomies before they became aware of the problem. They then caught and held onto the uprights of a merry-go-round fitted with wooden horses. This bold act gave them back their freedom.

'Your appointment wasn't upstream, I hope,' said Armand, brushing crumbs of gingerbread from his waistcoat.

'Heaven forbid!' replied a perspiring Odilon. 'No one could swim against this current!'

Strangely, once clear of the throng it became very simple to move about. Access to the attractions was unimpeded and the touts swinging their rattles seemed to be addressing them alone.

'A couple of office-workers out for a good time!' one bawled into his megaphone. 'Well, they've come to the right place! See the fountains of Versailles – as good as the real thing! And to finish off, the Rhine Falls at Schaffhausen!'

'A free afternoon and a few pence for a waffle! Here, feast your eyes on this! We have dancing and acrobatics on the tightrope performed by the lovely Mademoiselle Freluche, sole pupil of Madame Saqui, who, after a long and glorious career, has gone into retirement.'

From stalls to walk-in shops and from marquees to backdrops, the fair offered strollers a wide variety of entertainment and as many opportunities to lighten their pockets. Every taste was catered for, every vice pandered to, all against a common background of mendacity, dupes and masters of which found one another naturally in this environment.

Those who worshipped strength such as soldiers and farm labourers were shown wild animals, lion-tamers, adventurers who fought crocodiles or the 'iron man' who smashed boulders with a single blow of his fist.

Lovers of the exotic could admire Red Indians in teepees, a pair of Siamese twins decorating plates or Masai warriors in ceremonial dress who were paid to bite members of the public as a sign of the baseness of their instincts.

Even better served were the voyeurs, those who were drawn to spectacular malformations. For them, the fair offered the horse with five tails, the hydrocephalic child, the pygmy deer that jumped through hoops and any number of albinos, hermaphrodites and anatomical deformities floating in jars of alcohol.

Finally, humble folk were able, at the Gingerbread Fair, to meet minor celebrities, still of some interest albeit fallen from grace: the dentist to the Emperor of Brazil, the Queen of England's chiropodist, the man who made razor-strops for the Tsar and last but not least the woman who told the Austrian

Arch-duchess's fortune.

She occupied a caravan tucked away at the bottom of a field where the hippopotamus trainers grazed their beasts.

Not many visitors sought her out. People had little curiosity about what the future might hold in an age where this often seemed pre-destined: hospital for the absinthe drinker, Bicêtre Asylum for the wealthy neurotic, the Dubois Nursing Home for the man of letters.

In terms of decoration, the fortune-teller's caravan was a composite affair in the purest fairground tradition. It featured shutters painted in the Tyrolean style, complete with imitation snow and pots of geraniums, as well as a stuffed owl that was more Romany in inspiration. An accordion with a broken bellows adorned the roof, where the gutters also sported a garland of holly.

A panel hanging from the door informed the passer-by about the fortune-teller's talents: 'Madame Sérafin, cartomancer.' This difficult word was explained by a little drawing of Madame Sérafin taking an ace of hearts from a pack of cards. Rather than knock, one shook a cowbell, the gentle ringing of which conjured up a vision of Alpine meadows. Odilon shook it.

'We have an appointment with a fortune-teller?' Armand asked incredulously.

The door opened and grey skirts brushed the sill. The woman was Apolline Sérafin.

'You've brought him with you?' the young woman wished to know immediately.

Odilon indicated Armand, who, after a moment's hesitation, touched a hand to his hat.

'Excellent, excellent… He knows nothing?' she asked again.

The Parisian shook his head. At Apolline's invitation, the

twins stooped and entered.

The interior of the caravan was in stark contrast to the outside. Bare planks, unpainted and unvarnished, enclosed a room that was utterly basic. The sparse furniture comprised a chair, a table and a bed. On the table lay a number of books with tattered bindings but no writing materials and not even a lamp; only the gas-powered sign of a nearby marquee cast a modest light.

It was not how Armand had imagined a clairvoyant's consulting-room. The one he had now entered contained neither a Chinese screen nor a single Oriental pouffe. No gilded idols stood in wall niches and no incense-smoke rose from lidded cassolettes.

But most disconcertingly, there was no pack of cards. How did the clairvoyant practise her art? A wary unease came over Armand.

'Who are you? What is this place?'

'Please, sit down,' said Apolline, avoiding his questions.

Armand hesitated. It was ill-mannered to take the only chair in the presence of a woman. Nevertheless, he did as he was told.

Apolline and Odilon sat on the bed. They joined hands. Armand noticed the ring gleaming on the cartomancer's finger. Odilon took one just like it from his fob and slipped it onto his finger. His friend could not believe his eyes: Odilon was married to this gypsy?

As if reading his mind, Apolline smiled broadly.

'It's our secret – will you keep it? We're man and wife.'

Armand felt awkward. His eyes sought Odilon's, hoping to read an ironic denial in those light-blue irises. How he yearned to hear that quiet, familiar voice intone, 'You're having a bad dream, none of this is true!' And the twins would have exited with a loud laugh, they'd have left the gypsy there in her caravan and the caravan at the end of the hippo paddock and gone back to the fair and to cosy reality. Perhaps it was just a prank, after all? The kind of practical joke they played on greenhorns at engineering college? Odilon was play-acting, of course he was! Under the clairvoyant's wig was the cashier from the office, he thought he'd spotted a resemblance!

But the Parisian, too, was transformed. He was smiling, as if relieved at no longer having to live a lie. And what was he doing now? Wasn't he unbuttoning his waistcoat? Putting his arms round the woman? And that dreadful clay pipe he'd picked up from under the bed and was now sucking by its curved stem!

Something in Armand snapped. Mumbling excuses, he got up to go. His hand was already on the door-knob, turning. But the door would not open. He tried again, grasping the knob more firmly. No luck.

What trap had he been lured into? Panic seized the young engineer.

'Open this door!' he yelled. 'Otherwise I'll break it open!'

'Calm down,' was Odilon's reaction. 'Are you out of your mind?'

His young friend was pulling and pushing with all his might.

'I want the key!'

'What key? There's no lock.'

This made an impression on Armand. He let go of the knob and saw that indeed the door was bare, with neither latch, nor bar, nor bolt – nothing to counter the pressure of his arm. A bead curtain would have offered more resistance. So why wouldn't the damn door open?

'He has the gift, this boy!' the gypsy said admiringly.

Armand started when he saw Odilon coming towards him. But all the Parisian did was place his forefinger against the door and when he gave a little push…it swung wide open.

'I don't feel well!' said Armand, the colour draining from his face. 'I need a drink!'

6

Armand, Apolline and Odilon had resumed their places around the table. The clairvoyant served lemonade in little glasses, even biscuits on a plate. Clearly, her home possessed hidden resources.

As the afternoon advanced, the bareness of that interior became less austere. Warmed by the light of a candle she found under the pillow, the old caravan even took on a cosy look. Sitting there, surrounded by its ancient planking, one felt one was between the pages of a novel.

With calm now restored, Odilon spoke first.

'Poor Armand, so many riddles! Your head must be spinning with all these revelations!'

Armand took a sip from his glass to clear his throat.

'It is indeed! I'm totally mystified. I assume you're single. I discover you're married. But not to some nice middle-class girl; to a fortune-teller, someone who reads cards at the Gingerbread Fair. And now this door I couldn't open! If a writer penned all that, they'd be taken for a madman!'

'It's entirely natural, your confusion,' said Apolline, refilling his glass with lemonade. 'The down-to-earth work of an engineer, the calculations with which you're weaving this 300-metre Tower, thread by thread. No doubt they have ill-prepared you for such things. But remember, only twenty years ago few people could imagine the telephone, the phonograph or electricity. Reality has many more faces than the one illuminated by modern science!'

'I know. I no longer doubt it, now that I've seen a mere door mock my physical strength!'

At this last sentence, a smile of communication passed between the other two. There was a moment's silence as Odilon stood up to light his pipe at the candle flame. When he sat back down, he asked:

'My friend, do you believe in God?'

A moment earlier, the question would have startled the young man. Now he accepted it without surprise, prepared to hear anything from someone he had seen change in so short a time from being an engineer to being some kind of poet.

Armand's reply was honest: 'I do from my upbringing. My mother was extremely devoted to the Virgin Mary. But to be honest I hardly ever go to church myself. Working with figures has given my mind a certain bent that sits ill with religion.'

'And do you still think there's life after death?' asked Apolline with a little cough. She had inhaled a copious amount of pipe smoke.

The young man from St. Flour answered carefully, though he had never given much thought to such things.

'Anyone who has seen a bird fall from a perch and seen that same animal, two days later, dancing on a bed of maggots cannot have any great hopes of the beyond!'

The Parisian plunged a thumb into the bowl of his pipe to

tamp down the shreds of tobacco.

'Clearly, we don't share the same view. As I see it, the physical body is simply an envelope, a garment we cast off when it wears out. It protects the spirit, which is eternal.'

'To be precise,' Apolline corrected, 'there is an intermediate envelope between the body and the spirit. It is subtler in nature than the body yet, being still material, it assumes human form. It's the diaphanous shape described by people who have seen ghosts. We call it the fluidic or astral body.'

'After death,' she went on, 'the spirit frees itself from the physical body. It enters another world where it meets up with relatives or friends who have gone before. Religion posits a heaven and a hell, representing the everlasting reward or punishment for this brief existence. We, on the other hand, see only a transitional phase: as soon as possible the spirit will be reincarnated. That is to say, it will take up residence in a fresh body.'

The clairvoyant became animated, 'Each of us has shared the fate of many beings down the ages! Who knows? Maybe you wore the uniform of a soldier in Antiquity, then became a potter in the Middle Ages and a pastrycook at the court of the Sun King! It's in the depth and density of thousands of lives, through the ordeals they constitute and the lessons they teach, that slowly, patiently, the spirit rises. This almost endless ladder leads to supreme bliss. Finally admitted among the Just, the disembodied spirit contemplates the Godhead...'

A glow of ecstasy shone in the fortune-teller's eyes. The same effulgence had entered Odilon's gaze. Both appeared to be in a state of high excitement. It fell to the young man to sum up, which he did as he emptied his pipe with the aid of a spoon.

'It is things like this – and many more besides – that our

doctrine proclaims. What is the principle behind it? The existence of a soul and its survival after death. What does it seek? Knowledge of the laws that govern the created world. What methods does it use? Conversing with spirits and studying what they have to tell us. The name of that doctrine is spiritualism. There's nothing new about it; Pythagoras, back in the 6th century B.C., championed the idea of transmigration of souls.'

Armand felt a huge guffaw welling up from his belly. He only just managed to stifle it. What wild imaginings! So this was what occupied the mind of the esteemed Odilon Cheyne, an engineer specialising in iron construction! Ghosts and apparitions! How hilarious! How truly hilarious!

Nevertheless, not wishing to be rude, he ventured a simple question.

'That's as may be, but it doesn't get me anywhere. What do spirits have to do with a door that won't open and those glass cases at the morgue splintering into fragments?'

Apolline drew the candle closer to her face, the better to illuminate the expression it bore, which at that moment was one of intense passion.

'To expound the whole doctrine of spiritualism would take too long. It's a world of its own! All you need to know is that conversing with spirits can only be done in the presence of individuals endowed with a special faculty – mediums. Some are aware of their gift and cultivate it; they are "elective mediums". Others, knowing nothing of these phenomena, ignorant even of the part they might play, these we call "natural mediums". It is our belief that you are a natural medium.'

To Armand, Apolline's statement came as a painful shock. As long as this nonsense remained external to him and the business of a colleague and his gypsy wife – he could find it amusing. But how could he bear his own name being associated with it? Abruptly, his face hardened.

'Me? A medium? I don't think so!'

Quick as a flash, Apolline came back at him.

'Armand, has anyone ever told you about strange happenings, things that would make a house seem haunted? Logs rolling across the floor, doors banging, objects rising into the air, dishes smashing with a racket – all of it, of course, in empty, draught-free rooms, for no apparent reason?'

Apolline's conviction was intimidating. Armand swallowed before replying.

'Probably, yes, I have heard of such things. The newspapers rely on them for their "In brief" columns!'

'Well, spiritualism can explain them. Such disturbances are the work of frivolous spirits who delight in making mischief. They'd be unable to operate without a man or woman serving as their intermediary. In other words, without a natural medium amongst the people nearby!'

'So?' said the engineer, losing the thread.

Odilon tapped out his pipe rhythmically on the edge of the table.

'Don't you see? You are the medium such spirits used to break the glass cases at the morgue? And it was by drawing on your fluid that they jammed the door!'

'What fluid are you talking about? No, don't tell me. I've had enough of your silly stories! I can just about accept a clairvoyant being on intimate terms with the dead and engaging them in conversation, but an engineer!'

'Spiritualism is not a matter of occupation or class! Our doctrine is spreading throughout society, particularly among the lower strata. We publish two journals in Paris called *Dawn* and *The Lotus* and many more in England. Thousands of initiates in town and country hold evocations every day. A painting went on show in Antwerp recently entitled *Interior with Rustic Spiritualists.*'

'There you are!' Armand hooted, unable to contain his laughter any longer. 'You numb the minds of humble folk with ideas they can't possibly comprehend, just as religion was used to baffle them in the past! Shall we never be rid of these ancient superstitions, these beliefs from another era? How long must we wait for the glorious triumph of reason?'

Shards of clay sprang from the pipe as it was crushed in Odilon's fist.

'Saints in heaven, you mean?'

'I don't believe in saints,' the engineer hurled back. 'Only one, anyway, who makes up for all the others: Saint-Simon!'

The Parisian was preparing a stinging retort when there came a cry from outside.

'Help! Help!'

All three jumped up and rushed to the door. Outside, a strange scene met their eyes. In the immediate foreground stood a young woman, her hand raised as if to knock on the door. Beyond, moving at a clumsy trot, was a large hippopotamus trailing a broken rope and farther off, running as fast as he could, was a bare-headed man. The second was pursuing the third; what the first was doing was not apparent.

The animal soon tired and slowed down, whereupon the fugitive cast a glance back towards the caravan.

'Look, it's the ragman from the other day!' Armand observed.

Awkwardly, Gaspard Louchon vaulted the fence.

'So, Roseline, your boyfriend's been spying on you, has he?' Odilon joked, stepping back to let the visitor enter.

'Him?' the newcomer answered with a chuckle. 'Never seen him before! I might have boyfriends, they spring up like weeds under a girl's feet. But an ape like that, with grey hair and a fat arse? Not on your life!'

The Parisian uncorked the bottle to pour a fourth glass.

'What did he want with you, then?'

Roseline stamped her foot.

'I don't know, do I? There was no one following me when I left the theatre. I know that because it's a time when I always keep a wary eye out. Lord, they certainly go for actresses, those middle-class men! There's always a bevy of them sniffing around…'

At this point Armand, who had remained by the door with arms folded, not sure whether to come back in or go out, shouted at Odilon.

'You don't get it, do you? I recognised that man… He was hanging around the Eiffel offices last week. The ragman – remember? He's spying on us!'

'You must be mistaken,' Odilon replied. 'The face says nothing to me.'

It was the actress who made sure they got the story straight.

'The gentleman's right! My admirers aren't any of them that ugly!'

Having this young stranger cast her vote for him spread a pleasant warmth through the core of Armand's being.

Admittedly, the actress's silhouette, which the candlelight only enhanced, would have been the object of any male interest and the young man from St. Flour was no exception. She had one of those figures that clothing, however loose, only constrains: the bosom overflowed the neckline with commendable generosity; the waist challenged the corset, making it crackle like tinder; even the legs seemed confined behind their curtain of material – craving more space, more light and air.

Over the hips, no contrivance made the skirt billow out, no horsehair bustle or compensatory drape, only a natural curve imparted by the flesh beneath. It was a simple, comfortable dress, from the mid-price range of one of the larger department stores, but with a touch of originality that gave it its elegance. The 'New Empire' style, it was called, and the dress really drew the eye with its sequined tulle overlay and panels of blue silk embroidered with flowers.

'What a beautiful woman!' mused Armand, making no attempt to curb his smile. Somewhat to his alarm, it was returned.

'Time's getting on,' remarked Apolline as the light from the nearby tent sign fell on her face.

'Let's go!' said Odilon. 'Not once in five years has the seance started late!'

Taking his wife's arm, the Parisian stepped through the door, with Roseline in tow. Then, looking back over his shoulder as if he had forgotten something of minor importance – blowing out the candle, perhaps, or drawing the curtain – Odilon addressed his friend:

'Armand, our group meets this evening to evoke spirits. Will you join us?'

The young engineer glanced at Roseline and, sensing encouragement in her gaze, felt his heart starting to beat faster.

'But of course! I'd be interested to see…'

Apolline wore the expression of a mother who has successfully subdued a naughty child. She asked Armand to close the door, but she need not have bothered. The door in question, so recently intractable, had slammed shut behind him.

Only a short distance from the caravan, Odilon picked up a badly battered hat. Curiously, the brim of the bowler had been bitten. The saliva-soaked fabric bore the clear imprint of a set of enormous teeth.

'Darling, throw it away! It's disgusting!' the fortune-teller protested.

The Parisian threw the hat towards a grazing hippo.

'You're right. I expect it belongs to our visitor, but I don't feel like getting involved in a police inquiry.'

The young people directed their steps towards a postern-gate at the far end of the paddock, which the fairground people used to go into the city. In a moment, they were in the street.

As they joined the crowd outside, Armand had found it quite natural to offer Roseline his arm. And she, indeed, had taken it quite unaffectedly, following the example of Apolline as she snuggled up against Odilon.

In truth, the couple walking in front served them as a model, their gestures and bearing inviting imitation. There was no question, of course, of their reproducing the embraces of a married couple emboldened by the gathering dusk, but they were able, all the same, in this temptingly symmetrical situation, to draw close together and take each other by the hand or arm – practising mild complicities that they would never have dared indulge in alone. The actress did so the more readily for the fact that Armand, still slightly stiff, gave the impression that this was his first experience of sensual pleasure.

'How dark it's getting!' the young engineer declared in a hypocritical attempt to allay any such suspicion.

Yet his heart was beating fit to burst at feeling a woman's hand in the crook of his elbow – a tiny hand, sheathed in a kid glove that seemed to him so delicate, like a wounded bird nestling on a scrap of cotton-wool in his pocket, so fragile that he was afraid of bruising it by a sudden movement.

Armand no longer dared move his arm or shoulder. The whole of the upper part of his body was as if paralysed.

'Are you all right?' asked the actress anxiously, having sensed a quivering communicated through the young man's elbow.

'Me? Fine! I've never felt better!'

He gave her a sidelong glance, which had the effect of enormously increasing his excitement. The animal body beside him was eloquently reflected in the girl's face: no cooler lips could be imagined, no cheek more voluptuous – yet the pupils were cauldrons where water rumbled, seethed and steamed.

Just then Roseline, with a woman's instinct for the right moment, pretended to stumble, almost throwing herself into the young man's arms. She recovered quickly – helped somewhat feebly by the engineer – but without quite returning to her former position. On the pretext that her ankle hurt, she now half-leant against Armand. Her head rested tenderly on the boy's shoulder.

'Ah, Madame!' he sighed, overcome with emotion.

Impishly, the actress corrected him: 'Not "Madame" – "Mademoiselle!" No one has yet slipped a ring on my finger.'

'The well-bred man lives with his mistress and dies at home with his wife,' Armand quoted, hoping it would make him look good.

'That's something men say to excuse their affairs! Bah! you really are all the same!'

Angrily, Roseline removed the pins that held her hat on and tore it from her head. The gesture took Armand's breath away. This was a major breach of convention – going hatless in public! Such boldness thrilled him.

'You're quite wrong there,' he mumbled. 'The present generation respects women.'

'And how does it show that respect? By letting them open a savings account or join a trades union or sue for divorce… Hardly great conquests, are they? I'll feel your equal, young sir, when I can leave the house without a corset!'

In a softer tone, lowering her eyelids over those tawny pupils, she added, 'It's a shame, don't you think – keeping nature imprisoned? I expect you can't wait to see me without this contraption…'

Was this an invitation? Armand believed it was and experienced a rush of giddiness. So this was love? This dry throat, this tingling skin, this drumming in his chest… Above all, words spoken apparently in jest that carried a commitment for ever. It was possible, then, in a flash, to lose one's balance and topple into a quite different life? One look was enough to reverse a man like a glove, to turn a lonely boy, embarked on a quiet career, into an actress's impassioned lover. And Odilon had said nothing! Why had he not introduced Roseline ages ago? Why all the useless time-wasting, the student outings to boring dances – when all that mattered was here, waiting for him at the Gingerbread Fair? Actually, how had the meeting been contrived? Had the Parisian anticipated this love at first sight?

Questions went rolling in all directions, upsetting his former notions like so many skittles, spreading great confusion through the young man's mind.

He in turn laid his head on the actress's shoulder. She received it with tenderness, rather more the mother than the lover, whispering sweetly in the young man's ear, aware of the frantic beating of his heart through his clothing.

Suddenly, Armand felt shame at this relaxed acceptance. In an access of virility, he thrust his lips towards Roseline's neck and stabbed blindly – none too clear whether he had hit skin, the material of her dress or the curls of her hair.

The actress turned her lips to his. Excitement in Armand's case, concern to do the right thing in Roseline's, led them behind a lamppost. They kissed till their breath ran out.

The actress delighted in the boy's fresh skin, smooth and velvety like cream that has never been beaten, innocent of wrinkles; she felt sure it had never received any but his mother's lips till now. She moved her hips slightly to embolden a hand that had descended to that slope but hesitated to venture upon it.

Armand was making his own discoveries: the writhing of tongues within mouths, the soapy taste of lipstick, the rubbing of a pearl necklace, the scent of fresh linen between breasts as it wafted upward. Swollen against each other, their bodies turned pain to pleasure. There was so much to feel, so much to learn, that excitement somehow ceased to mount...

Not knowing how to finish, the young engineer was relieved to hear Odilon's voice.

'Armand? Roseline? Where are you? You'll make us late!'

His inexperience extending to his manners, Armand released Roseline unceremoniously to button up his coat. She, forgiving this loutish behaviour, even offered to help. A moment later, the couple stood before Odilon.

'Ah, there you are!' the Parisian grumbled. 'My colleague, the laggard! Let's get a move on! I don't want to keep our friends waiting...'

The young man from St. Flour was struck dumb.

Gaspard selected a stove-pipe hat from the display. It was covered in shiny stretched silk and was as smooth and black as a seal's skin. The inside was lined with crimson satin, resplendent with the hatter's trademark: four letters in modern English writing, embroidered in gold thread and underlined with an elegant flourish. Deep down inside were the silver-plated springs that would restore the hat's shape once it had been flattened.

'A very fine topper, this!' said Gaspard, one eye closed in admiration. He set it on his head. In the mirror placed there for customers to use, he saw reflected a fat face that overflowed the celluloid collar in soft, doughy folds. It resembled an underdone brioche escaping from its baking-tin. The hat perched on top finished off the reflection in a ludicrous, almost burlesque way reminiscent of a piece of fruit stuck on a bun.

Laughter rang out behind Gaspard, who quickly removed the head-piece.

'Such elegance! Don't tell me – you're invited to dine with the ambassador!'

Gaspard spun around – to find himself face to face with Gordon Hole.

'Sir!' the Frenchman said in a strangled voice. 'What are you doing here?'

'I come here on rainy days,' the American disclosed, taking the stove-pipe from Gaspard's hands in what was clearly an act of confiscation. 'This store has the advantage over the museum of the same name that it costs nothing to enter: a man can get under cover for free. Also, the hotel is nearby… But what about yourself? Didn't I ask you to do a job?'

Gaspard placed a hand on his heart as if to make a vow.

'I've done it, sir! Oh, you wouldn't believe the things I've seen! Incredible! And to start with, my bowler hat – left between the teeth of a hippopotamus!'

Hole, who was a head taller than the Frenchman, bent down to sniff the latter's breath.

'It's the honest truth!' protested Gaspard. 'But it's a long story, which I'll tell you later… All you need know is that this Odilon, Armand Boissier's friend, has a liaison with a gypsy fortune-teller. I've seen the caravan where they meet.'

Hole listened with his head down, staring at the curved brim of the hat. The fancy took him to try it on himself. He did so with a theatrical gesture that caused folds of grey material to spill from his sleeve. The opera hat suited him perfectly.

Gaspard was trying to think of something complimentary to say but the American got in first, saying harshly:

'I'm not paying you to shadow Odilon Cheyne but Armand Boissier. Have you anything to tell me about him, or do you just want money?'

'Wait!' the Frenchman gulped. 'I'm coming to that! Armand was there, of course he was! Four of them went to a funny place where they put dead bodies in glass cases…'

'The morgue?'

'The morgue – that's it! Well, did you know there's a secret staircase there? A spiral staircase hidden under one of the cases, behind a marble panel. You go down between the corpse's legs. Honest! That evening they'd just brought in a murder victim and there was blood dripping onto the steps. I thought I was going to pass out…'

The memory made the Frenchman feel queasy. Instinctively, his hand went to a certain inside pocket of his coat. But the bottle he had expected to find was no longer there… His gaze narrowed with suspicion as he looked back up at his employer.

'That's a good start!' Hole conceded as he looked in the mirror, assessing the effect of the hat. 'But what did you do then? They didn't leave you a key, I presume?'

'I bribed the attendant. He's a good man, that Old Man Modesty – understands the language of the rustling banknote. Anyway, there was a crowd of them to greet Armand and his friends, twenty at least. Men and women, all dressed as if they were going to a funeral, trooping down the stairs behind them… I could have mingled with the group and not stood out. My false beard often comes in handy!'

The American had turned away from the hat display, wearing the topper, and was now strolling through various other departments. Gaspard scurried after him.

'So,' the Frenchman resumed, 'I followed them all down into the basement of the morgue. The staircase came out in a large room with a wardrobe near the entrance, behind a screen. That's where I was able to hide. In the room there was a circular table, large enough to seat all those people, with the appropriate number of chairs. But just the right number, notice, not one too many, not one too few. So this was a gathering of regulars…'

'Which chair would you have taken?' Hole enquired slyly.

The innuendo passed Gaspard by.

'Over the table, casting a bright light on its surface but not much on the people sitting around it, was a chandelier of curious design. Its candles were red, sir, and they threw a very frightening blood-red glow that put me in mind immediately of some witches' sabbath…'

Hole had stopped in front of a display of toilet articles. A sidelong glance revealed two salesmen following them, no doubt because of the hat that still adorned his head.

The gentleman's hand promptly shot out and snatched a

Swedish razor, a string of Venetian sponges, a bottle of mouthwash and various other expensive items. As he took them, he loaded them into the arms of the flabbergasted Frenchman.

'What are these for?' asked Gaspard.

'You'll see in a moment… Follow me!'

Hole walked quickly towards the little train waiting only a few paces away – in mid-store! The management had had the idea of installing this miniature railway to carry customers from one side of Les Grands Magasins du Louvre to the other, thus relieving them of a tiresome walk.

The pair installed themselves in the front car, joining some unruly children who were playing a game that involved leaping from seat to seat. The salesmen climbed aboard too.

'Well? What happened next?' the architect enquired as the tiny train moved off.

The grinding sound of the wheels forced Gaspard to raise his voice.

'Right – the people present sat around the table like I said. The seat of honour, which had arms, was taken by the fortune-teller. There's no doubt about it, she's the priestess of this brotherhood. All eyes were on her and she was the first to speak. Cheyne sat on her right, taking notes, like the clerk of the court at a trial. I did the same – look!'

The Frenchman tugged at the sleeve of his shirt. The stretched material revealed several lines of scribbled words, jotted down in a hurry.

'Congratulations!', Hole said approvingly. 'Excellent piece of improvisation!'

Gaspard smiled with pleasure.

'At your service, sir! So here's what the gypsy said for him to take down: "Seance began at 6 pm on Wednesday, August 31st 1887. Weather thundery; sky overcast; strong northeasterly wind; barometer at 510; temperature inside, 18 degrees. Present: Odilon Cheyne, Armand Boissier, Roseline Page, Samson…"'

At that moment the train entered a tunnel, where there was not much light. Gaspard was obliged to stop reading. A clamour arose from the children's bench: they were afraid of the dark.

'Get to the point!' the American said, moving to another seat.

'Alas, sir, what happened then I didn't understand at all. It was like this… The people all joined hands like children when they want to dance round in a circle. The gypsy woman said a prayer in which the words "spirit" and "guardian angel" occurred several times. Then Cheyne came over to near where I was hiding – very near; it made me sweat – and fetched a sort of miniature table: a three-legged toy, two of the legs ending in little ivory balls to enable it to roll about and the third in a pencil. Meanwhile someone else, staring wide-eyed, was performing a sort of pantomime in front of the gypsy's face. His two hands swung from side to side, forward and back, like snakes before they bite. Made my flesh creep, sir!'

'Magnetic passes,' Hole explained. 'The man was hypnotising her.'

Gaspard shrugged.

'If you say so. Anyway, the fortune-teller soon slumped in her chair. I thought she was going to fall asleep, but in a moment she started these feeble hand movements…then a shiver ran up her arms, passed through her shoulders, and made her head roll – suddenly and very violently. A sort of groan rose from her chest and grew into an agonised scream. Honestly, sir, you'd have thought she was hysterical, like some crazed Salpêtrière inmate! I was trembling behind my screen.'

'And the others?' the American wanted to know.

'The others did nothing. They stayed holding hands and

they looked as if they were deep in thought. It didn't bother them in the least to be sitting in the company of a madwoman. In fact, one of them, once she had calmed down a bit, took her wrists and guided her hands towards the miniature table. The tiny toy started to roll back and forth in all directions, wherever the gypsy pushed it. So did the crayon attached to the third leg, which traced a frantic scrawl on the tabletop – loops, lines, whatever her fancy dictated... I ask you, sir, is that any way for right-minded people to behave?'

'Go on! What happened next?'

'Cheyne slipped a sheet of paper beneath the point of the pencil. I was too far away to see, but I think that was when the thing – how shall I say? – settled down. It no longer scribbled, it was writing. I mean it, sir, the pencil was tracing letters! For a good hour, it continued to cover the paper – sheet after sheet of it, as Cheyne replaced the full ones. Then, quite abruptly, the gypsy's hands went limp and no longer propelled the little table. Her head fell back against the chair. Someone asked for light. I lost my nerve and left...'

The train had just reached the end of the line. The driver, who wore the livery of the store, rang a little bell and announced, 'Ladies' fashions!' Hole alighted first, using his umbrella to part the children.

'Your story has a certain piquancy,' the American conceded, halting on the platform. 'But where does it get us in the end? Two of Monsieur Eiffel's engineers indulge in a bit of spiritualism and the most rational enterprise of the century is served by men who believe in ghosts! Big deal! It would barely make the "News In Brief" column. Not even your *Petit Parisien* would look twice at such a snippet and that's a paper that can never get enough scandal. So what now?'

The Frenchman blushed deeply in his embarrassment. He

could think of nothing to parry Hole's stinging rebuke. Fortunately for Gaspard, his employer said immediately:

'You mentioned a fourth person just now. You said, "Four of them…". Cheyne, Boissier, the gypsy – who else?'

'A young woman, Monsieur Hole. A pretty one, too. She's an actress who plays minor parts in some boulevard theatre. I've seen her face on a poster.'

'A member of the spiritualist group?'

'Possibly! A very good friend of young Boissier's, anyway… They did a bit of billing and cooing when the other two had their backs turned. And it seemed to me that, when everyone joined hands during the seance, they did so rather more enthusiastically than some.'

A fresh thought shone in the American's eyes. The point of his umbrella moved lightly over the floor, apparently tracing a shape – the bulge of a woman's bodice, perhaps. 'Promising! Very promising!' he mused, his brow furrowed with the effort of thought.

At the same time, Hole's gaze strayed into the middle distance, where a series of small canopies broke the monotonous lines of shelving. This part of the store was devoted to women's fashions and the management had inaugurated a number of new services for the comfort of customers: a 'lighting salon', where ladies could see what a dress looked like either by candlelight or in the very different illumination cast by gas; enormous weighing-machines with luxuriously upholstered armchairs on them; a buffet with refreshments; a reading and letter-writing room… Hole seemed to be scanning this decor for inspiration.

It was at that point that they were accosted by the two assistants who had been following them since they left the hat department.

The American glared at the newcomers.

'How rude! Can you not see we're in conversation?'

'I'm sorry, sir,' said one of the salesmen. 'It's 9pm. The tills…'

'In that case,' the architect interjected, 'we're leaving… this instant!'

The salesman touched his cap in a salute. It was not returned: Hole had taken Gaspard's arm and was steering him towards the revolving door.

'Excuse me, gentlemen! The tills are over the other side,' a clerk on the fabric counter pointed out.

'He's right, it's that way!' the Frenchman confirmed, looking over his shoulder.

'Don't worry about a thing… Come along, follow me!'

The American's pace had quickened. Gaspard was not exactly built for exercise, and with both arms heavily laden he struggled to keep up.

'Do we need all this stuff?' he panted. 'I'm rather hampered.'

'It's absolutely essential! Lose a single package and you lose your job!'

They were 30 metres from the doors when abruptly, without warning, Hole broke into a run. A sales clerk yelled, 'Stop that man!'

A whistle shrilled in Gaspard's ears. He would have cried out but panic had sucked the breath from his chest. Whatever had got into his employer? Terrified, he plunged toward the exit.

The American had already reached the revolving door but the young commissionaire had locked it. Coolly, Hole drew his revolver and fired at the glass. The pane shattered. 'Look out! He's got a gun!' came a shout from somewhere behind Gaspard. But the American had already grasped hold of his hired man and was dragging him out into the street. They fled, Hole still brandishing the revolver.

Rounding the corner of Avenue Victoria, the American holstered his weapon and the two men changed pace. They regained the hotel at a walk.

No sooner were they back in Hole's room than Gaspard collapsed on the couch with the packages. In his excitement he had crushed the bottle of mouthwash against his chest: shards of glass had torn his shirt to ribbons. The Frenchman, after hiccoughing two or three times, threw up.

'Disgusting!' hissed his master, dusting off the top hat.

Gaspard's tear-filled eyes peered out from beneath trembling eyelids.

'You're…you're out of your mind!'

The American spun on his heel with a dancer's grace.

'No no, my friend, no no! It was all thought out.'

'But why?' Gaspard asked, a little recovered.

Hole sat down beside the Frenchman and took his arm, as he had done earlier to draw him into a run.

'Why? To bind you to me, of course! I have a plan regarding Armand Boissier. It came to me in the store. But it will be tricky to implement, requiring total loyalty. I can't risk any betrayal.'

'Don't I already do everything you say?' pleaded the Frenchman, wiping his mouth with a flap of shirt material.

The American heaved a disillusioned sigh.

'You do what the money says, Gaspard. I don't blame you – anyone else would do the same. But now you're wanted as an accomplice to robbery. People saw you running out with me. Worse: a shot was fired, glass flew, I trained the gun on an employee… What better way to entwine our fates? Don't you see? It's like architecture – to lock two members together you join them with a cross tie! Are you likely to denounce me when with a single telegram I could send you to prison?'

'I could do the same!' the Frenchman countered pluckily.

'That would be stupid! You'd be giving yourself up. And don't forget – I'm an American citizen, I can only be tried in my own country. Before my case came to court you'd be an old lag, Gaspard!'

The cruelty of the stratagem and an awareness of his own impotence cast the Frenchman into a sullen silence.

'If you betray me,' said Gordon Hole with finality, crowning his associate with the stovepipe, 'you'll be the one wearing the hat – isn't that what you say in French? You'll be the one who carries the can!'

7

Making love, they say, helps old lovers get to sleep. Conversely, it may keep young ones awake; the prodigal expenditure of energy, the surfeit of exertion perpetrated by bodies in pursuit of pleasure, far from causing fatigue may bring as much relaxation as a good night's rest.

That was how it was with Armand.

The young engineer had not slept a wink since Roseline, weak with bliss, had lapsed into slumber in his arms. It was the middle of the night. The clock, he remembered, had last struck three, the hammer falling three times onto a little bell whose sound, he had thought, was far too loud in the now quiet bedroom. God! What if it woke Roseline? What if she then chided him because of it? So what had this attentive young man done? He had got up to stop the chiming mechanism, ensuring that it caused no further disturbance.

On the other hand, he had quite quickly abandoned the role of young squire brooding over his beloved with an enamoured gaze. Not that he was going off her, but the effort of holding Roseline in his embrace eventually began to give him cramp in the shoulders. And anyway – does the reader really need to have this spelled out? – he had less and less taste for the unrequited kisses one bestows upon a partner who has fallen asleep. Yesterday a caress, even a tender glance, had made the lad's senses reel; now only a greater intimacy could satisfy him. But young people are like that – they soon want more.

Unable to sleep, Armand spent the time like any lover in the home of someone who, that morning, had been a stranger to him. He wandered from room to room, picking things up and putting them down, then, growing bolder, leafing through letters – this without guile, simply as a different way of making the acquaintance of a woman who, after all, he knew little about.

These indiscretions taught him nothing, incidentally. The apartment was a typical single girl's love-nest, full of frills and furbelows. The things were either knick-knacks or toilet products – mainly perfume sprays, of which Roseline had a substantial collection. The letters were from admirers who all, some obliquely, others more directly, paid court to the actress in various ways.

The only thing out of the ordinary was the number of mirrors in the apartment. Glasses of all shapes and sizes, some new, some already speckled, graced every room. Even the smallest room contained one, a pretty Venetian model that no doubt gave every guest a fright. Armand smiled at the idea of the bourgeois visitors brought face-to-face with their reflected image in such humiliating circumstances.

Even knowing that an actress lived here, a woman who by taste and occupation treasured her own appearance, one was still astonished. Why so many mirrors, creating reflections that merged, mingled and ultimately interfered with one another? What was the point of a dwelling where the walls fell away and endless receding perspectives made a person's head spin?

The profusion of mirrors might well have upset the young man. That night, however, he was content with it. Normally averse to his image, he now felt a fresh attachment to it, almost an affection. He sought it out, pursued it from frame to frame; sitting in front of the tall cheval-glass in the bedroom, he interrogated it at length with a steady gaze. He was like a child confronting its double.

And Armand did indeed feel transformed through having lost his virginity. He could not get over the change. His face looked different to him in the depths of the mirror: less fleshy, more solid, lacking the shy mobility of youth. His gaze, too, had intensified, its volatile blue now almost green, the green of a plant that had sprouted, its roots now thrust deep into the earth.

The transfiguration of love had marked his skin. A spirited lover, Roseline had given him a tattoo of scratches; furrows of white or pink covered his whole body. These scars, taken in a single night as in a duel with knives, filled the young man with an awed respect. He counted them, measured each one with his fingers, even ventured a fingernail into a fresh cut – to give it permanence, perhaps.

Altogether, of the two 'firsts' – women and sensual pleasure – it was the latter that intrigued him most. He was less interested in the pale thigh emerging from the rumpled sheets and the quivering breast above the swirl of the quilt than in his own smile in the mirror. The unfamiliar tumult that flickered there was the true curiosity of this extraordinary night.

And what a night it had been! Was it possible for a life to be overturned in this way? Could a man change so quickly, so comprehensively? The Armand he had been the day before, that innocent visitor to the Gingerbread Fair, was now like a stranger to him. He'd have addressed such a stranger in the tones that a father might use to his son, calling him 'my boy' and liberally dispensing advice. The continuity of the different ages of man, how the child becomes a youth and the youth an adult, remained a closed book to the young man from St. Flour: he felt radically detached from himself, as a ship severs contact with the shore when it casts off.

'So now I'm a real man!' Armand mused with a rush of self-esteem. He saw himself strolling down the street next day, imagining the moment when, still warm from Roseline's embrace, he would strut along, doffing his hat to captains of industry, high-up civil servants, 'Good morning, sir!' Nothing now separated him from those imposing figures, those readers of newspapers and smokers of cigars who had once made such an impression on him. On the contrary, he now felt one of them, admitted to their company, having discharged his duty of virility. The 'great secret' was a secret no more.

With childish clowning, Armand assumed the expression of a 'real man' – lower lip extended, monocle screwed firmly into one eye – and submitted it to the large mirror in the hallway. Not a bad imitation! But for the slightly flushed cheeks, he'd have passed unnoticed at any bridge party. The thought of cards brought him back to Apolline and the Gingerbread Fair.

After the great upheaval of making love, the discovery of Odilon's clandestine wife and the revelation of his friend's esoteric practices counted for almost nothing. Admittedly, the young engineer retained a powerful memory of the spiritualist seance. How could he forget the ghoulish setting and the oppressive strangeness of the ritual? He had shivered, certainly, when Odilon had read out what the miniature table had written. Why, it was not every day that one heard the words of invisible speakers reported as freely as the comments of some petty official in the newspaper. What if there had been an element of theatricality? The mere fact of a voice from beyond the grave being able to ring in the ears of the living like that made his flesh creep.

There was no denying that it had been an emotional evening, of course it had, but the sharpest of those emotions, he had to concede, still clung to Roseline… Roseline who had squeezed his hand when they all formed a chain around the table, Roseline whose foot, having slipped its shoe, moved amorously against his own… Ah, Roseline! It had all been her doing; Armand had simply followed the lead of an enterprising woman.

How would their encounter have ended, without her initiatives? Quite otherwise – of that he was in no doubt.

For one thing, Armand would not have ventured that first kiss, which had permitted those that followed. Nor would he have tried anything as they left the seance, relying on luck or on the good offices of Odilon to bring the actress back into his life. The approach would have taken months, with letters perfumed with musk or verbena, little gifts left with the concierge – all that outmoded court that young fools pay through convention, wrongly supposing that is what women want. And the declaration? That would have taken even longer, or it would have occurred in so convoluted a fashion, with so much shyness and laden with such poetry that it would not have been understood. He had been fortunate indeed to meet Roseline, a woman who took matters in hand! A late-afternoon conversation, a mid-evening stroll, an embrace at nightfall… Here was someone who wasted no time!

Armand still found it hard to believe that things had gone so well. From the initial handshake to the most intimate caresses, no more than five hours had elapsed. The immeasurable distance between a kiss on the glove and a kiss on the lips was one this couple had covered even quicker; five minutes at most, a record!

Such impetuous haste caused the engineer no misgivings. He drew no conclusions from it as to the actress's morals, only noting the strength and truth of the love to which it bore such striking testimony. Only fate, he believed, allowed such rapid joinings. Minds were the more suited, the faster bodies came together. In their case, the match seemed perfect.

After a long time spent pacing the empty flat, Armand returned to lie down as day dawned.

Already at ease with her, he planted a kiss on the actress's shoulder and gently moved her over to make room for himself. The soft bed received him like a nest, filled with a honeyed warmth that he inhaled contentedly. How luxurious it felt to slide one's limbs beneath a stiff cotton sheet and a quilt stuffed with warm cotton wool, cradling one's head in a fine, lace-trimmed pillow! Was there any more hospitable place in the world?

The first ray of sunshine had just penetrated the net curtains and crossed the room, high up. What began as a sweetly welcoming thread of blond hair was soon a feather from an angel's wing. In its wake, colours awoke: bright knick-knacks appeared and pieces of furniture; whole swathes of darkness vanished from the mirrors.

Armand followed this revelation of a setting that, glimpsed only in separate, candlelit scenes, now presented itself to him as a whole, a richer, more complex whole than he had first thought. He took in the shot-silk wall-covering with its great bouquets of roses and the hardwood dressing-table with its paler inlay; the ornamental plant-pot with its extravagant sprays of palm and the foliage-pattern carpet in the lounge and its twin in the bathroom. Meeting the sun, a marble bathtub blazed into light: it was a key moment in the advent of the new day.

Roving idly beneath the sheet, Armand's fingers made contact with a bare thigh, which at first he mistook for the bolster. It was soft and smooth, like taffeta; simply resting a hand on it would, he felt, have left it creased.

'How right things are!' Armand reasoned. 'Pretty girls come wrapped in fine silks, peasant wenches in coarse cloth.'

The thought made him feel good. Suddenly careless of disturbing Roseline's rest he thrust back the covers, revealing her nakedness. The light, falling on this fresh prize, melted and dissolved; like an artist's brush dipped in carmine, it warmed the woman's skin. Her back, her buttocks and her legs all lost the polished coldness of an Ingres painting, swelling voluptuously in the manner of a Boucher. A smile of pride rose to Armand's lips. A choice morsel indeed!

But Roseline was now awake. Limbs spread like a starfish, she stretched voluptuously.

'Good morning, lover! What time is it?' the actress asked, her voice not entirely in tune.

'I don't know. The clock has stopped.'

They exchanged that crumpled morning kiss.

'Come to my dressing-room this evening, after the show. We'll have supper together.'

'At your service!' said Armand, giving a military salute.

And that was it. Slipping into a cambric shirt, she tenderly showed him the door. Her ablutions, she claimed, were not for young eyes. 'But I'd like to watch, I really would!' the engineer protested, grinning. Catlike, she eluded his embrace. He left the house a happy man.

Unfortunately, sensual indulgence is not an acceptable excuse so far as employers are concerned.

Armand learned this to his cost when he turned up at Établissements Eiffel around mid-morning. Monsieur Pluot met him with the long face he wore on bad days, while Odilon, who had guessed the reason for his friend's lateness, wore the look of contentment that graced his good days.

'I'm docking 2 francs from your pay!' Pluot announced implacably.

The young engineer mumbled an apology and meandered over to his desk, clutching at pieces of furniture to keep himself upright. It was a vain hope. The swivel chair that stood in front of his desk had just been oiled. Perfidiously, it gave way beneath his hand, dumping Armand in a heap on the floor.

'And you've been drinking, too!' Pluot roared, brandishing his T-square.

For Odilon's nerves, already tickled by his friend's comic entrance, this was too much to bear, and they found release in a great shout of laughter, a kind of spasm of the chest muscles, so sharp and so sudden that his braces slapped against his ribs. Monsieur Pluot levelled a furious pencil at the Parisian – then swung it on round as Odilon's neighbour in turn lost control of himself. A third man, then a fourth, burst out laughing at desks nearby. The hilarity was becoming universal.

'Right, fines for everyone!' the office manager yelled, scribbling names in his register.

From end to end of the office every draughtsman, every technician and every errand boy gave way to the contagious mirth. Months of effort and fatigue, long evenings spent nodding over squared paper, exploded in a paroxysm of delight, as irresistible as it was ungovernable. Not even Gustave Eiffel, who came bounding out of his office livid with rage, was able to restore order. Nothing could be done until his staff had let off steam completely, then the storm passed of its own accord, leaving an expression of warm contentment on every face and tears of joy in countless eyes.

The only person who did not laugh, apart from Messrs. Pluot and Eiffel, was Armand himself. The enjoyment he had occasioned was one he could not share. In fact, it almost overwhelmed him, battering at the headache that made his temples throb.

Head in hands, fingers drawing his eyelids taut, the young engineer gazed vacantly at a plan unfolded on his desk. He stayed like that all morning. Eventually, towards noon, a friendly hand shook his shoulder.

'Come and have lunch!' Odilon suggested. 'That'll make you feel better.'

Finding a table near the stove, young Boissier ordered soup and scrambled egg, foods whose consistency he felt would suit his confused thoughts. But Odilon disagreed. Summoning the waiter back, he had him bring a well-cooked steak, something to exercise the jaw.

Indeed, after three athletic mouthfuls, Armand felt wide awake.

'Odilon, what a night! You have no idea…' the engineer began, sawing off another piece of meat.

'Save your breath. I know Roseline.'

'Meaning?'

Odilon winked.

'Come on, we know her power over men. It's a trait all actresses share, but she has it in a highly developed form. They're all good at seduction but she's a genius. Her lovers would take up half of *Who's Who*. There's perhaps not a wife in the whole of Paris who doesn't have reason to be jealous of her.'

Armand flexed his hand to stave off cramp. Holding the knife in two bent fingers, which had the effect of making an innocent utensil for cutting meat look like a weapon about to strike, he retorted gallantly.

'Roseline isn't like that. Or if she was, she's changed... Do you think I'd fall in love with a tart?'

'Fall in love?' the Parisian picked up with a twisted smile. 'You poor fellow! That's a ticket to despair. You don't want to fall in love with Roseline!'

'What do you know about it, anyway?' Armand burst out. 'Were you ever her lover?'

Odilon took a sip of lemonade which went down the wrong way. He subsequently wiped his lips at great length, giving himself time to think.

'Yes, I was her lover once... The man who sat next to you yesterday, he was her lover before me and two others in the same group. Even Pluot could have aspired to the position had he ever shown the least inclination for womanising!'

This announcement failed to produce the effect that might have been expected. Some body blows are absorbed by muscles tensed through instinct. So it was with Odilon's disclosure: Armand rode with it dully, his only reaction a quiver of the lip as he chewed away at his piece of meat.

'All right, you slept with her,' the engineer conceded in a voice that was well under control, 'but between her and me, it's quite different. We love each other! Believe me!'

Odilon looked down, fearing that his eyes might automatically register a note of ironic doubt. He opted for a conciliatory course, listening without complaint as his friend, so it seemed, attempted to swamp him with amorous effusions. Armand, his serenity recovered, decided to return the compliment by feigning an interest in spiritualism, saying that he wished to attend another seance.

'As long as Roseline's there, is that it?' the Parisian quipped. 'All right, agreed! I'll introduce you to the group. Yesterday you were a guest, on Wednesday you'll be a member.'

'Wednesday, as early as that?'

'Seances are held once a week, at six o'clock on Wednesday evenings. They're always at the morgue, down in the cellar, where we were last night. We also have outings on Sundays.'

'Outings? What sorts of outing?'

'Museums, monuments…all places of interest to our discipline. Oh, there's no shortage of those in Paris! You can't imagine how many churches, for instance, have crypts that used to house seances just like ours. People have always practised the evocation of spirits.'

'Where have you visited recently?'

'We have regular outings to the Champ-de-Mars. Apolline is a great believer in the magnetic virtues of the Tower. She says its shape and make-up will be ideal for amplifying spirit signals. A spiritual antenna, if you like. Once the Tower is up, we'll be holding all our seances in a special room below the north pier.'

Pensively, Armand wiped a crust of bread round his plate.

'The Tower, an antenna…and you, working under Adolphe Salles, who has asked you to look at electrical phenomena? Why, you're in the ideal job!'

'I didn't get it by chance, either,' his friend confided, lowering his voice. 'The fact is, Monsieur Salles is himself extremely interested in what we're doing.'

The crust snapped as Armand's grip involuntarily tightened.

'Salles, an occultist? Fantastic! Is Eiffel one himself?'

Odilon's only reply was to tap his cane against the side of the marble tabletop. The waiter brought the dessert. Armand asked for extra sugar.

'You grow greedy!' his Parisian friend observed. 'Falconers keep their birds hungry – it makes them fly higher.'

Did this abstruse remark disguise a lesson? Armand declined to ask. He knew his friend's liking for recondite sayings, but he also knew how pointless it was to challenge Odilon's stubbornness.

They ate their dessert in silence.

For the rest of that year, Jules Boissier was a benevolent witness to his nephew's affair with Roseline Page.

Armand had made him a party to it on that very first evening, taking advantage of the express-message system then in operation to send him a *petit bleu* – a note posted by pneumatic tube – from the Café Napolitain. 'Don't expect me back this evening,' it read, 'either for supper or for the night. I have other plans. Your loving nephew.'

The uncle found the telegram puzzling. It was not so much Armand sleeping out that intrigued him; it was being informed in advance. Several times now the lad had stayed over at the office without notifying his 'landlord', indeed without a word of explanation next day.

He quickly guessed the truth. Undoubtedly, some love interest had entered his nephew's life… Ah, the exuberance of youth! What was she called? Was she nice, at least? One elbow propped on a pile of books, he pondered the matter deeply.

Once again, as when Armand had been taken on at Eiffel's, a dash of envy injected itself into his approval of the young man's excellent character. Why had he, Jules, never encountered her, the beauty with the hourglass figure a man is so proud to parade on his arm? Why had he never felt as Armand felt now, the young engineer bursting with life and vigour who was successful in everything, in love as well as in his equations? This dancing city of laughter and non-stop parties was one of which Jules Boissier knew nothing. The Paris he had found on coming up from his village in the Auvergne sixteen years earlier, just after the Commune, was an ugly city, burnt and stinking, still cluttered with barricades.

Suddenly bitter, Jules fell into his armchair. The chair groaned. He cuffed his old cat. Cups of cold coffee lay abandoned on the table: he emptied them one by one, each at a gulp, like swallowing strong drink.

The tantrum soon passed. The old man felt silly, in the end, being jealous of a nephew less than half his age who looked to him for trust and protection. Many an old bachelor like himself would dearly love a family, their own parents having abandoned them. How lucky he was, now in his sixties already, to have a young face to greet him with a smile every day!

Something else, that evening, helped to lighten the old man's mood: his work. Jules sat at his desk now, elbows resting on drawings of machines laid one on top of another, piled higher and higher – so high, in fact, that he had forgotten what colour the wood was underneath.

He had only to cast a glance over a line, any line, and his brain was away, pursuing and pinning down problems, solving questions of force and friction, gearing and gravity, caught up in the old ardour of work. There was so much to do! He still had to complete his model of a ship propelled by explosions, his method of fishing using electricity, his idea for an automatic cab meter…and what about that journal that was waiting for an article? He must get down to it. Jules donned his spectacles, dipped his pen in the ink and threw himself headlong into his calculations.

So while Armand was whispering sweet nothings in Roseline's ear, his pensioner uncle was paying court to hyperbolas traced lovingly onto squared paper. They were no less voluptuous than thighs, those algebraic curves, and they inflamed Jules quite as much. Occasionally, his pen trembled over an asymptote and made a wrong mark, whereupon Uncle Jules would reach for the blotter, blushing like a lover who has perhaps ventured too far…

That evening, women being on his mind, what Jules meant to work on was a design for a corset. 'You never know…' he told himself. If he came up with an invention, perhaps he might try it out on his nephew's bride-to-be? There was a certain gallantry, he felt, in harnessing his genius in the service of a future relative.

Boldly, Jules drew with a skilled hand what he knew of the corset – less from experience, alas, than from illustrated advertisements or the indiscretions of former colleagues.

The result, captured in black ink on a sheet of white paper, was an arched armature in which steel wires had replaced whalebone. The latticework of laces behind and the row of hooks and eyes in front made the whole arrangement appear pear-shaped in profile. A hatching of blue crayon inside the corset suggested volume. Jules imitated the silk brocade that sheathed the wealthiest bodies.

'Look at it,' the old man thought, 'this ghastly contraption that women endure, a piece of apparatus that bears so little relation to their anatomy that when ordering a new one they must answer such questions as: "Does the bosom go high or low and does it need enhancing?" "Is the belly big?"

"Do you have any delicate parts that can't take pressure?"'
One heard so many anecdotes of women fainting, even
suffering injury, because a corset was too tight.

In an instant, the eye of the artist became the eye of the
engineer. Jules contemplated his working drawing and
wondered how it might be improved. He did not have to
ponder long. Of course, the waist must be widened. The fact
was, men preferred bosoms, which were often in greater need
of enhancement than bums. What was the point of torturing
women lower down?

In this spirit of liberalism, the engineer struck out the entire
lower portion of the corset. That left the gussets enclosing the
breasts... They were a good idea, when you thought about it,
those stiff pockets lending breadth to the least favoured
bosom. The question was, how could they be supported
without the rest of the garment? In a flash, Jules had the
answer: he drew one strap encircling the torso, two more
passing over the shoulders, and he reduced the gussets to
elegant half-moons that were like hands cupping the breasts in
their palms.

And so it was that, late one night in September 1887,
retired engineer Jules Boissier invented the brassiere.

What did Uncle Jules do with his discovery? Very little,
unfortunately. He submitted his drawings to a political and
literary journal that had a scientific section, only to have them
rejected on grounds of propriety. The patent office likewise
wanted nothing to do with them. As for the corset-makers,
not only was the idea of limited practical interest, but in their
view, it also constituted an insult to their very profession. In
one of the establishments he visited Jules Boissier nearly had
an eye poked out by a seamstress working on lace holes with
a stiletto.

The incident cut short the old man's efforts to market his discovery. He rolled up the drawings and forgot about them. It is not known how the design fell into the hands of Herminie Cadolle, the young woman whose name came to be associated with the invention two years later.

With the bra project behind him, Jules Boissier still needed something to fill the rainy evenings of that autumn and winter. His work began to explore other paths, though without leaving the field of female accessories. It was as if the uncle, through the medium of his inventions, was able in his way to share his nephew's passion for Roseline. He designed the first handbags with Roseline in mind, dedicated a prototype zip-fastener to the young woman, created the self-warming garter-belt for her, the reversible skirt, the waterproof cape...

He thought of the actress as a china doll, an object to be groomed and dressed.

Armand, of course, had no notion of his uncle's interest in Roseline. How could he have done?

After that first meeting, the young man spent most of his time with the actress, moving most of his things to her flat. The case he had brought from St. Flour made daily trips between Rue de Bruxelles and Allée de l'Observatoire. Armand had not dared take everything at once for fear of hurting his uncle's feelings. So he moved by instalments, as it were – shirt by shirt and stocking by stocking – as far as possible without the old man knowing. It was a vain precaution: who could have failed to guess what was happening as the young man's wardrobe gradually emptied?

The biggest problem were Armand's visits – there was no other word for them, now that he was living somewhere else.

He made it his duty to eat at his uncle's house at least once a week and to 'pop in and say hello', as he put it, on two other evenings, when Roseline was doing shows. But the remedy was worse than the ill; uncle and nephew sat facing each other over bowls of tepid soup, conversing through yawns, between them a broad expanse of bare table lit by a single candle.

Armand was the first to lose heart at these dismal reunions. With unintentional rudeness, he glanced at his watch. What would Roseline be doing at this moment? Would it be time to make up already? Or would she be doing one of those interviews for the gossip columns in a flower-filled dressing-room? Ah, to be at her side!

He closed his eyes and imagined himself in his seat at the theatre. It was an expensive seat, in the front row of the stalls, so close to the stage he could hear the prompter. His neighbours, all high-ranking, all wearing decorations, cast intrigued glances at this very young man. Doubtless a complimentary ticket, whispered the powdered wives, fluttering their fans. Three blows were struck on the invisible stage. What? Time for the first act already? Armand's gaze flew to the curtain with its array of advertisements for, 'Viruega scented flea-powder,' and 'Labouille – condiments for fish'. A tremor ran through the expanse of velvet, which rose to reveal the set. 'Ah!' the audience exclaimed. Whistles came from the upper balconies, where working-class folk, ill-bred – and with a dreadful view – sewed disorder by dropping orange peel on the bald heads below. But the attention of the stalls was elsewhere: on the sumptuous, overly ornate stage-set now revealed in the harsh glare of the oxyhydrogen lighting. 'The star! The star!' cried the spectators in unison. With perfect timing she made her entrance. A thunderous ovation of the kind that makes the ears ring and the palms ache burst from the auditorium. In the boxes, ladies slid lorgnettes from crushed-velvet cases. Up in the gods, there was a riot: paper darts swooped hither and thither, catching fire in the candelabras. Armand, overcome with emotion, joined in the applause, knowing that, since it was addressed to her, some of it was for him. The lovely Roseline was on! Two enchanted hours went by before the end, before Armand, elbowing aside crowds of admirers backstage, burst through the dressing-room door and could at last enfold his beloved, still gasping from her performance, in his proud, proud arms. Ah, those evenings at the theatre! So very different from his suppers with Uncle Jules! And Armand, on the edge of his seat now, gulped down the last of his chick-pea purée.

What, meanwhile, were the old man's thoughts? Few, in fact. The stove had gone cold, that was a godsend: Jules could give himself a bit of exercise, re-lighting it. The same went for the leaky pane, the three steps over to the window constituted a walk.

Old age and living alone had no doubt inured the old man to silent mealtimes. He felt no awkwardness during their flagging conversations, only a certain annoyance at his nephew's impatience. Would he ever have the courage to ask Armand about his conquest, invite the couple to supper, perhaps? It might be the occasion to place his inventions before the young woman. No, not yet…

As soon as he had swallowed his dessert, in two spoonfuls, Armand made a rapid escape from his uncle's house. A luxurious carriage hired for the evening was waiting outside. A major expense, but what of it? Imagine trying to hail a cab! He'd wasted enough time already. The young man leapt in, and the carriage moved off at a spanking pace. Judging by the traffic in the street, he would arrive at the end of the show or soon after. In his haste to see Roseline again, he stumbled on the theatre stairs.

Armand entered the dressing-room with the usual gift – he always brought a box of glazed fruit, a bunch of wallflowers, or some small token wrapped in pink and blue ribbons – to find the young woman seated at her mirror. Her powdered cheeks, with their adorable half-moon dimples, lifted in a sweet smile. He bent to kiss her, then fell into her arms like a child seeking consolation.

'My love!' he cried passionately. 'My beautiful darling!'

As the actress finished removing her make-up, Armand toyed with the implements laid out before her: the plaits, the ringlets, the false hairpieces of real hair, the cartons of pearl white, the lipstick, the box of lettuce soap and the flask of aged cologne. His favourite trick? Blowing into a little bowl of very fine powder to make the whole room disappear in a heliotrope-scented cloud. Such cries of pleasure! Such wild laughter!

Armand was well aware of the privilege of being allowed into the dressing-room and of witnessing the supremely intimate moment that is the change of costume. The stage-star's lover is able to cherish his mistress twice over: once as an ordinary, mortal woman and again as the sylph, the milkmaid or the odalisque she plays onstage. Had Armand ever grown weary of the real Roseline, a glimpse of one of these other characters would have sufficed to rekindle his flame.

The actress's make-up sessions offered all the glamour that befits the theatre without foregoing the refinement that marks out the woman of taste. Depending on the role she was playing, she appeared now in a draped, Grecian-style dress, now in a Russian dress opening to reveal a lace pinafore, now in one or another of the historical costumes – Directory

Period, Louis XVI, Medici Florence – that were indiscriminately coming back into fashion. The fabrics, in uncertain colours called 'lotus blue', 'mandrake', 'carob' and the like, were chosen to suit the colour of her eyes as well as the subtly shifting textures of her wonderful skin. Whether they were raw or processed silk, velvet, crepe or muslin, all garments were weighed down beneath a fantastic quantity of trimmings and embellishments from gemstone stars to artificial roses and ruffles of machine-made lace.

The get-up took nothing away from the grace of her acting; on the contrary, it lent it fresh breadth. On her knees before the altar or recumbent after a stabbing, the actress took on an aura that was almost divine, a radiance both spiritual and sensual that won her the hearts of perhaps a hundred men sitting in the audience. 'She's mine!' Armand would breathe then with excusable vanity.

However, the outfit that most pleased the young man was not a stage ensemble. It was a sombre costume that Roseline donned after the show, a sort of antidote to the excess of light, a simple fitted jacket over a skirt of dove-grey serge, trimmed with astrakhan and, on cold days, complemented with a velvet cape. Armand was crazy about it. 'Please!' he would beg, holding out the little fur hat that went with it, 'Wear the grey costume this evening!' And the actress, delighted to satisfy her lover so inexpensively, would put on the garments requested.

The young people left together by the stage door, hands clasped inside a fur muff, cheeks pressed together, and nothing, at that moment, could have equalled their happiness.

As the solid citizens of Paris hurried by on their way to bed, Armand and Roseline began their evening's entertainment. Supper with his uncle did not count. Armand was ready to dine a second time in the company of his beloved. They chose a table in a boulevard café and let the soup grow cold in front of them, staring into each other's eyes.

'Hey, shall we do what students do when they go out drinking, write our names on the mirrors?'

The actress smiled as she always did at the young engineer's childish ideas.

'Why not? But I've no diamond to scratch mine with. You've never given me one!'

This half-reproach took his breath away. Armand resolved to visit a jeweller next day.

'Diamonds are old-fashioned. If I give you a ring it'll be an electric one! I know a craftsman who makes them. In fact, he advertises all over Paris.'

'Yes, I've seen it, a tiny cab wreathed in incandescent lamps drawn by a horse with an electric headstall. Poor creature!'

They were on the subject, so why not now? Taking a deep breath, Armand blurted out a proposal.

'Shall we get engaged?'

It seemed to come as a shock to her. For fear of hearing a 'no', the young man jumped to his feet and left the restaurant. Outside, there was a vending machine against a lamppost and to give himself something to do, Armand bought a packet of sweets and offered them to some beggars. A moment later, the staff of the Café Napolitain saw the customer from table nine, the lout who had left his pretty woman all alone, abruptly reappear.

'Yes!' was Roseline's reply.

Overjoyed, Armand inadvertently plunged both elbows into his lobster soup.

The weather was excellent that autumn. There was to be nothing solemn about the engagement, nothing starchy. No white-gloved presentations, no announcement in the press, no traditional basket of flowers. Nor was there any question of inviting the families; Armand's parents lived a long way from Paris and Roseline's mother had disowned her daughter's profession and virtually struck the girl from her will. As for the actress's father, she never mentioned him, preferring to conceal the fact that she had lost him in childhood.

The betrothal mass was a very private occasion, attended only by Odilon, Apolline and Uncle Jules. It was followed by a simple meal at which there was more merriment than good manners. For the old engineer and Roseline, it was their first meeting, and they formed a high opinion of each other immediately.

'I like your uncle enormously!' the actress confided to her fiancé, who soon received a similar confession from Jules. 'She made a big impression on me, your bride-to-be. She's quite lovely!'

The months that followed were to prolong the echo of that happy day. Armand and Roseline seemed to have been designed for each other. A flawless intimacy marked their every gesture, their every word; in the eyes of their friends, it took on the character of an absolute. Odilon humbly revised his former opinion of Roseline as a flighty young man-eater.

'I was wrong!' he admitted to his friend. 'It seems every woman is destined to belong to one man alone. And you are hers. Congratulations!'

There was much praise for providence for having brought them together and much blame for the fate that had kept them in ignorance of each other for so long. How, indeed, could one help but think of all those lost years, the nectar of their youth that they had already drunk? Roseline particularly blamed herself for having had so many lovers, 'a total waste,' she thought. They must make up for lost time, and they set about doing so with great zest.

The cool season, when everyone seeks shelter and lights the stove, was like a new summer for them. They made excursions into the country, which at this time of year was deserted. At Argenteuil, at Bougival, at Poissy, all they wanted was to walk alone down muddy tracks, gathering pears or grapes since there were no longer any flowers to pick. Armand had to promise a handsome tip and Roseline some complimentary tickets before a restaurant agreed to open especially for them.

'Would you like this table near the fire?' the proprietor asked.

'No, the arbour outside, please!' was the engineer's response.

'I've a fricassée of game cooked in Sancerre on the hob…'

'Take it off! We want something deep-fried, like in June. And some accordion music! Sweep the dance floor for us!'

Such caprices were expensive. They resigned themselves to more economical outings, every other Sunday: 'Punch and Judy' shows on the Champs-Élysées and strolls in Buttes-Chaumont Park or the Bois de Boulogne.

They had the Bois to themselves until winter should bring the ice-skaters. Their carriage with its large lantern was the only vehicle along the fortifications, except for the occasional tipcart driven by a dustman. At Boulogne itself, their favourite retreat was a lakeside bandstand. Snuggled together in the precious warmth of a large fur, they watched the few passers-by, poor folk braving the rain and the park-keeper's vigilance to scrape a living. Guessing the nature of these clandestine occupations was a game the couple loved to play. What was that man doing? He was collecting pinecones for the charcoal burners. And that woman? She was raking up moss for bird-sellers, or possibly she was pilfering ducks' eggs. As for those two, scurrying furtively beneath the branches, they were no doubt inspecting squirrel traps. Attracted by all these things that the lovers believed had been invented for their amusement, Armand and Roseline spent the afternoon conversing in soft tones and kissing with eyes half-closed, as if dazed with bliss.

When snow threatened, they abandoned the wood for the avenues of the capital. Their pastime then was to stroll the length of the northern boulevards from the Bastille to La Madeleine Church, staring scornfully at the Parisians huddled behind café windows. This was a chilly exercise in the depths of winter and often made their faces burn red like roaring stoves. The actress only looked the more charming while her lover became the more deeply ensnared.

In such weather the water-seller, with his three-cornered hat and his portable fountain, rarely came out, but the newspaper sellers, the postmen in their green tunics, the organ players and street singers continued to walk the pavements, their unassailable preserve. Roseline kept a special eye out for the chickweed seller, who as well as selling food for songbirds plied a rarer trade in gold-painted nutshells carrying a divinatory message.

'Do you want to know your future?' asked Armand with a smile. 'Nuts won't help. You need to consult a mindreader. I know one near Solferino Bridge.'

'Oh, no! Those clairvoyant women frighten me. They have a real gift, you know? One of them found a hairbrush that I'd been looking for in vain for two months. She said: "The brush has rolled under your wardrobe." And that's where it was!'

'But that's good, isn't it?'

'No, I'm not going to a mindreader. Suppose she had bad news – like that you were going to die or fall in love with someone else? That would kill me, it really would!'

'Well, all right…'

Having spent the whole day out walking, the lovers regained the Allée de l'Observatoire apartment. Armand lit a huge fire in the grate, Roseline changed out of her damp costume into a dressing-gown and eventually they both slipped between the sheets. The book they were reading together fell open. At the end of each page, the young woman asked if she might turn over.

'Finished?'

'Giving you pleasure? Never!'

A feeble enough syllepsis, but one we can forgive two young people so besotted with each other. Love, like childhood, will always be forgiven. 'Idiot!' the actress said, laughing. But she kissed her fiancé all the same, and again, and again…until the last embers expired in the hearth.

Gordon Hole tossed a small coin into the hand of the man behind the news-stand, then added a second by way of a tip. He was a good man, after all, not to have baulked at unfolding every publication on display – and there were dozens of them – to satisfy the American's whim. He wanted a large-format journal printed on thick paper and containing a large number of pages. 'What's it for?' the kiosk attendant had asked, finding it strange that one and the same customer should be interested in an ecclesiastical review and a magazine for soldiers. But Hole chose not to reply, except with a gesture: a finger on the lips adjoining silence.

The kiosk had a good position, where the Luxembourg Gardens met Allée de l'Observatoire, only metres from the Bullier dance hall, whose Moorish façade added spice to the grey day. Southward, the path led gradually back to stone and the city – a shock that was lessened by a series of squares that, with their flower-covered gates and railings, presented almost a contagion of greenery. Hole set off in that direction.

The architect marked off the paths with a regular tread, his legs swinging like a metronome. It was the time of day when men of fashion stroll with women of fashion, leaving pairs of footsteps in the wet sand behind them. Nannies pushing perambulators winked at handsome cyclists, men riding machines called 'Swallows' – the early model, with pneumatic tyres and rim brakes – the handlebars of which reared up with delight. Children could be seen pushing hoops or throwing tops, greatly to the displeasure of those among their mothers who feared for the shine on polished boots. 'Beg, children, beg and you shall have windmills!' called an itinerant toy seller.

A break in the cloud had been all it took to bring all these people out, until the next shower drove them back into the cafés.

Half-way along the path stood a drinking fountain, unused on this chilly autumn morning. The tin cups hung neglected on their lengths of chain. Standing opposite No. 15 Allée de l'Observatoire, this public facility formed a convenient angle from which to keep an eye on No. 21. Pleased to have found it, Hole leant against the drinking fountain and opened his magazine.

Three hours elapsed. Apart from the comings and goings of the caretaker, the handsome building with the gilded cast-iron balconies showed no sign of activity. No one had gone in and no one had come out; not so much as a curtain had twitched in the windows. Even the pigeons, those rowdy birds that bring animation to most urban house-fronts, seemed to shun this one. Whenever Hole looked up from his magazine, the same scene met his eyes; nothing had changed.

'A well-maintained property,' the American noted. 'Shiny

steps, plenty of doormats, the gutters never become blocked and the chimneys are kept swept and draw efficiently. Lucky folk, these actresses!'

As time went on, the architect paid less and less heed to his role. He no longer bothered to leaf through the magazine, which in any case offered a very insipid diet of society gossip. He also dispensed with the poses, such as smoking a cigarette or winding his watch, that he believed lent credibility to a long wait. Like certain animals keen to dupe a predator, he preferred immobility to pantomime.

Suddenly, all was movement. The front door of the building opened and a woman emerged, alone. It was Roseline! In his surprise, the American let go of the magazine, which splashed in the mud at his feet. 'Bloody hell!' he burst out, kicking it away. Fortunately the actress, pausing to adjust her hat, heard nothing.

The pavement was deserted. Hole waited until Roseline was some way ahead, a good stone's throw, before crossing the road to follow her. Immediately, he matched his step to that of his quarry in order to allow her footfalls to muffle his. He had also raised his coat collar and pulled up his scarf, like many people walking the streets in that autumnal wind.

In this way, moving as one but separated by a regular distance, they proceeded for several kilometres.

Not once did Gordon Hole take his eyes off the actress, whose silhouette, whether in profile or from behind, entirely lived up to the flattering portrait painted of it by Gaspard. This really was an extremely pretty woman and thoroughly desirable in her town dress of woollen tartan. Many a man, the American mused, must have felt that fur boa tickling his nose! He himself began to feel excited, following such a beauty, like a young suitor embarking on a trail. Ah, if his call-girl were from the same mould! How he would leap on her then! No erectile disfunction then, oh no!

Abruptly, Roseline turned into a street that climbed. The architect took the precaution of ducking behind a handcart. From his hiding-place he saw the actress stop at an ivy-covered gate, check the name and knock. Someone opened the door and host and visitor disappeared inside the house.

A quarter of an hour later, Gordon Hole took the same route. A green marble plaque bore the words, 'Monsieur Lavastre, painter'. The American undid his cravat and re-knotted it in the bohemian style, with two ends emerging from the shirt collar. His hand went up to the knocker. The gate swung open to reveal a very young manservant whose smooth cheeks were speckled like palettes of paint. Hole was ushered into the painter's presence.

The studio, on the second floor, admitted light through a wide sloping window. The floor, the platform and a number of easels held canvasses stacked several deep. Their wet edges had left paint marks on the wood. Others occupied chairs or were propped around a roaring stove. Of all these paintings, only one was the right way around: the large full-length portrait on which the artist was currently working.

As he entered the room, the American's gaze fell immediately on the model where she stood in the daylight falling from the big window. She was dressed up as an Egyptian queen, draped in one long piece of fabric that covered her bosom, encircled her waist and terminated in billows of silver at her feet. On her brow was a cobra diadem set with imitation gemstones and in her right hand she held a lotus.

A wig prevented Hole from recognising her immediately. But surely…yes, of course, this was Roseline! A stab of awed excitement pierced his heart. To come across her thus, half naked, in a strange house!

But the artist was also thinking of his model. He handed her a wrap, which she drew around her.

'Sir, how may I be of assistance to you?' Lavastre asked, approaching Hole with his hand extended.

He was a tall man, well-built and dressed more for the street than the studio. One would have searched in vain for the slightest fleck of paint on the alpaca jacket that moulded his shoulders. His sleeves, too, were protected against splashes of paint by leather arm-guards. Accustomed to visitors, he affected not to be disturbed by the American's intrusion.

'Ah, maestro, what an honour to be admitted to your studio!' the architect gushed, exaggerating his American accent.

He began to pace up and down with long cowboy strides, lifting pictures, overturning tripods, peering into every nook and cranny with impossible nonchalance – the trait that the French most resented in his fellow-countrymen.

Fearful of jeopardising a possible sale, the artist said nothing. He waited, jaws clenched, until the American had finished his tour.

'Marvellous, my dear maestro! The colours, the subjects! Such talent! Where do you get it from?'

The artist launched into a reply that Hole cut off with a pretence of shame:

'I'm so sorry! Allow me to introduce myself: Stephen Swimson, citizen of the United States of America. Our embassy has asked me to carry out a survey of Parisian painting – the good stuff, naturally… The New York museum is terribly short of items by French artists. We're in the market, maestro, we're in the market! And your work has caught our eye!'

Lavastre bowed modestly.

'What we need,' the architect went on, 'is about ten pictures – no, say a dozen! Any subjects you fancy: bunches of flowers, weddings, first communions… But they've got to be French, OK? With champagne and pretty girls!'

As he said this, the American's gaze darted to where Roseline sat on the edge of the platform.

'This young lady, for instance, what are you doing with her?' Hole asked, jabbing a forefinger in the direction of the actress.

The painter moved to his model's side and made her stand up. At the same time, at a nod from him, she consented to drop the wrap.

'It's a subject for a medallion. As you know, we're getting ready for the Centennial Exposition to be held in Paris. In the international exhibition hall, around the central dome, there will be a grand frieze representing the nations invited by France. Mademoiselle Page will symbolise the North-African countries: Abyssinia, Morocco, Egypt…'

The American contemplated the actress with an air of authority (though he could not take his eyes off a certain fold in the drapery, between the legs, that owed nothing to the way the fabric fell).

'Just what we need for Liberty!' he exclaimed, clapping his hands.

'I beg your pardon?'

'Yes, we're looking for a model to hold the torch of freedom at a Franco-American reception at the embassy. This young lady has just the right figure, broad hips and a large bosom, just like Bartholdi's statue! Can we hire her?'

The painter hesitated: 'Well…it's up to…'

Hole strode over to Roseline, taking out his wallet.

'Young lady, can you sing? We want our French guests to hear the Marseillaise.'

'But that's my job, sir! I'm an actress!'

'Bravo! The very thing! My dear maestro, I'm taking her from you for a couple of hours. The fact is, at the hotel where my delegation is staying we have on loan from Monsieur Edison his latest phonograph with a cylinder for recording voices. I'd like to record Mademoiselle Page to play back to the ambassador.'

'Oh, dear! My sitting...' Lavastre protested timidly.

Hole held out a banknote to the painter.

'Here are five hundred francs for your trouble! And twice that for the young lady if she'll be so kind as to come with me. You'll have her back tomorrow, my dear maestro, you have my word on it. As for the dozen paintings I was talking about, I'll take delivery of those in a couple of months time.'

'Ah, sir! I'm honoured!' the artist gloated, pocketing the note.

'No more than your talent is worth! But let us not delay. Young lady, would you mind getting dressed? We leave immediately.'

After many compliments and farewells into which Lavastre put much warmth, Gordon Hole and Roseline found themselves out in the street.

The actress had dressed in a hurry, as her profession, with its swift costume changes between scenes, had taught her. The effect was a certain casualness – a button undone here, a lace trailing there – that served only to enhance her charms. Certainly, that lovely little face had to draw itself into all sorts of contortions to manage the look of sulky rebellion it wished to present.

'I want an advance!'

'Of course!' the American replied, prepared at that moment to grant her every whim. 'Half the amount, do we have a deal?'

Roseline agreed unenthusiastically, a seasoned pro whom nothing could astonish. Folding the blue and pink note up like a love letter, she turned her back and tucked it under her garter-belt.

They climbed into a cab. On the pretext of the cold, Hole wound the scarf twice round his face and drew down the blinds. Luck gave him a driver who showed no interest in his pretty passenger, and luck continued to smile on him at the hotel, where neither bellboys nor receptionist seemed to pay any attention to Roseline.

'This is the room that I share with Monsieur Casper, another member of our delegation. Be so good as to enter...'

The actress did so but refused the chair that Hole proffered. Nor would she consent to remove her cape. She stared in alarm at the strange machine standing on the table: a golden horn emerging from a shiny wooden box about the size of an accordion, linked by a number of wires to a demijohn filled with some liquid.

'But you must sit down if we're to make this recording...'

'Does it hurt?' the actress asked, with a tremor in her voice.

'No more than exercising your vocal cords. Here, take a seat!'

Roseline sat down in front of the phonograph. She flinched when the American pushed what appeared to be some sort of inlet duct closer to her mouth but relaxed when she realised she felt nothing.

'This is the prototype of an entirely new model using a wax cylinder, which is a big improvement on the old one with a metal disc. Now the recorded voice no longer has that 'Punch and Judy' quality that spoils those early engravings. Sound is reproduced with amazing fidelity. So, would you like to be phonographed?'

'What do I have to do?'

'Just talk,' the American explained as he fitted a new wax sleeve onto the cylinder. 'Say whatever comes into your head. Recite a speech from a play you've been in recently, or a poem.'

'I know *Clouded Diamond* by Charles Cros★.'

'That'll do fine. Go ahead.'

Roseline took a deep breath, which narrowed her powdered nostrils. The waisted jacket inhibited her. She asked the architect to loosen the lace at the back a little. Hole did so, but very clumsily. Re-tied by him, the knot was even more oppressive.

'Oh, never mind! Let's get on with it!' the actress protested irritably.

Gordon Hole pressed down on the writing stylus to bring it into contact with the wax. The cylinder began to turn, driven by a small electric motor.

'I'm ready!' said Roseline.

The vibration of her words, acting on an invisible plate, made the needle move. It traced a furrow in the soft skin, close behind a miniature plane that smoothed the surface of the wax. The American signalled to Roseline and she proceeded to recite:

Certain diamonds display such special highlights
That, if snatched by thieves or mislaid in the street,
They always come back to the kings who own them.
Thus I recovered my lost darling.

Yet sometimes the stone will be split up
And sold on to various dealers, unless some special quality

★An ironic choice since the French poet-engineer Charles Cros (1842-88) invented the phonograph slightly before Edison but has never received credit for it.

Spares it this fate. By their hues and by their flashes
The scattered fragments would betray the brute destroyer.

So I no longer fear, you faintly clouded diamond,
Unique, nonetheless, in your veiled magnificence,
That I shall lose you. Always, my darling, you'll return
To me, your sole lover, from the hands that stole you away

The architect, unable to help himself, himself, blurted out:
'Splendid!'

But the next instant his hand fell brutally on the stylus,
knocking it out of its groove.

The gesture took the actress by surprise. The American's
face had undergone a change. Losing the affability it had
worn in the painter's studio, it now reflected not just the
voluptuous fascination that Roseline was used to inspiring in
men but an evil determination, a wish to inflict harm that put
fear in her heart...

Suddenly, the young woman appreciated the full danger of
her plight: she was alone with a strange man in a hotel room
and the only person at all aware of her situation was a painter
who hardly knew her. She felt fear coursing through her veins.

'Sir, I demand to be paid!' the actress protested, shrinking
back.

The architect replied quietly, his American accent gradually
becoming less obtrusive.

'Paid? But of course, young lady. You shall have your due.
However, there's one more thing you can do for us, one very
simple thing: inhale deeply!'

Roseline's cry was immediately stifled by a broad cloth pad
pressed against mouth and nose. The chloroform fumes mingled
with the air in her lungs, rapidly inducing unconsciousness.

With Roseline laid out on the bed, for a moment the two men did not know what to do next.

Having worked smoothly so far, the American's plan had run into its first difficulty. Should they kill the actress or let her live? The criminal option was immoral but would greatly simplify their task: with a corpse there are no risks. If they did not kill her, the opposite was true: they would have fewer misgivings but more problems.

The choice was entirely free since Hole's plan would accommodate a live actress as it would a dead one. He decided to spare Roseline. Murder was not a job just anyone could do. Even the hardest men are aware of a reluctance to commit murder – which only extended practice will relieve or alternatively, since the invention of firearms, the simple act of pressing a trigger, thus dispensing with the bloody work that killing once required. Moreover, if Hole did possess a revolver, it was one of those pretty models with a mother-of-pearl grip and round bullets that in his country was favoured by ladies. The weapon, wisely, was not removed from its holster.

'Shall I start, then?' Gaspard asked, opening a bag.

Hole nodded.

At the bottom of the bag was a collection of bottles held in place by silk ribbons. Three of these served to concoct a mixture with an irritating smell. So strong was it that the enamel of the dish was apparently being attacked, yellowing in places. Preparing it, Gaspard had to protect himself against the acid vapours it gave off by holding a bunched handkerchief to his lips.

'Ugh! Will she swallow it, do you think?' Hole enquired, attempting to clear his throat.

Gaspard rolled up his sleeves with something of a swagger.

'I've drunk it many times, I have, dissolved in soup. Nothing like it for playing dead on the battlefield. It's so strong you don't even feel the bayonet going in. One little glass and you're away!'

The time having come to administer the potion, Gaspard felt it superfluous to use a spoon. He preferred to stick his thumb between Roseline's jaws, force them open and simply pour the half-litre in.

The body responded to this harsh treatment with a dreadful groan. For a second, legs and arms flew about in violent spasms, which turned into nerve tremors as they gradually subsided. The actress remained unconscious throughout.

'Right, that's done!' Gaspard commented, mopping his brow. 'Now we wait for it to take effect...'

The American drew a chair up to the bed. The effect of the poison manifested itself immediately. First a general pallor became apparent, with the breathing becoming slower and even apparently stopping altogether. Then, stranger still, the same contraction of the muscles occurred beneath the skin that happens with a corpse. The illusion was perfect.

'She seems quite dead!' Hole said in alarm, feeling the weak pulse.

'Hibernating animals don't look much more alive. Take your hedgehog or your badger in the middle of winter. Trust me, they always come round. Now let's see to the trunk!'

The American had to be summoned twice before rising from his chair. A curious torpor had come over him. Was it remorse at having done something wrong or was it the shameful desire he still felt for this woman, now in a state of helpless surrender?

On his feet, Hole was seized by a sudden impulse. His hand slid beneath the actress's dress and pulled it up to the waist.

Her legs were now in full view, white as plaster against the unbleached fabric of the underwear. They were still desirable, despite the stiffening caused by the poison and even though blue streaks were visible along the thighs. The American's arteries began to hammer furiously. In a moment of madness, he climbed onto the bed and began unbuttoning his trousers.

'Sir!' exclaimed a terrified Gaspard.

Hole looked around. His teeth were chattering in his arousal. At the cost of an immense effort, he stepped down from the mattress and rejoined his associate. The cloth of his trousers betrayed a mighty erection.

'Not a word to Roseline, of course,' said Hole, regaining control of himself. 'Neither about that, nor about anything!'

The trunk that Gaspard had supplied was a spacious model, designed to hold the contents of an entire wardrobe. It would not have accommodated a person standing up but there was plenty of room for someone seated. Holes in the sides to air any furs that might be stored in it ensured sufficient ventilation.

Roseline was a tall girl and no scarecrow either, which complicated the job for a start. Another problem was the rigidity of the body. The arms, for example, had to be worked like the handles of a pump that has begun to seize up; i.e. with powerful, repeated strokes to force them into the right position.

'Careful! You'll break her bones!' the American warned as his associate forced a recalcitrant knee in by kicking it repeatedly.

After many contortions, the two men eventually achieved what they were aiming for: the actress was seated in the trunk in the attitude of a fakir, chin between bent legs.

'Whew! She's in!' Gaspard breathed.

There was no reason for clients of a good hotel to carry so voluminous a piece of luggage themselves. Hole got two bellboys to do it for them.

'Where shall we put it, sir?' one of them enquired.

'In the carriage we've hired. It's waiting outside the front door.'

'Are you leaving the hotel, then?'

'No, it's a trunk that got mixed up with my own. They both came over on the Transatlantic steamer *Champagne*, then by train from Le Havre. I'm going to return it to its owner and recover my own.'

'We can take care of that, sir.'

'Thank you, but I want to give the baggage-handler a piece of my mind. There's no excuse for such a mix-up!'

The trunk was loaded onto the cabriolet. After a brief detour in the direction of Montparnasse Station the carriage, with Gaspard driving, turned off towards the Seine. Crossing the river, it followed the Right Bank along Quai de la Mégisserie, on past the Louvre and the Tuileries Gardens and into Cours la Reine before re-crossing the Seine by Pont d'Alma. On the Left Bank, a wide gap in the line of façades revealed the four piers of the Tower, now linked by a horizontal structure.

'Look, they've started to build the first platform!' Hole remarked. 'Huh! The Tower's not going to rise much beyond that!'

The two men drove on a little way then unloaded the trunk near the edge of the water.

A sandbank covered the crumbling wreck of an old boat.

'This is the ideal position!' the architect murmured. 'Let's get to work!'

The trunk was emptied of its contents. Hole lingered for a moment, composing the scene in his imagination. Meanwhile, Gaspard was anxiously watching Pont d'Iéna, only a short distance downstream.

'Let's get a move on, sir! The police patrol this area!'

The American followed his accomplice as Gaspard climbed the steps to the parapet, the empty trunk on his head. In a matter of minutes they were back at Hôtel Britannique.

Around the site, parked against the fence now darkened with rain, the carriages made a sombre gathering.

The showers that had succeeded one another without respite since the morning had driven the coachmen from their benches. They were waiting beneath the hoods, well-sheltered behind raised windows. From time to time, one of them would glance through the rear lunette to see whether anyone was coming. Some had even dozed off, confident that they would be shaken awake when it was time to leave.

Not one of them had wished to view the huge iron structure being erected only metres away. They could not have cared less, for instance, that it had grown since the day before or that the already substantial number of rivets and girders had passed another landmark figure. Those who drove engineers to the site day after day were familiar with every aspect of the strange machine including the front view, side view and the views from Quai de Grenelle farther down the river and Avenue de Suffren, bordering the Champ de Mars. They knew it all by heart and no longer felt any surprise. For them, Monsieur Eiffel's Tower was already part of the Parisian backdrop – long before painters and photographers set about fixing it there.

Their passengers, on the other hand, the small group of men who, on alighting, strode towards the monument beneath their rubberised capes, had eyes for nothing else. They fell into ecstasies at first sight of the Tower, ecstasies that intensified as they approached it and as they became more keenly aware of its enormous size in contrast to their own insignificance.

'What?' they asked themselves in amazement, 'This is the thing we designed? This is the form our calculations have assumed? The solid product of our geometrical abstractions?'

So breathtaking was the apparent gap between drawing and object, they doubted whether they could claim any responsibility for what met their eye. The young ones especially, some of whom were seeing the Tower for the first time, felt violently stirred. This was either by a surge of pride as they recognised this or that component that owed its curvature to their pencil or on the contrary by a crisis of humility, as if suddenly made aware of the alarming repercussions of groups of figures that had emerged from their heads. The latter group trembled at the matter-of-fact audacity that made them perch girders weighing hundreds of tons at so immense a height. They looked upon Eiffel, the boldest of them all, as both madman and god.

Armand and Odilon registered neither of these opposing emotions. Standing in the front row of the group of engineers, arms entwined like good friends, they contemplated the Tower with the dispassionate interest of craftsmen before an unfinished task, comparing its present state with the way it had looked yesterday, discussing all the changes.

And changes there had certainly been! The structure they were now looking at contrasted in spectacular fashion with the early sketches. The term 'Tower', provided by the public, was at last appropriate. After soaring skyward in isolation for five months, the corner piers, which were built at such an angle they had looked in danger of collapsing, were now joined together by a platform. Henceforth the four legs now supported a table linking their tips.

'Nothing like it has ever been seen before!' Odilon breathed admiringly. 'A dining table for Gargantua!'

The Parisian removed his top hat in a gesture that was quickly imitated by several young colleagues.

'Hats off, gentlemen! Science has just delivered a formidable snub to ignorance. Those who prophesised that the Tower would collapse at least had a case so long as all that had been built was a square of piers leaning on wooden props. But now they can prophesy all they like. No one will listen. Not any more. Common sense is against them. A table's not going to fall over…'

'To Eiffel!' cried one comrade, tossing his bowler in the air. 'Hip, hip…'

'Hooray!'

Monsieur Pluot, who was averse to any kind of effusion, approached the group of engineers.

'Less noise, please! Your shouting will disturb Monsieur Eiffel. Come closer if you wish to see.'

Forming lines like schoolboys going back into class, the engineers followed Pluot to the bottom of one of the piers. There Gustave Eiffel and his foremen stood with a number of labourers. Two of these were operating a pump to inject water beneath the pier while a third, the strongest-looking one, drove in fixing-blocks with a sledgehammer. Eiffel's attention alternated between the team on the ground and another team high up in the scaffolding. The latter were supervising enormous sandboxes whose valves opened from time to time, releasing a stream of dry sand.

'It's a crucial moment!' Monsieur Pluot announced, levelling his umbrella at the Tower. 'They're aligning the girders of the first platform with the uprights, using hydraulic jacks to raise the supports and adjusting their angle of inclination with the aid of sandboxes. The work requires enormous precision! One or two centimetres out and the holes will no longer coincide, making it impossible to insert the rivets! And to think of all that being done at the height of the Towers of Notre-Dame!'

The office manager's enthusiasm found ready acceptance among the young men, and a chorus of 'ahs' and 'ohs' accompanied each episode of the assembly job. Only Eiffel, his forehead creased with worry – the same crease he wore on paydays – seemed untouched by the mood of excitement. So absorbed was he in the current operation that he was not even aware of the rain cloud passing over the Champ-de-Mars at that moment: his umbrella remained unopened.

Hours elapsed before Eiffel and his foremen together agreed that horizontals and uprights were in proper alignment. The positions of the huge iron members had been checked and re-checked countless times as the former were straightened and the latter inclined until eventually they presented an impeccable match.

The riveting, on the other hand, was accomplished in an instant. First extracting the bolts red-hot from the fire, workers inserted them in the holes in place of temporary plugs. A few blows of the sledgehammer were all it took to join horizontals and uprights two by two. So perfect was the fit that not once was any filing required to touch up the points nor reaming to enlarge the holes.

When all tasks had been completed, a ripple of applause was heard at the foot of the Tower. A bell clanged noisily and the 'chimney-sweeps' descended swiftly, sliding down the uprights of their ladders. Everyone on the site converged on a series of large trestle tables that had just been set up and loaded with bottles and glasses.

The engineers were served first and they drank to the Tower and to the triumph of science. Some who had always insisted on being addressed formally now offered first names and chatted like old friends. There many a hearty handshake and from the way toasts were proposed and embraces exchanged they might have been celebrating not an interim achievement but the climax of the whole enterprise.

How, indeed, could anyone doubt a successful outcome, seeing this solid square linking the four piers? By bringing horizontality back into an upward thrust, above all by posing and accepting a major construction challenge, completion of the first storey infected everyone like a shot of optimism. The rest of the Tower – the 250 metres yet to be built – seemed almost a trifle after this supremely difficult achievement.

Even Gustave Eiffel, a normally cautious individual, that day betrayed some emotion. Deserving members of his staff found themselves offered a bonus, whereupon others overcame their timidity to put in their own requests.

'My children! My children!' Eiffel kept saying, passing from one group to another with a face like Father Christmas. He lingered particularly with the younger engineers, whose boundless admiration flattered his pride. Addressing this tyro audience, Eiffel – who was in any case partial to giving advice – readily talked shop, revealing his ingenious brainwaves for the Tower.

'Have you any idea how far metal construction has come since the early days? Once upon a time our piers used columns of cast iron, with diagonals made of a different metal: look at the La Sioule Viaduct on the line to Orléans. Then I had the idea of replacing cast iron with wrought iron, which is stronger. The new piers were formed of cutaway columns, sealed together longitudinally to withstand the effects of wind. You can see that system in operation on the Duoro Bridge and the Garabit Viaduct. But it still didn't represent the ideal solution because for very great heights the weight threatened the equilibrium of the structure. So I decided to get rid of the diagonals and to curve the ribs, a method I have utilised for the 300-metre Tower. Remember one thing, gentlemen: the Tower is simply a bridge pier rising free – the ultimate bridge pier!'

With the older engineers, men who had been with him since his earliest projects, the 55-year-old harvested memories. They talked about the old days, when Établissements Eiffel, then a modest set-up, threw bridges over every abyss in France to open the country up for the railway. The conversation was littered with the names of outstanding international achievements, such as the Oporto Viaduct in Portugal and Hungary's Pest Station, as well as those of colleagues since deceased.

The eraser twins were the last to receive a visit from Eiffel. By then the entrepreneur had drunk many toasts, a great deal of champagne had passed his lips and clinking his full glass against Armand's he spilled its contents down the young man's jacket.

'I don't know what to say!' stammered the great man with a drunken hiccup.

Politely refusing the proffered handkerchief, Armand murmured the sort of indulgent remark that subordinates come out with in such circumstances.

As he was doing so a workman, soaked from head to foot, burst into the circle of engineers shouting, 'Monsieur Eiffel! Monsieur Eiffel! Something dreadful has happened!'

The apparition caused a stir around the tables. All eyes converged on the mud-caked trousers, the smeared face, and the rope-soled shoes that left trails of filthy water. Two or three of the sturdier engineers crowded round Eiffel, shielding him with their bodies. People feared for him because of the polemics his projects aroused – first and foremost, this defiant metal Tower to which opposition was almost unanimous. The protective instinct of members of his staff was that of sons towards their father, as well as of workers towards the source of their income.

'Oh, come on, it's me…' the man protested, wiping his face, 'Arthur, the ganger!'

There was a fresh stirring within the knot of people. This time, people crowded round the suddenly familiar figure.

'Well?' Eiffel asked. 'Spit it out! What's happened?'

The man removed his cap, revealing a shock of fair hair which was surprisingly bright against that blackened face. Earth clung to the locks at the nape of his neck.

'Alas, sir! Gaston and me, we were digging out the Seine ditch, the one that'll take the Exposition sewage pipes, when we saw…no…,' the ganger quickly corrected himself, 'Gaston saw it first. Yes, he saw it first!'

Arthur stabbed a forefinger at a second man, who was just approaching. He might have been pointing out a criminal.

'Saw what?' Eiffel demanded, beside himself. 'What did you see? Get to the point!'

'A body, sir! A woman's body sprawled in the sand, hair matted in a bunch, skirts rucked up to her thighs! Her tongue was even sticking out, like she'd been strangled! Saints preserve us!'

A sob distorted the man's final words. Doing what he felt was the polite thing, he blew his nose in a fold of his sleeve.

Meanwhile Eiffel, whose brow had instantly furrowed on hearing the bad news, now appeared reassured. Phew! The site was apparently safe. This was a worry that never really left him – that an accident of some kind, or a strike might delay or even compromise construction of the Tower. Compared with such calamities, the discovery of a body was a minor inconvenience.

'Right you are, my good man!' Eiffel was almost affable. 'Well, what are you waiting for? You must call the police.'

'They came without being called, sir. They're already at work: combing the shore for clues, they call it. At first they talked about sending for an ambulance, but seeing that the body didn't move and journalists were beginning to turn up, a wagon came from the morgue. It's just this minute left.'

'Journalists?' Eiffel asked, disturbed. 'What journalists were they?'

The second labourer, who had by now rejoined his colleague, supplied this information in a gasping voice.

'They came from various papers. I counted ten of them at least! There they all were, scribbling away. One of them even had one of those things for taking photographs. He posed this shot with the beach in the foreground and the Tower behind – should look pretty good!'

'Did they ask you any questions?' Eiffel enquired anxiously. 'I'll say!'

'About the Tower?'

'Why not?'

At this, Eiffel exploded with rage. Such explosions were very much a feature of his character, and his employees never forgot them – as they never forgot his Christmas bonuses.

'Why not? The fool asks me why not! Because, my friend, tomorrow morning every rag in France will be holding us up to ridicule! It will be on every front page, how the Tower has now killed someone. Imagine the headlines: "The Tower commits murder", "Body Found in Shadow of Tower"or "Eiffel in the Dock"! As if we needed anything else to turn opinion against us! The press! They're our worst enemy!'

So savage was the outburst that for a moment the two labourers were silent. They looked down at their hands, like guilty children who, playing with a loaded rifle, accidentally let it off. Arthur was the first to recover enough to make a suggestion.

'But in that case let's go and talk to them! The gentlemen are still down on the beach. It can all be sorted out.'

'No!' Eiffel shouted. 'I've nothing to say to those hacks! It's their bosses I'm going to telegraph and right this minute!'

Almost knocking the two men over, Eiffel strode off in fury. A great silence fell over the assembled staff. No one felt like celebrating any more. Putting down their glasses, they slowly dispersed.

Only the labourers remained, still under the effect of the shock they had received, and one young engineer whom the receding wave of his colleagues had left like a piece of wreckage on the shore. It was Armand.

'Are you coming?' asked Odilon, looking back.

But the young man from St. Flour was frozen to the spot as if turned to stone. A dreadful intuition had occurred to him, one of those intuitions that constrict the chest and force long needles down the veins. His skin felt feverish and shivery by turns.

'Listen, you don't suppose…' he said falteringly, twisting the knot of his cravat. 'That woman… It couldn't be…?'

There was such fear in Armand's gaze that Odilon felt alarmed himself. He made a supreme effort to keep his tone light.

'What are you thinking of? Roseline is at home, waiting for you in her room. Come on, let's go!'

Hearing the actress's name, the second labourer turned to look. Arthur murmured something in his workmate's ear, then came over to where Armand stood.

'Are you Armand Boissier?'

This stranger stepping up to him and knowing his name seemed quite natural. It all fell into the terrible order of things of which Armand had had a presentiment. Already trembling, the young engineer began to shiver so hard that he could not speak, he could only nod.

'Then this is for you,' said Arthur, taking an envelope from his pocket. 'It was tucked into the woman's belt... I shouldn't have looked, but it said, "Armand Boissier, an employee at Eiffel & Co., Builders". And with the police prowling round, you know... It was a matter of helping out a comrade. Tell me, did I do the right thing?'

Armand stared in terror at the letter in his hand. Circles of sweat grew over the surface, marking the position of each finger. He saw his name written in large black letters. Visible through the thin vellum was a sheet of paper covered in writing, a letter addressed to him.

'Ah, Odilon!' Armand cried out with a look of distress.

The Parisian arrived in time to take his friend's weight. Sapped by emotion, Armand's legs would no longer support him.

'Someone should keep an eye on him,' said Arthur, helping to carry the young man to a chair. 'He must have been crazy about that woman!'

THE SECOND STOREY

8

Had matters been left to Armand, the letter would have ended up as a crumpled ball in the gutter; or else, expunged by the damp heat of his fingers, which fiddled with it constantly, it would mercifully have become illegible.

To the engineer's mind, no place was the right place, no time the right time to devote due attention to it. The emotive settings in which most love letters are perused, church gate or rain-drenched square, struck him as unworthy of his fiancée's missive. He wanted something better, something bigger, something superhuman; the crater of an erupting volcano perhaps, the disintegrating prow of a ship about to go down…

In the event, Odilon, grown weary of walking, suggested the back room of a café. They ordered a bottle of wine.

'Ah, Odilon! This letter! I can't open it.'

'Give it to me,' Odilon offered. 'I'll read it for you.'

Armand handed the letter over. Immediately, he regretted the gesture. Too late! Odilon had seized it and was already tearing the flap.

'No! Give it back!' beseeched Armand. He was like a child whose toy has been confiscated.

But the Parisian brandished his cane between them.

'Come on, pull yourself together! What will people think of us? Two brothers opening a will, perhaps. Anyway...' Odilon added, his eye running swiftly down the pages, 'there's nothing in this letter to be alarmed about! In fact, you could almost say it's encouraging...'

Armand's laugh rang out, black and tortured.

'Encouraging! What possible encouragement can there be in a letter from a dead woman?'

'I ought to reproach you for saying that!' Odilon reacted, taking a sip of the heavy wine. 'For the spiritualist that I am and that you have become there is no death, only a passing. Roseline is alive, somewhere else and in some other way...'

Armand swept away his full glass with the back of his hand.

'Rubbish! Empty phrases! How can you trot them out at a time like this? I don't know what stops me from hitting you in the face!'

Alerted by the noise, the café proprietor now appeared, wielding a big stick. His gaze went from the broken glass to the two drinkers. It lingered on the young man from St. Flour, whose arm was raised to strike. Odilon, however, flashed a charming smile, as if to say: 'Don't worry! We'll pay for any breakages!' Reassured on this point, the café-owner tolerantly withdrew.

'Just calm down and listen!' the Parisian ordered in a low voice. 'The letter begins: "Armand my love..." '

'She wrote that?' the engineer gulped, craning to peer at the piece of paper in his friend's hand.

Odilon went on:

Armand my love,

Today my heart is heavy and my hand balks at writing these words, probably the last you will ever read from me… These are my tears, the purest tears of my heart, that are mingling with the ink, making it run. I can barely write, so great is my yearning to weep.

'Ah, such sincerity!' Armand sighed admiringly.

'She's quoting, I think… I seem to remember reading that last sentence somewhere.'

Armand, my sunshine, my angel! Do you remember, dear heart, the fiery kisses we stole beneath the lime trees, the lazy lemonades we drank through two straws?

'Do I remember?' Armand breathed, licking the sweet wine from his lips. But then, immediately afterwards, 'No, I don't remember actually! She hated lemonade!'

Odilon clicked his tongue reprovingly.

Alas! Those heady moments are gone for ever. In a few hours time I shall disembark on the island where the dead sojourn. On that same bank of the Seine where we strolled arm in arm, soon they will fish out a drowned woman…

Armand's chest heaved with a deep sob.

It pains me to take this step. No one can decide lightly to end it all, I less than anyone, for life has given me so much. Yet today it is the only step that I can take. Perhaps I shall have your understanding, if not your forgiveness, when you learn the appalling fate that has driven me to this extreme…

'Go on!' cried the young man, squeezing Odilon's shoulder.
'I will, if you'll stop interrupting! Where was I?'

Dear Armand, what do you know about me? What the gossip-columnists write, a little pillow talk… Not much, anyway. A woman, you know, will give less of herself away to her lover than to anyone.

You are ignorant, for example, of the fact that my father is a great American engineer and architect. His name is Gordon Hole. It is to the genius of this man that the people of that great country across the Atlantic owe their boldest constructions, most notably a huge building in Chicago. His love of France frequently brought him to this side of the ocean, right from his earliest years. It was here in France that he studied, worked, and loved. My birth was the fruit of an affair with a Parisian call-girl.

Oh, Armand! You cannot imagine how much suffering that unworthy parentage has caused me. Others might possibly have killed themselves before this in order to escape the jeers and taunts, but my love for my father, a quite exceptional man who for twenty years brought me up on his own, triumphed over all my resentment.

'How does she go on?' Armand asked impatiently.

But let me get to the point. The time has come for you to hear my terrible secret, a secret that now weighs so heavily on me it makes me seek out the grave…It so happened that my father studied at the same college as Gustave Eiffel. They learnt to be engineers together. The fact was, my father had more talent for the disciplines taught at the college, particularly metal construction, than his French fellow-student. While Gustave struggled, cobbling together clumsy sketches, an inspired Gordon, nourished by phenomenal intuitions, was laying the foundations of modern metal architecture.

But Eiffel was an opportunist, so what did he do? He copied.

Initially, he copied in order to secure his degree. Then, once he had entered the profession, he fell back into his old habits. His bridges, his viaducts and even the Tower itself, are simply laboured projections of my father's ideas. Imagine how Gordon Hole felt when he saw his brilliant inventions borrowed wholesale by a former colleague! And not only that: also earning the usurper wealth and fame!

'I can't believe what I'm hearing!' Odilon exclaimed. 'Eiffel, a fraud?'

Armand was frowning.

'It's possible, certainly… I knew already from my uncle that the idea for the Tower wasn't his.'

My father, of course, took him to court. But alas, how was he to prove so sophisticated a crime – one having to do with architectural solutions that judges understood nothing about and that in any case had never been patented? The actions were quashed, and my father was ruined. It took him twenty long years to recover to the point where he was able, in America, to acquire the fame that was his due.

All that time, my father and I had lived in abject poverty. Our only comfort came from cursing the name of Eiffel daily and spitting on his picture whenever it appeared in the papers. You know how hatred can turn to rage in the heart of a child…

When Odilon introduced us, I was unaware that you both worked for Gustave Eiffel. Finding out yesterday, by chance, was a horrifying revelation. You, Armand, in league with that vile person? Actually working on the Tower, that infamous structure for which my father had as good as drawn up the plans?

The horror of it choked me, and cries welled up in me at the same time as my tears. All day I have thought of killing you – breaking with you was not enough. A dagger was to serve the purpose and I was awaiting your visit with one in my hand.

Entirely unexpectedly, it was my father who dissuaded me. Fate dictated that he should visit me a few hours before yourself. His loving heart prompted words of appeasement. He spoke to me of your innocence – that of a young engineer called to work for a celebrity of whose turpitude he knew nothing and whom he naively looked up to as a role model. I am quite sure my father thought he was doing the right thing, explaining all this to me in his gentle, patient voice. He could not know that his remedy made matters worse. Death, robbed of you, sought out fresh prey and this time found me. Words that had been your salvation became my perdition.

Now you know everything, dear heart! The lifeless body you will find washed up on the bank of the Seine is that of a woman torn in two… Like so many before me I have fallen victim to that primal conflict: the love a woman feels for a man versus the respect she owes to her father.

I shall go to my death at the foot of the Tower, hoping the scandal will sully both Eiffel and his edifice. That will be some small compensation for the wrongs he has done me, having made me first a miserable child, then an unhappy lover. Forgive me if you can.

I love you. Farewell.
Roseline Page.

Armand let out a great cry, which brought the café-owner back with his big stick. This time, though, the young man was in such a state that neither Odilon nor the proprietor could calm him down. The former tried with soothing words, the latter with blows of his club – though all these did, in fact, was to add yells of pain to Armand's cries of woe.

Eventually, with the help of three stout fellows who had come through from the front, the deranged Armand was subdued. He was deposited fairly roughly in a chair and pinned there by the café-owner's fist.

Odilon, who had been picking up the scattered sheets of the letter, now brandished one excitedly.

'Look – the last sheet has writing on the back! There's more!'

So he resumed reading in the presence of the burly proprietor. Squirming in his chair, Armand resembled a rebellious prisoner in the dock at the moment of the verdict.

'Yes,' the Parisian confirmed. 'The letter goes on after the signature. But the writing is different, hurried and undisciplined. The ink's fresher, too. Maybe this was Roseline setting down her final wishes?'

Armand, my love, a few more words… I must hurry because at any moment you might appear and then I shall no longer have the courage to do what is my duty.

As bodies we shall soon be apart for ever but our souls will live on, and in their survival I, like Apolline and Odilon, am a fervent believer. Oh, my love! Would it not be a solace to our pain if, beyond death, in the special manner to which spiritualists have access, we could transmit our thoughts to each other? Our love might still shine and we be reunited in spirit! In the world I am going to, sadness and rancour are no more…

What a lovely idea, my angel! And what a comfort to me if you carry it through. Remember that spiritualist circle we attended together… Call up my spirit there! Why not?

Now that I think of it, my father himself used to converse with the dead in America. If you should chance to come across him, invite him to join the group so that he may hear my messages. Believe me, you will have my gratitude! I can imagine no greater joy for a departed one than to see her father and her lover reconciled before her tomb.

Odilon repeated the last word with a falling intonation,

because the first time he had left it suspended, as if in the middle of a sentence. There was in fact no full stop. This second reading ushered in a silence rather than the loud cry that had followed the first. The only sound was the rustling of the pages as he refolded them and slid them back into the envelope.

'Still…' Odilon mused, 'one thing intrigues me. This letter was in the water for as long as it took Roseline to die. Right? Yet the paper is scarcely damp! She must have thrust it very deep into a pocket for it to be taken from her sodden clothing virtually dry, surely?'

Armand added his thoughts in a dreamy voice.

'There's something else. In the letter, Roseline calls me *vous*. She never did that. And then… I don't know, that wasn't the way she talked. She used special words, special turns of phrase that don't appear in the letter.'

'Would you recognise her writing?' Odilon asked, looking at the name on the envelope.

'No, of course not! Why correspond when you live together? I had two or three notes from her, but those I've lost.'

With the conversation clearly taking a private turn, the other men had the tact to go. The twins found themselves alone, the letter lying on the table between them.

'There's a mystery here,' the Parisian concluded, using a hand to sweep up some shards of glass. 'I cannot believe Roseline resolved so quickly to take her own life and for so feeble a reason. Maybe she was being blackmailed? A jealous lover, for instance…'

'Gustave Eiffel?' suggested his friend, eyes lighting up suddenly.

'Let's not lose our heads… Above all, we must go to the morgue where the body's been taken. Will you come with me?'

'Of course!'

'It won't be pleasant...'

'Never mind, I can take it. Until I've seen her with my own eyes I'll never believe she's dead.'

Leaving the price of their drinks on the table, plus something for the broken glass, the engineers left the café.

Old Man Modesty counted the money as meticulously as a scientist might enumerate the organs of a millipede.

The man whom everyone tipped with a coin, whose very wages came with a metallic clink, felt awkward in possession of banknotes. The figures printed in the corners of the large bills were a challenge to his reckoning ability. They were disproportionate to the moderation instilled by fifty years of relative poverty, of wine at sixteen sous a litre, a dish of split peas for two sous or a cup of black coffee even cheaper...

Had he dared, he would have asked his visitor to convert the notes into coin, the kind you can bite to test its value. What was he to do with these bits of paper? They might as well pay him in pieces of torn-up newsprint. At least that would cover the broken pane in his window!

Still, Old Man Modesty reflected, supposing those 100 francs were really within his reach? A months wages! Was there not a risk of upsetting his benefactor by going on about it? Worse still, the man might take back part of the sum! Oh, no, he'd rather say nothing, 100 francs was good money for the little he was being asked to do!

He would get 25 francs down if, when the policemen came with the body of a young woman, he could usher them out before they took too close a look at it; another twenty-five if he classified the corpse as 'dead from drowning' without consulting the doctor who usually carried out the examinations; and another twenty-five if, when people arrived, he told them that the man offering him the inducement was the young lady's father.

This last request had to do with the removal of the body – which would qualify him for the remaining 25 francs – and here Old Man Modesty had a problem. He did not like anyone taking bodies from a morgue that, when all was said and done, he was employed to guard. That could harm his professional standing. Besides, since the body in question was that of a pretty woman found with her skirts up on the bank of the Seine, there would inevitably be an inquest, the pathologist would carry out an autopsy and there was no depriving the police of the object of a crime.

'All you need say is that the family claimed the body,' Gordon Hole insisted, making it appear a simple matter. 'Or that it was stolen! Someone broke into the morgue, knocked you out, and carried the body off through the window. If that's all it comes to, I'll be delighted to tap you on the head with the butt of my Remington.'

The appearance of the revolver lent fresh weight to the American's arguments. Old Man Modesty made no further objections but merely asked for details of the role he was required to perform.

Actually, this was not the first time that eccentrics had had designs on bodies before they were laid to rest. Many of them paid less well than this stranger. Mistreating cadavers, having carnal possession of them, extracting their fingernails or hair, practising dissection on them – he'd seen it all! Such dark impulses illuminated a facet of the human mind concerning which, true to his nickname, Old Man Modesty observed a decent silence.

With the deal done, it remained only to await delivery of the corpse.

The police presented themselves at the end of the afternoon. Old Man Modesty helped them carry the body in under a sheet – not, as one of the stretcher-bearers explained, because it was horrible to look at but because it remained desirable in death; the police had to be protected against improper desires. No one joined in the young man's throaty laughter.

'Over there!' the attendant ordered, pointing to the empty table that Hole had selected.

Roseline was laid out on the marble slab. Then, following the instructions he had been given, Old Man Modesty dismissed the policemen without offering them the customary tot.

'Who's being tight today, then?' commented the young stretcher-bearer, who missed his glass of absinthe.

As announced, the twins turned up at nightfall. Hearing their footsteps in the passage, Hole rubbed his eyelids with an onion ring. Tears began to flow from his irritated eyes. He then proceeded to disarrange his dress, undoing buttons and twisting the knot of his cravat. Old Man Modesty gaped in astonishment.

It was Odilon who spotted Roseline's body first. He tried to hold his friend back but was too late. As if sucked towards her, Armand had already hurled himself at his beloved's feet or rather at her face – that familiar countenance that he no longer dared caress but instead encircled with his trembling hands, touching it with his fingertips as if it were something very hot. Unlike Gordon Hole's, very real tears welled up in his eyes.

'Odilon, she's dead!' he wailed. His reedy voice, which sounded as if it were expiring, nevertheless echoed something of the serenity of reunion. This confrontation counted for more than absence, this corpse was worth more, somehow, than a letter.

It was a painful moment. Armand, on his knees beside his fiancée, wept freely. Odilon stood a few paces behind him, accompanied by Old Man Modesty. As for Hole, leaning against the table, he drew inspiration from Armand's grief to give credence to his own performance. The father borrowed the son-in-law's tears and sighs, adding a dash of chaste remoteness that he felt more appropriate to his role. His kisses were on the forehead, not on the lips. He hugged where the lover caressed.

Odilon looked closely at the American. The face was not unfamiliar – where had he seen the man before? Taking advantage of an opportune moment, he accosted the architect.

'Monsieur Gordon Hole, is it?'

'How do you know my name?'

The Parisian respectfully removed his hat.

'A letter found on your daughter by the people who discovered her.'

The American saw the letter Odilon was holding and suppressed a smile.

'A letter? What letter? The police told me nothing about that.'

'Sir, would you be so good as to dine with us tonight? I believe we have much to tell one another…'

The dinner duly took place, if a rustic stew of pork and beans heated up on Old Man Modesty's ancient stove can be dignified with the name. It was all the mortuary attendant could provide for his occasional guests. Generations of policemen, gravediggers and pathologists had graced his table, which the fashionable world also held in high regard. Every boulevard dandy loved to give himself the shivers by imagining that the board on which the meal was laid came from the mortuary itself and that the ancient kitchen knives – blunt enough, it is true – had once been used to dissect corpses.

Old Man Modesty was well aware that people visited him out of a taste for the macabre, but he took no offence. He preferred company, even of a frivolous sort, to the burden of solitude in his sanctuary of death.

That night, his guests were in no mood to savour the exotic nature of the setting. To loosen tongues that circumstances had made rather stiff, they ate lightly and drank heavily, emptying bottle after bottle from the old man's cellar. There followed mutual introductions and much talk of Roseline and her death.

Hole could not answer every question without giving himself away, so he fell back on weeping each time he was caught short. The ruse worked well enough, even if the twins were a little surprised to see him burst into tears over a trivial question about theatrical seasons.

The bottle of *eau-de-vie* that was broached with the dessert – and that alarmingly contained a human ear in suspension – encouraged the young men to pursue their investigation further. Mentioning spiritualist gatherings to a father who had just lost his daughter seemed a little tactless, to say the least. However, contrary to all expectation, the American evidently welcomed the subject. Indeed, why not call up Roseline's spirit? And why not right now?

'Right now? What do you mean by that?' Odilon enquired with a chuckle, alcohol having begun to cloud his faculties.

'Well, we're all three of us spiritualists, aren't we? Here's a table, here's a candle. Why don't we hold a seance right here?'

'Impossible!' Armand protested. 'We need a medium to make contact with the spirit, isn't that right, Odilon?'

The Parisian seemed annoyed. He wanted to agree with his

friend but felt forced to gainsay him.

'Armand...you're a medium!' he said in a low voice. 'A natural medium, a very gifted medium! Have you forgotten how that power was revealed to you and to all of us in Apolline's caravan?'

He then turned to the American who was savouring this difference of opinion between the twins.

'You're right, Monsieur Hole, we can hold a seance. Your daughter's spirit will probably have been released by now. They say that suicide delays the disjunction of soul and body but also that a spiritualist can easily effect it. As an initiate, Roseline will undoubtedly have performed the necessary procedure very swiftly. So, if Armand agrees...'

At this consultation, Armand banged a fist on the table so hard that the ear seemed to twitch inside the eau-de-vie bottle.

'No, I'm against the idea! Not here, not like this... I've never played the medium's role, I wouldn't know... And anyway...evoking Roseline!'

Hole made a gesture of appeasement.

'I know precisely what you're saying, young man. It's a deal, then: we won't call up my daughter's spirit this evening. We'll wait a few days, our chances of entering into communication can only improve. When does your group meet?'

'Wednesday night,' Odilon replied.

'May I attend?'

'You'll be welcome!'

The American signalled to Old Man Modesty, who had been dozing in his chair. The attendant fetched a fresh bottle – the sixth – and in a moment the glasses had taken on the same colour. Hole served his table-companions liberally but took little himself on the pretext that too much wine made him 'doleful'.

When he reckoned the collective drunkenness sufficiently advanced, the architect picked up the conversation where they had left off. 'I have a suggestion to put to you. A compatriot of mine, currently in Paris, is a famous medium back home. She's someone they call a "talking medium", or in other words, the spirits speak through her mouth. She passes on not just their words but also their intonations and their accents – which, I think you will agree – rules out any idea of trickery. Would you be willing to invite her to your meeting?'

Odilon was tipsy, hence his slowness in framing an objection.

'The thing is... The woman who leads our group is a medium herself. She specializes in writing...'

'What does that matter?' put in Armand, who took his drink slightly better. 'Two chances are better than one! And I shall be delighted to hear Roseline's voice!'

Hurt, his friend made a vague gesture of consent.

'Fine!' said Hole decisively. 'So I'll bring her with me. The seance is on Wednesday, you say? Wednesday is also the day of the funeral. Unfortunately, Roseline's procession will be a very short one. She had virtually no family apart from myself.'

'Don't you believe it, sir!' said Armand, wishing to be kind. 'All those theatregoers, all the people who applauded her...'

'...will be elsewhere, applauding someone else! Come on, I know men! But let's leave a painful subject... We all believe in Roseline's survival, so keeping these long faces would be an insult to her. Let's drink to her new life instead! Hey, it's like drinking to a newborn child!'

Indeed, the end of the meal was relaxed, almost joyful. Old Man Modesty's rough wine proved a better, faster fraterniser than the smoothest vintage. So riotous did the wake become towards midnight that a visitor who did not know otherwise might have taken it for an engagement party. Hole and the twins parted the best of friends.

Returning to the hotel, the American found Gaspard waiting for him with a bottle of champagne cooling in a bucket. They toasted the faultless execution of their plan.

Next morning was difficult.

Gordon Hole and Gaspard Louchon recovered consciousness in the bathtub of the hotel room, whither some idea that in their inebriated state had seemed quite logical must have led them twelve hours earlier. The American, who was in a particularly foul mood, accused his accomplice of having got him drunk.

'Wasting time drinking on a day like this! Come on, get moving! You have to dash round to the morgue and arrange for Roseline's removal. What if the police have already investigated and Old Man Modesty has told them about us? There's not a moment to lose!'

For the twins, the day began equally badly. They had slept at the morgue and, waking mid-morning, were very late leaving for the office. At that time of day there was no hope of escaping Monsieur Pluot's censure: the office manager was unbending and no drama, even of the most private kind, let one off work.

And then, for Armand in particular, drunkenness had given way to a sombre mood. His thoughts of the previous day, made messy with hatred and grief, still clung to his mind. He missed his fiancée, of course he did, but he also, increasingly, nourished an aversion for his job at Établissements Eiffel. If the man really was as the posthumous letter had described him and if he was the root cause of Roseline's death, how could he, Armand, decently remain in his employ?

His decision was soon made.

'I'll go to work,' he announced in lugubrious tones, 'but only in order to hand in my notice.'

'Hand in your notice? What will you do then?'

'Simple – I'll find a job somewhere else. I'll go and see Victor Contamin, the engineer in charge of metal buildings at the Exposition. Gustave Eiffel mentioned a Hall of Machines being erected at the foot of the Tower, built entirely of iron, apparently. That's something I could apply my talents to!'

Odilon did his best to hear his friend out kindly. But such naivety grated on his nerves.

'Are you crazy? Those posts were filled long since! Look, we live in a depressed economy, jobs are few and hard to come by. What's the Exposition for, do you suppose? Entertaining tourists? Cocking a snook at the British? Nonsense. It's all about providing work for the thousands of unemployed workers who, without it, might cause another revolution…'

'I'm not a worker, I'm an engineer!' corrected Armand in haughty tones.

The Parisian brooked no interruption.

'Even if they were still taking people on, they wouldn't take you. Who'd want a quitter on his team? The news of your resignation will get around, you can be sure of that! It's a small world, iron construction…'

'Then I'll leave the profession! That's it! I'll become a coachman, a button-carver… Anything rather than work for a monster like Eiffel! Uncle Jules can put me up for a bit longer… That reminds me: I'll have to move back the things I'd taken to Roseline's. As I can't stand the idea of sleeping there on my own.'

The thought of undoing his once-triumphant removal plunged Armand into sadness. He sank to the ground where they were, in the middle of the road.

'Come on, get up! You'll be arrested. Anyway, we've lost too much time already – it'll cost us dearly!'

'Cost us? On a day like this, you're worried about having your wages docked? Go on, then, run to the office, if you must! You haven't lost a fiancée, I'm aware of that. You're not in mourning…'

'Watch what you're saying!' Odilon riposted. 'Roseline was as dear to me as she was to you!'

Armand taunted him with a smile.

'Poppycock! City people feel nothing and engineers even less. Believe me, it will be a real pleasure to part company with them!'

This provoked a kick, which the young man from St. Flour, sitting there in the road, took in the ribs. In revenge, he sank his teeth as hard as he could into Odilon's leg – the one nearest to him. A fight started, which in a street teeming with cabs and trams was risky. A crowd formed, not to separate the combatants but to egg them on, because some of the passers-by enjoyed watching a good scrap. However, as soon as they had let off enough steam, the eraser twins threw in the towel before any bets could be taken.

'You're scum!' Odilon swore, fingering a loose tooth.

'And you're a scoundrel!' Armand replied as he rubbed a painful elbow.

'I'm older than you, you should show me some respect! At least take my advice and don't hand in your notice in the heat of resentment. Decisions taken in the cold light of reason are often the best.'

Armand made this concession to their friendship.

'All right, but don't imagine you've changed my mind! I know my duty to Roseline, as you should know yours!'

The twins continued on their way, limping. By chance, that

morning Monsieur Pluot had stayed in bed with a temperature and they escaped without a fine.

9

From the end of November, the Hotel Britannique housed a most curious guest.

She had registered as the 'Countess of Artois', arousing employees' suspicions from the outset. Not that anyone doubted the reality of the title – in Paris, one had only to make a claim to have it accepted, and dukes were as common as manholes – but it fomented mistrust that so highborn a lady should travel alone, with no companion. To the bellboys, wealth was associated with numbers and prodigality; rich people, traditionally incapable of doing anything for themselves, brought along a whole host of lackeys from cooks to chambermaids to corroborate their rank.

Those same bellboys quizzed one another in the corridors: how was this enigmatic woman to be described? Was she a *genreuse*, as they put it – meaning a genuine aristocrat – or a *pschutteuse*, a smart woman of uncertain social status?

The suspense did not last long: December was but a few days old when the Countess of Artois signed her restaurant chit as 'Princess of Batavia', thus exposing herself as one of those liberal embroiderers of the truth who usurp noble titles. No one looked round any more as she passed in her dress with its long train, the sweeping folds of which concealed a pair of horribly noisy mahogany-heeled shoes.

It soon became clear that this was not the only trait that marked out Salome – her real name – from the hotel's well-behaved and somewhat dull clientele.

On arrival the young woman had had carried up to Room 11, on the second floor, a very large trunk with two enormous padlocks. Along the sides of this piece of luggage ran canvas straps bearing wax seals. The traveller had specifically asked for the trunk not to be touched, adding the solemn qualification, 'If your staff value their lives.'

This was sufficient to ensure that there grew up around Salome a dense network of surveillance involving half a dozen chambermaids and as many grooms – such a network as, apart from dedicated intelligence services, only the personnel of a large hotel, with time on their hands, know how to organise. Three days later, Salome's entire routine was public knowledge. All staff members knew the time when she performed her toilet, her favourite dessert, how she wore her hair at night and even, thanks to the shameless intrusions of one bellboy, precisely how often she pleasured herself.

Eye-witness accounts exhibited subtle differences but on one thing, at least, all were agreed: no one had ever paid the young woman a visit.

That, in fact, was where the mystery lay, as from the rooms occupied by this solitary inmate came the sound, at all hours of the day and night, of voices engaged in discussion. People said they clearly distinguished those of a man and of a small child. Such conversations were brisk, even violent, suggesting a couple having a row. Soon complaints from people in adjoining rooms started to pile up on the manager's desk:

They heard screaming, crockery smashing, furniture being moved around – there was no getting a wink of sleep!

One afternoon, the noise reached a climax. Through the door of the room, a man could be heard shouting while a small boy begged, 'Papa, mama, stop fighting! Please!' The shouts carried down to the vestibule, where passers-by began to congregate.

The manager called the police. Ten minutes later, a sergeant wearing a tricoloured belt appeared with an escort of constables and dogs. The officer ordered Salome to open her door. Her only response was to bolt it from inside. When the officer insisted, she exclaimed, 'Leave me alone! Mind your own business! What's going on here is no concern of yours!' The din resumed, rising even higher this time.

Eventually, the door was forced open, revealing this unnerving sight: Salome stood alone in the centre of the room, looking at a large trunk from which issued the plaintive voice of a child and at a wardrobe that resounded with male oaths. The police stared at the young woman, who was quite calm, with a mixture of fascination and terror. Two of them seized her with considerable force, while others set about opening the heavily padlocked trunk and wardrobe.

The wardrobe was empty. Inside the trunk they found a smaller container from which out popped a jack-in-the-box, nearly striking an astonished policeman on the nose.

'Thank you, officer!' the jack-in-the-box said. 'You've gone to a great deal of trouble! I'm a cardboard toy and my mummy's a ventriloquist!'

The police, the assembled members of staff and the other customers were all utterly bewildered...

Newly arrived in Paris, Salome the ventriloquist had

worked up this number with a view to securing a music-hall engagement.

And doubtless she would have done, the way the newspapers fell over one another to tell her story and give her free publicity. However, Gordon Hole got in first, knocking on Salome's door, which happened to be quite near his own, later that very afternoon.

The American was a master of the art of persuasion – unless the talent had more to do with the apparently endless stream of banknotes that flowed from his pocket. Five minutes after their conversation began Salome the ventriloquist had been engaged by Gordon Hole and accompanied her new employer into his suite of rooms. There she met Gaspard and discovered what the affair was about.

'Is that all?' the young woman asked in amazement when her role had been explained.

'That's all. But watch out – the execution has to be perfect! The slightest departure would put us all at risk. Then I wouldn't be able to guarantee your safety.'

A residue of caution prompted Salome to ask, 'Why are you doing this?'

'Think of it as a farce,' the American replied with feigned casualness, 'a little practical joke I'm playing on a friend!'

The ventriloquist swallowed her curiosity. A meeting was arranged for the following afternoon, which gave Salome time to learn her lines and practise the right tone of voice. Gaspard gave her the phonograph with the engraved cylinder, explaining how it worked.

'And if the recording is poor?' the young woman asked, still slightly mistrustful.

Hole tapped the appliance in the manner of a jockey patting the neck of a thoroughbred.

'This, mademoiselle, is Edison's very latest model. It reflects the most recent technical developments in the field of sound recording. Let me tell you, this machine took ten years to perfect! So you need have no fear. Moreover, I am prepared to listen to you whenever you please. I know the person to be imitated and I recall her voice precisely.'

'In that case...'

With Gaspard helping, Salome carried the phonograph to her room.

'I have every confidence,' the American said when his accomplice returned. 'That young woman has talent and integrity. You see, that's the trouble with this kind of intrigue: you have to surround yourself with honest people, otherwise you're lost – people who'll agree to serve a dishonest end – otherwise you've no chance. There's only one way to do it: conceal from them the ultimate purpose of what you are asking them to do!'

'Oh, Salome will fit the bill, I'm sure of it! But how did you know that a mimic was about to arrive at this hotel?'

'I had no idea! It was pure chance! Actually, the Britannique does have a reputation for putting up stage people, particularly from England and America. The big Châtelet Theatre and the *Opéra-Comique* are just around the corner. Our friend must have known that.'

'Ah, sir, your plan's working like clockwork!'

Jules Boissier was indeed extremely surprised when he opened his front door one morning to find young Armand standing there, flanked by two canvas suitcases – the locks no longer worked, hence the liberal use of string to hold in the bulging sides.

With his unconventional luggage, and his upper body

squeezed into a dark jacket from which several buttons were missing, the young man from St. Flour looked like some impoverished violinist just back from a tour. The neighbours were bound to be spying from their windows.

'H–have you come for supper?' the old man stammered. 'But it's much too early!'

Armand pushed the larger of the two cases with his foot.

'Help me get this inside. It's all but pulled my arms off, dragging it from Roseline's place.'

Uncles and aunts, quite as much as fathers and mothers, are advised to observe a discreet silence when a young man who has left the house to go and live with his mistress suddenly returns. Jules did not say a word, not when his nephew emptied one of the cases into a wardrobe nor when he downed the contents of two coffee cups that he found on a table.

On the other hand, when the old man saw his visitor tearing up armfuls of flowers from the garden, he did feel he had to intervene. He cared nothing for the state of his borders, to which he paid little attention, but he did mind what the neighbours thought. As he aged, Jules was acquiring a desire for respectability.

'Whom are the flowers for?' he asked as he brought a vase.

'For Roseline,' his nephew solemnly replied.

As he did so, from one second to the next his nerves gave way. He let out a sob and tears reappeared in his eyes, tears like those he had shed in such abundance over the past two days.

Jules Boissier was good at offering consolation. In place of words, which often only sharpen grief, he preferred action. Taking the flowers from Armand's grasp he arranged them tastefully in the pot he had brought.

'You've had a row, I take it? Don't worry – a passing shower! At your age, the sky is swept by a constant wind that drives off every cloud. She'll like this bunch of flowers. Except…these chrysanthemums…are they right, do you think? Watch out – women read intentions into everything.'

Whereupon Armand fell into Jules's arms, crushing the flowers between them.

'Oh, uncle – Roseline is dead!'

There followed much weeping, by both parties this time, and a lengthy confabulation in the house with the closed shutters.

When the time came to leave for the funeral, alert neighbours saw the door of the house open and two men in black suits emerge to walk down the steps arm-in-arm. The younger man wore a spray of bright-coloured flowers that clashed with the dark suits and that the watching gossips, given what they assumed to be the circumstances, found badly out of place.

At the same time, a cab with lowered blinds was proceeding towards the cemetery to keep the appointment fixed by Gordon Hole. Odilon re-read the telegram that Roseline's intimates had received that morning.

'All the same,' the engineer confided to Apolline, who was seated beside him, 'it's no way to arrange a funeral! I mean, no mass, no procession… I wasn't expecting a church draped in black as if for gentlefolk, but even so… We shan't even be able to give Roseline one last kiss, the coffin will already be closed, ready for burial. It's appalling!'

The young woman reacted boldly: 'No, I approve, actually! A sincere spiritualist ought always to bury loved ones this way. If you all really believed in the soul's survival after death, you wouldn't feel any grief at funerals. Instead, you'd experience a sort of sweet melancholy, as when saying goodbye to someone on a railway platform. Weeping, processions, endless recitals of *De Profundis* – all those formalities are an insult to God! Ultimately, they show how little faith you have.'

'That's easy to say!' Odilon objected indignantly. 'Possessing a soul doesn't stop me having a heart – and feeling that heart when a dear friend disappears!'

Apolline shook her head but declined to continue the discussion, choosing instead to pluck a periwinkle from the wreath on the seat opposite, tear off the petals one by one and suck them as if she were eating an artichoke.

'That reminds me,' the Parisian added, in a mood to quibble, 'I find your habit of eating flowers disgusting! Look, you've ruined that lovely arrangement.'

The young woman held out a petal to him, revealing the shiny imprint left by her teeth.

'In the language of flowers, white periwinkle means, "the delights of memory".'

'Yes, I leafed through the same magazine where you read that stupid stuff! Now we know what a women thinks about on a day like this: what to plant in the garden! I suppose you'll be wanting to stop off at your dress shop to choose material for your mourning frock? I'm going to trump your white periwinkle with foxglove – for insincerity!'

Apolline shot her husband a withering look. Taking the suede fan that hung from her wrist, she opened it with a truly Spanish flourish.

'White camellia: "perfect beauty"! Locust-tree: "fondness that lives on after death!"'

The Parisian cut short the argument with an imperious gesture.

'Enough! This is neither the time nor the place for a scene.'

Just then the driver banged on the cab roof, which was

his rather unsubtle way of informing passengers that they had arrived.

As Hole had predicted, Roseline's funeral attracted few people. Apart from the four friends already named and the American himself, those who braved the winter wind to attend would not have filled one pew. They included the owner of the flat the actress had lived in, no doubt there to claim back rent, and the assistant manager of the theatre, worried about the cancelled contract. And as for the athletic-looking character, his height and the heavy moustache clearly marked him out as a gentleman of the law.

The American had not wanted a larger crowd. For one thing, the expense to which he had agreed in advance for this pretend burial already struck him as excessive, but also, he felt that the greater the number of guests, the greater the risk of being found out. Fate had decreed that Roseline had virtually no family and friends. Hole preferred not to tempt it.

The burial took only a moment. A small quantity of earth was shovelled onto the empty coffin, then Gordon Hole, dreading questions, summoned his carriage, which was parked up one of the paths of the cemetery. This hurried departure was put down to paternal grief, and no one dared to approach the American.

Even the police, who are occasionally shameless, showed surprising respect in the circumstances.

'Just a poor young woman who wished to end it all,' the inspector confided to Odilon. 'There are plenty of those in these wretched times. The men hang themselves, the women prefer drowning…'

The Parisian took the opportunity to vent his bitterness.

'I should have liked to pay my last respects to the deceased. Why was there no lying in state?'

'It was the wish of Monsieur Hole, given the particular circumstances of his daughter's death. The body was placed in the coffin the day after it reached the morgue. My men were not able to examine it.'

'But that's unheard-of!'

'Ach!' went the policeman kindly. 'Why upset the family? The girl wanted to die. May she rest in peace, I say.'

The case was closed to allow the mourning to begin.

In the bedroom of his top-floor furnished flat, Gaspard Louchon watched over the troubled awakening of Roseline Page.

Getting the young woman back from the morgue had been no easy task. Gaspard's muscles still felt the strain, as his nerves retained the memory of the frequent alarms that had punctuated his illegal journey across the capital. Was the American at least aware of the risks his associate had run, being in possession of a body stolen from Old Man Modesty? Did he have any conception of the punishment that awaited him if the police had got wind of the affair? Of course not! Gordon Hole took the easy, gratifying jobs – a letter needed writing, some playacting was required. While poor Gaspard got landed with the thankless tasks, the hard – and dangerous – graft!

Consulting his watch, he poured a fresh spoonful of antidote, the yellow, creamy liquid he was making Armand's fiancée drink. The blood was gradually returning to the young woman's cheeks, indicating progress. Nevertheless, Gaspard felt it was taking too long and he was worried. Sometimes the poison had side-effects. Unless what he was seeing were the equally debilitating consequences of the subject's many hours without food or water.

Towards noon, having clambered back through every level of consciousness, the actress finally opened her eyes. They seemed empty and uninhabited at first, but the next moment, in some indefinable way, intelligence slowly filled them. Gaspard, leaning over the convalescent, ventured a smile.

'Where am I? Who are you?' Rosaline asked between yawns.

The questions had been inevitable and Gaspard chose to answer them straightforwardly, knowing he could not have hidden the truth for long in any case. Without pause he recounted the kidnapping, how they had left her body beside the Seine, and her stay in the morgue. He passed over none of the steps in their carefully planned deception. Roseline learned that her friends thought her dead and that her funeral had been held that very morning. She discovered that Gordon Hole was passing himself off as her father.

'My father?' was her reaction. 'But he was killed on the barricades of Paris when I was a baby!'

Such was Roseline's confusion of mind that Gaspard had to tell the story three times over, modulating certain sentences whose meaning was either too dense or too abrupt for her to comprehend as yet. Eventually, she understood, and when the truth finally hit her, an expression of such distress appeared on her features, such horror at her situation, that Gaspard feared for her sanity.

'But it's all over now!' he concluded naively. 'You've come round and you're well! Monsieur Hole has asked me to look after you and I will!'

Only Roseline's head and, to a lesser extent, her hands had moved since her recovery. A sudden panic prompted her to try to get off the bed and see if she could stand. She sent a violent impulse to her legs and arms but to no avail. Twice she tried, but all that her desperate efforts accomplished was to turn her onto her side, where she was even less comfortable. Feeling dizzy after this manoeuvre, she threw up. Gaspard returned her to the prone position.

'Please be sensible, I beg of you! I'd hate to use force. I'm going to have to tie you down.'

And with the aid of a length of rope made ready in advance Gaspard proceeded to bind the actress's legs together.

'What are you going to do with me?' Roseline croaked.

'That for Monsieur Hole to decide. If you want my opinion, you're rather in his way. He hasn't the heart to kill you but neither can he let you live a normal life. No doubt about it, you're a problem so far as he's concerned!'

'But why kidnap me in the first place? Why pretend I'm dead? I don't understand.'

Gaspard looked at Roseline as he drew a knot tight against her thigh. He tied the knot quickly as soon as he saw the lovely face distort in a grimace.

'You refuse to answer,' the young woman observed. 'At least tell me this, shall I be allowed out?'

'A dead woman walking the streets of Paris? I don't think so.'

'But can I write? Send a letter to my mother?'

'That neither.' Gaspard said gently, not liking the role of censor. 'But on the other hand you have my promise that I'll bring you magazines and little delicacies. We'll have long chats, play dominoes and backgammon. You can knit if that's what you like doing!'

The reluctant gaoler did all he could to distract Roseline and present her imprisonment as a period of convalescence – all treats and play. Far from showing gratitude for his attentiveness, the young woman grew irritated at what she saw as a fresh stratagem.

'You're lying! You've made the whole thing up! It's all a

macabre rigmarole! Which jealous actress is paying you to frighten me? Is it Gabrielle Réjane, whom I just beat to a part at the *Ambigu-Comique*. Or perhaps Julia Bartet, I know the talentless wretch hates my guts… Come on, whose tool are you? Own up!'

'I'm telling the truth, Mademoiselle!'

'Prove it!'

Gaspard selected two newspapers from the pile on the table, one bearing that day's date, one from the day before. The second showed an engraving of the Tower in its most recent state, with a flimsy-looking first storey. The structure threw a latticework shadow over the Seine that resembled a giant net, a net whose meshes enclosed a female figure bearing Roseline's features. 'The Unhappy Siren' read the caption.

The first, the one published that day, contained a brief mention of the actress's passing in its deaths column. This was an 'economy' insert of four lines with no border or ornament of the kind placed by the lower middle classes when burying an uncle who has left no one anything. There was no indication of when or where the ceremony would take place. A succinct text simply invited readers to 'add their prayers' to those of the bereaved family.

'Quite moving to see your own name on that page, isn't it?' Gaspard observed ironically. 'Do you know how Moïse Millaud, founder of the *Petit Journal*, made his name on the modest rag he first worked for? He was in charge of the deaths column and he arranged for the names of the deceased to be followed by those of their attending physicians! How about that for an idea!'

But Roseline did not feel like laughing. Having the evidence placed before her in this way drained her last hopes. Then this lovely woman, who had never been seen to weep –

except on stage, of course – whose deepest sorrows had seemed to evaporate like morning mist, produced two large tears that rolled down her face and splashed onto her pearl necklace. Gaspard's heart turned over.

'No, don't do that, it's not right! You're trying to trap me emotionally and I'm doing everything I can to be nice to you! If that's the way it is, I'm going next door! I mean it! And don't try shouting, either, otherwise I'll gag you!'

Throwing several newspapers onto the bed, where Roseline could reach them, Gaspard left the room feeling deeply disturbed.

Night was falling when Gordon Hole, with Salome the ventriloquist on his arm, presented himself at the door of the morgue.

At that time of day, and in view of the circumstances, it would have seemed feeble to the American simply to ring the bell. He preferred to scratch at the door and, when it opened a crack, to look around cautiously and slip inside. These certainly excessive precautions bothered the young woman. Wherever was he taking her? Her unease turned to fear when she saw Hole exchange a sign of complicity with the attendant.

'Sir, I'm not coming a step further,' the ventriloquist said very rapidly. 'Keep your money. I'll just go.'

The American tightened his grip on her arm.

'Out of the question! I told you about this. Come on, brace up! It's a game, a masquerade. You're not in any danger.'

The full spiritualist circle was already assembled in the morgue. Twenty or so young persons were waiting, lounging unconcernedly against the tables reserved for the corpses. Their dark clothing blended into the funereal setting. Some looked like gravediggers who had come to take delivery of a customer. Others, of doubtful health, resembled corpses themselves and with their elbows propped on the marble slabs looked as if they had just got up from them. A glance suggested that these people did not live in the real world, nor were they entirely at home in their bodies.

Such a gathering might have inspired fear. However, on Salome it had the opposite effect. True stage artistes are like that, their nerves disappear as the curtain goes up. Recognising Apolline immediately, the ventriloquist strode across to greet her.

'How delightful to find a colleague here! I'm very pleased to meet you!'

The hint of an American accent, the slightly urchin bow – these fitted in brilliantly. Here was exactly the character that Hole had imagined and whom, from his description, the spiritualists might have expected: a New World medium, cheerful and high-spirited, whose occultism lacked the sophistication of its French counterpart but had an entirely transatlantic familiarity.

Across the ocean, people conversed with the dead as with a next-door neighbour. A physical workout with the arms and head put mediums in a condition to operate, in line with the American belief that any obstacles to communication lay within the body. Modern technologies and electrical charging in particular came to the aid of failing sibyls. Theirs was a pragmatic school and Salome was clearly a good pupil.

Apolline returned the greeting with a smile. Contact was good and no one sensed any mistrust on her part towards the newcomer. This did much to relax the atmosphere. Without further ado, the spiritualists formed ranks to descend to the cellar.

It was the first time that two mediums, neither of whom

took clear precedence over the other, had sat together at their table. This unusual case prompted a debate about protocol. Which of the two women should open the seance? Who should say the prayer to the spirits?

For reasons of courtesy, it was decided to allow Salome to conduct the evocation itself, while Apolline remained responsible for leading the evening's proceedings. The seance began.

This meeting, with strangers present, called to invoke the spirit of a dead woman whom they had all known, was unique in character. Apolline was keen to observe the formalities. They began, as their master Allan Kardec had laid down, with a reading of the spirit communications obtained during the last seance and their clarification. Then came a short report of the correspondence the group maintained with other occult societies. Odilon proposed a review of press coverage, which was indeed very dense, showing the interest that spiritualism was arousing in all quarters. The finest authors had made sacrificial offerings at this fashionable altar. The late Théophile Gautier, for example, had published the novel *Spirite* twenty years earlier, while the contemporary Yveling Rambaud was about to produce a series entitled *Force Psychique*.

Hole, who thought of spiritualism in terms of a fairground attraction and had expected the same comical affectations, was surprised by the seriousness of the gathering. The discipline of the proceedings and the unwavering authority of Apolline put one in mind of a college of philosophy where exalted matters are gravely debated. The meeting even included a special officer charged with keeping order, who on two occasions had excluded a member for speaking out of turn. As an outside listener, the American was required to keep silent.

By the time Odilon gave his report, an hour had already

passed and the evocation had yet to take place.

The waiting was a nagging torment to Salome. The closer the moment of her 'entrance' came the greater grew her fear of botching it. She felt increasingly uncomfortable in this richly adorned soothsayer's costume with its gold-spangled veils and jangling bracelets. How could anyone take her seriously? Who would fail to guess, as soon as she opened her mouth, the obvious fraud that was being perpetrated on them?

Suddenly, Apolline signalled to Salome that she might begin. Taking a deep breath, the ventriloquist recited the prayer of evocation:

'I beseech Almighty God to permit the spirit of Roseline Page to communicate with me. I also beseech my guardian angel to see fit to assist me and to banish all evil spirits!'

Although at that moment everyone had their eyes closed, Salome opened hers to gauge the effect of her words. She had succeeded. The twenty or so persons present sat with hands linked, listening in attentive silence. She continued.

'Spirit of Roseline Page, are you there?'

She spoke the question three times, as three knocks are sounded in the theatre.

'Spirit of Roseline Page, please answer me!'

It was time to deploy her skills. Recalling the actress's voice as she had memorised it from the phonograph cylinder, Salome borrowed it to say:

'Yes, I am here.'

The mimicry worked. A tremor ran through the assembled company at the sound of that familiar voice, which each one recognised from its rather solemn timbre and charming pronunciation defect – her way of substituting a sibilant for a palatoalveolar fricative; what teachers of speech production term a 'lisp'.

'Yes, I am here,' Salome said again.

The role of questioner had been assigned to Armand. He, however, was so overcome with emotion at hearing, as he believed, his beloved that he was unable to perform it. Odilon stepped in.

'Are you the actress Roseline Page, our friend who has gone from us?'

'I am,' the voice declared.

With each fresh answer, the young woman improved her technique. From this point on, she spoke between closed lips: a ventriloquist's trick that she hoped would underline the supernatural origin of what she said. Her colleagues might animate a puppet or an animal but she could give life to a ghost.

'A letter was found on you,' Odilon went on. 'Did you write it yourself?'

'I did.'

'Can its contents be believed?'

'I wrote nothing but the truth.'

The initial series of questions, which was quite protracted, aimed to confirm Roseline's identity. This, in fact, was the thing that most often went wrong at evocations: a spirit was summoned who did not come but was replaced by another that everyone took for the first.

The following questions served a different purpose. Written down by Odilon at Armand's dictation, they sought to make up for the letter's lack of precision on certain points.

'Your absence grieves us deeply...,' Odilon declared. 'We need to know more about your reasons. Someone moved you to make this unfortunate gesture, is that right?'

'Yes.'

'What is that person's name?'

'Gustave Eiffel.'

In the ten minutes since they had linked them, the spiritualists' hands had become moist and slippery, making them unpleasant to hold. They tried hard to maintain contact nevertheless, not wishing to break the chain. However, at this moment it was broken when Armand gave a start. The engineer re-formed the link with his neighbours.

'What has Monsieur Eiffel been guilty of?'

'He is the cause of our family's misfortune. He stole my father's talent and his ideas. Above all, he took on the man I love as a member of his staff. This insult drove me to kill myself.'

'But in taking this young engineer on, could Eiffel have known he was doing wrong?'

Salome hesitated for a moment. When she resumed, she chose her words carefully.

'Wrongdoing is not always intentional but that is insufficient to excuse it. The man who throws away a match and sets fire to an entire forest may not have meant to do so but that does not make him any less responsible.'

Silently, Hole congratulated Salome for dealing with the problem so adroitly.

'You chose to die near the site of the Tower. Was that to harm Monsieur Eiffel?'

'Yes, indeed. I hoped to compromise him. But the press hardly helped.'

Odilon had reached the end of his questions. He touched Armand on the shoulder, and the young man from St. Flour, having pondered his question at length, formulated it in a timid voice.

'Roseline... Can we...is there anything we can do for you?'

'Avenge me!'

This vehement reply, so out of keeping with what had gone before, caused a stir around the table. Apolline stifled it with an imperious 'Hush!'

'How?' the engineer asked.

'Destroy the Tower!'

The stir revived and swelled in volume. This time, Apolline was powerless to restore calm. Nor did the officer in charge of discipline have any greater success, although he had already expelled the most talkative members. In an instant, the spiritualist seance was transformed into a typical Parisian salon, where people conversed in lowered tones with those sitting next to them but in loud voices with colleagues across the table. Their discussions rose steadily in volume, mounting to a hubbub that was further amplified by the resonance of the stone vaulting.

Salome leant over to Apolline, who was sitting beside her.

'What a bear garden! I blame myself.'

Her fellow-medium took her hand.

'It's not your fault – nothing to do with you, in fact... The evocation went very well. I envy you your gift for making the voice of the deceased one audible. But you must understand how our spiritualists feel. Two hours – that's a long seance! They can't wait to discuss what Roseline said. The agenda tends to get forgotten.'

'The spirit had not finished, it seems to me. The noise sent it flying. Could another seance be arranged?'

A smile appeared on Apolline's face, as if from a master to a promising pupil.

'Very well...'

'When?'

'There's no need to fix a date. Come when you can, you'll always be welcome! We meet every Wednesday evening.'

With a wink Salome confirmed to Hole that the mission had been accomplished. The American reciprocated with a discreet indication of his satisfaction.

Across the table, Odilon and Armand were swapping impressions of the seance. The young man from St. Flour believed in the reality of the evocation, while his friend took a more critical view.

'Odilon, how extraordinary! Roseline is asking us to destroy the Tower!'

'Listen to you! To begin with, was it really Roseline?'

Armand gulped in amazement.

'Who else can it have been? We heard her!'

'It is not unknown for certain ill-intentioned spirits to have fun at the expense of humans. Mimicking a voice is surely not beyond them. Anyway, was the resemblance so striking?'

'But what she said! The details she gave…'

'There I'm shocked. Roseline was a passionate woman but she was a stranger to bitterness. I didn't recognise her in those vengeful words. Nor did you, judging from the way you switched to *vous*. You told me you always called her *tu*.'

The argument hit home. For an instant, Armand hesitated.

'I felt intimidated… Talking to a ghost is not like talking to a live woman!'

'And finally,' Odilon pursued, sticking to his idea, 'I was surprised she should mention the Tower. It's a shabby trait, don't you think, and one unworthy of our friend — seeking reparation in the form of an act that's going to kill large numbers of people?'

'Ah, but she didn't demand Eiffel's murder!'

The Parisian greeted this nuance with a dismissive gesture.

'In the peaceful realm that spirits inhabit, earthly passions have no place…except among base souls, which is how we recognise them as such. Roseline cannot be counted among their number. No, I'm sure of it, it wasn't her talking this evening.'

'Well, I'm sure it was!' the other retorted. 'There's no point in discussing it. Let's leave it till the next seance.'

The meeting over, the spiritualists left the morgue and dispersed on the embankment. The twins walked together at first, then Armand caught a bus that took him towards his uncle's house.

10

Further evocations of Roseline were undertaken in the months that followed.

This posthumous conversation became a regular, even a commonplace event, replacing the spiritualist group's other communications. What was the point of calling up anonymous dead people when there was this chance of accessing someone they all knew? Why interrogate confused or laconic souls when Roseline spoke so well, displaying all the eloquence of a former actress?

Coached by Gordon Hole, Salome contrived her effects. It was always towards the end of a seance that the spirit performed best, the foregoing exchange having served only to create suspense. As for the final few words, which were frequently opaque, their function was to make the audience want to attend the next show.

These invariably successful evocations, with no more hesitations or periods of silence than were necessary to make them credible, did a great deal for Salome's reputation.

Curiously, no one doubted the genuineness of a gift that

was well outside the human norm. People accepted that the newcomer was immediately able to make the dead talk as if by snapping her fingers, though this was something that others tried in vain to do for month after month.

Possibly it was a thirst for miracles – simple worship of those who dominate effortlessly, who triumph almost without trying. Their disciplined spiritualism, weary of too much humility, needed a hero.

But undoubtedly it was thanks to the American and his superb idea of giving Salome Roseline's voice. And repetition of the miracle disarmed even the most obdurate sceptics. So completely did the two women form one in the minds of those attending the seances that carping at the medium amounted to criticising the spirit herself. The live woman and the dead one made common cause – and the former benefited enormously.

Faced with so well-tuned a lie, only Apolline entertained any misgivings. She knew the job and in all probability, to her trained mind, many little details betrayed the ventriloquist's deception. So why did she never charge Salome with imposture, instead giving her every encouragement? How could she tolerate her colleague's assertion that she was called to be the spiritualists' unofficial guide rather than Apolline herself?

Clearly, the group's regular medium was in thrall to the visitor. The obscure ascendancy that some beings have over others, that makes the mother give in to her child, the tiger retreat before its trainer, some such phenomenon placed Apolline in Salome's power. The ventriloquist was aware of this interest – indeed, shared it to some degree – but was unable fully to respond. How was she to become friends with someone she was duping? Whatever happened, she must keep her distance. Faithful to Hole's instructions, Salome mixed with none of the group outside meetings.

Week by week, the new medium gradually supplanted the old, usurping her powers and her prerogatives. It was now Salome who chaired seances, drew up the agenda and signed correspondence. No longer was the spiritualist circle Apolline's group with Salome as a guest, so to speak. It was more like Salome's group, in which Apolline was still accepted.

With the ventriloquist now in charge, the shape of their meetings changed radically. Gone were the old dismal, starchy seances when everyone waited hours for spirits to show themselves! Gone too were the scribbled messages, which had given the poor interpreter headaches!

From now on seances were pleasant, diverting occasions. People attended as if going for a night out at the music-hall, with a spring in their step and a flower in their buttonhole. They came away repeating Roseline's parting quip like the latest refrain. The recommendation to be discreet went by the board. Some spiritualists talked of inviting their friends, since the group was now so entertaining. In fact, many cabarets, those whose musical acts had trouble filling three rows of seats, might have envied its success. A new decadent venue in the basement of the morgue? Word got around, spread by neighbours who had seen noisy revellers emerging from what they knew as the house of the dead.

Most spiritualists, having been attracted to occultism by a taste for the sensational, approved of the reformed seances. Only Odilon and Armand found fault, the first on the grounds of his spiritualist convictions, the second because this was about Roseline, and Roseline was sacred...

The Parisian's attempts to reason with Apolline drew a blank.

'You're upsetting yourself over nothing!' the medium responded. 'Salome knows what she's doing… Anyway, you have to admit that the seances are more fun this way!'

'Fun? Evocation of the dead?'

'Why not?'

'For heaven's sake, woman!' Odilon explained, seizing his wife by the shoulders, 'You're possessed! This isn't the Apolline I love, the Apolline I married! The American woman has turned your head!'

'I'm tired, Odilon… Five years of chairing the group have drained the strength from me. Salome came along at just the right time to take over.'

If the Parisian's insistence had any effect it was to weaken the bond between the couple, which was closely identified with a shared belief in spiritualism. Once their ideas drifted apart, it seemed their bodies must do the same. The rings on their fingers, already worn furtively, now disappeared altogether. Apolline was the first to leave hers off and Odilon, not to be outdone, followed her example. Those who knew them anticipated an imminent separation.

With Armand, things were very different. His beloved belonged to the other world. Once a week, she performed for the pleasure of a circle of interested spectators, mostly men, in a smoke-filled cellar not wholly unlike a brothel.

These exchanges were extremely disagreeable so far as the engineer was concerned. He did not like them being public. Talking to Roseline in front of all those men made him feel he was parading his fiancée in front of a crowd of voyeurs. How was he to touch on certain very private subjects when he knew that everything they said would be minuted? Roseline herself clearly found this oppressive. Hence the impersonal tone she had adopted, addressing each person present – including him, her fiancé – as *vous*… She even called him 'Monsieur Boissier'!

After two months of this treatment, people lost sight of the fact that he and Roseline had been lovers, or rather, it was remembered that other spiritualists had enjoyed her favours. But when Armand's role as questioner was challenged, he defended it fiercely, as he would have guarded his wife against rivals. To such posthumous jealousy there was no remedy, other than consulting Roseline in the puerile manner of the suitor asking, 'Which of us do you prefer?' Armand's pride still found that option repugnant.

One evening, at his wits' end, the young man from St. Flour cornered Gordon Hole.

'Monsieur Hole, can we talk?'

The American bowed courteously and himself steered the engineer towards two chairs set a little apart.

'I have to speak to my fiancée, I mean, speak to her in private, as it were.'

'My dear friend, you do so already,' the American observed perfidiously. 'All the time, day and night, in the privacy of your heart!'

'This is something else. I need to converse with her spirit. I have certain very urgent questions I want to ask but I hesitate to put them during seances.'

'This desire for privacy is very natural. Alas, how are we to go about it? Roseline has never come to us outside our meetings.'

'Let's organise a private seance – Salome, yourself, her and me! What do you think?'

'Only Salome could answer that,' Hole said at first, ducking the issue.

Then, feeling he had tormented the engineer sufficiently, he consented.

'Why not? I'll have a word with her.'

Armand's face lit up like a child's at a firework display. 'He adores her!' the American realised, with a stab of envy.

'Thank you, Monsieur Hole, thank you! You've saved my life! When will our seance be?'

'A minor detail. We'll agree a date with Salome.'

Whereupon Gordon Hole touched the brim of his hat and left the room in the wake of other departing spiritualists.

Certain works of equilibrium are admirably long-lived: the small pebble supporting a huge boulder that rocks under one's hand, the menhir that against all probability stays upright for millennia while houses with the finest foundations collapse after a few hundred years.

So it was with Gordon Hole's plan. Highly dubious, heavily dependent on chance, seemingly at risk from innumerable unexpected factors, it nevertheless worked – almost to its creator's own surprise.

Four months had elapsed without placing a single serious obstacle in the way of its success. The police had not opened an inquest, Old Man Modesty had not exposed Hole's bribery and Apolline had not challenged Salome's gifts. Above all, no one from Roseline's circle had ever doubted the reality of her disappearance. 'That girl sure is alone in the world!' the American sometimes thought as he continued to collect the post from the actress's flat.

Even so, one person did create problems, the one who had been thought least likely to occasion any – Roseline herself!

Since the young woman had come round, Gaspard's life, and indirectly the American's, had been nothing short of purgatory. The mistake they had both made had been to assume that the actress was like other Parisians plying the same trade: flighty creatures who lived for dresses and bouquets and whose greatest ambition in life was to have a nice little apartment in which to grow old without wanting for anything. For such a person, being a prisoner was indeed a tolerable fate. Many a girl spent her life as a recluse, barred from going out by a jealous husband – who did not always, like Gaspard, have access to a princely budget with which to cushion their whims.

However, Armand's fiancée was anything but a kept woman. More than presents, she needed people – ideally, an audience. The smell of the theatre, the atmosphere of the fashionable stalls and of first nights, these she missed most. What did she care for champagne, fine dinners and books with gilded edges? What every fibre of her being cried out for was to return to the world, to be reborn into that happy city that, once tasted, is never forgotten…

In her campaign to persuade Gaspard to let her go out, Roseline had tried everything. Four months is more than enough time for a woman to drive a man to distraction. The actress had deployed all her skills to display, by turns, authority, charm, love, esteem and madness; she had said 'I demand!' then 'I implore!' and finally 'I beseech!' Every nuance of human emotion had passed over her face in an extraordinary performance given for a single spectator inside a locked room, a performance that, in other circumstances, Gaspard would have applauded warmly.

Many a time, indeed, the poor man had been on the point of giving in. It was not within his power to resist a beautiful woman murmuring through pursed lips, 'I love you, untie me!'

'All right!' Gaspard roared. 'I'll set you free!'

He went so far as to undo one or two knots.

But already the consequences of his actions loomed up in

his mind: prison, forced labour, possibly the scaffold. Or else, if he was lucky enough to escape the law, he would have to face the rage and hostility of Gordon Hole, a fate almost worse…

'I shan't tell on you, I promise!' Roseline pleaded, twisting about to loosen the rope.

The well-honed blade of the guillotine sounded its dull thud in Gaspard's ear and the old man, yanked back to his senses, retied the knots and refastened the gag. His lips babbled, 'sorry, sorry,' over and over again, to which the actress did her best to respond with volleys of swearing.

These painful scenes occurred mostly during the day, when Hole was not there. When the American came to call on his associate, which was usually on a weekday evening, Roseline maintained a haughty silence, turning her head away or feigning sleep.

The young woman made it a point of honour to ignore the architect's questions. He needed stories to keep the spiritualist seances going. However, he was a gentleman, despite everything, and he could not find it in him to punish such stubbornness.

'Yes, you have the best part!' Hole observed, slightly bitter. 'For your average theatre audience, the scene would not be hard to read. Here is the evil monster, holding an innocent victim prisoner; there is the virtuous damsel, suffering a thousand ills from her capture. How straightforward! But life is not theatre. If you knew the cause to which I have dedicated myself, the injustice I am fighting, then you might look on me differently!'

Roseline said nothing. Hole shrugged and went into the kitchen, where Gaspard was waiting for him.

A troubled mood had come over the American since the

departure of winter. In terms of his stratagem, it was not unlike the emotions that afflict the architect as his building nears completion: everything has gone well so far but...a storm, a labour dispute – anything might happen, demolishing the work of a year in a couple of hours.

To start with, Roseline's imprisonment could not be prolonged indefinitely. One day it must end. But how? Death, once again, seemed an attractive solution. A gunshot or two or a spoonful of poison was all it would take. Roseline's tie to life was already so tenuous; vanished, buried, she would be quickly forgotten...

And then, Gordon Hole's faith in his associate was declining daily. Leaving the actress in the keeping of an ageing man undermined by drink and drugs would inevitably give rise to problems. She would make short work of poor Gaspard if he began drinking again! Well, the American had already found several empty bottles under Roseline's bed and some of them bore the unmistakable smell of absinthe...

Meditating thus, Hole nourished his own unease. He needed an antidote to such pessimism, a confidence booster. The architect had been delighted to learn that Armand wanted a private seance, with just the three of them.

'It's the chance I'd been waiting for!' he confided to Gaspard. 'Those public gatherings, don't you see, hardly suited our purpose. Fifteen spiritualists listening to Salome were fifteen witnesses against us if things went wrong. Now we'll have Armand to ourselves. What a godsend! I'm telling you, in less than three months the Tower will just be a pile of junk messing up the Champ-de-Mars! Victory will be ours at last!'

Gaspard's vision did not reach that far. He brought the discussion back to a more pressing point.

'Sir, I'd like to change my job. Guarding a prisoner means

being shut up with them. And guarding Roseline has become more than I can stand! I can't go out for a loaf of bread without being afraid she'll play some mean trick. The other day I found her banging her head against the wall to alert the neighbours! Then the following day she was quoting me some law from 1878 that fixes the minimum volume of air in a room at 14 square metres. "This room isn't big enough!" she shouted. "I'm suffocating in here!" Can you tell me, sir, how an actress knows all about building regulations?'

'I expect she made it up... You'd believe anything!'

'Well, I've had enough, sir. I'd like to be relieved, if you don't mind.'

The American spread his hands, palms upward.

'How I wish I could meet your request, my dear Gaspard! Alas, who would I get to replace you? You're the only person I can trust. You're loyal, faithful, devoted... Couldn't you hang on for a couple of months? Give me time to carry out my plan? Then, I promise you, you'll have your freedom back.'

The Frenchman had served this master long enough to know that an uncompromising refusal underlay the diplomatic words. He did not insist, but went on as before.

On April 8th 1888, shortly before supper, there came an importunate knock at Jules Boissier's door.

At the time, the engineer was tracing the curve of a hyperbola, a delicate task if ever there was one, and the sudden loud noise caused his wrist to jerk. This in turn made the old man's pencil leap across the paper, spoiling a perfectly good drawing with a line that had no place in it and that – worse still – ended, so sharp was the point, by disappearing through the paper.

Jules hated visitors. They always came at the wrong moment,

just when he had a pen in his hand, an idea in his head and was about to solve a difficult problem. It was as if they did it deliberately. Uncle Jules would, at a pinch, have permitted a knock on his door for a good reason; from an esteemed colleague, say, come to present him with the respects of the Academy of Sciences, or a manufacturer armed with an exclusive contract for him to sign. But no one of that sort ever ventured as far as his humble door. The spyhole revealed only the same dreadful faces, over and over again, the postman bringing bills, the neighbours with their carriage. Damn and blast it!

In such a mood, Jules was in the habit of opening the door sharply, almost wrenching it open. The resultant sudden draught whipped the importunate caller's hat off – except for ladies, of course, whose hats were pinned on – which usually helped to speed their departure.

The old man was true to his habit that day. Imagine his discomfort at finding that the man standing on the threshold was his much-loved brother Hippolyte!

'A thousand pardons!' Jules gulped, hurriedly picking up his visitor's hat.

'Good Lord! What's bitten you?'

'I'm so sorry!' the engineer kept on saying. 'A mistake… I took you for a creditor.'

'Are you in debt, then, that you greet creditors in this way? Our mother was quite right to call you her "little dreamer"!'

'And you her "problem youngest"! Did you have a good journey?'

Hippolyte puffed out his already chubby cheeks.

'An exhausting day. Paris is a crazy city. Just now, in the street, I saw a wagon loaded with trees!'

'Those will have been plane trees for the Universal Exposition.'

'Whatever. Lead me to an armchair and serve me a beer! My legs are killing me!'

It was while helping his brother off with his coat that Jules noticed the blackened buttons. The scarf, too, was grey with smoke. Even Hippolyte's beard, now he came to examine it, seemed shorter by a third and had strange curly bits.

'What's happened to you?' Jules enquired. 'Have the volcanoes of the Auvergne begun erupting again?'

'You won't believe this! Do you know, St. Lazare Station went up in flames today? My train was just coming in when it caught fire. We were very nearly burned alive! Wooden compartments – you can imagine! In the end, though, the fire crews smashed the windows and I managed to get out!'

'St. Lazare Station? But that's not where you get off, coming from St. Flour…'

Hippolyte scratched his head, dislodging a small snowfall of ashes.

'Is it not? Oh well, I must have got the changes wrong! Trains and I have not always hit it off too well.'

'Dear old Hippolyte! Only my brother could fall into such an adventure! Even as a child you used to scrape the skin off your knees chasing coaches! And what about those times working on site? Whenever a stretcher or an ambulance went past, you knew without fail, it was for Boissier the carpenter! Always his arm in a sling or a crutch in his armpit! Ah, I'm glad I chose engineering as a career!'

Hippolyte blew into his gloves to get rid of the soot.

'Well, let's talk about engineers! You have a good life, I grant you, but what about the worry for everyone else! Armand hasn't sent word for six months…'

'Is it him you've come for?' Jules asked, rather more coolly. Brother Hippolyte placed his hands on his knees, fists closed in the manner of a workman unwinding. His vigorous movements and stocky frame recalled something of the heavy work he had once endured. He was the sort of man who, when he shakes you by the hand, you are half-afraid will crush it. But this tough shell hid a sensitive, almost timorous soul. In particular, Hippolyte was incapable of telling a lie, so he replied truthfully.

'I've come for Armand, yes! It's a father's duty. He doesn't write any more. I don't know how many letters he's failed to answer – ever since the autumn! Enough to heat your stove all winter through!'

'That's just what they did do.' Uncle Jules put in fiercely. 'Armand never opened them. He said he hadn't time.'

Hippolyte made a gesture of resigned impotence.

'He's turning his mother's hair grey! She said to me: if you don't go, I will! A woman of Bertille's age, lost in Paris. Can you imagine it? So I bought a ticket…'

'How long are you staying?'

'A couple of days, maybe three. Long enough to give Armand a piece of my mind before I jump on a train home. If they're still running, that is!'

As an old bachelor, Jules understood nothing of fatherhood. This was his brother, but it was with a poor grace that he served supper to a man who had come for someone else. The place was laid carelessly, the stew was lukewarm. Not that this mattered to the carpenter, who was concerned only about his son. He asked question after question, with Jules replying between mouthfuls. Hippolyte heard about the life Armand had led since coming up to Paris: his recruitment and promotion by Établissements Eiffel, his affair with Roseline, the actress's suicide and the young man's recent infatuation with spiritualism.

'Spiritualism?' Hippolyte picked up with difficulty. 'What's that?'

'I'm not too sure. Armand doesn't confide in me much. I think it's something to do with calling up the dead.'

'Calling up the dead?' echoed the carpenter, who had little time for this new language. 'That's a fine thing for a young man to be doing! It's the way old women pass the time, isn't it, nattering about their late husbands?'

Jules explained what he understood by evoking the spirits of the deceased, at which Hippolyte expressed complete amazement.

'What a weird idea! At his age I cared as much about the departed as about stuff between my teeth! And if my girlfriend had popped her clogs. I'd have taken another one! What are young folk coming to?'

Then, adopting the prying tones of the merely curious:

'And what's this "calling up"? How do they do that? Do they use a telephone, that strange contraption you have in your house?'

'No… He meets friends and they close their eyes and recite prayers. All winter, the meetings took place once a week, but now it's every day! Armand's going to another group, where he's the only one that talks.'

'Talks? What do you mean – to dead people?' Hippolyte guffawed. He took none of this seriously.

'He talks to Roseline and Roseline answers him. I know it seems funny to you, I had a good laugh myself, but your son is very clued up! These chats beyond the grave, he believes in them as much as in a face-to-face encounter – trembling beforehand, whistling afterwards… You'll see how he starts pacing the room when it's nearly time to go out!'

'And what do they say to each other?'

'There's no way of knowing. If you want my opinion: nonsense and sweet nothings. As one does at the age of twenty...'

'Pah!' Hippolyte concluded, 'I don't see much wrong in that. Armand is in love with a ghost. That won't kill him. It's better than the booze, which is the road most lads of his age go down. That reminds me, I seem to recall a rather good liqueur that granddad left you in his will. A liqueur so potent, he used to say, that "Napoleon could have lit his cannon with it"! Do you have any of that? The thing is, the fire has left me with a terrible thirst. I could drink a pond dry!'

While the Boissier brothers were catching up over grandfather's liqueur, two friends were out walking the streets, looking for somewhere to eat.

Odilon knew of a place in the neighbourhood but Armand was feeling more adventurous, he wanted a cheap eating-place out at the barricades.

'You want to eat in one of those? Under a rickety wooden roof, where you'll fork up as many lice as potato peelings? Are you out of your mind?'

'Odilon, this is a blessed day in my life! Your bourgeois will choose to dine out at one of those swanky places, with the champagne flowing. I'd rather sit down with the poor.'

'What sort of sense is that supposed to make?' the Parisian wondered.

As they left the good districts behind them, the streets underwent a rapid and alarming transformation. Hardly had they left the boulevards when the handsome signboards and brightly-lit windows disappeared. Before long they were in the suburbs where the last trappings of prosperity fell away. Tiles were missing from roofs, panes of glass from windows, crumbling stucco fell from balconies... Not wretchedness yet, but certainly indigence was written all over those roughly-plastered, squat, warped hovels whose leaking gutters dripped perpetual tears. A number set on the wall between closed shutters, adorned certain façades.

'Licenced brothels.' Odilon remarked. 'You won't find a church nearer than 10 metres. That's the rule laid down by the police!'

There was little lighting here on the outskirts of Paris. Inside the poor buildings the lights were out to save tallow. Outside, the street lighting provided by the municipality was not working properly. Every other jet no longer emitted gas, either because it was out of order or because prowlers had stopped it up, darkness affording cover for their crimes. One walked in darkness or in a dim greenish glow, and one hurried to reach the next lamppost in the shortest possible time.

After walking for an hour the twins came to a sinister-looking quarter that Odilon refused to enter.

'That's it! I'm not going a step further! What is this place? One of the anterooms of hell?'

'It's called "California"! Or, if you prefer, "Montparnasse Gate". We've reached our destination. What say you to supper at the *Azart de la Fourchaite*?'

Armand pointed to a wooden shack on a piece of open ground, at the point where two streams met. Foul-smelling vapours poured from every gap in the planking. The place must be a steamroom inside.

'What's on the menu?' the Parisian enquired ironically.

'That depends… In the cheapest option, you help yourself just once from a pot of boiling water in which various titbits are cooking: hambones, carp spines, mussel shells, cats' heads, horses' hooves, rabbits' tails and such like. For this delicate dish, you get a tablecloth to match – i.e. a sheet of newspaper.

Shall we go in?'

'The gamble doesn't tempt me.'

'If you'd rather, the house menu includes various set dishes. Still for the same price, you can have a plate of beans with oil, a slice of rotting cheese…'

'I'm off, Armand! Just smelling that smoke makes me retch! You're welcome to it!'

Odilon turned on his heel, but Armand stopped him with a gentle trip.

'Have you forgotten? Last year you took me all over Paris – including to the morgue! Now it's my turn to be your guide! This address is recommended in Privat d'Anglemont's *Unknown Paris*, the bible of explorers in this city! Trust me!'

The Parisian gave his friend a look of amusement. Together, taking a deep breath, they pushed open the door of the *Azart de la Fourchaite*.

One is suspicious on finding a good restaurant empty but if it is a greasy spoon one likes it the more. By the time the two engineers arrived, the regular clientele had already eaten. Only one table was occupied, by two fellows in caps who held beers in their hands in an oddly symmetrical composition reminiscent of a card game.

Armand and Odilon ordered at random and were required to pay in advance. The dish was placed on the table, where neither of them touched it. It was enough to have come in, there was no point in risking an upset tummy as well!

'All right!' Odilon began, brushing a cockroach from the edge of his plate. 'Are you finally going to tell me what's put you in such a good mood?'

'Roseline loves me.'

Odilon put his hands together in prayer. Armand motioned to him to wait as the best was yet to come.

'You're aware, possibly, that I've been skipping the seances at the morgue? I found it a strain – evoking Roseline in front of all those people. It was like having witnesses at our most intimate moments. I told Gordon Hole how I felt. He agreed to organise private seances at which Salome would call up Roseline just for me. We met and since then my life has been transformed!'

Contentment comes out differently in each individual. There are those whose faces it causes to expand, quite soon tracing wrinkles of optimism around the eyes. In others, the sense of satisfaction remains internal, concealed – a nectar savoured unobserved.

Armand belonged to the second category. The only outward sign of his joy was a little Mona Lisa smile, with perhaps an absent-minded whistling, a drumming of fingernails on the table or some other harmless diversion. That evening, his battered fork tapped out against his wineglass a figure he had learned in the army.

'So Hole came up trumps so far as you are concerned?' Odilon asked, to prime the pump, as it were.

'What a charming man! Have you noticed how he slips away at the end of seances? I see that as a mark of exquisite tact: he keeps his grief hidden for fear of imposing it on us. Such discretion on the part of a father who has lost his daughter!'

Odilon's equally battered knife joined his friend's fork in its tapping against the glass. The two implements began to beat in time.

'I don't know Monsieur Hole. We've hardly exchanged...'

'He's a brilliant architect, responsible for an enormously tall apartment building in Chicago. That building includes innovations of which he's extremely proud. Most notably, a system of rubbish chutes that enables each resident to empty his or her rubbish without stepping outside. Our rubbish bins seem to him very old-fashioned by comparison.'

'You discussed the subject?'

'At length! Rubbish is his hobby-horse! You can't get him off the subject, once he's started!'

Odilon let out a guffaw, making his knife knock even more loudly against the rim of the glass.

'Well, let's not do the same! What news of your fiancée? Have your private conversations changed her in any way?'

'You can't imagine! She's quite different. As different as a young lady can be as between the way she is with her parents and the way she is with her lover. The seances at the morgue terrified her, it was like appearing before a court! Whereas with only the four of us Roseline really lets her hair down. She comes across as sweet and considerate, the way we knew her. Apparently, the idea came from her; she passed it on to me in my sleep. I didn't know spirits could do that – influence our decisions!'

'Now you really are a convinced spiritualist!' the Parisian remarked, the blade of his knife executing a dry roll against the glass.

'I've Salome to thank for that! Before I heard Roseline speaking through her, I didn't have much faith in spirits at all. Love certainly works wonders!'

Just then, the man who did the cooking appeared at the two friends' table.

'You want something?'

'I'm sorry?' said Armand, drawing away from a large ladle that was dripping onto the table beside him.

'You're tapping fit to burst a bloke's eardrums. I assume you want some grub.'

'No, no, my friend, not at all… We were doing it without thinking. Forgive us for disturbing you!'

'I came, didn't I? So it'll cost you!' the man roared, pointing his dripping ladle at Armand.

Odilon took out a coin and tossed it to the man. Satisfied, the latter went back to his stove, that is to say, he pushed past a barrel that marked the frontier between kitchen and restaurant.

The Parisian took advantage of this diversion to steer the conversation elsewhere.

'Funny place, this, don't you reckon? You'd think it was the sort of place where you could make yourself at home, but lo and behold, no tapping on glasses! In a year, this'll be like the best cafés in Paris: dominoes forbidden, pipe-smokers banned, whispering compulsory… Everywhere has its rules. And the Eiffel offices are no exception!'

The clumsy link aroused Armand's suspicions.

'What's Eiffel got to do with dominoes? Tell me that!'

Odilon decided on the direct approach.

'Look, one of the duties of friendship is to be frank. At the office, there are rumours doing the rounds – rumours about you. If they've reached the boss's ears, I don't give much for your engineer's grading. It'll be back to the eraser for you, my friend!'

Armand's insouciance collapsed like badly erected scaffolding.

'What…what rumours are you talking about?'

'You haven't been the same since Roseline died – that much is obvious! Where we used to talk about the Tower, now we talk about your fiancée.'

'Is it a crime to be in love?'

'Armand, be reasonable! A boss is paying you to help build

the Tower, he's even made you part of the delicate task of designing the elevators, that's how much faith he has in you! And what do you do with this splendid position? You squander it! For weeks now files have been piling up on your desk, gathering dust. You're late every day. In fact, many days you're not there at all! Monsieur Backmann is starting to mistrust your calculations, which are often approximate, your drawings need revising...'

'Stop! That's enough!' said Armand through gritted teeth.

But the Parisian was merciless. He went on implacably:

'It's been worse since these private seances started. You leave the office at four o'clock in the afternoon! We've all seen you! Monsieur Pluot doesn't know how to punish you any more, because if he levied all the fines you've incurred your whole salary would disappear.'

'But I'm a widower!' the engineer pleaded vehemently. 'A widower in full mourning! For another six months yet!'

'Roseline and you were not married...'

'We soon will be!'

At which Armand took out a little box, which he presented to his companion. Inside, two greyish rings nestled on a velvet cushion. This ghoulish charade made Odilon feel sick.

'What's that metal? Iron?'

'This is no ordinary iron, it comes from my blood! I had a chemist extract twenty litres of it to make a little ingot of metal from which these two rings were forged...'

'You're mad!' the Parisian exclaimed in horror. 'You're completely insane!'

Then, controlling himself, he continued:

'Armand, you've mourned long enough. It's time you returned to reality! I beg of you: destroy these rings, take off that crepe armband!'

Odilon's lunge to rip off the strip of material was intercepted.

'Stop right there!' Armand cried. 'That I'm keeping!'

Then, with his hand still clamped around the Parisian's wrist:

'Have you gone crazy, losing your temper like this? Is this going to end in fisticuffs, like just now in the street? All right, I have been neglecting my work a bit. Roseline takes up all my thoughts. It's as if one dead woman matters more to me than all the living. And whose fault is that? Who initiated me into spiritualism? Who dragged me along to seances?'

It was true, what he said, but still… Sullenly, Odilon slumped back in his chair.

'I didn't realise people were talking about me,' Armand continued. 'That bothers me. I don't want to lose my position!'

'In the winter, though, you were thinking of giving notice!'

'Now it's different. Roseline has entrusted me with a…mission. To perform it properly, I need to keep my job at Établissements Eiffel.'

'What mission?' the Parisian enquired ironically. 'Toppling the Tower?'

Armand gave him a sharp look.

'A mission – that's all. Thank you for the warning. I'll be more careful from now on.'

The engineer, wishing to bring the conversation to an end, stood up. But Odilon had not said all that he had to say. Sitting squarely on his chair, he addressed his friend curtly.

'I know nothing of your plans, but rest assured, I won't let you destroy the Tower! You'll find me constantly on your tail!'

The young man from St. Flour received this declaration of hostilities in sober silence. The engineers left the restaurant and set off back to the city, still not talking.

Back in the restaurant, the two men in caps still sat at their table while the proprietor stood yawning behind his pots.

'Time to think about going!' the latter remarked, having concluded there was no more money to be made that night.

One of the men – the younger of the two – said to his companion:

'It's a funny thing about the rich… They rabbit on about their womenfolk while we, some days, don't get enough to eat!'

The other man rolled an exhausted quid of tobacco around his mouth before spitting it, vigorously, straight at a passing rat.

'I recognise 'em, those two. Work over Levallois way. Remember when that American paid us to do that job? I saw them in the crowd. Jacket, cravat, the lot… Couple of swells, aren't they?'

The proprietor, who did not like saying things twice, picked up a sizeable bone in his fist and advanced towards their table.

'All right, we're off!' said the older man, pulling his cap down over a cauliflower ear.

Silence returned to California.

11

Returning late that night, Armand went to bed without knowing there was another visitor under his uncle's roof. Moreover, he had decided to get up early, and father and son missed each other again next morning. Hippolyte taking this coincidence as a snub, was aggrieved.

'You know, I get the definite feeling he's annoyed with me,' the carpenter sighed, spotting his son's still-steaming bowl on the breakfast table. 'What do you think – maybe it would be best if I went away? You've given me news of him, that's what matters. I don't want to be a burden on his account.'

Jules had no idea how to reassure his brother. The result was that Hippolyte repacked his things, still creased from the suitcase, and left the house by noon to catch a train home.

But it's an ill wind... Armand's early start and consequent punctuality delighted Monsieur Backmann, who had never seen the engineer arrive at work so early.

'Congratulations, young man! You've clearly turned over a new leaf! Hang on to this healthy habit, bring some discipline to your work and we'll make a success of the task Monsieur

Salles has set us.'

'I will, sir, I promise. I'll work hard from now on.'

And he was as good as his word. The talent and enthusiasm that had marked out the eraser twins were reborn in Armand. He plunged himself into the question of the elevators and became passionately involved in the major and often unprecedented problems with which it appeared riddled. Since he and Odilon hardly spoke any more, it was with Monsieur Backmann that he discussed the subject, all day long and even during the lunch break.

'As I understand it,' he summarised with an air of great competence, 'the vertical transport of visitors raises a number of difficulties: first of all the height of the Tower, which is very much greater than that of an ordinary building; then sheer numbers, as there will be thousands of visitors each day; and last but by no means least, the variable angle of the piers.'

'Plus,' Monsieur Backmann put in, 'the need to provide stops at the first and second levels in case visitors wish to redescend!'

'What solutions are envisaged?'

'None is completely satisfactory. Elevator technology is in its infancy and the companies that manufacture them have not had a great deal of experience. We've had steam winches for thirty years, but they can go no higher than forty or so metres because of the size of the drums onto which the cables wind. We also have screw and travelling-nut systems available, but they also present difficulties. They're slow and again there's a height limitation. And lastly there are elevators that use a plunger piston. The trouble there is the length of the piston. In the case of the Tower, we'd have to dig a pit 67 metres deep!'

'What do you think of the American method?'

Monsieur Backmann gave an indulgent smile.

'It's interesting, certainly. Nevertheless, such an arrangement is out of the question for the Tower and that is for two reasons. The first is that having the cabin suspended is risky. In France, we consider it safer to push elevators up from below. The second is the contractual obligation imposed on Monsieur Eiffel to use national suppliers. If we backed the American Elevator Company bid, the Exposition committee would be bound to block it.'

'I see,' Armand said resignedly. 'In that case, there's no way out!'

'That's where you're wrong, my young friend! I shall shortly be presenting a mechanism of my own devising in which two cabins move along a helical axis. The energy is supplied by electricity and each elevator has its own power source, it's revolutionary! I have no doubt that the committee will give its backing to so innovative a project.'

But Monsieur Backmann's system was deemed too complex and was rejected in June 1888. Armand and his colleague had to go back to the drawing-board...

Odilon took a harsh view of Armand's new commitment to his job.

His friend's return to favour with the senior staff struck him as precipitate, if not undeserved. Had not the young man from St. Flour virtually absented himself from work for the space of four months? Had not the design of the elevators been held back in consequence? Odilon felt fed up. Was that all that was needed – one or two good marks – to wipe out the memory of pages of poor results?

Many a time, through rancour and sheer malice, the Parisian was tempted to denounce Armand's plans regarding the Tower. 'I'll go and see Eiffel – it's my duty,' Odilon told himself, not unaware of his real, secret motive. Yet common sense counselled him to do nothing. For one thing he could adduce no proof of his allegations, and besides, the threat was still vague, as his indictment must also seem.

Basically, Odilon was in a quandary. He remained the model employee he had always been and continued to be respected by his superiors but inside a spring had broken. He in turn lost enthusiasm for his work.

The exciting discussions that took place between Armand and Monsieur Backmann had no equivalent between Odilon and those who worked with him. The question of the Tower's electrics, which he had found fascinating at first because of its mystical dimension, concerned him less and less. What did the secret properties of the structure matter to him now, when he was about to leave the spiritualist group? What was the point of continuing to support Apolline's ideas when he no longer loved her?

Monsieur Salles, who unobtrusively subscribed to matters occult, continued to push the group's plans, notably by accommodating a room where seances could be held within the foundations of the north pier. Each time Eiffel had to make a decision here, Salles used his influence to obtain the constructor's consent.

'But look here – why do we have this room in the hoof of Pier 1?' Eiffel asked once, amazed. 'And this staircase at water level? There's no justification for them whatsoever!'

Adolphe Salles disagreed stoutly.

'The room serves a definite purpose! It will house spare cables and other equipment for the elevators.'

'Does it need to be so large?'

'Probably. The cabins will be operating for the first time so there will inevitably be breakdowns and accidents. We'll have to have large numbers of spares available.'

'But this staircase coming out by the Seine, that will be very awkward, surely, when the river floods?'

'That will enable equipment to be brought by barge without disturbing the running of the Tower.'

Eiffel thought for a moment. Regarding overall solutions, he always had the final say, but so far as particular solutions and details were concerned he was happy to rely on his staff. That was what he did now, informing Salles:

'Do as you think fit! But don't forget: that where you're planning to put the room is right next to where the lightning conductor is earthed. Are you not concerned about the equipment stored in it if there's a storm?'

'The problem has been looked into,' Salles countered. 'The location of the room involves no risk at all.'

That same day, he secretly consulted Odilon, telling him of Eiffel's objection.

'You're quite right, there's no risk at all! Not for the spiritualists in the room nor for visitors to the structure. The system is extremely safe. Think about it: at the very top of the Tower, surmounting the spire, there's one lightning conductor with copper tips; there are eight others of the same design fixed to the balcony of the third platform and down at the bottom you have twenty-metre-long cast-iron pipes sunk in the ground. This arrangement guarantees that atmospheric electricity will be lost in its entirety. It protects not only the Tower itself but also a large area around it.'

Adolphe Salles continued to frown.

'That's not what the Americans say! They insist that the Tower, by altering the electrical conditions of Paris, will actually promote storms. As for our French opponents, they advocate installing alarms for the rapid evacuation of visitors in case of lightning!'

'Yes, I read that somewhere,' Odilon smiled. 'It's also been claimed that the Tower threatens to electrocute the fish in the Seine! Such assertions are quite unfounded. They prove only one thing: the puerile envy of all who gainsay us!'

'And if lightning struck anyway?'

'If lightning were to discharge itself through the lightning conductor, there might be some projection of molten metal, just a few drops, on the upper terrace. The Tower would probably reverberate like a huge tuning-fork for four or five seconds. That's all, and visitors would be in no danger.'

These confident words reassured Adolphe Salles.

'Forgive my anxiety. I'm concerned about your spiritualist friends. I'd hate to have to remove charred bodies from the room under the north pier!'

'It won't happen. The earthing arrangement is no threat to anyone. On the contrary, I hope it will create especially favourable conditions for what we are trying to achieve. As you know, spirits have affinities with electrical energy. So just imagine what a crowd of them might arrive in the wake of a bolt of lightning! It may be that we shall witness things never seen before, never dreamed-of before…'

'How I envy you, pushing back the boundaries of knowledge like this. Beside such a noble, innovative achievement, engineering work seems very routine to me, uninteresting, almost. Have I perhaps missed my vocation? Ah, Monsieur Cheyne, my dearest wish – I don't mind telling you – would be to attend one of your seances one day…'

'But why not?' the Parisian offered encouragingly. 'I'll tell Mademoiselle Séraphin. Outside listeners are not often admitted to our circle, but for you we'll make an exception!'

Such exchanges, on subjects that no longer held the least interest for him, put Odilon under very considerable strain.

He dared not confide in Adolphe Salles his growing detachment from the spiritualist group or how he was tempted to abandon the room under the north pier. Quite apart from the fact that he would have been placing his job at risk, the plan was too far advanced to be put into reverse now. Prudence recommended the opposite course: to let nothing show, to go on as before. That was what Odilon opted to do, under the mocking gaze of Armand, who could guess at the Parisian's state of mind.

Relations between the twins had worsened steadily since the evening at the restaurant.

They remained friends, that is to say, they exchanged non-committal handshakes, but mistrust had crept in between them, as frost will insinuate itself into a tree. Odilon kept an eye on Armand; Armand spied on Odilon. If occasionally they spoke, it was of harmless, unimportant matters, never of the subversive projects – sabotaging the Tower, planning the room under the north pier – they were working on without Eiffel's knowledge. Each looked harshly on the other, seeing him as a traitor, a plotter, without admitting his own crime.

The tension between them was at its greatest in the evening.

Then, the bulk of the staff having left the office, the twins were alone but embarrassingly in each other's way. These quiet times were ideal for combing drawers, unfurling plans, leafing through books and all things that the rules forbade but that furthered their purposes. Yet how was one to go about it with someone reading over one's shoulder?

'Aha!' Odilon scoffed on one of these occasions. 'The plan of the first storey! Is that where you mean to place your explosives?'

Armand retorted immediately:

'And what about the structural calculation on your desk? Are you afraid the north pier will collapse?'

Such sallies were designed to wound and they invariably did so. Odilon, for instance, set out his defence.

'The pier collapse? No chance! The Tower puts very little weight on the ground, just four kilograms per square centimetre. That's less than a wall 9 metres high and less than you – even with the weight you've put on! – on that chair with its very thin legs!'

Armand brushed the argument aside.

'If the Tower collapses and it's your fault, I promise I'll visit you in prison!'

'If it's blown up, you'll have my support when they guillotine you!'

Eventually, this sparring became unbearable. As a last vestige of their dying friendship, the twins concluded a non-aggression pact. They also moved into different offices at opposite ends of the building.

If relations between the eraser twins were not good, among the staff as a whole they were brilliant.

A spirit of healthy competition reigned at Établissements Eiffel, which found expression in fresh momentum throughout the site, seeming to boost construction of the Tower itself. The iron monster now had its own heart, a massive steam engine, kept fired up day and night to power the hoists, and prehensile hands, lofty cranes following the path where the third-storey elevators were to go and raising into place successive topmost members. The result was a clear increase in the progress of work. The average height gained per month, which had hovered around 10 metres in the early stages of construction, now stood at thirteen and it would shortly make a prodigious leap, reaching twenty-two. The Tower was not only growing; its growth was accelerating.

A splendid piece of news was soon brought to the engineers, following hard on the heels of the announcement that what was referred to as the '100 mark' – the first 100 metres – had been passed. The new announcement was that the second storey would shortly be completed.

'Then you'll see how beautiful my tower will be, with this further platform in place,' exulted Sauvestre, the architect. 'Before long the four piers will not just be linked but joined together to form one. A single shaft of steel will shoot upward along the axis, challenging the very sky and throwing down the gauntlet to the gods themselves!'

The second platform was reached just in time to celebrate France's national holiday on July 14th 1888.

A firework display from the Tower had been planned, something never seen before. Up until then the Tower had appeared bare and dark, save only for the showers of sparks given off by the steeplejacks' hammers at night. An austere simplicity, such was the impression given by this soaring iron member, clad in a web of finer metal. Through this one saw the bone and muscle, forming a sort of cutaway of an immense, upright cadaver, though not the skin that clothes it and gives it form.

Illuminated, it would all look different. The light sources emitted by the display would give body to the building. They would fill out its volumes and plug the many gaps and interstices with which the engineer, aiming to save weight and give less purchase to the wind, had riddled the steel structure.

A vast concourse of spectators had assembled when the display was announced: thousands of mayors, who had come together for a giant banquet on the Champ-de-Mars, the entire Eiffel staff and all the idle curious that Trocadero Hill could accommodate, jostling one another as they waited impatiently for the Tower to become a blaze of light.

From the moment when the first burst of crackling was heard, countless hearts started to pound in unison; most with excitement, some in terror at the sight of storms of illumination that recalled the recent war and the Prussian guns at the gates of Paris. There are disturbing similarities between the beauty occasionally manufactured by man's more murderous inventions and that produced by his least offensive creations.

Flashes of brightness – at once glorious and impetuous – spurted from every point: Roman candles on the second platform, rockets ascending from the corners of the structure, tricoloured fountains, exploding saucissons... So great was the heat given off that the metal of the Tower became burning to the touch. In fact, the pyrotechnists were astonished at how much the Tower heated up. It was behaving like a body when the blood starts to circulate: the skin takes on colour, the lips pulse – the whole being comes alive.

As members of the engineering team, the eraser twins enjoyed a choice position near the front. Odilon clapped enthusiastically, but Armand was oddly subdued, hardly looking and showing even less appreciation.

At one point, the Parisian became aware that his friend was no longer at his side. 'Good riddance!' was his reaction. 'He was spoiling the atmosphere with his long face!' After the display, Odilon went over to join Salles, who was drinking champagne with other members of the Eiffel staff.

Armand was walking towards the Tower with a large package under his arm.

He had started off briskly, then slowed down, thinking that a natural gait would draw less attention. Twice already one of the burly blacksmiths guarding the approaches to the Tower had accosted him.

'Sir, that way is out of bounds!'

The first, recognising him, had mumbled a confused apology. To the second he had identified himself. Both had let him pass without causing difficulties.

'How easy this is!' thought Armand delightedly as he neared the barrier around the north pier.

Here a third guard had been posted. He was an imposing fellow, whose triangular upper body stretched the woollen he was wearing; in fact, it was unravelling at the shoulders. Beneath the leather peak of his cap a badly rolled cigarette burned intermittently, a puff of smoke being followed by a feeble glow that the firework display put to shame.

He spotted Armand's frock-coat a long way off, noticing also the polished shoes that stepped carefully round the puddles. Who was this smartly dressed gentleman heading straight towards him? What if he was one of the senior staff, even Eiffel himself, whom he had never met? Unwilling to risk blotting his copybook, so to speak, the workman opened the barrier and stood aside.

That this obstacle fell of its own accord rather annoyed the engineer. What, after all, was his exploit worth if no one put up any resistance? The young man from St. Flour consulted his watch and looked up at the sky, now streaked with orange lines. The grand finale was still some way off, apparently. Plenty of time to exchange a few words!

'Good evening!' Armand said with a sort of military salute involving three fingers held together and the thumb folded over.

The workman returned the courtesy.

'My name is Armand Boissier. I work for Établissements Eiffel at Levallois. I'm an engineer.'

The guard whipped off his cap.

'Monsieur Eiffel has asked me to investigate how hot the Tower is getting. Apparently, the fireworks are roasting the ironwork. Some members are even glowing red.'

Sweat had etched lines on the workman's brow but whether this was from emotion or because it was very warm, Armand could not tell.

'Would you like to search my bag,' he asked, moving to undo the straps. 'I've brought some measuring instruments...'

'Pass!' the workman said in a strangled voice, taking at least three steps back.

Saluting again, Armand squeezed through the gap. He was glad to have courted danger and survived. What if the guard had looked inside the bag? There would have been dire consequences, of that he was in no doubt.

In a matter of moments he had reached the huge block of masonry that formed a hoof under the northernmost pier – pier number one. He had chosen to begin his climb where he would be shielded from the gaze of the vast crowd of people assembled across the river on Trocadero Hill. The firework display, oriented for their benefit, left this place conveniently shady.

A kind of joyful lightness took possession of Armand at this crucial moment when he was truly moving into action. Criminals, they say, experience a similar euphoria, which temporarily removes every inhibition. His mind felt calm and his thinking clear. He was also aware of a tremendous agility of body, which would certainly be an asset in the task he was about to undertake.

He leapt onto the metal staircase that rose inside the iron limb. The Tower was already provided with means of access, which were installed progressively to make it easier for the workmen to climb up and down. Only the last few metres were not yet equipped with stairs, up there the steeplejacks moved about with the aid of ladders and wooden gangplanks.

It was dark inside the north pier, as dark as a factory chimney. Despite the occasional bursts of light cast by the fireworks as they threw false dawns over the Seine, the staircase remained in shadow and Armand climbed blind. It was like exploring a spider's web – one woven in multiple layers.

Armand made effortless progress, climbing with a smooth, regular movement. In his left hand he held the bag whilst his right followed the handrail. He remembered Gustave Eiffel's words of advice, 'Climb very slowly, holding the rail with arm outstretched, swinging your body from side to side to give extra momentum,' but he did the exact opposite, taking the steps two at a time and the landings at an athletic run.

The workmen took six minutes to reach the first platform. Armand improved on that time. Soon he had reached the point, above the first platform, where a spiral staircase took over from a straight one. This was where he had to leave the normal route and descend into the web of steel.

The engineer took stock of himself at this moment when his enterprise became perilous as well as illicit, but his pulse was still steady and his breathing normal. He threw a leg over the rail.

For a further 10 metres, Armand was able to follow a suspended platform of the kind riveters place under key members. After that, emptiness… From the yawning gulf beneath him, criss-crossed with metal spars as a crevasse is with fallen tree-trunks, there rose that special quality of vertigo that lines abysses. Paris, already far below, could be made out through the diamond web of spars. Seen from up here, the city had the stillness of a panorama.

His time was limited. Executing the series of movements he had rehearsed, Armand took from the bag a hat, a hollowed-out candle and some phosphor matches. Lighting the second with the aid of the third, he poured a few drops of wax to cement it to the first. This modest version of a miner's helmet shed a yellowish light to a distance of a few metres. It was sufficient to find one's way, if the environment was familiar. Moreover, this limited field of vision reduced one's fear of the void. The engineer congratulated himself on his invention.

Armand set out along a gently sloping beam that led in the right direction. Reaching the end, he risked stepping across onto another, narrower member, which he followed like a tightrope-walker, carefully placing one foot in front of the other. His equanimity in this potentially fatal situation continued to amaze him. Did he owe it to excessive optimism or was he already resigned to die? Again he listened to his heartbeat, which was calm and slow.

On his journey through the latticework of the Tower, Armand observed that it was already equipped to accommodate climbers. Some day these steel members were going to succumb to the threat of rust and would need to be replaced or repainted, for which purpose handholds, cables and manholes had been provided at points that would present difficulties. So Armand was not the only one to make this trip, he was simply one of the first. He found the thought encouraging.

He soon reached the place identified on the plans where four key structural elements met. Without giving himself a moment's respite, Armand took from the bag a bundle of red sticks, each with a fuse emerging from one end. Inside each stick was a powerful charge of gum dynamite, an explosive used in quarries to deal with particularly hard rocks. Getting hold of the stuff had been easy, the site stores had whole boxfuls of it, presumably for the labourers employed to dig the foundations.

The eight fuses were woven together into a single strand, which was wound round a large spool. Having fastened the sticks of dynamite to the structure, Armand began unrolling the strand by turning the cylinder. This was the riskiest part of the operation and constituted a real challenge. In effect, the whole trip with its dizzying climbs and leaps across empty space had to be repeated in reverse, holding the spool.

It took the young man three minutes to reach the stairs that would take him back to the first-storey platform – three minutes balancing on narrow steel bars, at the mercy of a sudden gust of wind or a false step. In them he lost all his self-possession, the pain that had been lurking in his muscles suddenly flared up. A large firework going off behind him tore a gasp of fear from his throat. He turned around and saw the sky filled with multi-coloured flares.

'The grand finale… I shan't have time!'

First wedging the end of the fuse under a brick, Armand ran towards the west pier to set the next charge. On the way he passed a number of pyrotechnists carrying demijohns filled with sand. He even saw two or three visitors, who preferred this elevated viewpoint to watching the spectacle from the ground. One corner of the platform appeared populous and busy so he wondered if perhaps there was a party going on there? In any case, no one took any notice of his scurrying figure, bent under the weight of a large bag, except for one smartly dressed gentleman who exclaimed:

'Ah, the pyrotechnists' runner, delivering the final rocket! He's late!'

The journey up the west pier was exactly the same as that up the north pier. In five minutes, Armand had made both trips and was tying the two wicks together.

'Now for the east pier! Hurry! Hurry!'

Placing the charge on the east pier was easy, thanks to the light cast by the firework display. However, the south pier presented an unexpected problem. This side of the Tower, where they were letting off the Roman candles, was wreathed in smoke and floating ash. There was a real risk of his losing his way or being blinded. Armand decided not to proceed.

'Too bad about the south pier! It'll be left standing!'

Instead, the fourth charge was laid in a position where it would back up the first, but closer to the staircase. As a result, the engineer predicted, the Tower would topple over towards the Seine and many lives would be saved.

The four fuses snaked away into the darkness, their ends gathered in Armand's hand. The other hand held a match.

'Don't hesitate! Do it! Now!'

He struck the phosphor match, which lit slowly and as it were reluctantly. His hand was black with escaping powder.

It was at that moment, as Armand was bringing the flame to the fuse-ends, that a strange light caught his attention. He looked up, dreading to see a lantern – and therefore a guard – approaching, and his eyes met the thing…

30 metres above him, in the upper reaches of the edifice, hung a luminous shape.

Anyone but Armand would have seen a tattered cloud of smoke, a chance concentration of fumes given off by the fireworks. Anyone else would then have looked away as from an irrelevant distraction. Did he not have far more urgent business? But the engineer not only went on looking, he actually locked onto this apparition in some very private and mysterious way.

The match burned right down until it seared his fingers. He hurled it from him as far away as he could and dropped the fuses he had been clutching.

The object was rectangular in shape, stretched out at the extremities. In paintings of the 'Last Judgement,' the figure of Christ in majesty is surrounded by a halo – sometimes called a mandorla – that is not dissimilar. This was the same bright and radiant substance, with the same nebulous outlines, in which the practised eye can make out casings enclosing one another, as inside an onion. Without the thing having a life of its own, the wind or possibly the friction of solid objects gave it a faint degree of movement. It was drifting slowly away from him towards the upper reaches of the Tower.

'A cloud, a wreath of smoke,' Armand told himself, though without conviction.

He wanted to look at the thing up close. But how was he to get at it where it floated above him? He glanced down at his equipment, the four fuses, the packet of matches, and threw a sack over it all.

'I'll come back!' he promised himself.

He sprinted towards the spiral staircase that led up to the second storey.

As he climbed, Armand kept his eyes on the shape through the meshes of the ironwork. Still remote, still unapproachable… It seemed to have that quality of distant objects like the sun or a chain of mountains, whereby the movements of the observer do not affect them; they present the same profile when viewed from every angle. Far from putting Armand off, this fresh mystery thrilled him further.

On the second platform, the pyrotechnists were moving along banks of skyrockets. This was the grand finale, an incredible deluge of fire and light.

'What a shame!' said the engineer with regret. 'I won't have produced the star turn!'

One of the pyrotechnists spotted him and made an ambivalent gesture that might have meant, 'Look out! It's dangerous here!' or equally, 'How did you get up here? Who let you through?'

The young man from St. Flour took no notice. He was looking for a way to reach the summit. When wooden ladders took over from the metal staircase, Armand continued his ascent without pausing. Up and up he climbed, using planks and pieces of frail scaffolding.

There came a time when his head broke through a pall of smoke and he saw nothing but sky above him. He had reached the very topmost point of the Tower...Above him now there was only the star-studded firmament. The drifts of smoke from which he had just emerged glowed red and blue as fireworks burst and burned beneath him.

His gaze focused greedily on the thing, there it was, floating in thin air. Part of the night sky appeared through it, dull and indistinct. It might have been a bride's veil, caught up by the wind to dance unwitnessed in the upper atmosphere.

Armand selected a comfortable plank and sat down. Now that he was reunited with the thing, a feeling of well-being spread through him – the restful ease that follows exertion. The cloud from which it came filtered out all his evil thoughts and all his fears. Above was the peace of the firmament, eternally undisturbed. How well he felt! Why go down again?

The young man from St. Flour gazed steadily at the shape. If it shifted to the east or to the west, his head bent in the same direction; if it rose, he leapt to his feet, suddenly anxious at the thought of losing it, but each time the shape returned, as faithful to its patch of sky as a pair of scales is to the point of balance.

Time went by...minutes that seemed to him like hours. Then, quite clearly, the thing began moving closer... Armand closed his eyes, rubbed them, then opened them again. Beyond any doubt, the thing was coming towards him.

As it came, the shape seemed to weaken, losing brightness and body. At the half-way point, only a pale medallion remained, a wisp of vapour shredded by the wind. Then that too disappeared. Where the shape had been, now there was only a trace, a last disc of vapour that was soon gone completely.

At that moment, it seemed to the young man that the restless breeze modelled a face, a human countenance, smiling at him. The phantom face met and joined itself to his own in a long-drawn-out kiss.

'Roseline!' breathed the engineer at the touch of her soft, warm lips.

An incredible feeling of sexual pleasure came over him. He was aware of it streaming out between his thighs. His arms closed on nothingness, which he hugged as if it had been flesh.

A moment later, Armand let go. They found him asleep, balanced on a plank of wood, right at the top of the Tower.

THE THIRD STOREY

12

Once the riddle of Salome the ventriloquist had been solved, the Hôtel Britannique staff looked for something fresh to satisfy its need for intrigue. Which customer presented the strangest profile? Which had the oddest whims and excesses?

They consulted the hotel register. The candidates lacked a certain consistency. A sea-lion trainer occupied the nuptial suite, together with his animals, whose toilet requirements called for five saltwater baths daily and whose diet consisted of thirty baskets of fresh sardines. There was also a Red Indian, in Paris on an official visit, who had set light to his room by building a bonfire of table-legs in the middle of the carpet...

However, these cases only seemed to be original. Scratching the surface revealed quite ordinary personalities leading conventional lives – nothing like sufficient to hold the interest of the hotel staff.

It was at that point that an elevator-boy brought up the name Gordon Hole, the American customer on the second floor.

'A character – no question about it!' the elevator-boy continued, arguing his case. 'Suspicious, morose, never tips and would sooner use the stairs than the elevators... He also has a revolver, which he keeps feeling for in his pocket. According to a prostitute who goes in there, he and his sidekick – a fat Frenchman – are both queer. They certainly make a curious couple, you can take it from me!'

The motion was put to the vote and won a comfortable majority. The silver teapot that they used as a ballot-box – a precious bequest from Monsieur Baxter, who had founded the hotel in 1861 – was found to contain twenty 'for' votes and only three 'against'. The member of staff who acted as scrutineer pronounced the surveillance campaign against Gordon Hole open.

As for the method, investigations conducted at the Hôtel Britannique were modelled on police procedure.

The first step was to open a file which in reality meant assembling a pile of papers higgledy-piggledy, including documents, witness statements and records of various indiscretions committed by the suspect. This task was assigned to the establishment's accounts clerk, who was known for his attention to detail as much as his taste for irreverence. He summoned each member of staff to the laundryroom for an interview, of which he kept a written record.

In the case of Gordon Hole, these depositions were many and substantial. Each and every one of the hotel's twenty-eight employees had a story about the American, who turned out to be a promising subject indeed.

The best-informed sources were the receptionists, whose work combined with long periods of idleness inclined them to keep an eye on the guests. That Monsieur Hole regularly received a call-girl (one hundred and eight times over the year), that he granted hospitality to an old man with the forename Gaspard (on two hundred and thirty occasions), all such facts could be proved from their notes. They had recorded the American's every coming and going, and careful cross-checking revealed some interesting anomalies.

'What, for example?' the investigator wanted to know.

The receptionist leafed through his notebook.

'On December 7th 1887 a woman entered his room and did not re-emerge…'

'That sounds serious! Are you sure?'

'Unfortunately not. That afternoon, unusually, I had to leave the desk for a quarter of an hour during my shift. No one took my place. It's possible, albeit highly unlikely, that the visitor left the hotel during that quarter of a hour.

'What does the commissionaire say?'

'He doesn't remember and nor do the bellboys. One of them alleges that Monsieur Hole left the hotel around one o'clock, accompanied. I myself saw the two men return mid-afternoon, carrying a large trunk.'

'Well, thank you for the information. Rest assured: I shall make a note of it. Next!'

The second phase of the inquiry consisted in describing in as much detail as possible what the American said and did within the hotel. Word went out to every employee to lay siege to No. 16: between laundry-maid and cook and between groom and bellboy, the number was whispered back and forth like a secret password. A permanent watch was set up at the corner of the corridor in a convenient recess from which the door could be spied on without attracting attention.

That was how they discovered the curious comings and goings between Room 11 and Room 16.

Each day, towards the end of the afternoon, Salome (Room 11) left her apartment wearing somewhat unusual clothes, which one lookout referred to as 'gypsy clobber'. She walked a few metres along the corridor and knocked at another door, that of Gordon Hole (Room 16). The American bid her enter. A moment later, a young man who had given his name to reception as 'Armand Boissier' knocked at the same door. The three remained closeted for about an hour, then the two visitors left in the order of their arrival.

This was relayed to the accounts clerk, who had now been promoted to the rank of chief inspector. He detailed a bellboy to listen at the door. Cunningly, the boy was chosen from among the less highly regarded members of staff; that way, should he be caught red-handed his dismissal would not deprive the hotel of a valued employee.

So this is what one Frédéric Volle, bellboy, heard when he glued his ear to the door of Room 16 on July 15th 1888:

'Mademoiselle Salome, I have some bad news…'

'What is it, Monsieur Hole?'

'Our seances are about to come to an end. I shall soon be paying you off.'

A tense silence followed the American's words.

'May I ask why? Have I not been giving a satisfactory performance?'

'Oh, absolutely! This is something else.'

'What do you mean "something else"?' the ventriloquist insisted.

'It's all the fault of the young man who brought us together in the first place. Armand, that good-for-nothing… How I regret ever choosing him! I'd have done better bribing the first newspaper-seller or shoeshine boy I came across!'

The way the voice fluctuated in volume enabled the spy to picture Hole: on his feet, pacing up and down inside the room. Salome was apparently immobile.

'But for heaven's sake, what has he done?'

'What has he done?' the American exclaimed. 'He's ruined my plan, that's what he's done! Months of effort and preparation! His mission was simple enough: dynamite the Tower. Anyone with a scrap of resolve could have done it! Yet for some unknown reason Armand pulled out at the last minute.'

'Possibly he had second thoughts?'

A derisive sniff was heard through the door.

'Pretty late for that if he did! No, I don't think so. He was well hooked. Armand was under Roseline's spell so he should have seen it through!'

There was a pause in the conversation. Alarmed, the bellboy moved away from the door. Salome's voice brought him back.

'Where did you get this information? From the newspapers?'

'That at least would be some consolation. No, no, the journalists know nothing, they're being kept in the dark. I learned everything from a barrowman on the site, over a jug of cider.'

The American evidently flung himself into a chair at this point, judging by the squeal of springs. He then continued.

'This morning, while they were clearing away the equipment used for the firework display, the pyrotechnists found some fuses, which they took at first to be leftovers from their own appliances. During a display, two or three fuses may not burn, a common mishap, apparently. However, these lines led not to ordinary fireworks but to big bunches of dynamite lashed to the piers of the Tower! What do you think the pyrotechnists did? They alerted Jean Compagnon, the site foreman. Eiffel was told later in the morning.'

'And Armand?'

'He's a strong suspect. Granted, no one saw him actually set the charges but several people say they saw him walking around on the Tower, carrying a large bag. At dawn, a riveter found him asleep on the second platform. Imagine: a criminal who dozes off at the scene of the crime! Huh! The scatterbrain deserves what he gets. To start with, he'll be sacked from Établissements Eiffel! Then the investigation will establish his guilt. Prison or penal servitude will take him off our hands for a long spell!'

The bellboy heard indignation in Salome's retort.

'Listen to you! What a way to talk about someone who's done your bidding, risking his career and his very life!'

'He'd have done my bidding if he'd blown up the Tower. But with the Tower still standing, he's actually done me harm! I've wasted my time and also a great deal of money!'

There was a sound of movement in the room. Hole had evidently resumed his pacing.

'If Armand turns up, we'll need to use Roseline to tell him he's not wanted any more. Improvise something; after all, his fiancée has good reason to be angry. In sparing the Tower, surely he's broken his promise to her? Have her chide him with that! Have her heap abuse on the fellow! He'll not dare come back and this seance will be the last!'

'I can't do what you ask!' the ventriloquist rebelled. 'It would kill him!'

'Piffle! At his age you get over everything...'

Just then, the bellboy, who had one ear on the alert for sounds from the corridor, heard the door of the elevator clatter. He swiftly withdrew in the direction of a broom cupboard. That was the end of his report.

Odilon took a step inside the room. He had kept his hat on, like a man in a hurry who has no time for the niceties. The cane with the warthog-tooth handle was tucked in the crook of an elbow. He had run from the omnibus stop, presumably. Taking a handkerchief from his sleeve, he mopped his brow and temples.

Hole and Salome stood frozen in attitudes of astonishment. The American was the first to recover.

'We weren't expecting you to call!'

'Is Armand with you?' the engineer asked, casting his eye about the room.

Hole interposed his broad shoulders.

'No, he's not here.'

'I'm thirsty.'

With unruffled nonchalance, Odilon passed the American and flung himself into a chair. Hole considered the intruder, weighing up whether to receive him or throw him out. But his hand, having reached for the bell, veered towards the drinks table. An aperitif was served.

This simple gesture altered the whole tone of the encounter. Just as a turntable changes a stage set, replacing all the furniture and props, the spiritualist cell was transformed into a Parisian drawing-room: the candles were blown out, the mirrors uncovered, the curtains thrown open… Even Salome, seeing fit to lighten her dress somewhat, removed the sequinned shawl that had covered her head. In a moment, all sense of mystery was banished.

'We shan't be evoking the dead, then?' Hole remarked ironically, noticing Odilon's amazement.

His words might have given the game away. Fortunately, the nuance escaped the engineer, who in any case was not listening.

'Armand is nowhere to be found!' the Parisian began. 'Last night… '

'Get to the point! We know what's happened!'

Instantly, an expression of surprise formed on the visitor's face. Salome, alarmed by this oversight, glared at her partner.

'Oh, the rumour's got around, you know,' Hole added smoothly, very much at his ease. 'It's the talk of the Structural Engineers' Club.'

The explanation satisfied Odilon, who went on:

'So you'll be aware that a riveter found our friend up at the top of the Tower. At the time, the dynamite had not yet been found. The site foreman put a benign gloss on his behaviour, called it a drunken escapade after the fireworks banquet… More than one drinker had boasted, under the influence of champagne, of scaling the Tower one-legged or wearing stilts! They put Armand in a cab that dropped him off at home.'

'Presumably he didn't turn up for work this morning?' the ventriloquist offered.

'He did, but very late…which is hardly surprising after a night spent up there. The rest of us joked about it; in fact, Armand seemed quite good-humoured himself. Unfortunately, no sooner had he hung up his hat than a furious Eiffel came storming in. Twice over, he pointed a forefinger at Armand and then at the door of his office. Our friend obliged. A minute later, he came out again with a letter in his hand – his dismissal…'

The American was secretly delighted.

'What does Eiffel mean to do? Will he sue?'

'He's reserving the right to, he told Monsieur Salles. Actually, I think the boss is very worried about the whole business. Appearances are most certainly against Armand – hence his dismissal – but there's no proof. Imagine the scandal if the investigation confirms people's suspicions! Eiffel betrayed by one of his own engineers!'

Hole's look of concern emphatically did not reflect his state of mind.

'Armand was in a good mood, you said… That's a surprise!'

'I can't understand it. After the interview, while he was calmly packing up his things, I went over to talk to him. He wore a smile the whole time. The look on his face was so out of tune with what had happened, I feared for his sanity. Sometimes a violent shock can unhinge the brain – isn't that so? "How are you feeling?" I asked him. At which, rolling empty eyes towards me, the eyes of a mystic, he said: "I've never felt better! I saw her, she came to me, she kissed me! Do you understand, Odilon? I don't need the seances any more. From now on, we're joined."'

'He was talking about Roseline?' Salome ventured.

'I assume so, but that was all Armand said. He put on his hat and went out of the door, his full cardboard box under one arm. I should have followed him then, but Monsieur Pluot motioned for me to stay and disobeying him would have put my own job at risk! Later, I ran round to his Uncle Jules's house in Rue de Bruxelles but Armand wasn't there. Neither was he at Roseline's place, nor at the site, nor at the morgue, nor in any of our usual cafés. As a last resort, I've come here…'

'To no avail!' Hole threw in. 'Armand has missed his appointment with us and presumably he'll also miss the others. So is that it – no more seances? A good thing too! It's torture for a father, hearing his dead daughter's voice. Eventually, the remedy becomes another poison. Mourning needs silence.'

The Parisian said how much he disagreed, his initially faint voice becoming gradually stronger:

'I'm sorry, sir but with all due respect, I take the opposite view. Armand has disappeared. There's some danger he may take his own life, given his present state of mind – if not in a moment of distraction, then in order to be with his beloved again! There's only one thing we can do: keep watch on all the places where he might reappear.'

'Well spoken!' Salome said approvingly. 'Let's keep the seances going – same time, same place! I suggest Odilon joins us.'

In a movement of irritation, Hole knocked over his glass. His drink extended a gleaming tongue towards the edge of the table, fell in a curtain to the floor and was soaked up by the carpet. The American trod it in as one tramples a spreading fire.

'As you wish! Go on with the evocations! I shall not be there. Roseline is dead, Armand has lost his wits and it's time to draw a line, that's all I'm saying! Ma'am, sir – I bid you good day!'

The American leaped up from his chair, took his coat as he passed and strode towards the door. His hand was already on the knob when he realised that this was his room: it was for them to leave! Ostentatiously, he stood aside. The others understood and duly made their exit.

As Salome crossed the threshold, the architect grabbed her arm and hissed in her ear, 'Don't expect to be paid for this little farce. Our contract is broken!'

The ventriloquist went on out without replying, followed by Odilon. The door slammed behind them.

'Monsieur Hole won't want to see us again,' Odilon sighed. 'Where shall we meet in future?'

Salome glanced towards her door but looked away immediately.

'I'll take another set of rooms on this same floor. Reception will tell us if Armand presents himself.'

They agreed on this solution and made an appointment for late afternoon the next day.

The train had left the station an hour ago and was now steaming through open countryside.

From east to west and from north to south, one continuous swathe of textiles clothed the hills, woven by the hand of man from materials provided by nature: the deep pile of fields of wheat, the chenille of woodland, the rippling silk of rivers and streams – all were sewn with paths of gold thread and darned with villages, whose church spires lined the horizon like knitting needles.

Despite the noise, despite the stink of burnt coal, the passing train added a personal note to such rustic peace. It did not travel very fast; the cows had plenty of time to stretch out their long necks towards the passengers waving from the windows; they were able to sniff, muzzles aloft, at the smoke and steam spiralling from the shiny chimney.

As they entered each village, children ran up to pay homage to the great iron horse. They leapt and somersaulted all along the train, much to the alarm of the level-crossing keeper. Apples and peaches plucked from the local orchards were offered to the passengers, who reciprocated with handfuls of nougat or boiled sweets. What fun they were all having! How they laughed! They were happy – as they had been before the war.

Armand, his forehead glued to the window, shared his secrets with the scenes unfolding beyond the pane.

In the many tunnels that the line traversed and that obscured the windows one by one, the engineer rolled a piece of bread on his thigh. It was left over from a snack he had eaten at the station and with his stout shoes and the shirt on his back it was all that remained to him of the capital. The box of things retrieved from Levallois he had left on a bench somewhere.

The young man's mood was one of contrasts, much as light and shade continually replaced each other at the windows of the carriage. On the one hand, he was glad to have got away from the capital and impatient to be home once again in St. Flour. On the other hand, he felt bitter at the thought of the time he had spent in the shadow of the Tower.

How far off it seemed, that day when he had alighted from a hired carriage at Gustave Eiffel's door! Since then, Armand had learned a profession, made love to a woman, and even, by special dispensation, become initiated into the secrets of the beyond, into that knowledge of the spirit world that few men attain before they die. The credit balance looked pretty favourable!

On the debit side, none of it had come to anything. He was leaving Paris without having made his way in the world, without having acquired a wife and poorer than on his arrival since he was returning home luggageless. Oh well! What young man of twenty-four can boast of being truly happy? In fact, how many have experienced lasting pleasure?

The way of the world is such that nothing whatever can be entirely accomplished in youth. Youth, for us all, retains the disappointing tartness of unripe fruit. It is an age of sudden leaps and, therefore, also of stumbles. One falls, one struggles, one recovers, one goes on. There seems no end to it. Secretly, though, the circle is a spiral and one day bursts through into the light of maturity.

Armand got off the train at Neussargues. The stormy night battered like a sea against the station door. Unhesitatingly, the young man crossed the square and set out on the stony path that led to his village.

13

Armand's return to St. Flour was celebrated as if a prince had called in unexpectedly. All the way down its long history, the citadel had opened its gates to mighty leaders on their way to Spain, looking for somewhere to rest their escorts; King Charles the Seventh, scourge of the English, had once sought shelter there.

A son, too, is a king when he returns from afar and has been feared for. When father Boissier opened the door of the small family house in Rue du Thuile-Haut, he nearly fainted to see Armand standing on the threshold.

'By the bells of heaven!' roared Hippolyte, who swore like a curate.

This resounding proclamation of the news spared Armand's mother, Bertille, the initial shock. She dropped her embroidery hoop and ran to the door, sweeping the whole household along in her wake. There were tears, hugs and also muttered prayers of thanks, for the Boissiers were good Christians and never neglected to praise the Lord whenever they felt the effects of his grace.

Only Armand's little sister, Hortense, hung back from all this effusiveness, half for fear of being crushed in the press of grown-ups, half because she was a little afraid of this brother who had come home unannounced. Like cats, children are averse to having their world disrupted. She also observed, this time out loud, that Armand was luggageless. Hortense took a smack for this, but the remark was heard.

'She's right, for heaven's sake. Where's your case?' Hippolyte wanted to know, having paid for this fine object, made of real Russia leather – 'a travelling-bag fit for a bishop', as he had called it – out of his own pocket.

Armand improvised, on the spur of the moment, a mendacious account of the item's final fate. He claimed it had accidentally fallen from the moving carriage and been savaged before his eyes by stray dogs following the train.

'My God, is such a thing possible?' exclaimed an astonished Bertille, twisting a handkerchief in her fingers. 'Dogs going for a suitcase! You'll never catch me visiting Paris, not for anything!'

Hippolyte shrugged, because what did Paris have to do with it? Still, there was general lamentation over the wickedness of the world.

The loss of the suitcase, in a modest family that still used spirit-lamps, threw a jarring note into this joyful reunion. To start with, the open front door was now pushed shut to guard against the neighbours spreading malicious gossip, should they catch wind of some misfortune. The point was raised specifically by Bertille: had Armand bumped into anyone on the streets of St.Flour?

'As long as no one saw you!' the mother added in her capacity as domestic strategist. 'The eldest son, walking home, knocking on the door like a common beggar! That would be awful!'

'Not the neighbours again! You sound like Uncle Jules! It must run in the family!'

The insolence of this remark was not lost on Hippolyte. Sadly, he noted this emancipation on his son's part, which was no doubt due to the bad air in Paris.

Supper had long been over, but that did not stop Bertille from re-laying the table in Armand's honour and to show her son that they were not stingy with food here. Father called for the Sunday roast to be prepared.

'The leg of pork?' gulped his wife, not believing her ears.

A furious look from Hippolyte sent her scurrying to the stove.

While the oven was being lit, Armand breathed in the good smell of the room, made up of the aroma of food that had been cooked earlier, coupled with subtler emanations from familiar household objects: the horsehair broom that stood behind the door, grandmother's wall-mounted coffee-mill, the copper pans hanging in descending order of size from the line of nails. It was a fine smell – with elements of varnish and wax polish, of housecoal and washing-blue – the calming bouquet of *home*, reminiscent not so much of times past as of time in suspension; for nothing ever changes in the family abode, only the inhabitants who, one by one, take their leave…

Yet even this rustic setting had seen the dawn of progress. This took the gleaming form of a brand-new, galvanised-steel clothes boiler that Bertille had installed on a table of its own; a tabernacle, so to speak, of the new cult. The engineer also noticed, not without emotion, an engraving of the Tower, cut from a magazine and pinned up next to a photograph of himself in student dress.

'Oh, God bless St. Flour!' thought Armand, taking a sip from the small glass of white wine that his father had just poured him.

The meat was served without vegetables, for to garnish the noble dish would have been to spoil the mood of celebration and show a lack of respect for their guest. Nevertheless, knowing Armand's taste as she did, the cook filled a side plate with yellow lentils, a local speciality of which the boy was very fond.

It was time for the formalities. Hippolyte lit his pipe, the badge of the patriarch, and opened the dialogue in which no one was to speak but father and son.

'Armand, we are delighted to see you again. As Jules must have told you, I came up to Paris recently. At the time you were no longer communicating and we were worried about you.'

'Yes, Jules did tell me. He also said you had left much saddened, under the impression that I was avoiding you. That was a misunderstanding. In actual fact…'

Hippolyte interrupted him with a dismissive gesture as if to say, 'Let's not talk about that any more! It's all in the past!' He went on:

'Your visit, as I said, is a joy to us. However, I should appreciate knowing the reason for it. It's not like you to simply jump on the first train without telling anybody. If something's happened, speak up! You can be sure of a sympathetic hearing.'

For a moment, Armand was tempted to confess the truth, but confession was too risky a choice. How was he to explain Roseline, spiritualism and the rest of it? The least admission would involve lengthy discussions, obliging him to go into tiresome detail without any guarantee that he would be understood. He chose to lie.

'What do you mean?' he said, feigning innocence. 'Did you not get my letter? But I wrote in good time. Oh, my visit is perfectly straightforward, apart from that incident with the suitcase. Gustave Eiffel gave me a job to do with the elevators. That's finished now, so I've come back home for a while until he moves me to another position. It'll be a matter of a month or two at most!'

Hippolyte let out a sigh in which the young man thought he detected a tinge of disappointment. As the roast cooled down, the carpenter sucked at his pipe and said no more. It was Bertille who resumed the questioning.

'Are you sure your work was satisfactory? I know nothing about being an engineer, but surely if an employer values you he's not going to leave you idle? Your father will remember that as soon as he'd finished one job he was summoned to work on another site.'

'The Tower's different,' the engineer tried to explain. 'There are three hundred of us working on that and very few will see his labours bear fruit! Everyone has his special field, some work on tiny details like the prism of the beacon that will crown the Tower or the layout of the restaurants on the first platform. When a person has finished, he moves on, and someone new instantly takes his place. The days of full-time working from sunrise to sunset are history. In future, the working day will be no more than 10 hours and with the odd Saturday off too!'

'If that's the way things are going, it's a crying shame!' Hippolyte put in abruptly. 'How is a man to provide for a family on half-pay? I just don't understand what the government's thinking of!'

A rattling gurgle of the father's pipe underlined his anger and disgust. Having cleaned the object out with the point of his knife, he refilled the bowl and, between wreaths of fresh smoke, continued in a loud voice:

'But what about you – what are you going to do between

now and All Saints? You're not planning to lounge about the house, I hope?'

'Of course not!' Armand protested, thinking fast. 'I'll find a job here. Last summer you wrote that they were looking for a clerk at the town hall.'

'One's been appointed!'

'Well, something else, then! If they don't want my brains, how about my arms? I can cut hay, prune vines, burnish copper – I'll do anything! A bit of exercise will do me good, anyway, after more than a year in the big city! There, all you do is climb stairs!'

Hippolyte smiled readily in response to this sally. His pipe released a warmly opulent cloud of blue-tinted smoke that clothed these words of reconciliation.

'No hurry, no hurry... Take some time off, you've certainly earned it! Good God, it's not as if we couldn't feed you for a month or two!'

Hippolyte's good nature resurfaced completely and the whole table relaxed immediately. Bertille bustled about, serving coffee, and as Armand held forth on life in the capital, even the little ones – eight rapscallions who need not be named – burst out laughing like fire touching gunpowder.

The evening ended very pleasantly, amid an array of bottles and sweetmeats.

Country time is different from city time. It seems both longer – for the days stretch out – and shorter – because the weeks, months, and years count for nothing. One winter is much like another and summers are all the same. With nothing to hitch memories to, no post to moor the boat, one drifts along on the current, watching the passing bank, the passing years, life slipping irrevocably away...

Armand's stay in St. Flour lasted nine months but to him it seemed less than a Parisian season.

The first few weeks were the busiest. Indulgently spread about by Hippolyte, the news of his return had attracted awards, invitations to speak and even a medal. People learned to their stupefaction that someone from St. Flour had been involved in the enterprise of the century, the erection of this monument that was the talk of the Paris newspapers – and that the provincial press had taken up in consequence. The mayor himself had personally sought out the young man whom rumour had already dubbed the 'inventor of the Tower'.

'He drew up the plans!' the villagers breathed admiringly, looking deep into Armand's often lifeless, weary eyes for the fugitive spark of genius.

At the time, in fact, his fame almost eclipsed that of the structure, the people of St. Flour preferring this familiar hero who lived amongst them to the distant metal construction. It made little difference whether Armand had been in charge of the entire project or whether he had been simply a member of Eiffel's staff. In their eyes, the Tower *was* Armand Boissier!

Some of the more excited villagers saw the young man as an historic figure and wished to put up a statue in his honour: a standing figure of Armand, eyes raised skyward, his left hand pointing to a plan of the Tower while his right hand adjusted a very professional-looking pair of spectacles. The municipal council gave unanimous backing to the project. Only the cost of the bronze, which was indeed excessive, prevented its implementation.

The misunderstanding might have lasted and the farce have spread throughout the district had it not been for the calamity that struck the plateau's farms that autumn, namely a fever epidemic that killed hundreds of cattle. This disaster promptly dominated the headlines, casting Armand into abrupt oblivion.

The engineer no longer interested anyone except the odd joker who stopped him in the street and asked:

'How about the Tower, then? Any news?'

To which Armand, in his innocence, would reply:

'It's still getting higher!'

He lived in dread that one day he would meet someone in the know, someone who would see through him and expose the truth.

For this reason, Armand kept abreast of the mixed progress of the Tower's construction through the many newspapers and magazines that mined this lucrative seam. Indeed, there was no shortage of them. From village newssheet to fashionable gazette and from ladies' illustrated magazine to gentlemen's review, every publication or virtually every one had voiced an opinion on Gustave Eiffel's extraordinary undertaking. By combining articles drawn from various sources, it was possible to put together a complete portrait of the Tower and make a tracing, so to speak, of the original plan.

It was as a reader that Armand followed the progress of the Tower's construction from the summer of 1888 to the spring of 1889.

With the second platform completed, fresh inspiration infused those building the Tower. Now that the major difficulties had been overcome, now that the widely-spaced piers had come together in a single spire, no one doubted any further that the summit would be reached. The rate of assembly increased, the well-versed teams gave their all in a bid to meet, and if possible bring forward, their appointment with the 300-metre mark. This elemental vertical on which the whole organisation was focused seemed to many the ultimate straight line.

'The Tower is a bottle of champagne,' the workers quipped, 'and we're in a hurry to reach the top and pop the cork!'

As the Tower acquired its distinctive tapering shape, no longer in two dimensions on a sheet of paper but in terms of volume and space, Parisians began to find likenesses for it, and hence nicknames.

For the common man, it remained the 'Tower of Babel'. But poets, writers and other masters of eloquence sought more sophisticated comparisons. Some of these were well-meaning, but the majority were hostile.

For some, the Tower represented a 'bottle sheathed in painted wickerwork', a 'giant boiler-works', a 'skeletal belfry', a 'glorious ironmonger's' or a 'spider's web in which suns will get caught'. For others, it called to mind an 'oil well', a 'monstrous trinket', a 'lone suppository riddled with holes', a 'ludicrous mast on the ship of Paris' and a 'factory chimney under construction'. Finally, the more caustic critics, seeing it as a symbol of bourgeois presumption, denounced a 'new church in which to celebrate the divine service of the almighty Bank', a 'lofty dredger capable of extracting the gold-bearing sludge of the Stock Exchange'.

Some – the poet François Coppée, for example, who had been up the Tower mid-summer – penned disillusioned lines to it. The panorama from the Tower, he wrote, turned:

Palaces of history,
Wealthy arrondissements, starving suburbs,
Into toys from the Black Forest
Freshly unpacked from their pine boxes.

If the Tower was not the butt of jest, it was an object of fear. According to the papers, nothing could be more vulnerable nor paradoxically more threatening than this giant metal monster. Man in his pride was inviting heavenly retribution by sticking such a needle into the sky. Only the nature of his punishment continued to divide the prophets: would the structure be bent by the wind, shattered by lightning, or broken up by variations in temperature?

Early in 1888, the newspaper *Le Matin* offered the sensational headline, 'Tower Collapsing!' The article called upon Eiffel quite simply to stop work immediately. Other papers drew attention to the dangerous way in which the Tower was beginning to lean, though they were unable to agree on the direction. 'The Tower is plunging into the Seine!' argued some. 'No, it's falling towards Avenue de Suffren,' alleged others. Nobody, curiously, saw the inclination as being in the direction of the Champ-de-Mars and the Army College – probably because no one lived there.

These verbal attacks were accompanied by actions, particularly among literary figures, indicating varying degrees of hostility. Verlaine, when travelling in a cab, ordered the driver to make a detour in order to avoid passing the hateful Tower; Maupassant was in the habit of dining in a restaurant on the first platform, not for the purpose of enjoying the view but because it was the only place in Paris from which the Tower could not be seen.

To have his work thus abused was a source of some irritation to Gustave Eiffel, but deep down he was not displeased.

Novelties are not unlike illnesses: the more serious the attack, the more fiercely the body reacts. A work of value is recognised by the scandal that surrounds it, the mockery with which it is greeted. All things considered, these insults, these taunts, these petitions were evidence that the Tower had become part of Parisian life. In its cold, unyielding manner, like a nail driven into a solid object, it was gradually remoulding the mental landscape after being forcibly imposed on the physical landscape.

The earliest signs appeared at the beginning of 1888 and they asserted themselves with growing insistence as the year went on. If the artistic establishment continued to shun the iron mast, amateur writers and musicians no longer scorned to draw inspiration from it.

A mechanic from the Le Havre Ironworks, for example, wrote an epigram in response to François Coppée's poem:

> *Farewell! Withdraw to your Parnassian fastness!*
> *Your Immortality has lost its power!*
> *For now the Worker wields his hammer*
> *From atop the Eiffel Tower!*

Or take this old lady, of whose homely lines Eiffel was the dedicatee:

> *The Tower is restless, it beckons to me!*
> *I perceive my engineer*
> *At a glance I take him in*
> *When I see him he electrifies me*
> *He makes all my machinery thrum*
> *He makes my whole body hum*
> *To pay homage to the President!'*

The Tower also spoke to artists, with Georges Seurat and Douanier Rousseau both painting pictures of it, and even to fashion designers, prompting the Paris-Londres house to bring out their 'Ascensionist Eiffel' coat with its layered capes.

But it was in music that the immense resonance of the Tower found its fullest expression. Several cantatas were dedicated to it, as was the Valenciennes Choral Club's *Babel Eiffel*. Adolphe David composed a symphony in its honour, the various movements retracing the phases of construction:

Lento – the engineers and gangs of workmen arrive at the
Champ-de-Mars
Moderato – work begins on the foundations of the Tower
Allegro, sprightly – the iron workers
1st ascent, andante cantabile – 1st platform
2nd ascent – the Tower rises
Andante cantabile – higher than the hills
Moderato accelerando e crescendo until the end –
the crowds climb
Lento e grandioso – hymn to the French flag.

Such serious works had their frivolous counterpart in a wealth of objects and souvenirs from the cigar-cutter to the cheese label and from the fish-slice to the peppermill. Depicted on every conceivable support was the well-known outline of what all France knew as *La Dame de Fer* – the Iron Lady.

Some trinkets carried a higher price than others: these were items manufactured from original construction materials. Under an agreement signed when work first began, Eiffel had undertaken to supply Messrs Jaluzot and Co., owners of the Printemps department store, with all the 'offcuts, trimmings, and metal punch-outs' that came from the Tower site. With the iron thus collected, marvellous miniatures of the monument were cast. These had their 'authenticity guaranteed by the Paris Metallurgical Works' and could either be put to use, depending on the purchaser's whim, as vases, lamp-stands or pipe-cleaners, or else enthroned in splendour on the family mantlepiece. After all, a century earlier paperweights fashioned from the rubble of the Bastille had gone on sale.

So the business of the Tower was apparently well in hand. But what of the 300-metre Tower itself? Already famous, already much copied, it was yet to be completed.

After the optimism of the summer of 1888, that autumn and winter brought trying times that were to remain in Eiffel's memory as the worst periods of the construction process.

As early as September, seeing their pay diminish daily, the workers went on strike.

'We had a twelve-hour working day in the summer but in the winter that drops to nine!' the men argued. How were they to break even on such terms? Anyway, their wages ought to be keeping pace with the Tower: the higher they built, the greater the danger!'

Eiffel objected, 'The risk is the same at 200 metres as it was at forty. Either way, it's certain death!'

As was soon proved by an accident that happened to an Italian workman, who died in a fall from the first platform. Thanks to the insurance taken out by Eiffel, the widow was discreetly compensated, in exchange for which she undertook to go home to Italy. Two other misfortunes were to cast a pall over the site. One man died from his extensive injuries, another was left a cripple. But this was not much, compared with the dozens of victims of another major engineering project of the period, the construction of a bridge across the Firth of Forth in Scotland. In fact, the Tower site was held up as a model of good practice and Eiffel as an exemplary employer.

Nevertheless, the strike took hold. Showing great solidarity, the workers demanded a uniform increase of 20 centimes an hour. Eiffel offered 5 centimes, for certain specialized workers only. Three days of talks ended in a compromise, the hourly rate would go up by 5 centimes each month until the desired figure of twenty was reached. The work of assembly resumed. Unfortunately, the resumption was short-lived.

With the onset of winter, which that year was a severe one, working conditions for the men erecting the Tower worsened rapidly. Despite their thick woollen jumpers and otter-skin caps, the cold ripped at them like a wild beast. This fearsome enemy, fortified by altitude, attacked its human victims with elemental savagery. The workmen were obliged to defend themselves, as against a marauding pack of wolves, by lighting braziers to repel assaults. But even these were of little use at the top.

The men who worked up there fought a heroic battle against numbness and death. In terrible, icy gusts, with the temperature reaching 10 degrees below zero, exposed fingers froze to the iron. It became impossible to drive in rivets that hardened as soon as they emerged from the fire – which itself struggled to stay alive in the teeth of the wind.

Indeed, it was the riveting crews that people felt most sorry for. The 'boy' who heated the bolts in his mobile forge, the 'gripper' who picked them up with pincers and inserted them in the holes, the 'riveter' himself, who hit the other end to turn the metal over, the 'striker' who finished the job off with blows of his sledgehammer. These poor fellows were permanently in the front line, up where the wind blew strongest. Were they not in constant danger of falling, perched precariously on a wobbly wooden platform?

In the middle of December 1888, with the wage increases having already reached their ceiling, a fresh dispute broke out on the site.

This time Eiffel refused to give ground. Sticking to his strategy of rewarding merit, he promised a special bonus to those 'chimney-sweeps' who stayed on until the Tower was completed. He made one condition: they must turn up for work next day and those who did not would be dismissed.

A majority of the workforce accepted the deal and continued as before. On the other hand, those who had led the strike were excluded from assembly work. They were given a humiliating job that led to their workmates dubbing them 'the indispensables'; they had to erect the decorative arcades on the first platform. Access to the second platform was barred to them. The insult led several of them to quit.

Eiffel took effective measures to prevent a fresh downing of tools. These included creating a high-level canteen, which meant that workers no longer had to descend to the ground for lunch. It also had the incidental effect of discouraging visits to the neighbourhood wine-merchants. Competitive prices and the lure of two warm stoves gave the canteen a guaranteed clientele. Conversely, a certain discipline was imposed: an hour's break only, no alcohol and no visits outside mealtimes.

One further ordeal marked that difficult winter. In February 1889, the Seine burst its banks and flooded the site of the World Exposition. Workmen reached the Tower by boat, like the keepers of an enormous lighthouse in the middle of Paris. Fortunately, the flood quickly receded and normal work was resumed.

From this point on, time and space were severely rationed. It was a race for the summit.

This chronicle of the Tower, the episodes of which Armand followed week by week, became precious to him whilst at the same time grating on his nerves.

It was precious because of the nostalgia it brought, evoking the memories of a bygone era. Without really admitting as much to himself, Armand missed his job as an engineer helping to build the Tower; but he also – and equally – regretted his aborted mission to bring it down.

He would have liked to talk to his friends about technical details that the newspapers gave no hint of. The question of the elevators, for instance, had still been unresolved at the time of his departure; had it been settled since? At other times, his thoughts returned to the moment when the burning match in his hand had spared the fuses. How would he decide now, given another chance? There was no doubt in his mind: he would light them.

What mattered most, after all, was not so much doing the right thing as finishing, no matter what the cost, finishing with a flag planted at the summit of the Tower or with the smell of gunpowder wafting over its ruins. It was fitting that man should set the seal of his own finitude on his attainments.

At the same time, the daily reports of the Tower's progress aroused many other feelings in Armand's heart.

The fact was, there were problems with the suture between the Parisian life he had left behind – but of which all his newspaper-reading reminded him – and life in St. Flour. Indeed, they were like opposite poles. When he looked up from his paper and considered the landscape, his thoughts were troubled, as on the threshold of a dream.

All his young life had been dedicated to the Tower. But how much did it matter really? Did it merit the exaggerated importance conferred upon it by its relationship, when viewed on a flat plane, to other human constructions? Or the derisory importance to which it was reduced by the slightest unevenness on the earth's surface. Armand gazed in admiration at a particular mountain chain that rose to a modest height already five times greater than that of the metal Tower. He imagined the Tower stuck on the flanks of La Margeride. Nothing at all! A mere toothpick! A bristle! And that, the engineer mused philosophically, is the insignificant object to which I devoted my every effort, and for which I was prepared to die.

The doubts aroused in Armand by his reading did not spare his fiancée.

There had been a moment − the kiss at the top of the Tower − when their love had peaked. Armand sometimes wondered about the nature of that event. Had it been a hallucination, produced by his overheated brain? Or had his talents as a medium suddenly manifested themselves, offering to evoke Roseline for him without a go-between? There was no way of knowing.

What Armand remembered was the perfection of that instant when their lips had met, beyond the void and beyond death. The young man could conceive of no greater pleasure than that vaporous, fleeting, perhaps imaginary embrace; he denied the possibility of an intimacy more complete, more accomplished.

But what does the climber do when he has reached the summit of the mountain? He descends. Immediately on waking next morning, Armand had felt released from the unhealthy bonds still attaching him to the actress. His feelings were unchanged; however, the urgent need to hear his fiancée's voice and to evoke her spirit daily, these had left him.

He did not know what she would become for him, whether the adored ghost of the intangible caresses in whose form she had once revealed herself to him, or perhaps, as for many young people looking back on their first mistress, just a charming recollection, a cosy corner of his memory. Whatever the future might hold, a page had resolutely been turned.

Roseline had no place in St. Flour. In the same way as the Tower shrank to absurd dimensions in the landscape, the young woman lost substance like a dream about to end. For a while, she was in Armand's thoughts. Then he lost sight of her. All that remained was the love he had conceived – for love, one of the world's energies (no more and no less than the electricity that flows from the battery, the force exerted by the lever), is transmitted but never disappears. Armand's love was hovering somewhere, young and irresolute, soon to be available to someone else.

At the same time, material worries assailed the young engineer.

The promise he had made to his father, that he would find another job, proved difficult to keep. No one dared ask the scientific genius who had become the toast of the region to sift lentils or clear ditches.

'Good heavens, that's not for you! You deserve something better,' the farmers all told him.

Until the middle of August, Armand found no work anywhere.

In the end, it was a friend of the family who got him a job. The young man could not have dreamt of a more restful one. It was a real sinecure: it involved doing the shopping for the enclosed nuns of a Carmelite convent perched on the flank of the St. Flour plateau and carrying their mail to and from the citadel.

Easy and well-paid, the job also enabled him to strike up a relationship with the postman who brought the mail from Paris. That was how he managed to intercept the letters that

Uncle Jules sent his father, Hippolyte, for of course Jules was worried about Armand and wished to report on all that was being done to find him.

'If we've heard nothing by the autumn, I'm alerting the police!' the old man had said in a recent missive.

Armand wrote a note to let his uncle know that all was well. He was at St. Flour, in the bosom of his family, whose fond regards he took this opportunity to convey. 'Hang on to my suitcase, which I shall send for,' the engineer requested, adding as a postscript, 'Thank you for saying nothing to my father about my disappointments in Paris. He is not well and the shock would only make him worse. I shall tell him everything myself, as and when I think he can take it.' Uncle Jules complied, and the subject was never mentioned again. Armand stopped censoring his father's mail.

He sent letters saying much the same thing to Odilon, Salome, Apolline, Gordon Hole and even to Gustave Eiffel – to avoid a charge of having fled, should a suit be filed against him. That done, he felt he had discharged his duty to the law as well as to his conscience. On the other hand, having thus publicised his exile, he felt less secure. The lofty lookout-point where for hundreds of years sentries had been posted to guard the ancient hill town was pressed back into service by the young engineer, who was afraid the police might come in search of him.

Armand was not wholly reassured until a month later, when he received kindly replies from those he had written to – though not from Hole or Eiffel. Still, there was little likelihood, at this stage, of any action being taken again him. He ceased patrolling Terrace des Roches and peering out over the plain.

With this last concern removed like a thorn from a

wounded heel, Armand's daily round became extremely peaceful.

His job with the Carmelite nuns was very convenient indeed. Someone who knew the shortcuts could have all the letters delivered before noon, which left the hours remaining until sundown for strolling in the countryside. When not taking long afternoon naps propped against warm rocks, Armand visited his friends, all of whom worked on farms, to lend them a hand in the fields.

One problem of a minor order plagued him as summer gave way to autumn. This was his lack of clothes, particularly warm clothes, his own having allegedly disappeared with his suitcase. But here again destiny smiled on him.

It just so happened that one of his younger brothers, Alphonse, had a sudden growth spurt at the age of nineteen. From one month to the next, this youth found himself unable to don one of his woollens without tearing stitches or to wear a pair of his shoes without giving himself corns. Even his head had grown, though now it at least fitted a beret that had once been too big.

Luckily, his former measurements were close to Armand's, so the engineer had the curious experience of inheriting a younger brother's wardrobe. Armand wore the smock, trousers and the rest alternately with his Parisian garments, which he continued to use. One day he could be seen dressed for the office, sporting city shoes, and the next day he would be in his rustic outfit with wooden clogs on his feet. It was an amusing sight, and his brothers and sisters did not spare him their laughter.

From the day when he had a job and could dress properly, Armand felt happy in his provincial surroundings. He had no intention of returning to Paris but was slowly growing used to idea that his place was in St. Flour and that he would 'plough the furrow' here, perhaps in some notary's or lawyer's office, drawing up documents and pouring wax seals.

The skill he had acquired in handling his eraser struck him as his greatest asset on the threshold of this new career. He saw it not as a minor detail but as a key point, and he congratulated himself on having developed, alongside the useless knowledge represented by logarithmic calculations or the science of hydraulics, this very precious ability that was universally applicable, no matter what the job.

'I shall be a master rubber-out!' prophesied the young man, believing his life's pattern to have been laid down.

But the Tower, like the curse of the Pharaohs – or a strip of flypaper – never lets go of those who once touch it. While Armand was confident he had escaped it, its shadow, lengthening daily, was reaching out towards the engineer. Before long, they would be rejoined…

14

In Paris, Armand's departure ushered in a period of disturbance.

From Gordon to Salome and from Odilon to Apolline, they all suddenly realised that the focus of their joint endeavour was not, as they had thought, the Tower, but rather this young engineer, on whom all aspirations, all hopes, and all plotting centred.

With Armand gone, it was if a leg had lost its articulation: to avoid falling the walker must find crutches.

The first to lose his balance was Gordon Hole. At the instant of slamming his door behind Salome, that day in the summer of 1888, he had been visited by a swift, pellucid vision of the many disastrous implications. No longer could he hope to involve anyone else in his machinations; worse, he was allowing a person to walk free who knew everything and whom their difference of opinion had turned into a potential enemy. There was only one thing for it. From now on he must work alone, under cover. As a first step, the American loaded six bullets into his Remington.

Hole's last visit to his accomplice, occurring towards midnight on 15th July, was gloomy and tormented. Gaspard did not need to hear his employer speak to know that things had changed; Hole's face told the whole story.

'Bad news, sir?'

Hole's only response was to take from his pocket an 1859 Perrin pistol, 11 mm calibre, with a hatched walnut butt. He placed it in his associate's hand.

'Do you know how to use one of these?'

Gaspard, whose humour had never left him, grinned assent.

'Well, first off, hold it by the butt! The trigger is that little curved piece of metal. No, don't pull it now! The gun's loaded. You can kill a man merely by pressing that. A sharp crack and away goes the shot!'

'How simple it is, a firearm!' the Frenchman said admiringly. 'Even an idiot can use one!'

'They were invented for idiots, that's the whole point. But let's get on. I've lots to tell you.'

Hole's account, delivered in the manner of a cheap crime story, threw Gaspard into agonies of fear.

'But, sir – in that case, all is lost!' he wailed, brandishing the pistol.

The architect redirected the gun, which was pointing at himself.

'Let's consider instead that we are in a state of siege. Tomorrow, possibly, the police will come knocking at your door, demanding to be let in. What will you do then?'

'I'll fire through the spyhole!'

'No, you won't, stupid – you'll escape! You'll climb down this drainpipe and get away across the roofs!'

'And Roseline?'

'That's the snag! We've spared her up to now but in such a

situation leaving her alive would mean curtains for us. You shoot her.'

Gaspard felt the weight of the revolver in his hand, looked at the wall beyond which their captive was sleeping and heaved a long sigh.

'If I must!'

'That's good, Gaspard. You're showing courage and discipline. Thank you for that…'

Hole really did feel gratitude towards the man he had hired and he wished to indicate this in some way. He pretended to take a personal interest in him.

'How are you feeling, Gaspard?' he asked.

'Roseline is making my life impossible, sir! All I get from dawn to dusk is whims and complaints, anything to upset me! Take yesterday, for instance. She wanted a paper. So down I went and got her one. Except the one I'd got wasn't the right one. So I had to go back down to the kiosk and exchange it for another one. She didn't want that one, either – the fashion page was crumpled, she said. I made five journeys in all! Each time there was some problem: the copy smelt of ink, or another one stained her fingers, or a third one was marked by a customer's fingernails. You have no idea of the excuses she made up for sending me out again! She was enjoying herself!'

The American smiled indulgently.

'Gaspard, my dear fellow, you're too good!'

'Not any more, I'm not! From now on, it's the gag if she so much as sighs, let alone complains, even if she makes a noise chewing her food! I've decided this for my own peace of mind. Roseline knows what she can do and what she can't, she's learned the limits of my patience. I mean, honestly, who's in charge here?'

'You are, Gaspard, you are, and I congratulate you on your

firmness! Still, be careful not to harm her… How is she taking her imprisonment?'

'Very well, sir. She's a fit girl, that one! Of course, getting no exercise has weakened her muscles a bit and recently she's been suffering from bedsores from lying down all day. But I'm onto it, for 10 minutes each evening and again in the mornings I let her walk round the bed, which I've pulled into the middle of the room. Oh, I've seen plenty of prisoners in worse shape than her!'

Gordon Hole doffed his hat in approval. The astonished Frenchman grasped the hand that was held out for him to shake.

'It's time for us to part, Gaspard, and probably to say farewell. This will be my last visit! Trying something again after what happened this afternoon, now that the police may well be on our trail, that would be almost suicidal madness. I'm leaving you this pistol as your sole companion in the coming ordeal. My own will protect me for as long as God grants me life.'

These solemn words revived the Frenchman's fears, which for a moment the conversation had banished. He could not help grabbing his employer's sleeve as the American turned to go.

'Come on, man – let's see some guts!' Hole muttered. The childish impulse vexed him.

But Gaspard would not let go, and now big tears rolled down his cheeks.

'Oh, sir, sir… It's not weakness that makes me cling to you, it's sympathy! I feel so sorry for you! You've been defending your rights! You wished to avenge the insult Eiffel was dealing you! But look where it's got you: you're being accused, you're a wanted man, tomorrow they might throw you in gaol! It's so unfair!'

'Keep your sympathy!' the American hissed, curtly

removing Gaspard's hand. 'I'm not down yet, I've only stumbled. My mistake was to delegate when I should have acted alone from the outset. Be patient, Gaspard! Don't take your eyes off the Tower on opening day! That pretty flower may well be cut down in full bloom…'

With these words, Gordon Hole turned and left the room.

Following his visit to Gaspard Louchon, the American opted for a voluntary seclusion that was no less harsh than the one being undergone by Roseline Page.

He remained shut up in his room day and night, having his meals served there in semi-darkness, for he kept the shutters closed. The bellboy on surveillance duty neither heard a sound through the door nor detected the least ray of light beneath it. Gordon Hole, it seemed, had said goodbye to the world.

This new development proved frustrating for the investigation that the hotel staff had opened on him. The investigation had dragged on for months with not much to show for itself beyond the disturbing reports filed in the first few weeks. For this, the accounts clerk blamed the elevator boy, chiding him for drawing their attention to a customer who was turning out to be very ordinary or whose only distinguishing feature was his inconspicuousness.

'You were having us on! Your eccentric is actually a hermit!'

'It's just that he's changed!' the other argued in his own defence. 'We've all seen it! You must surely admit that the evidence gathered by our spy during that meeting of the three of them in Room 16 was pretty remarkable! Calling up the dead, sabotaging the Tower…'

'I grant you that. But it only happened once! So much effort for so little result! Anyway, we're not journalists or police officers. Our inquiries have one purpose only, to keep us entertained. If they don't do that…well, we wind them up.'

A vote as unambiguous as the first one brought the investigation into Gordon Hole to an end.

As it happened, the American emerged from his room that very evening. It was the first time he had done so for six months. He went straight down to the kitchens to the very place where, at a secret meeting, staff had just been discussing his fate. The chef was startled to see this pale, ill-shaven man enter his domain.

'Sir, I wish to learn to cook!' Hole announced.

'I'm sorry?'

'Teach me your skill, or at least the rudiments: preparing vegetables, concocting sauces, building meringue dishes and so forth. I'll pay well.'

Whereupon the American patted a pocket from which bank notes began to tumble like apple peelings.

'But why?' the chef asked in amazement.

'That doesn't concern you!'

The chef's misgivings dissolved as the notes continued to fall. With the tiled floor almost entirely covered in money, he invited Hole behind the stoves.

For the next four months, the kitchens of the Hôtel Britannique enjoyed the benefit of an extra assistant who, far from drawing a wage, was paying to learn. The diners noted that the service had speeded up but that unfortunately this went hand in hand with an equally perceptible decline in culinary standards.

'Waiter, this is a disgrace!' customers protested, waving a gritty lettuce leaf or a burnt slice of roast lamb. 'Look what comes of recruiting kitchen staff off the street!'

'I'm sorry, sir – you're mistaken. Our catering assistant is a wealthy American architect…'

As Gordon Hole pursued his laborious initiation into French cooking, Salome and Odilon foregathered, every day at the same time, in a room on the second floor of the Hôtel Britannique.

The two had thought long and hard about the form their meetings should take and what should be their substance.

Regarding the form, they quickly reached agreement: it was to remain that of a spiritualist evocation, with the costumes adopted for the seances in Hole's room. That way, if Armand should turn up, he would find the setting familiar, which he would certainly prefer.

The substance proved more controversial. Without saying exactly why, Salome was reluctant to go on calling up the spirit of Roseline. Those seances, she contended, had mainly concerned Armand and Hole and in the absence of those two relatives of the actress, they had no further object. Odilon, however, maintained that they should be continued, not for their own sakes but for the dead actress.

'Spirits are not beings of a different order, deprived of sensibilities. They love like us, they experience suffering and delight just as we do. We have a duty to show solidarity and help see our friend through her present ordeal. Isn't that what you'd do if she was alive?'

Such questions, coupled with the evident generosity of Odilon's motives, placed the ventriloquist in a painful dilemma. How long could she keep up the pretence? A dozen times she was on the point of admitting the truth to Odilon and a dozen times she shrank from doing so, not for fear of being punished but because she did not wish to hurt the American.

'He has helped me, after all!' Salome reasoned. 'I've been living on his money for nearly a year! If we did wrong, I was partly responsible.'

And so she gave in. She agreed to enter into communication with Roseline's spirit.

The consequences, however, were disastrous. Without Hole's instructions and without a script to learn which she had only to recite in the correct voice, Salome committed blunder after blunder. The new Roseline was shy, hesitant and self-conscious. Asked the simplest questions, she gave silly replies, contradicting herself at every turn or losing the thread through endless digressions. Even the voice no longer sounded the same, as Salome, in her growing concern about the content, neglected the vehicle.

'She's upset...' is how the engineer analysed Roseline's apparent distraction. 'Perhaps we're disturbing her? You were right. Let's stop these conversations.'

This time the desire was mutual and they decided to halt the evocations.

The decision regarding the private seances had of course to be extended to the public seances, which continued to be held in the basement of the morgue. One day when the whole group was assembled, Salome declared that evocations of Roseline would cease and at the same time announced her resignation from the group.

'I'm needed for other work in America,' the ventriloquist lied. 'I must take up my new post this winter.'

Salome's decision appeared legitimate and no one contested it, but she was criticised for the way in which she was going without preparing the group for her departure. From behind the agitated fluttering of a black fan, Apolline was her most vehement critic.

'Your attitude is unworthy of a professional medium,' she objected.

'I was only ever a guest amongst you,' the ventriloquist

reminded her.

'You have acquired a position within the group that places certain duties upon you. The question must be put to the vote!'

'Well, I'm leaving whatever the outcome! Be in no doubt about that!'

'That is not the way we operate. Read the rules!'

Apolline signalled to the discipline commissioner, who rose to his feet as two other members of the group took up positions on the stairs. The exit was blocked.

Fortunately for Salome, the ballot was in favour of her departure, albeit only by one vote. She had made herself sufficiently objectionable for the fickle opinions of the spiritualists to turn against her. The ventriloquist made her farewells, tactfully thanking each member for his or her welcome to her and contribution to the group. In the circumstances, the seance ended immediately.

As Salome embarked on the staircase leading to the morgue, Apolline moved to her side and climbed with her.

'I shall miss you deeply, Mademoiselle Salome! I have become very fond of you…'

This unexpected compliment disturbed the ventriloquist. She saw that Apolline felt no resentment against her but only sadness at their separation.

'I shall miss you, too!' said Salome to make up for her earlier harsh words. 'May our spirits remain friends beyond the grave!'

In a dark section of the staircase, Apolline gave way to a mad impulse. She threw her arms around Salome and kissed her on the corner of her mouth. The ventriloquist nearly lost her balance. Recovering, she looked around for the medium but saw no one. Apolline, her confession made, had fled.

The spiritualist circle dispersed in silence at the gate leading to the square. Odilon and Salome left together.

Salome may have quit the spiritualist group, but she never missed the daily appointment with Odilon.

It was a somewhat unusual situation, these two young people meeting every day at the same time, driven neither by inclination nor by any sense of duty but by a vague hope that they had themselves engendered.

And it was an awkward situation to present to their respective circles of friends, particularly so far as Odilon was concerned. His colleagues at Levallois had their own ideas about what motivated these encounters and they would not take 'no' for an answer.

'Come on, it's painfully obvious: you're nuts about each other!'

'It's not like that at all!' Odilon protested in perfectly good faith.

'What? You meet up with this woman every evening in a hotel room and you don't do anything? A likely story!'

The engineer was indignant.

'But it's true, I'm telling you!'

'Well, how do you pass the time?' his friends insisted. 'Do you count the flowers on the wallpaper?'

'We talk, that's all!'

'Listen, Odilon…The girl is evidently pleased to see you. Take advantage of the occasion! Seduce her! Otherwise, if you don't, be careful that others don't take your place! I know of several fellows who dream of having a mistress like yours: she's available, obliging – and she pays for the room!'

These conversations left Odilon troubled and thoughtful. He had never seen Salome in terms of a desirable woman. In the early days, his love for Apolline had kept him from doing so; latterly, it had been his preoccupation with Armand.

Now, with his eyes opened for him, Salome appeared to him as an extremely attractive young woman: one whose figure, general bearing and indeed face many men, himself included, might turn to stare after in the street.

Having never met her except when she was dressed as a medium, he wanted very much to see her in a street outfit, wearing patent-leather boots with heels that might emphasise her waist and give her a curved behind. And what kind of hair was she hiding under those peasant shawls that she had removed only once? Long auburn curls, as he remembered. How they must gleam against the white background of a pillow! Yes, indeed, she was a lovely girl!

This incipient fancy on Odilon's part completely changed the nature of their private meetings.

Throughout the summer, the appointments kept by these two young people had been a model of innocent friendship, the kind of thing that might exist between prepubescent cousins. The long conversations they had together on subjects as harmless as the theatrical season or preparations for the World Exposition kept strictly to the narrow limits – bounded by high walls and bramble thickets – of the most scrupulous decorum. Nothing was said that was not honestly meant and politely expressed. Anyone would have thought that, like angels, they had no bodies and no access to sensual feelings.

Then, one day, quite without warning, the engineer turned up with a bunch of flowers. Salome's surprise can readily be imagined. In fact, she gave such violent signs of it, with frenzied fluttering of eyelashes and a nervous cough, that Odilon became alarmed. He took the coward's refuge in cunning.

'I brought these to cheer up the room! I mean, look at that empty vase – how sad!'

However, Salome was not deceived, and with a woman's typical courage in matters of the heart said as she took the flowers from the engineer's hands:

'Don't tell fibs, Odilon, you brought them for me. How kind of you, I really appreciate it. However, I cannot accept…'

The young man was not so smitten that the rebuff caused him much pain. Proudly, he responded:

'I know – I'm not your type.'

'You are, you are…' Salome burst out as she gave him her first loving glance. 'It's something else.'

'You're betrothed, then. You have a husband somewhere or a lover…'

Nothing, in the boy's mind, could stand in the way of their love affair but indifference or another man. 'Typical male ineptitude!' the ventriloquist thought with regret.

She weighed up her dilemma: on the one hand, the sheer abjection of seducing a man one has lied to; on the other, everyone's acknowledged right to make mistakes and then mend their ways. Nothing justified throwing away the love here on offer. Casting her lot, Salome threw herself into Odilon's arms.

This was by far the best appointment either of them could remember. Usually, the chambermaid hardly needed to tidy the sheets, so little did Salome's chaste sleep disturb them, but that day they flew about the room. One was left hanging on a window like a bride's veil after the wedding.

Weary at last, the lovers lay quietly in each other's arms.

'Odilon, I have a confession to make!' the young woman whispered, choosing her moment.

'So do I! That bunch of flowers – I really did mean it for the vase…'

The engineer received a little slap to punish his lack of gallantry.

'This is serious, darling. Very serious, in fact. You'll hate me when you know.'

'Hate you?' the young man murmured with a tender look. 'Not possible!'

'You promise you'll be nice to me, even if you're upset?'

Odilon propped himself on an elbow, suddenly suspicious.

'What do you mean? You've got me worried now. Out with it!'

So Salome unburdened herself. Straight out, making no allowances, she told him everything about her ventriloquism, the arrangement with Gordon Hole, the phoney spiritualist seances and mimicking Roseline's voice. The more she confessed to, the more Odilon's features melted like wax.

'Are you cross with me?' Salome concluded in a timid voice.

Odilon was staring at her like a stranger. Before long, however, his face resumed its naturally mild expression and he pulled the young woman towards him. A kiss marked their reconciliation.

'It wasn't your fault. You were only carrying out orders, after all. You couldn't know what vile purpose you were being used for! All the same, I should have preferred to find out sooner.'

'Sooner? Before getting into bed with me?'

'Don't be silly!'

The words came with difficulty, for the engineer was still in the grip of emotion. So many memories crowded into his mind: false, distorted memories that had painfully to be untwisted to bring them into line with the truth. A whole year of his life – one of the most momentous – suddenly appeared in an entirely new light. It was as if an eclipse had passed over a sun-drenched landscape.

He might have stayed in this stupefied silence, eyes fixed on his discarded jacket, had not Salome resumed talking in a voice that had now become firmer.

'I know what Monsieur Hole is planning.'

There was a pause.

'He told you?' Odilon reacted. 'I'm amazed. Brrr! It makes me shiver to think that he's staying in this same hotel, only five doors away!'

Salome caught and held the arm of her lover, who had started up, brandishing his fists.

'Don't try anything! He's got a gun!'

'Oh, I don't know what to do!' the Parisian said, relapsing into uncertainty. 'My mind's all confused… I need to think.'

He pressed Salome to him, not in order to reassure her but to calm himself.

'The American told you his plans, you were saying?'

'He didn't mean to,' the young woman pointed out, 'but he's a smug one who can't resist bragging about his achievements. He's incapable of being discreet. His other flaw is thinking aloud.'

'A drawback, certainly, for a man in his position. Anyway, what did you learn?'

Using a mahogany lighter, the ventriloquist relit the bedside lamp.

'I know where his accomplice lives. His name's Gaspard. No doubt that's where Roseline is being kept.'

The engineer leaped out of bed, 'There's not a moment to lose!'

Salome gave him his shirt, which she had picked up off the floor.

'I agree. We must get the police involved!'

'Absolutely not!' Odilon said, hurriedly buttoning his

waistcoat, missing out half the buttonholes. 'Roseline would become their hostage. No, we must act alone!'

Salome came round the bed to hug her lover, who was struggling into his trousers.

'Just you and me?'

'With the help of someone else who'll be very happy to learn that Roseline is alive. I had a letter from this person this morning. He's living in St. Flour, with his family. I'm going straight to the station!'

'Whom do you mean?' Salome asked, fixing the engineer's tie-pin.

'His name's Armand Boissier.'

One day in April 1889 Armand, who had just bought a newspaper, saw in huge letters on the front page: 'TOWER COMPLETED!' His heart began to beat furiously, as if he had just read his name on a 'Wanted' poster.

'It's true, for heaven's sake! The Exposition will be opening soon!' the young man exclaimed, having lost all notion of time.

He scooped up an armful of magazines, paid for them all and departed with the bundle under one arm. But in his impatience he stopped part way home, leant against a wall and began to read, oblivious to the flies buzzing round his head.

The first publication he looked at was *L'Illustration*. Beneath the headline, 'The completion of the Eiffel Tower,' were two long columns, down which his eye skimmed:

On the stroke of half-past one, at the head of two hundred guests…Monsieur Eiffel began the ascent. Not until three-quarters of an hour later did the procession arrive at what might be termed the fourth platform, 273 metres up…but the ascent was not yet over. One storey higher, and the party came out beneath the round dome…

Above the dome, a beacon. Here there were no more stairs. An enormous hollow iron mast... leads to the top. This was the route by which a dozen officials, the only persons allowed into this part of the Tower, reached the topmost platform, a narrow circular terrace from which, the eye brimming with wonder roams unchecked over the horizon. Our picture shows this terrace at the very moment when Monsieur Eiffel hoisted the national flag at the summit of the Tower...

Armand glanced briefly at the engraving that accompanied the article before reading on:

Just then, twenty-one cannon shots rang out from the third platform...Several minutes later, the members of the official party...were raising glasses of champagne in a toast to Monsieur Eiffel, and soon they were back at the foot of the Tower, where the workforce had assembled for luncheon.

'And I missed it!' the engineer gulped, slapping a hand to his forehead.

His fingers came away sticky with bits of dead insect.

'You missed nothing. It was pompous and boring. It also rained non-stop...'

Armand's head jerked up at the sound of this murmured reply. With a start, he recognised Odilon.

'Good Lord, I must be seeing things! What are you doing in St. Flour?'

'How you've changed!' the Parisian remarked, seizing his friend's hand. 'You've lost weight, you're tanned like a redskin... And those muscles! It's true what they say: the country does wonders for the physique!'

Armand in turn studied the new arrival. Odilon was as he remembered him, a picture of bohemian elegance that looked out of place in the straw-strewn village street. The only difference was that a film of dust now took the shine off his pale-coloured shoes and his exquisite cuff-buttons. He also had a package beneath his arm, not a proper bag but a few things done up in wrapping-paper, after the fashion of city-dwellers who travel only rarely. The package appeared small, even for a short stay. Armand expressed surprise.

'No trunk? One's clothes get dirty in the country. They need changing often.'

'I just brought things for the journey. You see, I'm going back this evening.'

'Out of the question!' Armand retorted expansively. 'To start with, you're coming home with me for a refreshing drink. I'll introduce you to my father, a fine fellow who once worked as a carpenter for Gustave Eiffel. Then we'll go for a stroll in the countryside. I don't know what brings you here but you're very welcome. The fact is, I've rather been pining for the capital.'

Odilon was shaking his head. Placing his package on the ground, he took hold of his friend by the shoulders.

'I'm leaving this evening, Armand, and you're coming with me. Roseline is alive. She's been kidnapped by villains who are holding her prisoner. We must go to her aid.'

The expression that formed on Armand's face at that moment defies all description. It was not unlike the one that Odilon's features had so recently assumed – but more intense and certainly more tortured.

'Oh, my poor friend!' sighed the Parisian. 'This you'll never believe. It was all a plot. We've been duped – both of us!'

Armand wanted to hear everything immediately. So they sat down on bales of straw outside a barn door and the Parisian told the whole story.

'You're right!' Armand burst out as soon as he had heard all. 'We must do something! Stay right there. I'm going to climb into my room the back way to fetch a few things. No one will see me, and that will avoid a great deal of discussion… I'll leave a note on the bed for my father! Don't move – I'll be back in an instant!'

He was as good as his word. Just catching the Nessargues stagecoach, the two engineers arrived in time for the night express. They were in Paris the following morning.

15

The introduction of the revolver had radically upset the almost domestic relationship that, much against their will, was forming between Gaspard Louchon and Roseline Page.

When the hired man had first appeared with the weapon, the actress thought her last hour had come. She screamed.

'What's up with you?' grumbled Gaspard, who hated noise.

But when he at last understood what had so terrified the young woman, he mumbled some apologies and put the revolver back into his pocket.

It was not an easy thing to carry around – without ever letting it out of your sight, as the American had stipulated – this contraption whose little tongue could so temptingly, so easily, trigger a destructive blast and, depending on what it was pointing at, smash a vase, pierce a wall or kill a person.

Gaspard thought the weapon ill-conceived. It was normal for a lighter, say, or a pair of scissors to fit a man's hand; one used such things every day. But making so manageable an object out of this dangerous revolver – which could at best wound, cause material damage or prompt law-suits, and at worst bring about the death of a human being – that struck him as a deeply illogical decision.

Since the pistol was likely to occasion such drama, what should have been created was the most complicated and most cunning of devices, with buttons everywhere, wing-nuts, screws and a secure housing for the trigger protected by five locks with five different keys. Instead, you had this plaything, almost, that a mere child, without any comprehension of it, could turn into an instrument of death and, so far as he or she was concerned, a ticket for the scaffold. Who, Gaspard thought, had ever made aggressive use of a revolver without regretting it later, without paying for it with his or her life and liberty? Truly, the world was a poorly designed place…

With the pistol in his pocket, Gaspard lost his normally carefree attitude.

He felt that he, as much as the others, was both protected from and threatened by a fatal blunder. There was no denying that the object possessed a virile force of exaltation, like a pubescent youth discovering the novel properties of his penis. Gaspard felt stronger and more important for having this weapon at his disposal. How much damage can one do to a person without a pistol? Mere bruising of the sort that fists can inflict. Possessing a revolver, on the other hand, puts one in a position to deal death, a power that bestows more on men in terms of honour and prestige than the ability to give birth bestows on women. Avenues are named after generals, never after mothers of large families.

'She'll have to behave herself in future!' Gaspard mused occasionally. 'Otherwise I'll kill her!'

In fact, Roseline could not have had a gentler or more considerate gaoler. Since giving her such a fright, the old man never entered the room with the gun in his hand but either put it in his pocket or held it uselessly by the barrel to show that he meant no harm. However, in the adjacent kitchen and in the other rooms Gaspard's misgivings returned and the pistol reappeared in his hand, ready for use against a possible attacker.

Since owning a revolver, his life had become very much more complicated. Never allowing himself to put the gun down on the table but always wanting to have it in his hand – the left, for he was left-handed – Gaspard had become a sort of one-armed man for whom everyday tasks became inconceivably difficult. He had to cook with one hand, turn the pages of a newspaper with one hand, cut his steak with one hand... Roseline had much fun at his expense, asking him to do jobs for her that she knew would prove troublesome in the circumstances, asking for example, 'Gaspard, would you be so good as to give my plate a wash? I hate eating dessert that tastes of spaghetti.'

Apart from his visits to Roseline, his few outings to the local shops and other 'patrols' within the building, Gaspard spent the whole day sitting on a chair in the kitchen, gun in hand.

He had found a fairly comfortable position that was not too tiring, with his left elbow resting on a stack of newspapers, itself held in position between two heavy books. The table supporting the newspapers was steadied by a system of sand-filled saucers placed under its legs.

In this way, the barrel of the revolver pointed towards the entrance door opposite where Gaspard sat, or more precisely at a target a little below the spyhole corresponding to the position of the 'third eye' of a man of medium height. The arrangement did not allow for the assailant being either a dwarf or a giant, but such an eventuality was unlikely, and in any case nothing could be done about it.

Having made these preparations for the visit of the police, the old man awaited it almost with serenity.

One evening, as he was reading the racing news in a newspaper he had taken from the pile – a minor concession to his need for entertainment – Gaspard was disturbed by a violent knocking on the other side of the door.

The knocking signalled not so much a request for admittance as a desire to force an entry: here was a body of vigorous, resolute men assaulting a dungeon. Blows from shoulders and fists rained upon the woodwork and soon Gaspard saw the notched tip of a crowbar smash through just above the lock. As if on cue, Roseline started yelling from the next room as if her throat was being cut, augmenting the already considerable din.

Although he had expected and even looked forward to this invasion, Gaspard went to pieces at the prospect of conflict. His finger tightened more in nervousness than deliberation on the trigger and the first of the six bullets described an entirely harmless trajectory, embedding itself in the wall several centimetres above the door. Roseline's yells doubled in volume.

'Shut up!' thundered Gaspard as he closed one eye to aim his second shot.

The door was now more than half stove in. Having dealt with the lock, the visitors were concentrating on the upper bolt. Part of the frame had been breached and through it arms could be seen flailing about and faces grimacing wildly.

'They're not police…' the old man reasoned. 'Otherwise, they'd have used that hole to poke a pistol through and fire inside!'

Such a realisation might have prompted clemency: why fire at unarmed men? Gaspard, however, taking fright at these strangers, furiously pressed the trigger.

The second shot was even more disastrous than the first. Since Gaspard's hand was damp from gripping the butt all day, the pistol reared up out of control and fired more or less at random – as it happened, hitting a full bottle of Clos Vougeot that stood on the dresser.

'What a waste!' the Frenchman cursed, more annoyed at the loss of the wine than at the damage being done to his door.

It was at that moment that Gaspard remembered his master's instructions: 'Kill Roseline,' Hole had said, 'then make your getaway.' He rushed into the next room. At sight of him, Roseline's screams turned to insults.

'Will you be quiet, woman? You're not making my job any easier!'

He aimed the revolver and fired.

'Wretched thing!' the old man raged, as another shot missed its mark. Feathers were flying about the room from the burst pillow. Roseline had fainted with fear.

Gaspard's fourth attempt was ruined by a rugby tackle from behind. He lost his balance and fell on the bed. The pistol went flying against the wall.

'I've got him!' shouted Odilon, as Armand retrieved the revolver.

A blow with the butt knocked Gaspard out.

It was dark when Gaspard came round.

A paraffin lamp standing on the floor cast a smoky light into the room. The first thing he registered, not with his eyes but from the searing pain in his limbs, was that he was well trussed up. With the intention of causing him pain, a rope had been pulled tighter than necessary to bind his legs, his arms, his chest and even his neck. A large knot under his jaw meant that he had to hold his head back to avoid suffocating.

'I can't breathe!' the old man moaned.

The tut-tutting sound that answered his words told Gaspard he was not alone in the room. In fact he was flanked by two men, one standing on either side of him, their faces unrecognisable in the darkness beyond the lamplight. Roseline was sitting in the chair, from which he deduced that he had taken her place on the bed.

'Back with us, are you, scum?' one of the visitors – the one holding the gun – hissed between his teeth.

The voice bore into Gaspard's skull like a drill. A violent migraine made him clench his jaws. At the same time, his memory returned with full clarity and precision. He relived the door being forced, the three shots and finally the moment when one of the men had tackled him from behind and he had fallen on the bed. He glanced to one side. The kitchen was almost in darkness, with what was left of the door hanging from ruined hinges.

'Your neighbours took a lot of notice!' the other man observed ironically. 'To say nothing of the concierge! Funny house, this, where one can make so much noise without rousing anyone! Never mind, we'll alert the police ourselves!'

This statement led to a brief whispered consultation between the two men. Gaspard took short breaths to try to dispel his headache.

'My friend will take care of alerting the police,' the stranger resumed. 'He'll do it this evening. That's unless…'

'Unless what?' Gaspard articulated painfully.

'Unless you tell us what your boss is planning to do to the

Tower! In which case you'll not only save your life – we'll set you free!'

Gaspard hesitated for no more than a moment. His loyalty fell far short of sacrificing himself for the American.

'Monsieur Hole is planning to dynamite the Tower. He's going to try and do it on opening day. That's all I know…'

This spontaneous confession took the visitors by surprise. They had expected some resistance and had resigned themselves to employing whatever methods were required to overcome it: blackmail, psychological pressure, even – as a last resort – torture. This was to take the mild form of tickling the soles of Gaspard's feet.

'Opening day? When's that?' the man with the gun asked his companion. 'I thought the Tower was finished!'

'Eiffel went up the Tower with a small party of ministers, but the official opening has yet to take place. It's planned for 15th May, shortly after the start of the Universal Exposition… We've got a month!'

'A month to do what?'

'Good heavens, man! To thwart Gordon Hole, of course! I'm not going to permit a second attempt to dynamite the Tower!'

Sensing a difference of opinion between the two men, Gaspard thought it best to take no notice. He opened his mouth only to claim his part of the bargain.

'Don't forget your promise!'

'All right, vermin. We'll set you free!' said the man with the pistol. 'But don't try and contact your boss! We know what you look like and we're keeping your papers. One step out of line and you've had it!'

'Don't worry on that score,' Gaspard said hurriedly. 'Sir would kill me if he ever found out what's happened here! You let me go and I'll be off like a shot from that gun!'

One of the visitors took a knife and very clumsily severed Gaspard's bonds. With the pistol aimed at him the whole time, the latter was allowed a moment to choose how he wished to make his escape – whether through the door or through the window. He chose the window as offering greater promise in the event of pursuit.

As he threw one leg over the sill, the old man gave a final glance back at Roseline, who still lay sprawling, possibly comatose, in the room's one wretched chair.

'Mademoiselle Page, do please accept my apologies for all I've done! I had my orders, don't you know? Deep down, though, I was very fond… '

'Out, scoundrel! Out – or I shoot!' roared Armand.

Grabbing the drainpipe, Gaspard disappeared into the night.

A month was not a long time for these young people to acclimatise to the ways in which their lives had changed: Odilon separated from Apolline, now involved with Salome; Salome now free of Gordon Hole and with Odilon; and lastly Armand, back together with the fiancée he had believed dead.

For the actress, those four weeks were a period of convalescence, but for the others one of huge upheaval. The state of their relations called for certain adjustments which they made as soon as they could. Salome left her hotel room and moved in with Odilon; Roseline went back to her flat together with her fiancé, despite the young man's misgivings at resuming their love life so soon – misgivings that the first night of their reunion dispelled.

'Ah, my Roseline!' Armand confided, drunk with kisses. 'I thought I was happy evoking your spirit but I have to admit, I prefer your company in the flesh. Come, love me again. I want to feel my happiness!'

The actress gave herself willingly.

'Did you miss me, at least?'

'Like a woman who's gone away on a trip but writes every day…Still, I must confess, after a while I no longer yearned for you physically. A person doesn't stay in love with a memory for long. God, but the St. Flour girls are pretty!'

This was a little too frank for the actress and Armand had to blow very hard to re-light the wick he had so carelessly extinguished.

'Oh, I'm sorry! What a silly thing to say! It's true, though. You'd forget me too if I went under a tram.'

Roseline gave him a maternal hug.

'Oh no, my darling! I'd never forget you! One's memory improves, you know, when one's job involves learning lines. Anyway, you're not like the others…'

'A kiss for a splendid speech!'

'What a child you are!' smiled the actress, accepting his lips.

They spent another whole day in bed, busy doing what lovers do when they have been apart for some time. Eventually, Roseline started talking about going to see some theatrical producers. It was the time of year when they would be taking people on and a few visits were called for.

'But you must rest!' counselled the engineer.

'I've spent the last six months on a bed! That would be enough for the laziest of souls!'

The interviews were disappointing. The actress received appointments because she was a good-looking woman, but her name seemed to have been universally forgotten or worse: people recalled it as having belonged to a former star, one who was no longer in fashion.

'Roseline Page, Roseline Page…' the producers mused. 'Ah, now it comes back to me! You played the lead at the

Opéra-Comique before the big fire of 1887. A lovely voice, very expressive… Unfortunately, those years have gone! Nowadays, what the public wants are young girls who can kick high! Cabaret singers who are, as the saying goes, "well-endowed". Take the Moulin-Rouge, due to open shortly, they're advertising champagne, "oom-pah" music and jokes about garters!'

Roseline experienced five rejections in one morning. Eventually, a man who ran a small theatre specialising in historical productions was prepared to promise her a part. But that was less because of Roseline – of whom he said quite shamelessly that there were 'hundreds like her in Paris' – than because of Armand, who accompanied his fiancée to these interviews. Armand's engineering background intrigued him.

'So you actually worked on the Tower, did you?' the producer enquired. 'Congratulations on such a huge success! It so happens that we're putting together a show about the Universal Exposition. Your ladyfriend will be playing the allegory of science. Would you be interested in trying the role of foreman yourself? You won't have to look far for inspiration!'

'Me?' Armand asked, taken aback. 'Good heavens, I never dreamed of going on the stage!'

'But you have the looks for it! In fact, the caricaturists will love that slightly beaky nose. I'll take you on probation.'

The engineer clapped his hands together like a spoilt child.

'Oh, thank you, sir, thank you!'

'In return,' continued the producer, who never gave with one hand without soliciting with the other, 'my wife and I would be delighted to receive tickets for the Exposition…'

'Unfortunately, no one's handing those out, except for the complimentary tickets for the press and the exhibitors. They're so anxious to come in under budget.'

'I quite understand, I quite understand,' the producer replied frostily. 'So, I'll be calling you both in soon to sign your contracts. Rehearsals are from Tuesday to Friday, starting at half-past eight. We fine for lateness.'

Suddenly, out of the blue, Armand and Roseline had become a theatrical couple. Armand was delighted, since it meant he no longer needed to go job-hunting. They celebrated the good news over a bottle of champagne, then the engineer suggested a visit to the Tower.

'It's been nine months since I set eyes on it,' the young man insisted. 'I feel like a father who can't wait to see his child again.'

The walk took them past Pont d'Iéna where, out on the bridge, a hawker had set up an astronomical telescope. For 10 centimes, it was possible to watch the workmen on the Tower. Armand, however, chose to point the instrument at the flag waving at the summit – a colossal standard measuring 7 by 4 metres.

'Gosh, does that look bedraggled! It's like the Emperor's banner at Waterloo.'

'You're right there,' the hawker agreed. 'It's because of the wind. Terrific gusts – three times as powerful as down here. Since I set up my telescope, they've replaced it every week.'

'Eiffel's quite right about only the French flag having a 300-metre flagpole!'

Then the young man from St. Flour pointed the telescope at the first platform, where painters suspended from ropes where inscribing the names of seventy-two top scientists in gold letters.

'Here, Roseline – this is worth looking at!'

'I can't see your name anywhere…' the actress commented wryly.

'Wait a few years! There's hope for me yet! "Boissier" is a

short name: they're not honouring Geoffroy St. Hilaire because there isn't room!'

'By such details does destiny sometimes hang!' Roseline mused philosophically.

They paid the telescope man and strolled back to the embankment.

Armand felt less emotion at seeing the Tower again than he had expected to. Was it because he had worked on the plans so often that his eye had grown accustomed to its shape? The impact of the encounter seemed somehow deadened.

Roseline, on the other hand, had only seen the early stages of construction, that already far-off time when there was more wood on the site than iron. Faced with the finished Tower, she was like a child at a 'Punch and Judy' show: 'How beautiful! How tall it is!' Then, impishly, 'The more I look at the Tower, the more I'm aware of the disheartening futility of high heels!'

Indeed, during the final phase of construction the Tower had gained a great deal of height, doubling in three months the metre-count achieved in two years. This was a good thing in view of the parallel but antagonistic progress of the buildings of the Universal Exposition, which were beginning to clutter its base and interrupt its sight-lines. So much so, in fact, that, as they grew, what had been 'ground level' appeared also to rise, threatening to engulf part of the Tower in a jumble of roofs and glass canopies. The lofty exhibition hall of the Palais des Machines had already reached the height of the first platform.

'What a shame they built so close to the Tower!' Armand observed regretfully. 'The Tower was sufficient on its own.'

In the eyes of many of Eiffel's engineers, the Exposition site was of only secondary interest, viewed as a construction project, in comparison with the one they were employed on. The vast expanse of land that had been dug out, consolidated and built on at the same time as the Tower aroused at best their indifference and at worst their hostility. They often joked about the insignificance of the galleries and pavilions kneeling humbly in the shadow of the Tower. That the new era should have to share its space with the Brasserie Tourtel or the Norwegian chalet struck them as an insult, almost as a betrayal. Like his former colleagues, Armand felt only scorn for these puny arrangements of housepainters' scaffolding in which unglamorous workmen assembled bricks and stones as if building a house for a provincial gentleman of leisure.

'At least the Tower has a style of its own,' the young man said, perhaps rather pompously. 'Whereas those monstrosities... Pastiches of Ancient Greece and Rome, copies of Norman Gothic or Tours Renaissance, Louis XIV Versailles or Louis XVI Paris – architectural old hat wherever you look.'

Roseline backed him up, pleased to be taking part in a specialist discussion.

'Apparently, they couldn't find any architects willing to design the Tunisian and Algerian pavilions.'

'I'm not surprised,' the engineer grimaced. 'Those Beaux-Arts gentlemen of the arts establishment abhor anything that isn't old. Even the Eiffel pavilion is apparently Renaissance in inspiration though crowned by an observatory dome! What a curious blend that must be, a fashionable hat atop a hoary old pate!'

It took all the actress's skill, coupled with some of her most loving smiles, to persuade her fiancé to cross the threshold of the Universal Exposition as an ordinary visitor.

Even then he did so with a poor grace. For example, he refused to pay for an admission ticket, proudly informing the lady at the cash-desk that he was an associate of Gustave Eiffel and as such excused the 'obligations of the common man'. Since the cashier declined to give way and the queue was growing longer, Armand did eventually hand over the 10 francs; which, he claimed, would be refunded to him that very day together with 'moral and pecuniary redress' for the indignity suffered.

However, that was not the end of their troubles. Hardly were they through the gates than they were approached by a tout.

It was quite impossible for any foreign visitor or Frenchman up from the country to set foot inside the Exposition without encountering one of these gentlemen who, though dressed in the height of fashion, had the tongues of travelling salesmen and the tenacity of beggars. Their services, for which one invariably paid a high price, ranged from selling leaflets to giving guided tours. For this, they commanded an all-purpose line of patter in several of the languages of the civilised world.

From Roseline's bearing – a typical Parisienne, clearly – the tout instantly guessed where his customers hailed from. He accosted them in French.

'Sir, surely you're not thinking of visiting the Exposition without someone who could show you around? It would take you a week to find out where you were and still you'd have seen nothing. Whereas if you ask a representative of the great Centennial Agency to take you through the galleries, in five hours you'll have done the tour!'

'So, you say you can show us around?' asked Armand huffily, because the incident at the cash-desk still rankled.

'Absolutely! A guide is indispensable… Just imagine: this year we have thirty thousand French exhibitors and twenty-five thousand from abroad. Millions of visitors will soon be streaming through the Exposition's twenty-two gates.

Incidentally, do you know the grand entrance at Les Invalides, flanked by its two giant Oriental pillars? That you simply must see! Come, I'll take you there…'

'Just a moment!' interjected Armand as the tout made as if to lead them away. 'We haven't decided anything yet. Do you know your stuff, at least?'

The tout bowed stiffly. He had probably never imagined he would meet with such resistance.

'Try me, sir! The Exposition holds no secrets for me.'

'On the second platform of the Eiffel Tower the newspaper *Le Figaro* has set up a pavilion. They write, print and sell a special edition there, known as *Le Figaro de la Tour*. Every visitor can order a copy bearing his or her name as a souvenir. However, this morning, as he was setting the paper up, the compositor noticed that one lead character was missing from his collection. Which letter was it?'

'Which letter?' the tout echoed with a chuckle. 'Good heavens! It could be any one…'

Harshly, the young engineer answered his own question.

'It was the letter "B" that was missing… "B" for bats, bonkers, blabbermouth – all epithets that might be applied to you, sir. It is also the first letter of "Be off with you!" So why don't you take the hint?'

Armand's extended fist would soon have got rid of the fellow, who would indeed willingly have let them alone without further ado, except that Roseline, feeling sorry for him, purchased a guidebook before he could disappear.

'You're too good…' the engineer scolded. 'Those rogues should be burned, together with their guidebooks!'

'Still, his will come in very handy. The Exposition is a maze. We'd certainly be lost without the Tower!'

The Universal Exposition of Industrial Products held no

shortage of attractions for two young lovers out for a stroll.

This gigantic fair that took over the Champ-de-Mars for six months did more than present an organised display of the products of the civilised world. It constituted a faithful miniature of the entire planet – or at least of the hemisphere that knew the telegraph and the voltaic cell.

Of the twin themes that had inspired the Exposition, the first – the centenary of the first meeting of the States General at Versailles – remained unobtrusive. There were a few rosettes here and there, perhaps the odd extra flag, and instructions to the colonies to organise literary competitions to the greater glory of the motherland.

It was mainly the second theme, the advent of the machine age, which suffused the rich trappings of the Exposition. The legacy of 1789 was apparently, for most people, not the abolition of the *Ancien Régime* but the sweeping-away of the medieval guilds that had ushered in the industrial era. From that day, it was believed, people locked into the then *status quo* had lost their fondness for tradition and had broken out to aim for a fresh horizon: progress. They had invented machines, harnessing with their boilers the wild vitality of steam, and in so doing shown themselves so potent and determined that one national journalist could write: 'Seeking to oppose the march of humanity is like trying to stop a locomotive with a toothpick.'

The fact was, nowhere better than at the Exposition did Auguste Comte's famous phrase seem to be enshrined, that motto of the new era: 'Order and progress'.

Progress, first and foremost, took the radiant, cheerful, abundant form of electricity. For the first time at an international exhibition, incandescent lamps illuminated palaces, monuments, gardens and pavilions as well as omnibuses and boats on the river. Nor was this a curiosity; it was the new norm. Here the final improvements were being made before electric lighting invaded the streets. The arches and platforms of the Tower were electrified save for one or two gas jets modestly enclosed in glass globes. The white energy even lit up, right at the top of the Tower, a powerful lantern of the kind lighthouses beam out over the sea.

This mighty fire matched perfectly the other innovation of the Centenary: metal architecture. The Exposition confirmed its triumph. Metal architecture was everywhere: on façades, in roofs and domes, along ramps and balustrades. And everywhere it was present in such proud profusion, one might have thought the human race had entered a Second Iron Age.

In some places such as the Tower and the Galerie des Machines, the metal was boldly exposed, the purest projection of abstract calculation. In others, the big 'palaces', almost as a concession to modesty, it was clad in materials that covered up its private parts. The iron-roofed palaces had walls of painted lava, glass, brick, or stucco. The oriental blue of glazed earthenware and the pink of terracotta dominated their studied polychrome effects.

With their gilded masts, banners and pink and white canopies, the Exposition buildings gave an impression of lightness and freshness that was much appreciated by the public. The 'monstrous illusion' so decried by certain critics made willing victims of the vast majority.

Armand, from the outset, sided with the sceptics, for whom the name of Charles Garnier, architect of the recently completed Paris Opera House, had become a byword for bad taste.

'Typical Garnier!' he railed, contemplating the scene before him, 'Dazzling amounts of glass, stifling quantities of marble, plaster mouldings oozing like confectioner's custard over limp arcades...the whole turgid vocabulary of over-indulgent decoration!'

Denying any innovative quality to the Formigé palace or the Bouvard galleries, the engineer saw only painstaking copies of the past. Never, he concluded, had so much been commemorated as between these brand-new walls nor tradition been more celebrated than in the name of progress.

'A glance through this guidebook says it all!' Armand scoffed, taking the said object from his fiancée's hands. 'What does the Palace of the Fine Arts have to offer? A gallery showing a hundred years of French art, together with the usual decennial and international exhibitions. They're so big, apparently, you get around them in a wheelchair! And what's on the programme at the Palace of the Liberal Arts? A complete history of work, the trades, and modes of transport... The Trocadero gives us an inventory of comparative sculpture... Yet another retrospective! Has the last trump sounded? You'd think man had been summoned to appear before the Court of Heaven, so here he is, making a rapid, very rapid appraisal of his brief history.'

'An appraisal it may be,' the actress conceded. 'But it's a very positive one! The Grand Ball of Exhibitors, the Grand Colonial Fair, the Grand Mayoral Banquet... Everyone's having fun!'

'But are they really? Isn't it more that people are seeking distraction from their fears in pleasure and debauchery? It's only a step from a grin to a grimace. If I believed in God, I'd worry that the Apocalypse was indeed imminent. Never have the dying years of a century seemed so much like the end of the world.'

As they talked, the lovers had reached the ornamental pools

at the foot of the Tower. Their visit was beginning in a familiar setting. Roseline immediately took matters in hand.

'I should like to see the whole thing before looking around the individual buildings. What do you think? We have a choice: train or balloon?'

Methodical visitors could indeed start their tour either by going up in a balloon or by making a circuit in a miniature train. Armand chose the train because he suffered from vertigo, he said, in balloon gondolas. They set out for the little station.

A dense crowd was already waiting beneath the canopies of the departure platform. What struck the engineer immediately was how different this crowd was from those one ordinarily saw milling around music-halls and at racecourses. On the one hand, it was more homogeneous: solid citizens rubbed shoulders with working men and clergymen jostled tarts. On the other, it was cosmopolitan: on a sea of opera hats floated Turkish fezes, Russian fur caps and Indian turbans.

It was at this point that Armand became aware of what the Exposition represented: nothing less than a wide-ranging encounter between the French nation and the rest of the world. It was not the elite these visitors were meeting but the common people – these visitors whose numbers were continually replenished by several railway lines, two riverboat lines, twenty omnibus and tram routes, plus countless cabs and other hired carriages. As a columnist in the well-known journal *La Famille* wrote: 'The whole of Europe is in France, the whole of France is in Paris, and the whole of Paris is at the Exposition.'

When their turn came, the couple took their seats aboard the tiny Decauville train. There was very little room in a vehicle that had been designed for soldiers and had actually seen service in Tonkin, where it had been used to transport colonial troops. The seats were scarcely deep enough to hold the thighs and had so little width as to impose a potentially embarrassing promiscuity upon their occupants. Fortunately, this was something that Armand and Roseline enjoyed, and they squeezed tightly together on the wooden bench. A whistle sounded, and the train lurched into motion.

The small steam locomotive, a perfect miniature of a full-sized one, pulled the train along at a cautious pace not exceeding 10 kilometres an hour. It was not so much a train trip as a gentle rocking to the rhythm of the cross-ties between the rails. The narrow track ran along beneath the trees of the Orsay embankment and passed through tunnels under the Alma and Iéna bridges before entering a tight curve and proceeding up Avenue de Suffren. Fences on either side bore safety notices reading, 'Warning: Look out for trees! Do not allow legs or heads to project beyond carriage!' The national printing office had loaned its stock of characters to enable the notices to be published in twenty-eight languages – including Malay, Sanskrit, Volapük, Provençal, Latin, and even shorthand.

But Roseline was busy reading something else. She was engrossed in the Exposition guidebook.

'We haven't chosen our destination. Where do you want to go first?'

'No idea! What do you suggest?'

'Charles Garnier is offering a history of human habitation on the Champ-de-Mars. "Jules Verne dreamed of travelling around the world in eighty days; the journey can now be done in six hours!" it says here.'

'Garnier again! He's everywhere, isn't he? You needn't describe this architectural gem for me, I can imagine it – here a primitive cave, there an Egyptian building, somewhere else a medieval castle or a Louis XV town house… Not one for me, I'm afraid!'

The actress licked a finger and turned the page.

'There's been a lot of talk about this one: Rue du Caire. It's a genuine Arab street with carved gateways and mucherabys rebuilt from old demolition jobs. The buildings are copies. There's a mosque, a school, a palace… In the café, real Egyptians serve the drinks. They've brought over about a hundred natives to run the little booths that line the street: a weaver, a goldsmith, a saddler, a carver…and donkey-drivers with their mounts. Oh, please let's go there! It would be fun to see a belly-dancer, wouldn't it?'

The engineer rolled a cigarette with an air of boredom. Roseline looked for another cause to champion.

'Luminous fountains on the Champ-de-Mars: an interplay of water and light produced by electricity…'

'Of interest only to the idle curious!'

'Or the Japanese villa! Daily performances in the local manner: an attack by bandits, the execution of a man condemned to death, someone committing *hara-kiri*… Otherwise, I can offer you the Forest Pavilion, built from all the types of wood that grow in France. Whole beeches and maples form a colonnade… No? Well, what about the painted panoramas: "History of the Century" shows a procession of a hundred famous characters; "Transatlantic Liners" simulates a voyage on the high seas; "Ports of France" is a geographical mock-up featuring a harbour in Brittany and a Mediterranean quayside… Still no? Would you rather see the millionth-scale globe with a spiral gallery you can walk up?'

Each time Armand declined, shaking his head with the regularity of a metronome. Vexed, his fiancée slammed the guidebook shut and folded her arms. The young man saw the error of his ways.

'Sorry, darling, I'm being a spoilsport... But it's not my fault if the attractions drawing the crowds strike me as vulgar and boring! Let me have the guidebook. There must be something to my liking!'

Whatever her fiancé suggested, Roseline went along with. They alighted from the train and took rickshaws at the sign of the Green Dragon. The athletic legs of two Tonkinese men brought them swiftly to the Thomas Edison pavilion. A guided tour by the International Society of Electricians would be starting shortly.

'Just our luck!' the engineer cursed. 'We have to wait!'

The queue here was even longer than for the miniature train. Everyone was keen to try out the improvements that had been made to the American machines that had caused such a stir eleven years earlier, at the 1878 Exposition. Much was expected of the new Edison phonographs, whose mechanism was capable of reciting impeccably, in a clear, distinct voice, the thousand or so words recorded on a wax cylinder. This invention was accompanied by another, the theatrophone, which transmitted live performances via a cable from the Opéra-Comique.

While awaiting their turn to put the receivers to their ears, visitors relieved the tedium by 'taking a hit' from the wire fence: a current of around 100 volts electrified it at intervals, giving people a pleasurable thrill. Children especially enjoyed electrocuting themselves.

Roseline was already familiar with the phonograph, having tried one out in Gordon Hole's room. She was less interested in its delicate cogwheels than in the huge, powerful, brutal ones in the engines exhibited in the Galerie des Machines.

Situated at the eastern end of the Champ-de-Mars, the Galerie des Machines was a vast construction measuring 420 metres in length and a quarter of that in width. Its disproportionate size made it the younger brother of the Tower. In fact there was a comic song to the effect that, should the Tower collapse, the gallery would make a handy coffin. The two monuments did indeed have much in common: both used approximately the same quantity of iron, and each had cost a similar amount to assemble. Moreover, engineer Dutert had accepted almost as mad a challenge in roofing his building with enormous metal trusses that spanned the entire central nave without any intermediate support. There was nothing to hold the 45-metre vault up but a paradoxical play of forces.

'A fine piece of work!' Armand commented, knowing what he was talking about.

'Yes, it looks nice,' echoed the actress.

The Galerie des Machines appealed to them for different reasons: Roseline admired the graceful statues representing 'Steam' and 'Electricity' that flanked the entrance as well as the whiplash lines of the Art Nouveau decoration. Armand, however, preferred the high-level moving platform which, as it carried visitors down the length of the interior, gave them a bird's-eye view of the exhibits on either side.

They left the gallery well content, if a little deafened by the din of progress.

Armand was reluctant to leave the Exposition without looking at the so-called 'ancillary galleries', the only ones to be somewhat shunned by the public, despite the interest of what was on show there. All one met in them was a trickle – characterised by varying degrees of turbulence – of poets and drug addicts in search of fresh material for their waking dreams.

It was in such company that the couple successively visited, for example, the Meat Inspectorate display with its many items of carnal pathology including a 'pig's head stained black', a 'calcified horse liver', a 'measled ham' and some 'rotting sausages'. Then there was the display organised by the Department for the Insane, showing different types of rooms and cells complete with the equipment used to discipline inmates. There was one put on by the Cleansing Service with wheelbarrows, protective suits for sewage workers and bottles of disinfectant, but also full-size models of a healthy house with modern water closets and another that was less salubrious, with no balconies and bricked-up windows. Finally there were the dreary stands of the Libraries Department, which included glass-fronted bookcases and card-indice and those of the Public Finance Office with their early budget-books and ledgers.

Armand said he had never known a museum visit provide so much entertainment.

'I'm thirsty!' he said as they emerged. 'Where can one get a beer here?'

Roseline consulted the guidebook.

'"The Exposition contains 86 bars…"' she read. 'Quite a choice! The Bambara Café and the Creole Restaurant are particularly recommended.'

'I've found something closer: the Volpini Café. It looks all right – let's go in!'

The pair crossed the terrace of the Palace of the Fine Arts towards a large marquee.

A table had just become vacant. Armand took one seat and Roseline took the other, installing herself as comfortably as her elaborate skirt would allow. The women's magazines, which at other times told their readers what to wear on the beach or in the divorce court, had prescribed this particular model for a visit to the Universal Exposition: a plum-coloured costume decorated with embroidered flowerets, its sleeves trimmed with pale lace. What particularly distinguished the outfit was that it followed the lines of hip and waist quite closely – a fashion idea that met with Armand's full approval.

'What are you looking at?' Roseline asked, becoming aware not so much of her fiancé's interest but that of several other men who were giving her the eye.

'Something that it would be unseemly for anyone else to admire but me!'

Roseline smiled, revealing a row of perfect teeth – each one of them yet another reason for falling in love with her. Their hands touched beneath the marble tabletop.

In a moment, Armand's reappeared to take the menu that a waiter had just brought.

'What? Two francs for a bowl of soup! Five francs for a pear! Thirty sous for a portion of cheese! These are prices for Americans!'

'The prices are higher because of the Centenary…'

'In that case, we'll eat somewhere else and pay less. 5 francs is the price of a ticket to the 'Buffalo Bill' show at Porte des Ternes. I'd rather see a live horse prancing than a bit of horsemeat on a plate!'

But an orchestra had just occupied the stand: four uniformed young Russians wearing smart Cossack boots were tuning instruments decorated with interlacing flowers. Armand's attention was drawn to the adjacent tables, where the musicians were being given a rapturous welcome. Most of the customers were dressed like artists. Those at the more bourgeois end of the scale must have come from the nearby watercolour pavilion; others, more disaffected, had perhaps come to admire the modern canvases displayed around the café.

Having decided to stay, while they were waiting for their order the couple began to feel curious about this evidently unpopular art, which had opted for an approach that placed it radically at variance with academic convention. Although the artists had paid for the privilege, the works of these *impressionistes* and *synthétistes* were hung at the far end of the room between the counter and the buffet, hard by the beer pumps. Anyone who stopped to look at them ran the risk of being jostled by the waiters, whose route to the kitchens took them right past the paintings. Armand peered forward to decipher the signature on one of the canvases: P. Gauguin.

'Never heard of him!' the engineer muttered with that special disdain that artistic anonymity inspires.

Roseline was lingering over the next work, which depicted a group of Breton women.

'Who knows? Maybe this unknown will be a star one day… Fame is notoriously capricious.'

'You think so? P. Gauguin will become famous while Édouard Detaille, the winner of last year's Salon and now the favourite for the Exposition Prize, will be consigned to oblivion?'

'Why not? No one likes Le Pellerin de Flaubert any more, who once gave us that fine allegory of progress, "Jesus Christ Driving a Railway Train!" Established reputations are often inflated, and memory is a better judge than one thinks.'

'I hope so… Because then there'd be a chance that the Eiffel Tower would one day be renamed the Boissier Tower! The boss, after all, only really knew the Tower through his calculations. I nearly lost my life on it!'

Returning to their table, they sat down to enjoy a large glass of the currently fashionable 'coco Mariani', which they continued to re-order until the café closed.

After these private festivities in the company of Armand, Roseline's return – her resurrection, to all intents and purposes – was celebrated at a grand supper party given by Uncle Jules.

The Rue de Bruxelles house had never seen such a large crowd – nor one so youthful. It made the old man very happy, and he demonstrated by the quality of his cooking that he could be an excellent host as well as a dignified recluse.

After a starter of chicken in aspic with a hot sauce, the company enjoyed asparagus 'à la Pompadour' and salmon 'à la genevoise' – two recipes contributed by Dumas père that Jules had copied from his favourite magazine. The conversation was spirited, the atmosphere by turns jolly and emotional.

Then, having dwelt at length on memories of the past, over cheese the guests turned to a current matter: the attempt to dynamite the Tower.

The old man was granted the honour of opening the debate.

'My great age,' he began vigorously, turning to the young trio, 'gives me licence to address you as a father, even if I do not in fact have that status. I listened to the account of your adventures… Appalling! You behaved – how can I put this? – like stupid, mindless animals!'

'What do you mean, uncle?' Armand asked, wiping his chin with a corner of his serviette.

'After Salome's confession, there was only one sensible course of action: to notify the police!'

'We considered that, sir,' Odilon replied. 'There was a risk of the police taking Roseline hostage. In the circumstances, you yourself…'

'You read too many crime novels!' Jules broke in. 'Combating villains is all well and good for the heroes of newspaper serials! Not for you – creatures of flesh and blood! You took enormous risks! It would only need Gaspard to have been a good shot rather than a novice, and Roseline would be dead. As for Armand and Odilon, they'd probably be out of action. And what about Gordon Hole? He's still at large. He may even be on your trail.'

And so the sermon went on. Meanwhile, the young people kept their eyes on their Montlhéry cheese. When Uncle Jules had finished, it was Roseline's turn to put her point of view.

'Monsieur Boissier, I too tremble at the idea of Hole being at liberty. God knows what he's up to at this very moment! However, it would be no good taking legal action against him. What evidence do we have? How can we prove he is guilty or even an accessory? Hole said a great deal but he hardly ever wrote anything down. I doubt whether he's left any trace of his crimes.'

'You're forgetting the witnesses,' Uncle Jules persisted. 'There are plenty of those, apparently.'

'Unfortunately, even when repeated under oath witness statements do not make a crime. There's no law against attending a spiritualist group or even practising deception at one. Anyway, lots of people think the whole idea of calling up the dead is a hoax. Nor can Hole be accused of having usurped my father's personality. That's a moral offence, not a legal one…'

These arguments gave the old man something to think about.

'All the same, you were poisoned, kept prisoner…'

'Probably the most scandalous doings go on without anyone knowing. As for the visits the American made to his associate, they took place late in the evening and he was discreet. Of course, the concierge may have seen him on the stairs, and some evenings he did ring the bell… But that again proves nothing.'

'We're buggered, then!' Jules exclaimed with the familiarity of despair.

Odilon waited for the general emotion to dissipate before intervening.

'There is one thing we can do, sir. We know the American's intentions: to blow up the Tower on Opening Day. His plan must be thwarted at all costs. Thousands of lives are at stake.'

'But how are we to prevent Gordon Hole from gaining access to the Tower? There'll be masses of visitors!'

'Who said anything about stopping him? No, we won't try anything before he's set the charges. That way, we stand most chance of catching him red-handed.'

Jules gave a strangled cry: 'You're mad!'

'We've no choice!'

'But you have: tell the police! Hole will be arrested and thrown into gaol, and we'll be rid of that loathsome character for a long time to come.'

The Parisian shook his head slowly from one side to the other and back again, like a teacher confronted by a dunce.

'Do you suppose Hole would have stayed on at the Hôtel Britannique if he'd had the slightest fear of a visit from the police? Roseline is right: we have no evidence against him. If he was arrested, he'd be released immediately. The situation would then be worse: knowing what we'd done, he would most likely change his plans – in a direction we could not possibly predict.'

'Not only would the Tower be in danger,' the actress put in. 'Our lives would be threatened!'

The old man had to agree: acting alone, without the knowledge of the police or the Tower staff, was the safest course. The rest of the evening was spent arranging the details of the operation.

Towards midnight, Roseline having of necessity retired to a room upstairs, Uncle Jules contrived to meet her as she came down. Shyly, he accosted her:

'Mademoiselle Page, may I speak with you alone?'

'But of course, Monsieur Boissier!'

He led the young woman into a study where the shutters were closed. The only item of furniture in the room was a table covered with a velvet cloth – which seemed to have something else under it. Jules lit two hanging oil lamps of the robust kind used by the railway company.

'I shall be brief,' he began, standing by the table. 'I did not give you a present on the occasion of your engagement as tradition requires and the most elementary good manners demand. You see, everything happened so fast. Today it is time I repaired that omission.'

Roseline's response was to make a graceful movement of her chin as if to say: 'I didn't hold it against you. All the same, it's nice of you to think of it…'

'My gift,' Uncle Jules went on, leaning one fist on the table, 'is somewhat unusual. To start with, it is meant for you and you alone: it won't be any use or give any pleasure to your fiancé. In fact, it would be best if he does not know I have given it to you. Later on… Well, you'll understand.'

'I'm intrigued, sir.'

Without further ado, Jules removed the cloth from the table with the same sweeping gesture as, in his younger years, he had employed to reveal locomotive prototypes.

'Bless my soul!' Roseline exclaimed. 'Whatever is it?'

'I call it a "breast pouch", but perhaps "bosom support" would be a better name – what do you think? It's a device of my own invention for… Well, the name says it all, does it not?'

'And… And it's for me?' the actress stammered, struggling between amazement and hilarity.

'Ah, do you not like it?' the old man asked anxiously. 'You're shocked, perhaps?'

'Not at all, no, it's just…very unusual!'

Jules turned up the wicks in the lamps to give more light.

'The way it works is simplicity itself,' he explained, taking up the garment. 'No more corsets and all that time spent lacing! Look, you slip this strap over one shoulder, this one over the other, hook up behind…and it's on!'

Roseline had recovered herself somewhat. She kissed the old man on both cheeks.

'Thank you. Thank you so much, Uncle Jules. It's a lovely present.'

'Seriously?' the retired engineer beamed. 'You mean you like it?'

'I'm very pleased with it… You have no idea what women go through, wearing corsets. They're instruments of torture. To spend every waking hour imprisoned in that grill of steel – why, it's worse than being shut in a room on one's own all day. And I should know! Thanks to your invention, I shall be the only woman in Paris who can breathe easily inside her dress. However…would you mind a little anatomical observation?'

'I'm all ears.'

'Your device doesn't really fit me. The bust measurement, you know. I'd need it slightly larger...'

'I didn't have a model, you see,' the old man said in his defence. 'I was working…from imagination!'

Jules and Roseline agreed to make a new prototype, designed from nature. 'It will be our secret,' the young woman whispered. Having agreed to say nothing about the conversation they had just had, they took their leave of each other with all the furtiveness of an adulterous couple.

A short time before this, Armand and Odilon, concerned at Roseline's prolonged absence, had climbed the stairs to the first floor. There they found only empty rooms and closed doors, the latter bringing back painful memories for the young man from St. Flour.

'Odilon, there's a question I want to ask you. But first you must promise to give me a straight answer.'

'I promise,' said the engineer, raising his right hand.

'A while back, when we went to the Gingerbread Fair, I tried to open the door of a caravan and the door wouldn't budge... Do you remember?'

'As clearly as the day I lost my virginity!'

''Well, I have to know... Was there some trick? Was there a bar or something blocking the door from outside?'

A moment elapsed before the Parisian declared very solemnly:

'It was an ordinary door, Armand, a perfectly ordinary door.'

To which he added, by way of reassuring his friend:

'That's not to say there wasn't another person operating from outside. Our bowler-hatted friend, for example.'

Armand thought for a long time.

'And the panes of glass in the morgue that suddenly shattered?'

'That I can't explain. A gas explosion, possibly, as we conjectured?'

'Possibly...but then again, possibly not. The mystery remains. Oh, Odilon! I wish I could believe that all of it – mediums, seances, spiritualism – was just the product of sick minds. Roseline's voice was a hoax, why not the rest? The unfortunate fact is that there's no proof, but nothing invalidates it all, either... Always this quandary in which one finds oneself! Should one choose reason or faith, nature or the supernatural…?'

'There, my friend, I have no answer. Science will never remedy our ignorance of first causes and final ends. All we can study are effects…'

'It's dreadful!' Armand groaned. There was real anguish in his voice.

'Why? As Tallyrand said: "Hope is certainly no prerequisite for setting out, nor success for persevering." I would humbly add: "Nor understanding for doing something." Do you suppose soldiers would get anywhere if they gave so much as a thought to the meaning of their actions? Well, I too am at war. I'm opposed to Gordon Hole and his insane plan to blow up the Tower! There's a great cause!'

Odilon's confidence passed to his friend in waves of fresh energy. As after swallowing a tonic, Armand was aware of renewed vigour coursing almost instantaneously through his veins. He said nothing but shook the Parisian firmly by the hand.

At that moment, they heard Roseline's voice down in the drawing-room. The two friends descended the stairs in a rush.

For the sake of convenience, Jules Boissier suggested that his friends stay the night. Next morning, the young people shared out the domestic tasks, for the old man employed no one to maintain his household.

Roseline and Salome were dispatched to the local well to replenish the water supply, this method of distribution being thought healthier than pumping, while Armand and Odilon made a start on the pile of washing-up.

They had no idea – how could they? – that at the same moment, in a street not far off, Gordon Hole was himself washing dishes in front of a jury of examiners. This test followed one about handling a broom and one devoted to waiting skills, and was by no means the least demanding. The candidate was given a minute to restore to their virgin state five large dinner-plates, five champagne glasses and a pan lined with ancient grease – and to do so, of course, without causing the least chip or crack in the nielloed porcelain or the bohemian crystal. The only tools provided were a sponge and a cake of soft soap.

The American made the right decision: starting with the glasses, which hardly dirtied the water, before continuing with the dishes and finishing with the dreadful fish pan. The result appeared to satisfy the members of the jury, whose chins sketched a sign of approval.

'Congratulations, Monsieur Swimson! You passed our third test brilliantly.'

None of them shook the American's soapy hand, but they meant what their spokesman said. The last test investigated the candidate's culinary skills. It was theoretical rather than practical, the preparation of an actual dish solely for the purposes of the examination being considered too onerous.

Summoned to assist in the matter, the restaurant's head cook studied the certificates of aptitude that Hole had presented. The first was merely an elaborate forgery bearing the badge of the famous Delmonico's restaurant on New York's 5th Avenue. The second, signed by the chef at the Hôtel Britannique, testified to a four month placement as kitchen assistant, during which Monsieur Swimson had demonstrated a 'respectable command of the commonest French recipes' (there followed a long list of dishes) and 'considerable talent in the preparation of Anglo-Saxon recipes'.

'These testimonials certainly speak in your favour,' the chef remarked. 'Also, the fact that you have specialized in American cooking is a bonus for our establishment. Let's see… Is the recipe for Lobster Newport one of your regulars?'

'It certainly is, sir.'

'Which mushroom is usually associated with it?'

'The truffle. Two medium truffles are right for an 800-gram lobster.'

'Precisely. Now, can you give us the ingredients of a shrimp cocktail?'

The examination continued for a further quarter-of-an-hour, at the end of which, on the positive advice of the head chef, the jury pronounced itself in favour of taking Monsieur Swimson on at assistant grade. He would shortly be assigned to the Anglo-American Bar at the 300-metre Tower.

The usual congratulations followed, together with these special recommendations from the proprietor:

'The Bar will be one of four catering establishments to be opened on the first platform. The others will be the Brasserie Lorraine, the Russian Restaurant, and a French restaurant called Brébant. We expect large volumes of trade well before lunch. You will of course need to be there at the crack of dawn! Our cashier will issue you with a special pass providing access to the Tower… Be punctual!'

'Oh, I shall!' Gordon Hole affirmed with an indecipherable smile.

16

The inauguration of the Tower, a week after the opening of
the Universal Exposition, was the major attraction of the
exhibition and its dominant talking-point.

The slow growth of the Tower beneath the gaze of Parisians
but even more, now, its inaccessibility at the centre of a busy,
animated spectacle exasperated the public's expectations. Like
a special delicacy displayed in a confectioner's window, the
Tower drew every eye and whipped up every appetite.

People flocked to it from all over the world to admire it and
to contrive, as their aptitudes permitted, to climb to one of the
three platforms that formed a scale of merit: the first was open
to families, the second was accessible to walkers, the third was
reserved for seasoned climbers. The air at the top was thought
to be the best: healthy, pure, invigorating, even endowed with
certain healing properties against anaemia or whooping
cough, as established by one Dr. Hénocque. Eiffel sent his
grandchildren up there to cure their head colds.

Responding to the call of this new peak, as if a mountain
had grown at the heart of Paris, brave foreigners who could

not afford the train attempted some exhaustingly novel approaches. Their exploits passed into legend. There were the Italians who crossed the Alps on velocipedes, the Austrians who surmounted the same obstacle with a wheelbarrow, the Romanian who travelled by litter and the Tyrolean who took a sedan-chair. One Russian officer achieved fame by covering the distance from Warsaw to Paris on horseback.

The force that took possession of vast numbers of people deserved to be called something other than 'curiosity'. A Vogue columnist sought to evoke it with the words, 'Those seven million kilos of iron must exert some incredible magnetic attraction since the Tower draws from their homes people on both sides of the Atlantic, since every steamer in every port in all the world is setting a course for this amazing miracle.'

One or two voices did speak up against the Tower, accusing it of eclipsing the country's other monuments. Towns and cities throughout France found themselves suffering from their flat and seemingly crippled horizons since the erection of the Paris Tower. They complained that their treasures — including cathedrals with graceful, soaring spires and slender belfries — were rated purely in terms of their vertical performance. An advertisement began to appear in American magazines that was really addressed to France's National Tourist Office, reading, 'Must every town have its Eiffel Tower before you will appreciate the rest of France?'

Their efforts were in vain…

Like a mighty sceptre brandished above Paris, the Tower affirmed the omnipotence of industry, the sovereignty it meant to wield henceforth not just over the world of making — be it bridges, road, or railways — but also over the world of thought.

On that crucial day, Armand, Roseline, Odilon, Salome and Jules were not worried about tourism. They had only one thing in mind: thwarting Gordon Hole and his projected assault on the Tower. Each had been given a precise task in accordance with wishes expressed if not with means available.

Chivalry willed that the least risky jobs should fall to the women. So Roseline and Salome had been assigned an easy one: keeping a lookout for Gordon Hole's arrival at the foot of the Tower.

Not that this was an entirely simple matter – on the one hand, because of the huge crowds of visitors; on the other, because of an elementary but insoluble mathematical obstacle: two women had to watch four piers. Although Jules Boissier had been excused any onerous work on the grounds of age, he insisted on lending a hand. This brought the number of watchers to three, which was an improvement, certainly, but still not enough.

It quickly became apparent that there were going to be problems here. No one had expected the crowds to be so restless or so ill-contained. People surged against and frequently broke through the barriers designed to keep them in line, and the ticket booths were literally swamped. How were any of them to distinguish a particular face among all those hats, canes and sunshades, constantly stirring and shifting like a mass of molten lava?

The other difficulty had to do with the access routes. No doubt in order to distribute the load between the four supports, these had been increased in number. The staircases up occupied the northern and southern piers, which also housed the elevators to the second platform. The western and eastern piers held the staircases down and the elevators to the first platform.

Effective surveillance was impossible without a company of policemen stationed at every corner of the monument, checking the papers of each person wishing to ascend.

'It can't be done! We're wasting our time!' Uncle Jules sighed.

Roseline put a hand to the little mirror in her pocket that was to be used to flash a signal to the boys up the Tower that Hole had arrived.

'They're relying on us. We must stick to the plan.'

'But our lookout operation will leak like a sieve!' cried Jules, his pessimism growing all the time.

Salome sprang to her friend's defence.

'Roseline's right, we must do as we agreed. Who knows? Maybe with luck…'

'Huh! Fancy relying on luck!' the old man grumbled as, despite his misgivings, he took up his post under the northern pier.

While Jules and the two women were keeping watch at the foot of the monument, the twins had ascended the Tower to intercept the American.

Only Odilon was able to mingle with the official party currently invading the 'Iron Lady'.

A group of men in tail coats – amongst which, exceptionally, two or three more modern jackets could be made out – were pompously preparing to ascend the Tower. The bolder ones chose that intimidating novelty, the elevator, though never without crossing their fingers or reeling off a prayer. Among candidates for the vertical ascent, persons of note turned out to be the most nervous. The Shah of Persia, for example, Nasser ed-Din, after first dispatching his minions to test the strange invention, subsequently turned his back on it and chose the stairs; or take Prince Baudouin of Belgium, who entered the cabin crossing himself, following a lengthy telephone conversation with his parents.

The vast majority preferred the stairs. Apart from the safety aspect, which was their main advantage, they offered powerful men with a concern for protocol the possibility of staggering their progress in a satisfactory manner. The king went one step ahead of the minister, the minister two steps ahead of the councillor etc., in a fashion that preserved the age-old tradition of the palace steps.

Of course, as a mere engineer Odilon was not entitled to walk at the head of the procession with Gustave Eiffel, the king of Siam, the *bey* of Djibouti and similar luminaries. He was only permitted to tag along behind where his peers rollicked like schoolboys, noisily celebrating the completion of the Tower.

The mood among staff was very different from the sophisticated, strutting atmosphere that reigned in the foremost ranks. Back here there was dancing, people shouted 'hurrahs', bottles of champagne were shaken to froth them up, ready for the buffet to come. In fact, some of the golden liquid was imbibed straight from the bottle in cooling and not always entirely accurate draughts that stained many a shirt-front yellow. Already consolidating memories, younger members, their voices heavy with emotion, went back over heroic episodes from the history of the past two years or, in tones shot through with laughter, its few lighter moments:

'Do you remember the time when Pluot lost his spectacles? What a business! He accused us of having taken them, even wanted to go through our pockets! It was going to be fines all round unless the thief gave himself up!'

'Yes! And what about the time Sauvestre was so drunk he dipped his quill in his drink? He complained it was writing a funny colour! Good God!'

Yet behind the apparent merriment, there was enormous tiredness. Odilon's gaze alternated between these gaunt young faces, furrowed by long nights at the drawing-board, and the well-fed princes in front, whose only merit was to have alighted from a carriage and followed a red carpet. They led, while the men who had actually built the Tower came after. 'The world knows no justice!' the engineer mused philosophically.

Like his three associates at the foot of the monument, Odilon was becoming aware of the difficulties his mission presented.

From his official position within the procession, he had offered to screen its composition. There was no reason why Gordon Hole should not have infiltrated the American delegation. Numerous foreigners had accepted Eiffel's invitation including, of course, representatives of every scientific discipline. Hole would have fitted in. What a temptation that would have been for such a megalomaniac, detonating his bomb in the middle of the procession, simultaneously destroying not only the Tower but the elite of the civilised world! Would he even attempt to escape the explosion himself? Maybe not... The stakes seemed high enough and the man sufficiently unpredictable for a suicide attempt to be well within the bounds of possibility.

During the ascent, Odilon examined the people immediately around him as well as those he could glimpse, ahead and behind, through the struts of the great iron web. Unfortunately, the terms of admission to the official party had been very generous, at least three hundred people had received complimentary tickets and there were the inevitable extras who had hitched a free ride. Furthermore, interlopers were joining the procession all the time, employees from the restaurants on the first platform, journalists, workmen, elevator attendants... Although the Tower was still closed to the public, it seemed to have been invaded already, colonised by large numbers of insects swarming up its long iron legs. How could he scan such a throng?

Odilon consulted his watch: 11:40.

'Possibly at this very instant a flame is racing along a fuse!' the engineer breathed, surveying his companions. 'If they only knew!'

The selfsame thought coursed through Armand's mind as he contemplated the crowds milling around the piers 100 metres below, 'If they only knew!'

Of the five tasks, he had chosen the riskiest. Some of the risks were natural – deriving from the skills he must successfully deploy – while others, aggravating these, were external and had to do with his personal involvement.

What he was going to try to do was nothing less than to repeat, this time for the right reason, his earlier sabotage attempt. Armand put it like this. 'Redeeming a bad action by performing the same action in reverse.' In other words, he suggested that he should investigate the Tower in search of Hole's charges.

Of course, the American might set his explosives somewhere other than in the actual structure. The finished Tower offered countless hiding-places, and many had the advantage over a junction between two girders of being harder to spot. However, Armand believed that an architect, being professionally aware of the weak points of a building, would be tempted to exploit them.

'He's aiming to make the Tower collapse, not just to damage it,' the engineer reasoned. 'So, if he wishes to achieve that with a moderate amount of explosive, the weak points are where he must place his charges.'

As might have been expected, Armand's suggestion caused consternation among his companions:

'But that's suicide!'

'It's a challenge, certainly...'

'You'll kill yourself!'

'I'll be taking some risks, I admit.'

'Oh, no!' Roseline cried angrily. 'Am I to lose you just when I've found you again? It's foolishness and I forbid it!'

The young man from St. Flour took his fiancée's hand, but she repulsed him with a flick of her fan.

'Come on, Armand – think again!' Odilon put in. 'Your chances of succeeding are virtually nil. Even if you manage to enter the Tower, which considering the number of guards would already be an achievement, your first step out on a girder would expose you to thousands of eyes. It would be the middle of the day, don't forget, and crowds of visitors would be swarming all over the Tower. What would Jean Compagnon or Adolphe Salles say if they passed you on one of the staircases?'

'That's why I shan't be taking the stairs but using the elevator.'

'With the official party, I presume?'

'No, though we will be sharing the same cabin.'

They was no shifting him.

First urged and then pleaded with by his friends, Armand's reply was unchanging. 'I've done wrong. I must face the fact and make what reparation I can.'

That night, hours before dawn, Armand crossed the Champ-de-Mars and vaulted over the fence surrounding the Roux-Combaluzier elevator in the east pier.

The iron lattice-work had creaked under his weight. He lay flat on the ground and listened. The only sounds were the distant barking of guard dogs and hammering from the night shift working on the first platform. He got to his feet and stepped over the barrier blocking access to the elevator.

Despite its imposing size – two cabins, one on top of the other, capable of transporting one hundred passengers per trip – the elevator was simple to climb. Using the guard-rail of the gallery, then its delicate canopy, he easily reached the roof of the lower cabin. From there he was able to pull himself up onto the curved roof of the upper compartment, some ten metres above ground.

One question was bothering Armand. Once on the roof, he emptied his bag and held the coat he had brought against the metal vault on which he was standing. In the moonlight, the colours looked the same, a reddish-brown obtained by mixing iron minium with linseed oil. The engineer gave a sigh of relief. He spread the coat, lay down on it, and pulled the sides over him to leave only the upper part of his face exposed.

The rest of the night passed without incident. The elevator was inspected by the operations manager before being taken into service and the manager did not see his duties as extending to carrying out a check on the roof of the second cabin. As for the workmen descending the east-pier stairs, none of them noticed a roll of fabric abandoned on the sheet-metal cladding. They had better things to think about on the day the Tower was being inaugurated!

As the hours passed, an increasingly dense crowd gathered outside the gates of the elevator. A rising tide of conversation could be heard, mixed with the pawing of the horses belonging to the Republican Guard and the squealing of the Decauville railway. These nearby sounds tested Armand's nerves severely: wrapped in his coat, he felt like a condemned man, blindfolded, facing an execution squad. 'I must have been mad to embark on this adventure!' he said with sudden regret. 'It will be a miracle if I come through alive!'

'Atten – shun!' The order was followed by the sharp clicking of many pairs of heels. Automatically, Armand brought his own together. A forced silence had fallen among the spectators, possibly as some important personage went by. But suddenly a band struck up, large brass sections blaring out *The Marseillaise*. It sounded very close, only metres away. The thumps on the bass drum made the cabin roof vibrate. The engineer flinched, causing one foot to emerge from the coat. Gritting his teeth, he brought it back in.

A speech followed, with an interpreter translating it into some foreign language. More music, another barked order, rhythmic hoof-beats… Time passed with irritating slowness, like blood flowing silently from a simple cut – but threatening to drain the entire body.

At last, much to the young man's relief, the cabin dipped under the weight of the passengers climbing aboard. When both cabins were full, two blasts on a whistle indicated that the elevator was ready to depart. Armand felt it lurch into motion.

All hell broke loose. Armand had not anticipated that the movement of the machine would be so violent and so convulsive. The first few jolts nearly made him roll off the roof, and he was saved only by a reflex action: he grasped and hung onto the edge of the sheet-iron on which he lay. Then he had to deal with a series of almost unbearable shocks that caused his jaws to rattle like castanets and put the muscles of his arms under painful tension. Furthermore, an infernal din accompanied the whole operation as huge iron chain-links ground their way through ducts of the same metal.

Fortunately, the trip was a short one. Something like a minute after its departure, the elevator came to a halt with a final jerk at the level of the first platform. The doors slid open and a compact stream of passengers emerged.

This was the critical moment. Armand had literally to step over the crowd, reaching out across the sea of hats to the iron structure opposite him. If anyone chose that moment to look up, that would be it! Just as he had calculated, there was a hollow girder about a metre from his head.

'Don't think – jump!'

Gathering the coat around him, he leaped catlike to a point halfway along the strut. Fear flooded his muscles with new strength. With an agility he had not known he possessed, he pulled himself up by his arms alone and took refuge several metres farther along behind a bunch of cross-ties that hid him from view. His pulse hammered in his ears with a noise like field-guns firing.

He took a quick look to check that no one had spotted his move. As it happened, the elevator operator had just climbed up the side of the second cabin to inspect the roof. Possibly someone had heard the sound of his fingernails scrabbling for a hold. If he had left it a moment longer…

'The gods are with me!' thought Armand jubilantly, licking the sweat off the corners of his unfamiliar moustache.

Wrapped in the coat, the colour of which caused him to blend perfectly with the background, he waited until the now empty cabins redescended. Then his elusive silhouette could be seen crawling along girders, sliding down ladders and negotiating former scaffolding structures on his knees. Expending little effort, Armand made rapid progress. He seemed at one with the Tower, swimming like a blood corpuscle through the arteries of the organism to which it brings oxygen.

He quickly reached his destination, the exact place where he had once fastened his third charge of dynamite. A piece of string still hung from a hole. Alas, he saw nothing more…

'Don't hang around!' the young man urged himself in order to hide his disappointment. 'West pier next!'

The return journey was accomplished without difficulty. As Armand drew near the platform, he noticed that the elevator was still toiling upward and had reached no more than the halfway mark. Nimbly, he threw his coat into the bag and jumped across to the service gangway. A moment later, he set foot on the gallery of the first platform.

Beneath his camouflage coat, Armand wore a suit that was to enable him to cross the platform from one pier to the other, passing through the crowd without attracting attention. It was of the kind worn by people walking in the mountains. Indeed, many people thought of a visit to the Tower in terms of an Alpine excursion. It comprised a pair of trousers, a waistcoat and a jacket cut from the same Scottish tweed criss-crossed with red and green stripes.

Since on the other hand Armand ran the risk of being recognised by Gordon Hole or by one his former work-mates, he had rounded off his disguise with a pair of eyeglasses and a Norwegian fur cap with ear flaps that went with his outfit. He hoped his new moustache would dispel any lingering suspicions.

Running the same risk, Roseline and Salome had taken similar precautions. Armand's fiancée had worn an Alsatian black 'butterfly' in her hair, while Odilon's lover had sported the kind of bonnet young women wear in Arles. Only Uncle Jules – whom Hole had never met – and Odilon – as a member of the official party – presented their ordinary appearance.

When Armand reached the first platform, the inaugural procession was already winding its way up towards the second. The platform was empty, except for the Tower staff, who were taking advantage of this lull between the official tour and the arrival of the general public. It was beneath their gaze that Armand strode along the gallery towards the west pier, pretending to be a guest who had been left behind.

'Are you looking for the staircase going up, sir? It starts here.'

Who had addressed him? Armand turned slowly, twisting his face into an unrecognisable grimace, with his top lip drawn back to expose the gum and his eyes screwed tight behind his spectacles. But no... It was just a young attendant, he probably thought he was being useful. If only he would mind his own business!

In the time it took for his hand to go up to his cap and his lips to form a smile of gratitude, Armand considered what he should do. He could not ignore the young fellow's advice without a solid pretext. On the other hand, dressed as he was, the role of day-tripper was the only one open to him. In a word, he was trapped...

Inwardly seething, he turned away from the west pier. He soon found the staircase and set off up it unthinkingly with the cumulative momentum of rage and fear.

'Fancy failing so pathetically!' the engineer sighed resignedly. But what else could he have done? What evading action could he take, now that he had been marked out? Armand could feel the attendant's eyes on him. Dropping the bag, he quickened his pace.

A moment later, glancing over the handrail, Odilon saw this climber ascending the stairs two at a time. As unobtrusively as possible, he went down to meet him.

'Armand?' he asked, barring his friend's passage.

Armand leaned against the rail to catch his breath.

'It was all for nothing. I was caught.'

'But why are you coming up?' the Parisian asked in a voice both strained and calm, the voice one uses with mad people.

'I have to go somewhere!'

'Not up there! You'll be recognised. All the people from Levallois have come!'

Armand gave a protracted yawn as if to say, 'What do I care?'

'Stay where you are! On this landing, you're at less risk of bumping into the wrong person. And in an hour, meet me at the place we agreed!'

Odilon hurried back up to rejoin the official party. Armand for his part had stooped to undo his shoelaces.

'It'll give me something to do in case anyone comes.'

He settled down to wait for the appointment.

The fall-back plan if anything happened was to ask for 'Monsieur Guigne's table' at the Anglo-American Bar on the first platform. Shortly before noon the five announced themselves to the head waiter with these words and sat down at the same table.

Compared to the more luxurious French restaurant, the more rustic Russian tavern, and the more picturesque Brasserie Lorraine – where Eiffel himself came to eat sauerkraut, his favourite dish – the Anglo-American bar existed rather on the margin. The catering principles applied there were in the nature of a disease contracted by the distant gold-diggers and passed on to the more restless visitors to the Universal Exposition: customers were served quickly, sated quickly and as quickly replaced. Conversation there was casual and frequently political, with the same frothy emphasis as infected the beer and an over-indulgence in sauces containing too much sugar. Tobacco was chewed there, and the rusty smell of it mingled with the aromas rising from the grills. Proponents of progress came to drink there with ardent secularists or fervent republicans. God was frequently alluded to, but mainly in the phrase 'the almighty dollar bill'.

That day, the bar was playing host to the American delegation, who had come to Paris to 'take the temperature of the country' – which would of course be higher than normal at the heart of an exhibition dedicated to the glory of France. From one end of the bar to the other, the children of the New World were swapping impressions of the Tower.

'They're a noisy lot, they really are!' Uncle Jules complained. 'There's no question that we behave better in France!'

The four young people, infatuated like everyone their age with the wonder of America, took no notice of this outburst of an older patriotism. As the eldest, Odilon began to sum up their wretched day.

'Friends, I don't know what to say… The thing we have attempted appears to be beyond our capabilities. So it would be wise, I think, to refer the matter to the proper authorities.'

'Well said!' opined Jules, who had thought this all along.

The others pondered their failure in silence.

'But before we go to the police, what say you to an American lunch? It would be a way of paying tribute to Gordon Hole. Because – say what you think – the scoundrel has had us all, good and proper. And if that's as hard to swallow as this food, too bad!'

The idea found favour, and they opened their menus. Without forming an opinion about the dishes on offer, the young people chose the most expensive – Lobster Newport and prawn cocktail – the presumed splendour of which seemed to express the full measure of their defeat.

As for Jules, he refused to have anything American but asked if there was anyone in the kitchen who could prepare him a little mushroom omelette. The waiter replied in stumbling French.

'I'm sorry, sir, but I don't know whether we can do that for you. Cook has his hands full with this delegation that's just arrived. So a new recipe…'

The old man started. What was that? A 'new recipe'? Something that his own grandmother had liked to cook back in the days when France had a king?

But it was Armand, in a mood to pick a fight, who attacked the waiter.

'An omelette! Your man can't cook an omelette?'

The waiter twisted his apron between fingers stained with barbecue sauce.

'It's like I was saying, he's at the end of his tether. Besides, nothing's going right today. There aren't enough plates, we're short of bread, the gas-stove won't light, even the garbage chute is blocked!'

The mind makes mysterious connections at times and this final phrase produced an electrical discharge in Armand's brain. His eye lit up, not with irony, as a moment ago, but with interest.

'What did you just say: the garbage chute is blocked?'

'Hopelessly!' the waiter confirmed, rather embarrassed at being required to say more on this matter. 'There's this big tube, see, running down the east pier, with a hatch to close it. Any garbage we throw down there…'

'Where does the tube lead?' the engineer asked eagerly, this thirst for details greatly astonishing his table companions.

'Into a truck specially positioned at the foot of the Tower. The garbage department take it away when it's full. I should know, it's my job to get rid of the garbage! But a moment ago when I took some, I could sense it wasn't going to work, the bags slid a couple of metres down the chute, then stopped. There must be something in the way.'

By now Armand was in a state of great agitation. He shot a look at Odilon, who looked back at him in deep puzzlement, before declaring in ringing tones:

'Not serving an omelette in Paris is inexcusable. I demand to see the cook!'

The waiter's apron-twisting became positively frantic.

'All right, I'll ask him to come out…'

'No need!' the young man said peremptorily, getting up from his chair. 'I'm coming with you!'

Odilon put out a hand to restrain his friend.

'Are you mad! All this fuss over an omelette!'

'I have a hunch,' Armand whispered to him, 'a quite astonishing hunch. What if Gordon Hole is quite simply on the staff of the Anglo-American Bar – and has placed the explosive in the garbage chute?'

'My poor friend, you are indeed raving mad! The emotions of this morning have fried your brains…'

'Look, think back! Remember how proud he was to have installed garbage chutes in his Chicago skyscraper. "An invention that looks like nothing but will revolutionize the world!" was his boast…'

But there was no need for Armand to say another word. At that very moment, Gordon Hole himself emerged from a staircase and ran across the room. Still encircling his hips was a greasy apron, which he untied as he went. The cook himself appeared at his heels, resembling a wild beast with a mane of reddish hair whose roars soared above the din of the restaurant:

'Where is he, that wretch of a kitchen boy? Leaving saucepans on the stove like that…!'

But the architect was already out of the door.

The five stood up as one. They all looked to Armand for instructions: he was their leader now.

'The bomb first!' the engineer commanded. 'We'll split into two groups. Uncle Jules and I will take care of that. You, Odilon, catch Hole if you can!'

'What about us?' the two women chorused in unison.

'Too risky – both jobs! Which would you rather, be blown up by dynamite or shot with Hole's revolver?'

Armand had hoped to silence them, but Roseline spoke up bravely:

'We'll take Hole… I've a score to settle with that gentleman!'

Bursting from the doors of the restaurant, Odilon and the girls immediately came across the fake cook's discarded apron. They looked around in every direction but could not see the tall figure of the American anywhere. Gordon Hole had fled…

'Quick – the stairs!' Odilon cried. 'I'll take the east pier, you ladies take the west!'

The three dispersed.

Armand and Jules, for their part, had gone in search of the mouth of the garbage chute. What might a garbage chute look like? Or rather, what might distinguish it from the mass of tubes, pipes and ducts squeezed into the Tower as into a human neck?

On the other side of the central open space, the two men encountered fresh crowds milling in front of the ticket booths. They were queuing to buy white tickets to ascend to the second platform or blue tickets for the top. The public had just been admitted, and compact blocks of people were starting to emerge from the elevators, in serried streams from the staircases. Everywhere – pavilions, cafés, souvenir shops – teemed with impatient visitors.

Armand elbowed his way across to a hatch he had spotted slightly to one side, in a corner.

'This way!' the engineer called, beckoning to his uncle.

Taking great care not to be noticed, the two men slid back the bolt and opened the hatch. A fearful stench assailed their nostrils.

'How vile!' Armand coughed. 'It's blocked, there's no doubt about that!'

The duct was positioned in such a way that a person could reach the first few metres of it from the platform and even lower if he risked stepping over the handrail. In an effort to locate the blockage, Jules began to sound the garbage chute with a series of thumps and kicks.

'Stop!' his nephew reacted. 'Not that way!'

'Why?'

'If as I suspect the bomb is inside this duct, the slightest shock could set it off!'

'Not if we're talking about dynamite!' the old man protested.

'Do you see a fuse?'

Jules inspected the garbage chute carefully. No piece of cord emerged from it, whether from the mouth or from one of the joints.

'In my opinion,' the young man went on, 'Hole is using pure nitro-glycerine… It's a highly unstable substance, extremely sensitive to sudden motion of any kind. You'd only need to shake it a bit and that would be that – goodbye Tower!'

Uncle Jules considered the garbage chute again, visibly appalled.

'What a treacherous invention! Bur how would the sudden motion occur?'

Armand gave this some thought. 'A build-up of weight on the charge,' he concluded. This is a delayed-action device, each time a kitchen boy dumps a sack of garbage, he increases the pressure on the plug of explosive. One day it gives – and bang goes the Tower!'

Jules quickly loosened the knot of his cravat. He felt giddy all of a sudden.

'Armand, get away from that duct! This is a job for experts. Let's alert the attendants!'

'No time!'

'What, then?'

'Well, this…'

Opening the hatch, Armand inserted both arms, then his head. At the same time he wriggled in an effort to get the rest of his body in. With a diameter of half a metre, the tube was just wide enough to admit his shoulders.

Jules was too slow to grab his nephew by the ankles. Panicking, he called out to the attendant at a nearby ticket booth. The man came running.

At precisely that moment, Roseline, who was descending the west-pier stairs, caught sight of the American three flights below. She yelled at the top of her voice.

'Stop that man! He's a criminal!'

Gordon Hole turned in the direction of the voice. He took out his revolver and fired. But the actress, seeking to spoil his aim, had hidden behind her broad parasol. The bullet struck sparks off one of the iron steps.

'That's no way to treat a lady!' said a brave citizen, seizing the architect's arm. With a blow to the stomach, Hole sent him reeling.

During this brief exchange, the two women had descended a whole flight of stairs. They were leaping like madwomen, skirts clutched to mid-thigh, delicate shoes twisting on the steel steps. To gain more speed, Roseline wrenched hers off and continued barefoot.

'Stop him! Stop that man!' Salome shouted in a broken voice.

The American waited until he had recovered his lead before once again turning and taking aim at his pursuers. The actress's Alsatian bow was visible from a long way off. Taking that as his target, Hole pulled the trigger. A tear appeared in the black bow.

'Missed!' the actress hissed. 'Clearly, pistol-shooting is not your strong point – any more than it is Gaspard's!'

With a gasp of rage, Hole plunged on down the stairs.

On the next landing, an artist had set up his easel to sketch the Tower from inside. But this was not just any artist, this was Auguste Lavastre, for whom Roseline had once sat. When the painter saw Hole running towards him, his practised eye immediately recognised the man who had called at his studio the year before last. Then he remembered the 12 canvases the American had commissioned, without ever paying an advance. His blood came quickly to the boil.

'So! We meet again, Philistine! Wait while I teach you some manners!'

A storm broke over Gordon Hole. The pointed end of a jabbing paintbrush stung the American like a swarm of bees. He managed to bring up his revolver but lost it immediately when a backhand blow from Lavache's palette tore it from his grasp.

'I'm not afraid of you, for heaven's sake!' the painter roared. 'I've seen off bigger men than you in the exhibition halls!'

Next moment, Roseline and Salome reinforced the artist's stinging brush strokes with some savage punishment from parasols wielded with considerable force.

'Mercy! Mercy!' the architect begged, sinking to his knees on the metal steps. Roseline picked up the revolver and aimed it at him.

It was being threatened by a different weapon – this one belonging to a policeman – that persuaded Armand to emerge from the garbage chute. At least, that was what he meant to do, actually getting him out involved pulling him by the legs. The engineer re-appeared, covered with some of the refuse he had encountered down the duct, his jacket was stained with sauces of various colours, while his hair was intertwined with potato-peelings. A growing circle of onlookers gathered.

Contrary to all expectations, Armand's story found an attentive ear. The officer clearly reasoned that only an absurd motive would prompt a man voluntarily to penetrate a garbage chute. The engineer was therefore granted permission to use a gaff to hook out, one by one and with extreme caution, the bags of kitchen scraps that were stopping up the tube.

'I want those all put back, mind!' the policeman warned, holding his nose.

The last bag to be removed was large enough to block the pipe. Attached to the jute wrapping was a length of rope by means of which it had no doubt been lowered and which could be used to pull it up again. Jules offered his knife to cut the bag open. Inside was a carboy filled with an oily, golden liquid that looked like honey.

Armand was triumphant, 'Nitro-glycerine!' he cried.

Applause greeted this astonishing discovery.

'And that?' the officer enquired, indicating a layer of sandy material surrounding the bottle of explosive.

'Probably kieselguhr, an inert material that chemists use when handling explosives. It absorbs shocks. The carboy was protected against vibrations and was only to go off as a result of a violent impact, for example, when it smashed into the refuse truck after falling 100 metres.'

'Young man, you have my congratulations!'

The familiar voice took Armand by surprise. Delicately, he lowered the carboy to the metal deck in preparation for receiving Gustave Eiffel, as the constructor made his way through the crowd. Still tied around Eiffel's neck was a serviette bearing the badge of the Brasserie Lorraine. The older man took the younger man's hand and shook it warmly.

'You have saved the Tower!' Eiffel proclaimed, pointing skyward. 'By this courageous gesture you have defended the work of hundreds of men and the lives of thousands. We owe you a great debt of gra...'

Eiffel had broken off in the middle of his encomium to don his spectacles and stare at the young hero's face, a certain detail of which – the nose like the prow of a ship – spoke confusedly to his memory.

'But...that face?'

'Armand Boissier, sir!' the young man offered, shaking his head in an effort to remove some of the potato-peelings. 'I am an engineer and I used to work for you...'

Rival emotions appeared to be tussling for Eiffel's soul: irritation at recalling the events of the previous year; and indeed gratitude, for the young man had just rendered an enormous service. The latter succeeded in cancelling out the former, and a smile restored peace to the great man's features.

'Tell me what's happened!' the constructor asked. 'I really don't understand the first thing about this bomb story. I have my detractors, of course, and no doubt many of them would approve of the Tower being destroyed. Some have even talked of taking action themselves. But who would be mad enough to carry out such a threat?'

'This man!'

At these words, all eyes turned to the staircase. A path opened through the crowd to allow two women through, one of whom, barefoot, held a man at a respectful distance in front of her with a revolver.

As often happens, Eiffel's memory was quicker to dredge up this face from the past than to recall the very recent impression made by the young engineer. The former École Centrale student greeted his fellow alumnus effusively.

'Gordon! What a surprise!'

'Don't come too close, sir!' Roseline warned. 'This man has sworn your ruin and that of the Tower! It was he who made the bomb!'

Eiffel was reluctant to accept appearances at face value. As a man of solid composure, his first act was to take the gun from Roseline and his second to conduct all of them, plaintiffs and accused, to the police station.

It took all afternoon to explain the whole affair, despite the twins' attempts to suppress superfluous comments. The fact was, certain episodes placed them at odds.

It emerged from the statements that the two engineers were not entirely innocent themselves and had incurred minor fines because of their sometimes impetuous actions. However, Gordon Hole was quite definitely guilty – on several counts. There was general amazement at the number of victims this man might have killed as well as at the impunity with which those victims, as well as fate itself, had so long provided him.

The chief of police had a total of seven witnesses, for the painter and the cook from the Anglo-American Bar had also decided to testify. No doubt, as soon as the investigation opened other statements would be added to the file: Apolline Sérafin, Old Man Modesty, the staff of the Hotel Britannique, Hole's call-girl, the layabouts of Montparnasse Gate, Gaspard, if he could be apprehended – and how many else besides? Wherever Hole had gone, he seemed to have done something wrong.

'The Attila of crime!' the police chief called him.

Eiffel was good enough to pay his old student colleague a visit in the temporary cell that had been assigned to him – an empty room at the police station.

'Alas, my friend! Shall you be the next victim of the electric chair, that invention that has recently replaced hanging in the state of New York? What a degrading use for progress! Electric power will be the next great leap forward in the history of humankind!'

Gordon Hole had no answer to that. A door closed, and he was gone.

Gustave Eiffel gave a private party to celebrate the happy outcome, entertaining Uncle Jules and the four young people in his private quarters on the third platform near the top of the Tower. Here a small apartment had been set aside for his personal use, whether this involved receiving important visitors or conducting scientific experiments in the adjacent laboratory. Science and sociability, the aims of what became known as 'Eiffel's boudoir', faithfully mirrored the personality of its occupant.

An invitation to visit the constructor's private domain was an honour of which Armand and Odilon were immediately sensible. The former, particularly, was enjoying his return to favour. Yesterday's reprobate was today Eiffel's guest, almost, one might say, his close friend! The young man from St. Flour admired everything about the luxurious appartments, the walls covered in cream-coloured fabric with a blue pelmet, the squat chairs upholstered in velvet, the original bench forming a ring around a central column. Clusters of Edison lamps hung from the ceiling, spreading their radiance over the desk with its telephone. Every detail illustrated Eiffel's lavish taste, his liking for costly furniture such as adorned his numerous homes.

'Welcome, all of you!' the constructor announced, distributing champagne. 'It's a pleasure for me to have you in my little drawing-room. This is not for everyone, this place. I have just refused access to a young couple who wish to spend their wedding night here. Sit down, please...'

The guests chose seats as seemed to them most fitting. Uncle Jules laid claim to an easy chair opposite Eiffel's, Roseline and Salome shared the Louis-Philippe couch, where their voluminous skirts bunched up beside them, while with a nice sense of hierarchy the eraser twins opted for the bench, which was less comfortable because of the pillar at their backs. The champagne sparkled in their goblets as they raised them in a toast.

'There is nothing more boring than a compliment that drags on,' Eiffel continued, eschewing formality. 'I shall be brief, simply praising your sagacity, your persistence and not least your courage when the time came to act.'

Then, turning towards the couch:

'Heroism was also shown by you ladies. Had you not

intervened, Gordon Hole would have got away! Your high deeds deserve a reward… So tomorrow I shall give orders for copies of the bronze medal of the Tower, which I am awarding to the workers, to be struck for you too, with your names on them. Well done, then…bravo to you all! You have served our cause with intelligence and great brilliance! I did not expect such prompt collaboration…'

A certain inflexion in the boss's final words caught Armand's ear. Not daring to voice his suspicions out loud, he exchanged a knowing glance with Odilon.

Eiffel immediately removed all ambiguity.

'Yes, my dear friends, this was indeed a collaboration. I must now reveal the truth to you… The fact is, we have known everything for weeks!'

This dramatic announcement affected his listeners in various ways. Jules Boissier felt little emotion, since he considered Eiffel to be someone of altogether exceptional intelligence in any case and was quite prepared to add detective skills to the wide range of abilities he already believed the man to possess. The young women were only moderately surprised, their involvement being more recent. Only the twins were truly overwhelmed.

They froze on their bench, and against the background of the new wall-covering, champagne glasses motionless in their hands, they looked like two of the waxwork images that the Grévin Museum had just put on display in homage to the men who had built the Tower. White-faced, they begged Eiffel to continue.

'I had no conception of what Hole was up to. Possibly he told you that I had stolen his ideas, that he was taking his revenge on me? That was not his only motive, even if it was one of them. In actual fact, his plan was nothing less than to sell the Tower as separate parts. In the earliest days of construction, he rented an office in Paris and sent out a circular letter to various European scrap-metal merchants. The letter was headed: 'Swimson & Co., purchaser of materials recovered from the Eiffel Tower'.

'Incredible!' the Parisian breathed. 'What was in it?'

'A tissue of lies… The Tower, according to him, was to be demolished after the Exposition by order of the city council. Swimson & Co. had taken on the job of selling the iron: 7,000 tons at the price of 20 centimes a kilo. A bargain indeed! And there were scrap merchants gullible enough to take the bait. Hole collected 15 million gold francs in advances, some of which helped to finance his criminal activities. But then, instead of making himself scarce like any other crook with a scrap of nous, he stayed in Paris. What did he hope to achieve? To collect the balance of his commission? To defend an absurd right to the Tower materials, now that contracts had been signed with scrap-metal merchants? No one knows…'

Uncle Jules had been following Eiffel's revelations like a newspaper serial. Passionately, he asked:

'What's the connection with the bombing?'

'I'm coming to that. Staying on in France after his confidence trick would be a big risk for Hole. Our friend would have to face the consequences. In fact one of the dealers, growing suspicious, had the idea of writing to me to ask for confirmation of the deal. I quickly disabused him and at the same time opened an investigation into the author of the swindle. Too late! Sensing that the wind had changed, Hole had wound up Swimson & Co. and seemed to be concentrating his efforts on another project. We didn't know what at the time, but I suspected an assault on the Tower…'

'…with the idea of buying up the demolished ironwork

and honouring his commitments to the scrap merchants?'
Odilon presumed.

Eiffel reacted with a dismissive gesture, as if to say, 'What do
I care?'

'And then?' asked Jules, all attention.

'My first instinct was of course to notify the police. "But
you have no proof," the inspector objected. He was right,
Gordon Hole knew what he was doing. He had a borrowed
name, false signature, junior employees representing him in
dealings with the scrap merchants... He was a phantom. How
was I to get hold of him? I could hardly go to his hotel and
simply grab the man...'

'That was our reasoning, too!' Roseline put in.

'Attack was impossible, so I had to defend. And that meant
above all protecting the Tower against a hideous threat! A
patrol was created to inspect it at regular intervals. I also
recruited more attendants from among the riveters whose
contracts were coming to an end. What method would Hole
employ? When would he act and using what cover? We had
no idea but we held ourselves in readiness. That was how we
managed to find the nitro-glycerine in the garbage chute and
defuse it with sawdust some hours before you came along.'

Odilon made a choking sound.

'You mean...all that effort was for nothing?'

'Certainly not! It was you that set off the trap we had set
for Hole, making it possible to arrest him.'

Eiffel's revelations left the young people utterly confused.
They stared at one another in dumb amazement, not knowing
whether to laugh or cry, whether to feel sorry for themselves
or happy for the engineer.

Fortunately Jules, in his wisdom, showed them in a discrete
aside meant only for their ears how chance had smiled on

them: what if Eiffel, continuing his investigation, had discovered not only what Hole had been up to but also how far Armand had been involved? The twins' misgivings vanished immediately.

The whole company recovered their good humour and it was with renewed enthusiasm that the six champagne glasses were clinked together once again – and again, and again… The party in Eiffel's private drawing-room continued late into the evening.

THE TOP

17

The fourth storey of the Tower, a simple circular platform around the summit – possessed one curious feature: a lighthouse whose exceptional range made it one of the farthest-reaching beacons in the world.

Although the light was switched off by day, the beacon already shone because of its golden colouring, the culmination of a cleverly staggered colour-scheme that made the Tower look even taller than it was. This ran from the dark bronze of the legs below the first platform, which some said might have been 'dipped in cold meat juice', through an increasingly warm range of copper tones, to the pure gold of the tip.

At night, the beacon really came alive. Its light, a combination of a steady white beam and flashes in the national colours, could be seen for kilometres around. In clear weather, the towns of Fontainbleau, Chartres, Provins and even Orléans could see this point of light, whereupon tourists making for the capital would utter an optimistic, 'Nearly there!'

As well as the extended beam sweeping the horizon, the

lantern shone shorter beams almost at its feet into the streets of Paris. People who lived there were used to these brief flashes making the Île St. Louis, for instance, resemble an isolated rock and giving moored barges the appearance of trawlers about to set out on the high seas.

One such beam, which traced a circle of one kilometre radius around the Tower, travelled successively over the Palais Bourbon, the Champs-Élysées, Rue de la Boétie, Place de l'Étoile and the little La Muette Park. It shone on the houses of the prosperous middle class, bearing the bright message of progress into homes that were already well lit and whose inhabitants were not mean with the paraffin nor, before long, with the electricity.

Odilon and Salome Cheyne, now married, were still living in the young engineer's Rue de Berri apartment, just off the Champs-Élysées, and the reason may well have been this friendly beam that lit up the eighth arrondissement in black and white each night, prompting their small child to enquire naively:

'Daddy, Mummy, what's that up there?'

'It's the eye of the Tower!' Salome replied in a deep, resounding voice such as might be attributed to the iron giant.

'Is the eye looking at us?'

'It only looks out for naughty children, ones who don't do as they're told… So go to sleep now, otherwise the eye will find you – even under the covers!'

Another beam swept a wider path, reaching up to 4 kilometres from the Tower and visiting the theatre district, among other places. It took in Place Tivoli, the courtyard of the Louvre, Boulevard des Italiens, right round to the Luxembourg Gardens.

Here it visited the home of Armand Boissier and Roseline

Page, who were still in the actress's rooms in Allée de l'Observatoire. Since the place was full of mirrors, the beam split into a great many bright flashes, appearing to burst from every corner. The effect was like a firework display. Roseline liked it very much but Armand shunned the sight saying, 'One evening when fireworks were going off, I almost lost my life!' A bohemian couple, they still declined to marry, wishing to keep their love fresh in the temperate climate of a long engagement. They were happy that way, they said.

The same beam, alas, threw its light into an empty room, the one formerly occupied by Gordon Hole in the Hôtel Britannique. Light was something the American now hardly saw at all. As an American citizen, he had escaped capital punishment, but those testifying against him had carried enough weight and there had been sufficient evidence to send him to prison. Repatriated and held behind bars, Hole spent his days running his hands up and down the metal uprights and wondering why an initially glorious career had cast him so low.

A third beam, with a range exceeding 5 kilometres, ventured into the poorer quarters of the capital, the unlovely periphery where its luminous passage was no longer seen as a benefit but as a provocation, since it exposed the poverty of the workers and disturbed their sleep.

This beam penetrated much human anguish and distress. It plunged a dagger into the darkness of the morgue, the basement of which continued to accommodate meetings of the spiritualist group, alternating with the big room beneath the north pier of the Tower, which was used for larger gatherings. Regular seances had resumed, Apolline Sérafin propelled the miniature table to evoke the dead and occasionally, while the pencil traced a black spiral on the paper, her own memories. She missed Salome, in fact they all did – not simply as someone who is no longer there but as life itself.

Elsewhere, this third beam glinted off a shard of glass from a broken bottle, a forgotten leftover from some ancient dispute: one in which Gaspard Louchon had demonstrated his total incompetence in the matter of handling a firearm. The new tenants of the little apartment were not keen on housework and had never run a broom under the dresser. There the shard remained as a last reminder of a man who, rumour had it, had gone into exile in Cochin China, where he was growing rich from the opium trade when not stupefying himself with his own commodity.

The same wretched beam did in fact illuminate a certain amount of fine architecture, including the town house Jules Boissier had just sold for a godly sum in order to purchase one in St. Flour. With the rest of his savings, the old man set himself up for a life of utter idleness. He spent his days as a countryman very differently from his time in the capital. Having burnt all his drawings and deciding not to patent his new invention, though it was an important one, he devoted himself exclusively, henceforth, to playing cards with Hippolyte.

'Your turn, Jules… Come on, play!' the retired carpenter would say to his elder brother, who still had a tendency to dream.

For Uncle Jules allowed his surroundings to distract him. From time to time the scent of resin wafted up from the pine forests below. Jules luxuriated in it, eyes closed, hands on knees, dreaming that though in future iron constructions might rise even higher, posing an even more immoderate challenge to the sky, one would never, ever, breathe an air so pure as this.

He was back in St. Flour, and the eye of the Tower came nowhere near his country retreat.

In time, Parisians tamed their wrought-iron Tower. The crowds that had flocked to it during the 1889 Exposition stayed away during the next one, in 1900. Skyscrapers erected by Gordon Hole's disciples soared higher and higher, forcing the 300-metre Tower to its knees in their shadow. If some of France's finest writers poured scorn on the Tower, at least they paid it the compliment of taking an interest in the capital's new landmark.

One man, however, continued to look on it with pride and tenderness: the elderly builder to whose vision it bore witness and whose shuffling steps, when he grew very old, it sustained like an iron walking-stick. A street in Dijon already bore his name. That man was Gustave Eiffel.

'Everything that a man is capable of imagining, other men will be capable of bringing to fruition.' That had been written by one of his favourite authors – Jules Verne. And in his personal copy of *Twenty Thousand Leagues under the Sea* the passage had been underlined twice, by his own hand.

What actually happened was the converse: Eiffel brought his Tower to fruition, and since then man's imagination has known no bounds.

ACKNOWLEDGEMENTS

Writing this book meant gathering a large amount of documentation on a wide variety of subjects ranging from the workings of the phonograph to the pathology of syphilis and including the teachings of spiritualism, the hierarchy of the Parisian rag-and-bone trade, the technology of the first elevators and the patter of touts at the Universal Exposition.

Such an investigation requires a great deal of reading and much sustained correspondence, notably by e-mail, with experts in a range of disciplines.

I wish to express my great gratitude to all – whether conscientious professionals or enthusiastic amateurs – who agreed to let me share their remarkable erudition, notably:

- The staff of the company currently responsible for operating the Tower, the Société Nouvelle d'Exploitation de la Tour Eiffel or SNTE
- Monsieur J.F. Danjou, manager of the Hôtel Britannique in Paris
- Monsieur Agnard, who owns a museum in Sainte-Anne-de-Beaupré (Quebec) devoted to Edison and cylinder phonographs
- Madame Josette Martinage, a librarian at the French railway company SNCF
- Madame Sandra Oliel, who runs the tourist office in St. Flour
- Monsieur Frédéric Volle, who has records of the Universal Expositions
- Mademoiselle Laetitia Bouille, member of the European Institute of Deep-Sea Fishing and part-time spiritualist

MARION BOYARS PUBLISHERS: French translations

Thierry Paquot

The Art of the Siesta

Translated by **Ken Hollings**

'A short book…but a richly suggestive one…about the theft of people's time by modern society, and the effort we should make in order to reclaim it' Nicholas Lezard, *The Guardian*

The Art of the Siesta is a series of vignettes on the importance of the siesta in paintings, literature and sculpture. In *Preliminary*, we hear of the rhythm of sleep, including the fear babies have of going to sleep. In *The Midday Demon*, death in life and erotic dreams take form. The last vignette, *The Siesta Fights Back*, shows how the economic necessities of Western society are conquering the siesta. This is a translation from the French of a book that reinstates the value of sleep in waking hours. From mosques, where guards sleep under the protection of Allah, to 'slow-food' restaurants in Berlin in 2001, it explores the part sleep plays in the cycle of human life.

Thierry Paquot is Professor of Architecture at Paris-la Défense. He is the author of many books, including *Utopia*, *The Improbable Philosophy of Art*, *The World of Towns* and a study on Le Corbusier.

'Purely voluptuous…a charming volume' *Evening Standard*

'[A] daydream of a book' *The Independent*

£8.95 / $13.95   ISBN 0-7145-3092-1

Georges Bataille

My Mother, Madame Edwarda and The Dead Man

Translated by **Austryn Wainhouse**
With essays by **Yukio Mishima** and **Ken Hollings**

These three short pieces of erotic prose fuse elements of sex and spirituality in a highly personal vision of the flesh. They present a world in which the holy horrors of sex and the anguish of heightened awareness struggle against the stultifying spiritual inertia of social order and reason. Each narrative contains a sense of intoxication and insanity so carefully delineated by its author that it infects the reader. This volume also contains Bataille's own introductions to the texts, together with an autobiographical statement and essays by Yukio Mishima and Ken Hollings.

Georges Bataille was born in 1897 and died in 1962. A philosopher, novelist and critic who wrote on a wide range of topics, including eroticism, religion, anthropology and art, Bataille's combination of scholarship and creative genius assured his pre-eminence among his generation of French intellectuals. His work continues to exert a vital influence on today's literature and thought.

'Heaves with necrophiliac undercurrents' *The Observer*

£9.95 / $14.95   ISBN 0-7145-3004-2

Georges Bataille

L'Abbe C

Translated by **Philip A Facey**

Told in a series of first-person accounts, *L'Abbe C* is a startling account of the intense and terrifying relationship between twin brothers, Charles and Robert. Charles is a modern libertine dedicated to vice and depravity; Robert is a priest so devout that he is nicknamed 'L'Abbé'. As the story progresses, the suffocating atmosphere of the novel becomes increasingly permeated with illness, breakdown and eventual death. As in *Blue of Noon* and *Story of the Eye*, Bataille has succeeded in portraying the darkest and most profound aspects of human experience with amazing strength and dispassionate objectivity.

'Essentially a psychological novel in which the emotions of the characters determine the movement of the story from beginning to end; explicit sex is absent. The style is crisp and this translation is quite remarkable…always faithful to the spirit' *New York Times Book Review*

'Bataille is now recognised in France as one of the most challenging and original writers of our century' Leo Bersani

'Bataille intellectualizes the erotic as he eroticizes the intellect…reading him can be a disturbing kind of game' *New York Times*

£9.95/$14.95   ISBN: 0-7145-2848-X

Georges Bataille

Literature and Evil

Translated by **Alastair Hamilton**

'Literature is not innocent,' Bataille declares in the preface to this unique collection of literary profiles. 'It is guilty and should admit itself so.' Only through acknowledging its complicity with the knowledge of evil can literature communicate fully. Bataille explores this idea through a series of remarkable studies on the work of eight outstanding authors: Emily Bronte, Baudelaire, Blake, Michelet, Kafka, Proust, Genêt and De Sade.

'Bataille is one of the most important writers of this century. He broke with traditional narrative to tell us what has never been told before' Michel Foucault

'The power of Bataille's prose is still impressive, his capacity to shock still compelling' *Literary Review*

'Bataille's work deals basically with one issue only: the experience of the edge, that is, living at the very limits of life, at the extreme, at the borderline of possibilities' *Bloomsbury Review*

£9.95/$14.95   ISBN: 0-7145-0346-0

Georges Bataille

Blue of Noon

Translated by **Harry Mathews**

Set against the backdrop of Europe's slide into Fascism, *Blue of Noon* is one of Bataille's most overtly political works, exploring the ambiguity of sex as a subversive force and synthesizing the fetishes of violence, power and death that mesmerized an age. Troppman's sexual adventures with Dirty, Xenie and Lazare submerge him beneath the hallucinatory flux of erotic possibilities in a paradoxical world. The reader is taken on a dark journey through the psyche of the pre-war French intelligentsia, torn between identification with the victims of history and the glamour of its victors.

'Bataille denudes himself, exposes himself, his exhibitionism aims at destroying all literature. He has a holocaust of words. Bataille speaks about man's condition, not his nature. His tone recalls the scornful aggressiveness of the surrealist. Bataille has survived the death of God' Jean-Paul Sartre

'The writing is superlative…daringly imaginative, intended only for those awake and aware of the possibilities of excess – in literature and life. Along with Céline and Breton, Bataille writes as if he were dropping a bomb; in a foreflash he creates a world of demented funereal sexuality' *Detroit Free Press*

$14.95   **ISBN 0-7145-3073-5**

Georges Bataille

Eroticism

Translated by **Mary Dalwood**

Eroticism is a study of the underlying sexual basis of religion and philosophy, especially in its relationship to death. Bataille's great erudition enables him to range from Freud to Sade and from Saint Theresa to Kinsey. This far-reaching, provocative and often controversial book includes the results of Bataille's own research into the origins of taboo, religious ecstacy and the erotic impulse.

The author emphasises throughout the fundamental unity of the human spirit, the relationship between death and eroticism. We are asked to imagine man's existence in terms of man's passion. This important and stimulating work helps us to understand Bataille's vital influence not only on French writing today, but also on modern existentialist thought.

£12.95   ISBN 0-7145-2872-2

Georges Bataille

The Story of the Eye

Translated by **Joachim Neugroschel**
With essays by **Susan Sontag** and **Roland Barthes**

First published in 1928, *Story of the Eye* is most accurately described as erotic rather than pornographic, reflecting the extreme and excessive limits possible in human experience and imagination. Bataille explores in this book the forbidden grounds of adolescent sexuality and fantasy, unearthing hidden and suppressed images of man.

Susan Sontag's seminal essay 'The Pornagraphic Imagination' and Roland Barthes''The Metaphor of the Eye' discuss in depth the genre, style and language of this remarkable modern classic.

'*Story of the Eye* recounts its youthful characters' obsessions and deeds with poetic verve and a kind of gleeful serenity. It can be arch and witty, and yet also dark and cruel, with a sure sense of the grotesque and disturbing image'
New York Times

'*Story of the Eye* goes far beyond pornography. It is a multifaceted work both comic and serious. It is a 'metaparody', a psychoanalytic treatise, an enquiry into the bases of literature' *San Francisco Review of Books*

£12.95   **ISBN 0-7145-2627-4**

Jean Cocteau

The Art of Cinema

Translated by **Robin Buss**

For more than 30 years, Jean Cocteau maintained a passionate affair with the moving image. To him, film was a visionary dream-like medium, a glimpse of the phantoms that haunted the poet throughout his life. This posthumous collection of writings illuminates Cocteau's work for the cinema, with detailed discussions of his aims, responses to criticism and his reflections on the relationship between poetry, theatre and film. He also comments on the movie stars he admires – Marlene Dietrich, James Dean, Brigitte Bardot – together with such great directors as Georges Franju, Charlie Chaplin and Orson Welles.

Born in France in 1889, **Jean Cocteau** was a visionary poet, film-maker and artist. His films include the avant-garde masterpiece *The Blood of the Poet* and his later meditation on art and mortality, *The Testament of Orpheus*, both published by Marion Boyars as *Two Screenplays*. He died in 1963.

'Extremely discriminating, witty and astute' *The Times*

£9.95/$17.95   ISBN 0-7145-2974-5

Robin Buss

French Film Noir

Since the earliest days of cinema, film-goers have delighted in the depiction of violence, criminality and sudden death. Evil, whether portrayed in psychological, social or spiritual terms, has long held a fascination for our culture. This wide-ranging study of film noir analyzes the peculiarly French contribution to the crime thriller and gangster movie genres.

Robin Buss shows how such directors as Melville, Becker, Godard, Truffaut, Chabrol and Corneau have responded to the demand for films reflecting the dark side of French society. From the gritty political allegories following the Nazi occupation to the slick post-modern fantasies of today, Buss relates these films to French, American and British traditions of crime fiction, and shows how the genre has been used for both pure entertainment and stark social commentary. French Film Noir contains complete details of the 100 most important films discussed, plus plot details and a filmography.

'Incisive' *New Statesman*

£12.95/$16.95   **Illustrated**   ISBN: 0-7145-3036-0

Julian Green

Paris

An American born in Paris at the turn of the last century, Green accompanies the reader on an imaginative stroll around the French capital, revealing its secret stairways, courtyards and alleys and sharing his discoveries at every turn. From haunted visions of Notre Dame to memories of the old Trocadero, Green lovingly describes these strange and often little-known locations.

This special bi-lingual edition is illustrated with the author's own photographs and reveals the hidden delights of Paris in an intimate literary portrait.

Julian Green published over 70 books in France and was a member both of the Académie Française and the American Academy of Arts and Sciences.

'A series of love notes, subtle and charming' *Kirkus*

'Exquisitely literary in a traditional French manner'
New York Review of Books

'If you care for good writing and are interested in seeing Paris from an unusual perspective, then try this lovely and elegant book' *Gay Times*

£9.95/$14.95   ISBN 0-7145-2928-1

Raymond Radiguet
The Devil in the Flesh

'He belonged to the solemn race of men whose lives unfold too quickly to their close' Jean Cocteau

The Devil in the Flesh, one of the finest, most delicate love stories ever written, is set in Paris during the last year of the First World War. The narrator, a boy of sixteen, tells of his love affair with Martha Lacombe, a young woman whose soldier husband is away at the front. The liaison soon becomes a scandal and their friends, horrified and incredulous, refuse to accept what is happening – even when the affair reaches its tragic climax.

In the film *Le Diable au Corps*, Claude Autant-Lara recreated this story of the First World War with nostalgic tenderness. His sensitive dramatization treats the affair with such delicacy that many critics consider the love scenes to be among the most beautiful ever photographed. The film won the Grand Prix and the International Critics Prize.

Raymond Radiguet wrote *The Devil in the Flesh* between the ages of sixteen and eighteen, about his own adolescent love affair with an older woman. He died from typhoid fever at the age of twenty. His only other novel is *Count d'Orgel*, also available from Marion Boyars Publishers.

'A triumph of the poetic intelligence: a masterpiece'
New Statesman

£8.95   ISBN: 0-7145-0193-X

Henri–Pierre Roché
Jules et Jim

With an introduction by **Francois Truffaut**

Jules arrives from Austria in belle epoque Paris, where he is befriended by Jim. Together they embark upon a riotously Bohemian life, full of gaiety, colour and bustle. And then there is Kate, the enigmatic German girl with the mysterious smile.

Capricious, untamed and curiously innocent, Kate steals their hearts in turn, and so begins the moving and tender story of three people in love, with each other and with life. Francois Truffaut, whose film of the novel is one of cinema's greatest achievments, has called *Jules et Jim* 'a perfect hymn to love'.

Henri–Pierre Roché devoted his life to the arts, numbering Duchamp, Brancusi, Braque, Satie and Picasso amongst his closest friends. *Jules et Jim*, an autobiographical novel, was originally published in France in 1953 and was followed by *Deux Anglaises et le Continent*, which Truffaut also made into a film.

'A delightful account of people sharing and unsharing each other' *Times Literary Supplement*

£9.95/$14.95   ISBN: 0–7145–2958–3

SOME MARION BOYARS AUTHORS:

Georges Bataille

Ingmar Bergman

Gerard Beirne

Heinrich Böll

Jan Brokken

John Cage

Elias Canetti

Samuel Charters

Jean Cocteau

Julio Cortázar

Robert Creeley

Merce Cunningham

Elaine Feinstein

Nikolaj Frobenius

Mark Fyfe

Carlo Gébler

Witold Gombrowicz

Julian Green

Roy Heath

Ken Hollings

Ivan Illich

Charles Ives

Leos Janáček

Pauline Kael

Nora Okja Keller

Ken Kesey

Julia Kristeva

Federico García Lorca

Tim O'Brien

Kenzaburo Oe

Thierry Paquot

Raymond Radiguet

Lev Raphael

Tadeusz Rozewicz

Jeremy Sandford

Erik Satie

Arno Schmidt

Hubert Selby Jr

Shel Silverstein

Elif Shafak

Anthony Shaffer

Penelope Shuttle

Hjalmar Söderberg

Terry Southern

Fritz Spiegl

Karlheinz Stockhausen

Latife Tekin

Virginia Tiger

Frederic Tuten

Peter Weiss

Eudora Welty

Judith Williamson

Hong Ying

Yevgeny Yevtushenko

For further information on our list please contact:

Marion Boyars Publishers

t +44 (0)20 8788 9522

f +44 (0)20 8789 8122

24 Lacy Road, London SW15 1Nl

www.marionboyars.co.uk